Secrets of the Chest

Secrets
of the
Chest

Evelyne Morris

Copyright © Evelyne Morris 2014
First published in 2014 on behalf of the author by
Scotforth Books, Carnegie House,
Chatsworth Road, Lancaster LA1 4SL

ISBN 13: 978-1-909817-17-3

Printed in the UK by Short Run Press, Exeter

For my granddaughters, Julia and Millie.

*Thank you to Lorna Holdcroft for the enchanting
front cover painting.
Thank you to Sylvia Howe for your ideas and guidance
for my re-writing of The Chest.*

Contents

Foreword   1

Part One   Mary de Courtsey 1599–1666   11

Part Two   Maria Rochester 1791–1836
              Miriam Rosen 1878–?   117

Part Three   Marie Beauville 1944–2011   157

Afterword   259

Owners of The Chest

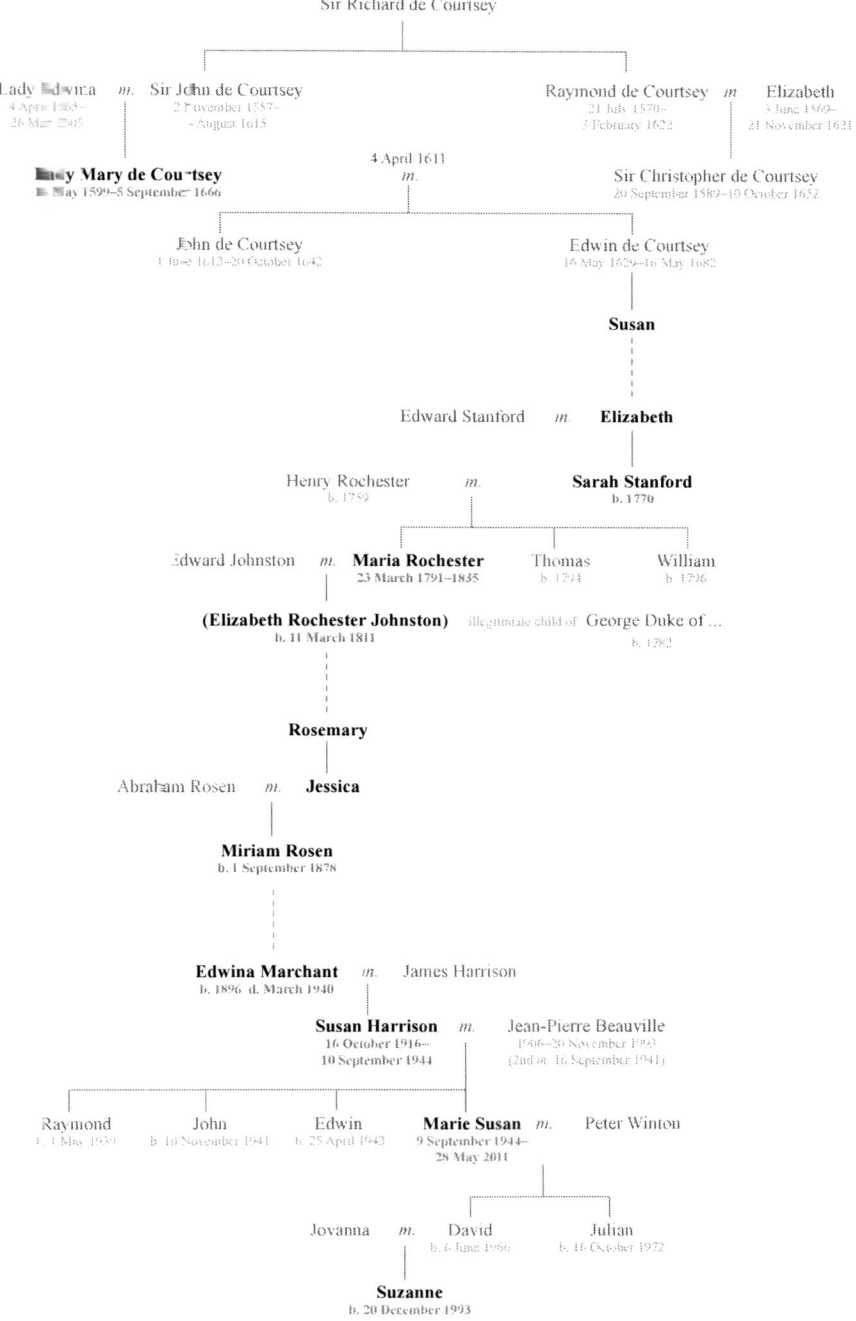

Foreword

20th December 2011

It was cold, and wet on the morning of Suzanne's 18th birthday, but she hardly noticed the weather outside; today she was expecting great things! Forget the 'A' Level history revision! The question was: now that she had passed her driving test, had her dad bought her the car that she had been angling for as her 18th present? She had even pointed out to him the bright red Mini that had been on the forecourt of Miller's Garage!

She had butterflies her stomach when she looked out of the window. She was not looking at the stunning views of the South Downs from their spacious country home; she looked at the driveway and saw that it was empty. No red Mini. Suzanne was disappointed, but her dad might still have it hidden somewhere as a surprise for her. With a smile on her face she skipped downstairs, doing up her watch strap as she went, and looked expectantly at her dad standing in the hallway. "Happy Birthday," was all he said, giving her a quick hug and handing her an envelope. Then he reached up for his car keys which hung from a hook fixed high on the wall next to the front door, and, without saying another word, he left for work.

Suzanne was really puzzled now. She sighed as her dad closed the door behind him, and then frowned when she looked down at the envelope in her hand. She recognised at once the handwriting of her grandmother Marie, who had died last spring. Suzanne smiled to herself as she remembered her favourite grandmother- Grandma

Marie. How she missed the laughs, the cuddles, the games of Scrabble that Grandma always won. She even missed the gently offered advice, sometimes taken sometimes not, but most often right in the end!

Suzanne went to the kitchen, made a cup of tea, and sat down at the table. She looked again at the envelope in her hand. So what was this? Her disappointment began to change to curiosity as she opened it and took out a long letter. It was dated 1st March 2011; just a few weeks before her grandmother had died. It read:

> *My dearest Suzanne,*
>
> *I am so sorry that I cannot be with you to wish you 'Happy Birthday' on your special day, but I do have a gift for you, and it is an exciting one. It isn't a car or an Apple Mac, or whatever you are yearning for!*
>
> *It's the old oak chest that your father has been keeping for you for the last few years, until you turned 18. I expect you remember me telling you when you were growing up that it would be yours one day. Not that you ever showed any great interest in it when you were young!*
>
> *It has been passed down the female line of my family from mother to daughter or granddaughter ever since it was made over 400 years ago. And now it's your turn to have it!*
>
> *When I first opened it up in the late 1980s, I found a collection of stories written by some of its previous owners. Letters, little belongings and memoirs of their own lives. But most important to me were the discoveries I made of my parents' past. There was the puzzle of finding my father's Birth Certificate. I always thought that he had been born in London, but the Birth Certificate showed that, in fact, he had been born in Constantinople (modern day Istanbul), in Turkey.*
>
> *But mostly I was deeply moved to learn the truth about of my parents' marriage and my own birth, in 1944, during the Second World War. And the discovery that I had an aunt, my mother's sister Monica living in Colchester. As you know it was too late for me to meet her, but after some digging I eventually found her two daughters, my cousins Emily and Lizzie who still live in Colchester, and are your second cousins! All the documents are there for you to read, and I think that at 18 you are now old enough to know the family 'secrets'.*

I had just about got over the shock of making my own discoveries, when I knew that I wanted to find out more about my father's birthplace, and his early life. So I set out to trace anything that remained of his family, and perhaps what they were doing in Istanbul. You were just a tiny baby when I made the first of my journeys to Turkey. You know all about my visit to the British Consulate in Istanbul, and my discovery of my cousin, Alina. You were 2 years old when you met her for the first time, and now you have been to Istanbul so often that I think that you could draw a street map from memory!

As for me, my new life as a Granny to you and your three cousins gave me all the joy and fulfilment that I wanted, and I settled down to that role with great happiness. Half a dozen visits to Istanbul had satisfied my curiosity about our Turkish heritage, and I didn't want to take my investigations into the family history any further. But now that you are 18 you might want to follow that Beauville trail to Malta to seek out the local History of the Knights of St. John. I leave that to you!

I have made a rather sketchy family tree of our female line going right back to Mary de Courtsey. With your love of history you might like to do some research to try to fill in the gaps. You may even want to do one for your grandfather's line – that would be a good project for you!

Now I must tell you of something extraordinary which happened on my 65th birthday, eighteen months ago!

I had celebrated my 65th birthday the day before, with your dad and uncle Julian, so, on the following, with memories of my mother fresh in mind I decided to clean up the old chest, which I had taken to using as a dumping ground for half read books and various bits and bobs. I cleared it, pulled it away from the wall and started to give it a good polishing. Then, when I was rubbing particularly hard on a knobbly bit of carving along the bottom edge on the right hand side, I was startled when something popped out at the front.

The chest has a false bottom, and the 'something' was a secret drawer. It is about 8 centimetres high, and about 40 centimetres wide, and almost the full depth of the chest. The edges of the drawer are cleverly hidden in the vertical lines of the front carving. I couldn't see anything inside at the front of the drawer, and I held *my breath as I felt carefully towards the back. At first I felt nothing. Then my insides leapt and I pulled my hand back when my fingers touched something horrid. It felt like a dead rat! I had to be mistaken. A secret drawer must have a secret, not a dead animal! So I took a deep breath, reached for my inner brave, and had another go. This time I realised that it was rotted fabric that I was touching, and I felt something hard within the fabric. I manoeuvred the large lump to the front, and carefully pulled out what turned an envelope of blue silk with something hard inside it. The silk was virtually worn through but some of the threads still flashed its original colour, a vivid peacock blue. The rest had rotted away.*

My hands were shaking as I peeled back the silk and found a book. It looked very old, and it was covered in what looked like well worn dark leather. I opened it up as carefully as I could. The pages were stiff but quite fragile, and a bit crumbly at the edges. They smelt very musty. Every page had writing on it which was still strong and clear. It was written in English, but the words were in ancient spelling, and they were very tight and small. Every word was hardly separated from the one before, and I found it almost impossible to read. Some of the pages had even smaller writing squeezed into the margins, which I could not make out at all.

But I saw clearly the date, 1615, on the first page, and the name Mary de Courtsey. The heading was: 'The Historie of the de Courtseys of Thornhill Manor from the Memorie and Memoirs of Mary de Courtsey...' It was the same name that is carved into the underside of the lid of the chest, which has the date, MDIC. (1599. Look at it and work out the Latin numbers!) I did not turn too many pages fearing that the book might fall apart, but I did notice that some of them were thicker than others, where there were letters attached to them.

I realised that if the book had been started in 1615, and the letters were genuine, then they would be almost as old as the chest itself. And if the book was genuine I felt sure that it might be very valuable, both moneywise and for its historical content. Without telling anyone in the family about my discovery, I decided to check for myself. I thought that if I were to take it to an expert he might be able to tell me if it really was as old as it looked. I found the telephone number of the British Library in London and I made a call. I was put through to a rather snooty sounding librarian in the

Reading Room, who, speaking in cool crisp tones, refused to take me seriously. He made it quite clear that he thought that I was another hopeful idiot, expecting to turn a worthless pile of dusty papers into a goldmine!

I refused to give up and my persistence won through. Eventually he passed me to a Dr. David Hennessy, a specialist in the rare books department. Dr. Hennessy was a different kettle of fish! I repeated to him the story of my discovery, the book dated 1615, and I told him of the name and date 1599 carved into the Chest that seemed to match the document. He was interested at once, but although he spoke with a much warmer and friendly voice, he was also a bit cool and cautious. He said that he was prepared to have a look at it for me. "When you bring it in," he said, "you must be extremely careful not to damage it. Do you have any bubble-wrap?"

I said that I had some. "Good," he said, "Make sure that it is new, and has nothing sticking to it. No Sellotape or anything like that. And be very careful how you handle it too. If it is genuine, and it has been shut away from daylight and fresh air for 400 years, then it almost certainly will become even more fragile if it becomes exposed to sunlight. If it is not parchment, it may even disintegrate altogether."

He said that he was a very busy man, but he sounded quite keen to see it soon as he could. He found a gap in his diary and made an appointment to see me the following Monday.

You can imagine the terror that Dr. Hennessy had instilled in me. I put the book aside, untouched, until Sunday evening. Then it was with shaking hands that I wrapped it, oh so carefully, in brand new bubble-wrap, and I slipped it in my handbag (the big one you gave me for Christmas last year). I was fretting about taking the book to London, and I hardly had a wink of sleep all that night. I was up well before my alarm went off, and minutes seemed like hours until I eventually set off from Eastbourne Station after the rush hour crowds were gone. I held my handbag close to my body to keep it safe, but all through my journey to the British Library I was alternately frightened that my bag would be snatched by a mugger, that I would get lost when changing trains, that I would be jostled by other travellers and the book would fall to pieces, or that, when I got there, Dr. Hennessy would just laugh at me and tell me that it was just rubbish, someone's idea of a joke!

Eventually I arrived at King's Cross tube station without mishap, and I found myself, in a daze of fear and expectation, walking towards the huge modern building of the most famous library in the world. I quailed at the prospect of showing the Journal to Dr. Hennessy, but unless my instincts were completely wrong, I knew, somehow, my journey had not been wasted.

I was still shaking when I met and was introduced to Dr. Hennessey in the Reading Room. He is a funny little man; short, totally bald and as round as he is high! But, my goodness, what a likeable and clever man he turned out to be! He started off by being cool and crisp, every bit the learned academic dealing with an ignorant woman. But as I unwrapped my parcel he peered closely at the book and became immediately interested, and he couldn't wait to look at it closely. He led the way down into the basement to a special room with dimmed lighting, where the BL keep ancient manuscripts, and he put on white cotton gloves before he examined the book. He told me that hardly any domestic writings from the early 1600s, have survived, and if the book was real, then it could be well nigh unique! The most famous diary of the 17th century is the one of Samuel Pepys, and this one was written 45 years earlier! After a minute or two he turned to me, smiled, grinning from ear to ear. His voice suddenly went up a couple of octaves. "I believe that it's genuine," he squeaked. "I will have to make a more thorough examination to be absolutely sure, but I do believe it to be genuine. The Journal of Mary de Courtsey. 1615. I can hardly believe my eyes. It's the real McCoy!"

He was almost babbling by then. I could hardly believe my own eyes! The cool Dr. Hennessy had changed from an aloof professional to an excited little boy!

"And it is written on paper! Commercial paper production was still in its infancy in the early 1600s. The first in England was made in Dartford, Kent, in 1588. It is even rarer than parchment documents from the same period. And to have survived so long is a miracle!"

His excitement was infectious. I was almost jumping up and down myself. "Did they really make paper in the 1600s?" I asked.

"Oh, yes." He said. "But commercially produced paper was still quite rare and very expensive, so it was hardly ever used for writing

memoirs." He started babbling again! I have never seen anyone quite so mad with delight!

"Does that mean that is valuable?" I asked

He calmed down a little and became more thoughtful, his voice returning to cool!

"What is value? To the social historian it will, indeed, be most valuable. In itself I really don't know at present. Because of its fragility I don't think that it could ever be on open display – the paper would disintegrate. I think that the Journal has survived in such relatively good condition only because it has remained in the darkness of that secret drawer for hundreds of years, possibly put there by Mary de Courtsey herself!"

He paused, and I could see him pondering on what to say to me next. "I think," he said slowly, "and I must make sure with further detailed examination, that this Journal will have to be placed in an air conditioned unit to keep it from disintegrating. As to its monetary value, I really don't know what its value would be on the open market."

He was able to make out the writing and, and with some hesitation and a little difficulty, he did eventually read out a few pages of vivid description and emotion that Mary de Courtsey had written about her life.

He stopped for a moment, then he exclaimed. "This is interesting. After a few pages she changes her way of writing. It is almost like a simple code. Look she is using just the capital letter for repeated names; C for Christopher, B for Bessie, and even F for Father! Now she begins to leave out some vowels when the word is quite understandable without them. Here is the word bedchamber, and she spells it bdchmbr; and garden, grdn; and Thornhill Manor is Thrnhll Manr. Absolutely fascinating! It's almost like modern texting."

I looked at the words that he was pointing to, and I could just about make them out. "I suppose," I said, "that she was trying to save paper and effort. I just cannot imagine writing using a quill pen. It must have been very labour intensive."

"Yes," said Dr. Hennessy. "When you think about authors like Charles Dickens, scratching away with his quill pens, writing hundreds of pages! Must have been a nightmare to alter! Anyway, back to Mary de Courtsey. Let's see if we can make out a bit more."

It was almost as if she was telling me her story today. And to think that Mary was my (our) very distant grandmother! Her Journal is a delight for you to read for yourself so I won't spoil it for you. I'll just say that the Journal appeared to have been written for the sons of Mary de Courtsey, but one of them died quite young, and the other seems not to have discovered it in the secret drawer, or found out the unpleasant truth about their father. What a pity!

After Dr. Hennessy had read some of the Journal and letters to me, we went upstairs to his office, taking the book with us. He managed to find just about enough room for us both to sit down amongst the piles of books and papers which were all over his desk, on the chairs and even on the floor, putting Mary de Courtsey's Journal very carefully on the desk between us.

"The first thing I want to say," he said, "is that I think that you should leave the Journal here with me."

I was about to protest. It was my treasure, and I wanted to take it home!

"I know that you won't want to leave it here, but I think that it is too fragile to take it backwards and forwards from your home to the British Library. I need to study it fully in order to authenticate it, but the first thing that I want to do is to have a specialist photograph or scan each page of the Journal. This will have to be done extremely carefully, but once it is done, then anyone who wants to study the contents will be able to do so without causing the Journal itself to deteriorate."

He insisted that I call him David. Doctor Hennessy was too formal he said. Then for the next half hour he wooed me by telling me how special the Journal was and how valuable to the nation it will become. I was very reluctant to leave my new found treasure, but he begged and pleaded with me to leave the Journal with him, and the British Library on permanent loan, for them to preserve it as only they can.

He looked at me very directly and said. "You must know by now that you really would not be able to look after it at your home. You really should leave it here."

I knew that he was right, but I was still reluctant to agree.

"And," he paused, "how about this for an idea? I am sure that once we have scanned the Journal I can persuade the directors of the British Library to have a facsimile made for you, plus I will make you a transcript in modern English so that you will be able to make sense of the 17th century language and spelling. How does that sound to you?"

That sounded such a super idea that, finally, but still with some reluctance, I did at last agree. Although I was almost heartbroken to go home without Mary de Courtsey's Journal, I knew that it would be best kept and preserved at the British Library.

David Hennessy was as good as his word. He got the agreement from his bosses, and five months later (it seemed to take forever to me), and after lots of excited telephone calls between us, he called me to come back to the Library to collect my copy of the Journal, plus his transcript written in modern English. This time I was so elated as I took the train to London again, that I could hardly sit still in my seat. Up until then, although I was almost bursting with excitement, I hadn't said a word to anyone in the family about Mary de Courtsey and her Journal. On my journey to the Library I came to a decision. I told David Hennessy that if the British Library were to make to make their find public, then they were not to reveal the ownership of the Journal, and I decided to keep my discovery and all that happened since, a secret from the rest of the family until you were 13, and then I had hoped to share it all with you in person.

But that was not to be, and now the chest and all of its contents belong to you, and the first thing that you will find in it is the copy with the letters attached in the same way. You will see that it has been bound in a deep red calf leather, with 'The Journal of Mary de Courtsey, born 1599' written in gold letters on the front. David's translation in modern English is also bound in matching calf leather, and lies next to it. He tried to keep the original feeling of the old text as much as possible, so although all of his translation is in modern English spelling, he has included some of Mary's original expressions. I love them both. It's quite a sad story, even brutal in places, but our Mary lived to triumph over adversity, and, fortunately for us, wrote everything down.

But – I must admit that I have been a little bit naughty! To make Mary's journal into more of a story I have made up a few lines which I have slipped into the modern translation at the very beginning and at the end.

Since we don't know the date of Mary's death, I have imagined that she was still living in London when the Great Fire broke out in September 1666, she would have been 67 by then, a great age for that period, and as this trauma overtakes her she finally fades away. I don't know whether I will ever be able to find Mary's grave, but with all this descriptive knowledge of her life in Thornhll Manor, I am going again to Thornton village, to the church to see again the de Courtsey graves, and the site which would have been the Manor grounds, and I will see everything again with new eyes!

So, my darling Suzanne, although technically now the Journal belongs to you, I would like it to remain where it is! Don't you think that it is exciting to have your family memoirs kept and preserved in the shadowy depths of the British Library? And, of course, you can go to see the original Journal at any time. Just make yourself known to David Hennessy and I am sure that he will give you a guided tour of the British Library. It really is a very important and quite amazing institution.

Darling Suzanne, this is my gift for you, the chest, and all its contents. I suggest that you read Mary's Journal first, and then the other documents and letters which will lead you through the years, (with many gaps), from 1600 right up to the end of the 1900s, and the secrets that I discovered about my own parents.

Remember that Mary de Courtsey's journal has so far been my secret. You are the first person, apart from those at the British Library, to know that you are a descendant of Mary de Courtsey, and I hope that you will feel proud to be part of her family. And now you have my blessing to share it with your dad, your uncles, and the rest of the family.

I love you with all my heart.
God Bless
Grandma Marie xxx

Suzanne was astonished. She let the letter fall on to the table and drew a deep breath. She was about to pick it up again and re-read it, but then she decided that she could not wait until her dad returned home to investigate the contents of the chest. She knew exactly where he kept the old iron key, and went straight to the top drawer of his desk…

Secrets of the Chest
Part One

Mary
1599–1666

5th September 1666

She was an old lady now. Her face was wrinkled, her back was bent and her dainty figure was a thing of the past. Her long, dark and handsome hair, which she had always considered to be her best feature, was now sparse and grey and hidden under her white lace cap. She had lived for an extraordinary sixty-seven years; and during that long life she had lived through the last years of Good Queen Bess, the most loved Queen of England, two disliked Scottish Kings, a terrible Civil War, a Republic ruled by a hated and joy crushing Dictator, and now England suffered the return of another frivolous Scottish King.

She had survived times of anger, abuse, danger and political turmoil, even the Great Plague of last year had passed her by, and now a great fire was consuming the City!

But with the crackling flames getting louder and louder, having already burned down the Royal Exchange and getting closer by the minute to where she lived halfway between the Royal Exchange and the Aldgate, all she could think about was saving the one possession that was really hers; her Bridal Chest and its contents.

The fire had started three days ago in Pudding Lane, in the King's baker's shop, which was many streets away from the Aldgate, but in London where houses were built so closely together, the flames had been leaping from one house to another and they caught fire in a flash before they could be doused.

Sparks were flying all around in the air, and she was becoming desperate. She had to save her Chest. It was so heavy, and whilst calling for her son to help her, she sat down upon it to rest for a moment. Even if the house were to burn down, her Chest must be saved. The contents could not be destroyed. Her Father's King James Bible and her little 'treasures' that she had saved since her childhood, were in the body of the Chest with many other things, but her Journal and her Confession were still in their hiding place, in the secret drawer.

Had she told Edwin about the secret drawer? She could not remember. She must do so soon, as after her death, which she feared would come soon, Edwin had to find out the truth about his Mother and Father. Then she wanted the Chest and everything in it be passed on to Edwin's daughter, her grand-daughter Susan.

~~~

The Historie of the de Courtseys of Thornhill Manor from the Memorie and Memoirs of Mary de Courtsey commenced during my recoverie from the beating given unto me by my Husband, which has nearly killed me, and has caused the death of our unborn child.

October 1615

Last August my beloved Father died, and now my son and I are left with no protection from my evil Husband, who is also my Cousin. Even now his wickedness still continues while my Uncle and I have been in deep mourning for my Father. Christopher is no respecter of other people's sadness, and he has shown that his apparent regard for my Father was all a wicked falsehood to estrange me from him. He has even dared to push aside his own Mother and Father, and has claimed the Lordship of the Manor for himself. Now he has killed my unborn child and almost murdered me.

One day I will need to give account of all that has happened to my dearest son John, so I have taken one of my Father's Journals, which Christopher insists he no longer needs, and I have decided to use it to write down all that has passed between me and John's Father, who is my Husband Christopher. In my writings I will include my family's history from before I was born right until the present day so that John will understand all. I shall keep this Journal away from my Husband's eyes, in the secret drawer in my Chest.

My Chest is the only place of privacy that I have in the whole of Thornhill Manor, which by birthright should belong to me, but is now entirely controlled by my hateful Husband Christopher.

I shall start this Journal with my earliest memory, which is of the day of my fourth birthday on 16th May 1603. It was for me so horrifying a day that, even though I was so very young, every word and image is forever burned into my memory.

The day started very happily for me. The Old Queen had recently died and church bells all around the countryside were ringing to welcome the new King down from Scotland. But I was Mary de Courtsey, I knew that I was a special young lady, and I thought that the bells were ringing out just for me, to celebrate my special day!

I have been told that I was handsome as a little maid, quite tall for my age, slender and with a smooth olive complexion that suited my dark hair and brown eyes. I was Mary, special Mary, the only child born to Sir John and Lady Edwina de Courtsey in their twelve years of marriage, and I was the heiress to a modest fortune.

I desire to tell you John, a little of our de Courtsey family history which will help to explain how your Father and I were obliged by our own parents to marry each other.

The de Courtseys are an old family. Our ancestors came to England with King William in 1066. They had been very much reduced in land and monies by the time of my great grandfather Sir Richard de Coutrsey, but service to Queen Elizabeth's father, King Henry, had been rewarded with lands and property that had been confiscated from a dissolved monastery near Chelmsford. My Father, Sir John, was Sir Richard's heir, and as I had neither brother nor sister, I was due to inherit all.

My parents were the Lord and Lady of Thornhill Manor and Thornton village, which includes all the houses, the blacksmiths shop, the tavern and St. Peter's, the village Church. The lands of the Thornhill estate, which are situated between Chelmsford and Colchester, also encompass many acres of woodland and several tenant farms, adding up to almost ten thousand acres, most of which is fertile farmland.

A smaller manor house, The Grange, is also part of the Thornhill estate. It was built in the valley six miles to the south of Thornhill Manor, and has only two small tenant farms attached to it. When I was four, The Grange was owned by my Father's younger brother, my Uncle Raymond, his domineering wife, Aunt Elizabeth and their son Christopher, who is my Cousin, and also your Father. They are our only kindred.

My Father, being the elder son, had inherited most of his Father's property, but he and Uncle Raymond, worked together to create wealth for the whole family. I saw my Uncle on most days, but I was mightily content that the six miles that separated our two homes were enough to keep Aunt Elizabeth and Cousin Christopher from visiting very often. I had no love for Aunt Elizabeth, and I had a great hatred for Christopher!

Thornhill Manor is an Elizabethan house. It was built on a hill overlooking Thornton village, forty years before I was born. The style is an enlarged 'E' shape, as were many then, to flatter the Old Queen. The main room is a large central hall which we call the Great Hall, where both you and I played in our childhoods. Do you remember how cold it was to play on the stone floor and how we liked to look up at the high ceiling decorated all over with patterns in white plasterwork? Do you remember the huge fireplace that burned logs all year long, except for a few weeks of high summer, to sustain some heat within the Manor house?

In the old days, when my Mother was alive, on Christmas Day, Easter Sunday and Harvest Festival, the local gentry were always invited to Thornhill, and we celebrated in the Great Hall. For these occasions a long trestle table was placed along the back wall and it was usually laden with a goodly amount of seasonal foods; roast goose, roast ox, mutton stews, fruit, sweetmeats, specially baked breads fashioned in all shapes and sizes and, occasionally, a suckling pig.

At Christmastide the huge Yule log, that would burn for the whole of the twelve days of Christmas, was dragged into the Great Hall by two servants while everyone stood around, drank mulled wines and sang merry songs until the log was well lit and burning bright. The Hall was decorated with fragrant wreaths of holly and ivy, but the highlight was a great garland of dried flowers. Red gillyflowers, large white daisies, cornflowers and marigolds were just some of those collected, and they were all intertwined with grasses, and long oat and wheat stems and hung in swathes all along the long wall and between and above the windows. The gardeners worked for months to produce this fabulous decoration, firstly gathering and drying the flowers, oats and grasses in the summertime, and then putting the garland together in situ. They hung up the huge twist of twine and dried grasses, and then each flower was wound into it one at a time. How splendid it looked, and all who saw it would gasp with surprise and delight. It was so sad that after the New Year festivities this wonderful garland was taken out and placed on the compost heap!

Part of my admiration for the Great Hall was the plasterwork which dominated the chimney breast above the fireplace. It had a large E and R, for Queen Elizabeth painted in bright crimson red, and the family crest bearing two falcons above a boar's head on a silver and green background. When I was a child my great contentment was to draw, and my favourite pastime was to try to copy the E and R, and the family crest, with a piece of charcoal onto the stone floor, until I was shooed away by one of the maids whose work included keeping the floors clean and well swept.

Above the Great Hall was my parents' bedchamber. Its main piece of furniture was an enormous curtained bed. When I was just an infant I would often climb onto the footstool at my Mother's side of the bed, creep through the curtains and into their bed to be held close between my Mother and Father. I was mightily pleased, and the smell of the bed comforted me. Even today I can recall that comforting warmth of my Mother's body mixed with the warm smell of lavender coming from freshly laundered sheets.

My Mother also had her own, separate bedchamber containing her guard robe, and a small withdrawing chamber wherein she kept her silks, wools and tapestries. My own pretty bedchamber was nearby, with a door between us so that she could visit me in the night if I was unwell or disturbed. These bedchambers, in the east wing of the Manor, were always warmed by the kitchens below, wherein fires also burnt all day and most nights, especially in wintertime when bitter east winds sometimes blew snow in great drifts to block the high kitchen windows.

That day, my fourth birthday, I remember looking out of my own bedchamber window into the sunshine and on to a fine display of spring flowers, nodding their heads in the breeze that blew over the gardens. I hoped that after breakfast I would be allowed to play outside with my Father's new hound puppy, Rex, who was sleeping in his kennel next to the stables. That morning I was dressed in a pretty yellow muslin gown by my playmate and nursemaid Bessie Smith, who then brushed my long hair which flowed free and grew to halfway down my back. Bessie is the daughter of the Thornton village blacksmith, and at nine years, with her straw coloured hair in braids that wrapped around her head, she was as big and strong as a young oak tree.

When I was ready I ran into my Mother's withdrawing chamber, for my birthday greetings and the surprise present that my parents had promised me. I was so excited that I hardly noticed that the window had been opened for the first time since last summer, and the fresh spring air which filled the room, adding to the fragrance coming from the bowls of narcissi that had been gathered from the gardens.

My Mother, the Lady Edwina, was sitting in her special chair beside her embroidery table and tapestry stand. She had already reached the great age of thirty-eight, but she always looked young and beautiful to me, with her slender figure, her long dark hair, and handsome green eyes. That day she looked particularly lovely in a peacock blue silk dress, with a yellow damask surcoat. She was always gentle and loving to me, and on this day she welcomed me, her cherished daughter, with gentle hugs and kisses.

"Slow down, Little Maid", said my Mother. "We give you greetings on this, very sunny and special day for you."

My Father, who did not often enter my Mother's withdrawing chamber, was standing beside her chair, and he was lovingly, or maybe nervously, touching her long neck. When I was a little maid I thought that my Father was a cross and stern looking man. At forty-six he was of an even greater age than my Mother. His hair was already white, and having a strongly lined face, he looked to me like an old man. I was often most afeared of him.

"Is my birthday gift in there? In that wooden box?" I asked excitedly, and I pointed to a large chest that was placed on the floor in front of my parents.

The 'wooden box' was, indeed, a large oak chest, my Chest.

It looked huge to me. I could even have climbed inside it quite easily! It was quite handsome too, having a plain lid and beautiful carved panels on the sides, and little legs that lifted the whole thing a few inches from the floor. There was a bright metal lock at the top of the centre front panel with a mighty iron key sticking out.

My Father went to the Chest and opened the lid. "This *is* your birthday gift", he said. I was much disappointed.

"A box? With nothing in it? Not even a pretty doll?" I asked. Tears started to well up in my eyes, and my Mother, giving a disturbed look to my Father, gathered me up in her arms. I remember my Father looking back at my Mother and shifting his feet uneasily. I did not understand the looks that passed between them.

"Let me explain" he said. "Because your Mother and I are ageing, we are not expecting to have any more children, and we have no son to help with our lands. So it has been decided that when you are older you shall be married to your Cousin Christopher. And this 'box', as you call it, is to be your Bridal Chest, in which, for the years between now and your marriage, shall be placed all manner of beautiful things that you will want to have as a newlywed young wife. If you look into it right now there may just be a small doll waiting in there for you!"

Cousin Christopher! I was stunned and horrified. Even the prospect of a new doll could not excite me now. As a little maid of four years I did not know what it would mean to be married to my Cousin, but I did know that he was vile and that I hated him!

Christopher was ten years older than me. He was already fourteen, and at fourteen he was considered to be almost a grown man. But he did not behave like a man. He was fat and lazy and cruel to almost everyone around him, especially if they were smaller and weaker than himself. At The Grange all the servants, farm tenants and especially their children, were afeared whenever he was nearby. He copied his mother by demanding their complete and immediate obedience. He pulled the ears of the children, and he whipped them like dogs if they made any mistakes or did not respond to his demands quickly enough. He found it mightily amusing to hide in corners of the dairy or behind milk churns and jump out at the milkmaids so that they were startled and spilt their buckets of milk, and were beaten by Aunt Elizabeth for their carelessness.

He was most cruel to animals. He kicked any stray dog that came his way, often until it was crippled. His own dogs cowered away from him, aware that they could be kicked or beaten at any time. When riding he would savage the mouths of his horses and kick and whip them until they did bleed.

I was just a little child, but I knew instinctively that he disliked me and was envious of me, because as the daughter of his uncle, the Lord of the Manor, my position in the family was higher than his. Indeed for the ten years before I was born he had been the only child of the de Courtsey brothers and during the years following my birth, which had been a joyful surprise to my parents, he had been obliged to cast down his attitude of self-importance together with his expectations of inheritance of all the family lands and monies.

Happily for me I did not see him often because of the distance between our two homes. Even though I was barely out of babyhood I had already had my own experiences of his vileness towards me. If he ever found me on my own he would pinch my arms or ears, or tease me by taking my dolls away. He would dangle a favourite doll or toy just above my head and out of my reach, until I cried in frustration, jumping up and trying to get it back. When I knew Christopher was coming to visit, or I heard his horse clip-clopping over the cobbles into the stable yard, I would run to my Mother's side and make sure that I stayed close by to her until he returned home.

The worst day in my young life had happened just five weeks before that fourth birthday. After weeks of grey damp weather with a cold east wind blowing, the sun had come out at last and I was so happy to be outside playing very merrily in the parkland with my new white kitten Blanchette. I did not hear Christopher's horse, or see him as he crept stealthily towards me through the trees.

Suddenly he was there, standing in front of me! He had a nasty sneer upon his face, as he leaned close and he snatched Blanchette from me. I did not know what he wanted with her, and I called out,

"Give me back my kitten. Leave her alone." I trembled and started to cry. "Please, give her back to me!" I begged, although I knew that he would not. He ignored all my pleading and my tears.

Then, to my horror, he swung Blanchette by the leg he threw her at a tree. I saw the terrified look in her eyes, and I heard the sickening crunch as her poor little body hit the tree. She screamed once, and crumpled silently into the laurel bushes below. I was too shocked to scream out at what had just taken place. I was rooted to the spot, too stunned to move.

Christopher just laughed out loud and ran away. My hatred of him boiled up inside me forcing me into action, and then I was able to run too. I ran, screaming and sobbing, to my Mother who was walking in the parterre garden and, between sobs, I managed to tell her what had just happened. She held me close and comforted me, and together we went to gather up my poor dead kitten. Mother cried too, and then she went quickly to tell my Father what had happened. My mother wrapped Blanchette's poor little body in a small woollen blanket, then later as she and I buried my little kitten in the garden, I held her hand tightly and asked, "How could anyone be so cruel and horrible?"

"I do not know, my little Mary," She replied, "but I have asked your Father to talk to your Cousin and Uncle Raymond, and have suggested that Christopher should be severely punished."

The next day my Father rode over to The Grange and questioned Christopher, but he denied killing my kitten, and told falsehoods to my Father, telling him that a fox had killed Blanchette; and he had just found the dead body and thrown it away! Did my Father believe him? I am not sure. He was never punished.

And now my Father was telling me that I was to be married to him! "I hate Cousin Christopher," I cried out. "You know what he did to Blanchette. I will not marry him!" Then I burst into tears and, sobbing in great gulps, I threw myself into my Mother's arms.

"You will have no say in the matter, and will do as you are told," said my Father, with a cold voice. And a dark scowl of anger crossed his face.

My Mother tightened her embrace around me. She had believed

me when I had told her about Blanchette, but she was without power to do anything to change my father's plans, although she knew just how wicked her Husband's spoiled nephew could be.

She shook her head in warning at my Father, and said softly, (I now think it was to convince herself as much as me), "Do not worry, Little Mary. It will be at least ten years before you will be ready for marriage, and I am sure that by then your Cousin will have become a perfect young gentleman."

"Yes," said my Father, a little more gently now. "You and Christopher will eventually be the Master and Mistress of all the lands around us, and he will need to learn the responsibilities of controlling so large an acreage. Before you and he are to be married, Christopher will come to live in our home. He will live in the west wing, which is now is being renovated, and will eventually become your marriage home. You will move in there with him after your wedding, and your Mother and I shall remain here, in this part of the Manor, to be near you and to guide and protect you."

This was even worse. I may not have understood what marriage to Cousin Christopher meant, but I did know what life would be like if he came to live in Thornhill Manor.

"I will not marry him, and I do not want him living here. This is my home," I screamed at my Father. My Father lifted his hand, but he did not strike me. He glared at me, lowered his arm and walked from my Mother's chamber, saying to her, "you deal with her. She is your daughter; and she must be taught to obey."

My Mother took me back to my own bedchamber and together we put my new little doll in the tiny crib which was next to my bed. She sat on the nursery chair, drew me on her lap and comforted me. Then she explained again how things would be, and how she and my Father loved me and would be there for years to protect me and see that I was content.

Then she had an extra surprise for me. She called for a manservant to bring the Chest into my bedchamber. When he was gone she closed the chamber door gently, knelt down on the floor in front of the Chest, and reached around to the side.

"Look." she said. "Watch what happens when I press on this little bit of carving just above the panel between the two legs on this side of the Chest. You have to push quite hard!" And then, as if by magic, a drawer in the front and at the bottom slid out.

"A secret drawer!" I cried, forgetting for the moment all that had passed in my Mother's chamber. "What's inside it?"

"Shush," said my Mother, "it *is* a secret drawer, and you must never tell anyone about it. Only Benjamin Haydock, who made the Chest and I, and now you, know about it. If you ever have anything very special and secret, you will be able to keep it hidden in here, and no one will ever know about it. And here is your first secret gift."

She took off a large pearl ring from her finger. "It will not fit you until you are grown up, but you can keep it safe in here until then. See I will wrap it in my handkerchief and put it in the drawer for you." She carefully wrapped the lustrous pearl ring in a small square of green muslin, and laid it at the front of the drawer. Then she pressed the carving again, the secret drawer slid back into place, and no one could tell that it was there.

"Now," she said, "for the present time you must forget about the secret drawer, and just use the Chest in the normal way. We do not want anyone finding out about it, or seeing you opening it, do we?"

So together we opened the lid of the Chest and put at the bottom the first of my treasures, my favourite doll and a prettily embroidered pillow that had been mine as a baby. Mother showed me how to lock the Chest using the great iron key, and although it was mighty heavy and weighed me down, I attached it to my girdle. I was proud to show everyone my key and tell them that I had my own Treasure Chest. To begin with it really was a place to store my toys and treasures rather than a Bridal Chest. (It was not until many years later that it became for me my Chest of Secrets, and the secret drawer became the hiding place for this Journal.)

My Mother also pointed out to me the inscription carved into the underside of the lid of the Chest.

"Look at this", she said. "I know that you cannot read yet, but you will soon be able to understand these words and letters. It says,

Mary de Courtsey, Thornhill Manor, MDIC

That is your name, this home where you live, and the year of your birth. So everyone will know that this Bridal Chest belongs to you. And maybe, one day, when you no longer need it, you might give to a daughter of your own." I hugged my Mother again, and for the moment I was comforted.

That comfort did not last for long. In spite of all my protests, within a few weeks, Christopher and I were Contracted to each other in my Father's library. I knew what was expected of me, and I did not want to go in. I resisted as much as a little maid could, and I clung to my Mother in a desperate attempt to stop the proceedings. She said nothing but I sensed that she no longer agreed with what was happening. My Father was angered with both of us and pulled me away from my Mother, roughly forcing me into the room where Christopher and Father Thomas of St. Peter's, the Thornton village church, were waiting.

Father shut the heavy door with such a thud that I felt the whole chamber shake. My Mother was excluded and I felt abandoned. I looked up at Christopher and saw a smirk of triumph upon his face. I was shaking in fear and had unshed tears in my eyes, but I had no further say in the matter, and I did not have my Mother to cling to or to rescue me. The only witnesses to the ceremony were my own Father and Father Thomas. I was made to place my hand on the Bible, then Cousin Christopher covered my hand with his. Even that filled me with disgust and made me tremble even more. I was determined not to cry as I was forced to agree that I would marry Christopher at some future date, and I was too young to realise the importance and the permanency of what I had agreed to.

The very next day Christopher was brought to live in the west wing of the Manor house with his own manservant, under the authoritative care of my Father. It is not uncommon for parents to contract marriages for their children, but each child usually remains within its own family until both sets of parents deem that they are old enough to consummate their marriage. This hardly ever happens before the girl has reached at the age of fourteen, and it was thus planned that ten years would pass before my Cousin and I would be wedded to each other, but in the meantime I was forced to endure his everyday presence invading my home!

I tried to avoid him as much as was possible. The manor house was large enough for us to have our own separate space, and he never came into the nursery, the kitchens or the work rooms where Bessie and I often played together. I was reassured to have Bessie always close at hand and with her at my side I felt strong enough to stand up to Christopher whenever our paths did cross.

Bessie was intrigued by my new Chest, but I did not show her the secret drawer. My mother had impressed upon me how it would only remain a secret if I told no one! But Bessie did know all about Benjamin Haydock, who is my Father's master carpenter, and she told me how he had taken many weeks to make the Chest using an old oak tree that had been blown down in the meadow in the previous autumn storms. I greatly admired Benjamin. He was a big man with broad shoulders and rough hands. Sometimes, when I was out in the woodlands with Bessie he would lift us both up into a tree, and pretend to abandon us there until we cried out to be brought down again. At other times he made me laugh and clap my hands in merriment at the terrible faces that he made.

Benjamin lives in a cottage next to the stables, with his young brother Godfrey. Like most of the other workers and servants on the estate, he works six days a week. His cottage is rent free, and he is paid a few pence each week for his long hours of labour. This leaves him some free time on Sundays after the church service, which always includes a long and boring sermon by Father Thomas, to make and sell his own pieces, for his own profit.

(How I hated those sermons when I was a little maid. I would often fall asleep or fidget and my Father would fix me with a stern look and threaten me with a beating if I did not pay attention—but he never did beat me!)

When I was little Godfrey was still an unlettered shepherd boy. I knew him well because he and Bessie were playfellows, and the three of us would often roam the pastures and woodlands when both Godfrey and Bessie had free time.

Benjamin loves his brother Godfrey, and since their parents had died two years previously when Godfrey was but ten years old, he had used some of his earned monies to pay Father Thomas to teach Godfrey how to read, write and count.

1604–1611

My Mother had knowledge of how much I hated my Cousin, and helped me avoid him as much as was possible. We were rarely together during the daytime, and the evenings, especially when we ate our supper in the family parlour, were the only hours that we were all together. Then my Mother was always at my side.

From my childhood days when I would write with charcoal on the floor of the Great Hall, I had shown an ability to copy letters and words, and my Father started to teach me. Paper was then most costly, so I learned my letters and numbers with chalk on slate. When I could read and write simple words my Father brought out his own treasure, an old book of Aesop's Fables printed many years ago, and he taught me to read from that. Although I still continued my lessons with my Father, I now had to share his time at home in the Manor with Christopher.

My Father was a good teacher and I knew that he was proud that his little maid was just as clever as any boy. He also started to teach me to write using a quill pen and ink. That was much more difficult to do, especially getting the amount of ink correct so that I could complete my task without a large blob of ink spoiling my work. The quills that we used were goose flight feathers which old Tom the gardener plucked from the geese which lived in the orchard. When I was old enough to use the special pen-knife, my Father taught me how to cut the end of the feathers to fashion our quill pens. He also had a small supply of superior swan's quills, which produced finer lettering. I was never allowed to use those, they were reserved for the writing of important documents and deeds – which now, unfortunately, included my own Marriage Contract.

Daily I spent many hours with my Mother and Bessie too. Although my Mother was the Lady of the Manor, she did not pass her days sitting in her boudoir in fine clothes, she was very much the Mistress of the Manor house. She had firm but gentle ways to ensure that everyone; Mistress Tadworth, the cook, Dick the cook's son and kitchen scullion and the other kitchen maids, the menservants, housemaids, dairymaids, laundry-maids and gardeners, all completed their tasks well. If any were sick or had difficulties in doing their work, my Mother would find them help. Everyone loved her. It was my Father who had control of everything else, the lands, the tenant farmers, the stables, the groom and the stable boys, although they also felt the tenderness of my Mother's care when they were sick or had need.

Bessie was also called upon to work when extra help was needed, but mostly she spent her days working or playing with me. We both like to play with Dick, in the few moments he had to himself. The poor boy worked all hours of the day keeping the kitchen fires clean and burning, washing all the pots, scouring the pans and drawing all the household water from the well in the courtyard. He was a funny little boy, only a year older than me. He seemed always to be content, full of merry smiles and winsome ways. Despite all the hard work that he was expected to do, he never complained.

Sometimes, when it was wet outside, Bessie and I played with a ball, a shuttlecock or jumping ropes in the Great Hall. Even with rush mats, the stone floor was always cold to sit on so we preferred to run around in our games. At other times we both sat with my Mother in her withdrawing chamber to learn stitching and sewing. As in all things, my Mother was a patient teacher and I began to become quite accomplished in the making of simple handkerchiefs, decorative stump work and the weaving of small tapestries. Bessie was all fingers and thumbs, and always produced lumpy and misshaped offerings. My Mother would just sigh!

A special pleasure and an occasional treat was when we went to 'help' Dick's mother, Mistress Tadworth in the kitchen, especially when it was really cold outside. Mistress Tadworth was fat and jolly, and always merry like Dick. It was a warm and happy kitchen. How we would laugh together when Bessie and I, and sometimes Dick, attempted to bake sweetmeats! I think that we ate more of the uncooked mixtures, licking them off our sticky fingers, than was put in the ovens. But in these cooking and baking tasks it was Bessie who outshone me, and soon became a most proficient cook herself.

One day as Bessie and I were making a great spotted dick pudding under the watchful eye of Mistress Tadworth, Bessie said to me, "I don't rightly know what my place is here in the Manor. When I am with you and your Lady Mother I seem to be part of the family. Sometimes, at luncheon times in the Great Hall, I eat off the pewter plates and drink from the pewter tankards at the top table with you. At other times I eat off wooden platters and drink from horn goblets with the rest of the servants at the lower table. What do you think I am, Little Mistress? What is my place? Am I a servant like Mistress Tadworth? I always do as your Lady Mother asks, but your Cousin tries to treat me like he treats his dogs. He orders me to fetch things for him, or to pick up things that he drops, and he scowls at me whenever I join in with you all at mealtimes."

"Oh, Bessie," I replied, "You are my Maid, but you are also my very best Friend in the World! I wish you were my Sister. I know that Mother loves you as much as I do, and she always wants you to be at my side. Just you take no notice of that hateful Christopher or his scowls. You belong at the top table with the rest of us."

That evening, as I was preparing for my bed, I spoke to Mother about Bessie. "Mother," I asked her, "is Bessie a servant or my companion? Does she belong in the kitchen or with me, you and Father? I want her to be like my Sister, and I like her to be at my side whenever Christopher is there."

"She is almost like a Sister to you, is she not? She is certainly your friend and companion as well as your personal maid," said Mother. "And I am most content knowing that she is forever watchful over you when you are together. I will see to it that Christopher accepts her place in the family."

So it was then that I became Bessie's sole responsibility. Whether it was dressing me or making my bed or playing with me, she had only me or Mother to answer to. Her truckle bed was brought down from the servant's bedroom in the attic and put into the nursery. And that made us both content.

When the weather was clement we played outside in the gardens or woodlands, often joined by Godfrey. We also like to assist Tom, the old gardener who had trouble with his back, to weed the extensive kitchen garden. My Mother had often told Tom that his two sons could do the work, and all he needed to do was to make sure that they worked under his supervision. She would always assure him that his home was safe, and that he would never be evicted from his cottage when he could no longer work. But still he came everyday to tend the vegetables or to clip the box hedges in the parterre of the formal garden.

How I loved my Mother. She was beautiful, gentle and loving. My special time with her was when we would sit together in my bedchamber, before I went to sleep at night. She would brush my long hair until it shone, and she told me stories of Fairies and Witches, or Princesses in far away castles where Princes would come and save them from Dragons or Wicked step-mothers. Perhaps the Dragons and Wicked step-mothers, (or Cousins and Aunts) were all the same!

Little by little, as well as learning to read and write with my Father, I also learned how to become Mistress of the Manor, with my Mother.

But no real contentment in my life had ever lasted for long. When I was just six, my loving and gentle Mother took ill quite suddenly. First she complained of a fierce headache, and then she took to her bed with a high fever that left her hands and feet quite cold. Aunt Elizabeth was sent for and during the next two days she and my Bessie nursed her, as I sat crying at her bedside, praying that she would soon recover. But she worsened with much vomiting, and Father was almost witless with fear. He sent for the doctor from Chelmsford, but before he arrived, Mother lost her senses and was taken over with convulsions.

There was nothing that could be done for her, and Jesus took her to Heaven on 26th May 1605, after only five days of her sickness. It was so sudden. No one could believe that my beautiful Mother had left us forever. I was bereft. I clung to my Father howling out in my distress, wanting him to make everything better and to bring my Mother back. It was the first and only time I saw my Father cry. He heaved great tears of unhappiness, and we tried to console each other, but neither of us felt relief.

Bessie had loved my Mother too, and as we cried together it was she who comforted me the most. It was with her that I would sleep at night, she holding me close as I cried into my pillow. Soft, warm Bessie. Big and strong Bessie with a soft and loving heart of gold. I would never have survived my Mother's death without her comforting strength.

Two days after she died my Mother was laid in a tomb close by the alter in St. Peters church. Bessie and I had gathered every one of the spring flowers from the Manor gardens, which looked bare and denuded as if it were their own recognition of my Mother's death. Father Thomas had filled the church with them, and their perfume was more powerful than the church incense. All the servants of the Manor and the tenants joined us in our prayers. Most of them were in tears too. I felt utterly wretched and lost without my dearest Mother, and this was the saddest day of my life. My father too was totally distraught and unable to give me comfort. Bessie was my friend and only support. Although Cousin Christopher came with Uncle Raymond and Aunt Elizabeth to the funeral, I was too unhappy to have any regard or fear of him that day.

Later that week my Father ordered a stone effigy to be made of my Mother which, a few months later, was placed on top of her tomb. With her two hands held together as though she was at prayer, the stone mason had captured the very look of her Mother, but the effigy was cold and hard, quite the opposite of her soft and gentle being, and it gave me little comfort. Father also had one of himself prepared, for when the time came for him to join her.

It was Bessie's idea that, with the help of old Tom's son William, that we plant a special corner in the Manor garden as a remembrance garden for my Mother. We chose her most favourite and fragrant flowers, narcissi for the spring, gillyflowers, roses, marigolds and lavender for the summer and autumn, pansies and all sorts of herbs for the winter and in between seasons. William made a little gravel path through the garden and set a small stone bench in the centre. I could see my Mother's special garden from the window of my bedchamber, and occasionally I saw my Father sitting on the bench, deep in thought. I so wanted to run to his side to comfort him and to be comforted in return. I longed to tell him how much I missed her too, but the thought of rejection by him always held me back.

Now I no longer had anyone to protect me from the plans and ambitions of Christopher, and especially those of my Aunt. Indeed, it was my Aunt Elizabeth, named for the Old Queen, who had given in to every whim and desire of her beloved son and had created the immoral monster that he had become. My Uncle, Raymond de Courtsey, had always been a quiet and gently spoken man, but his Wife Elizabeth was a large, dominating and demanding woman who was in complete control of her Husband's mind, home and monies. I had no knowledge, but I am sure that their marriage, too, must have been a contractual agreement, because I could not imagine my gentle Uncle Raymond choosing to marry such a disagreeable woman. My Mother had told me that Aunt Elizabeth was older than him by five years, and she had only to fix her eye upon her Husband for him to crumple and agree with whatever she demanded.

I am certain that for years Aunt Elizabeth had been most content that her Sister-in-law appeared to be barren and unable to produce an heir. Then after the disappointment of a living child being born to my Mother, she saw a new opportunity for her Son to inherit the whole of the de Courtsey land and property. Indeed, it was she who had first promoted the idea of we Cousins being Contracted in Marriage.

Not long after my Mother's death to my dismay, Uncle Raymond and Aunt Elizabeth left their home at The Grange and moved into the refurbished west wing of the Manor to join Christopher, who, after two years of living in our household was no more pleasant than when he first joined us. I still hated him! How I wished that a Prince, or even a simple Knight would ride up on white charger and rescue me, just as in the tales that my Mother had told me!

Christopher was by then sixteen and he had almost completed his training in the management of our large estate and the control of many people from craftsmen and tenant farmers to swineherds and milkmaids. Aunt Elizabeth took over the management of the manor household – and me!

As a six year old maid I had no say in the matter. I began to hate her almost as much as I hated Christopher. Gone was the love and laughter in my home. Gone was the privacy that I had enjoyed. Gone was the friendliness I had with the maids, the scullions, the cooks and the stable boys. Gone was all the laughter in the kitchen. Gone were the hours of contentment that Bessie and I spent making puddings sweetmeats with Mistress Tadworth. Aunt Elizabeth mastered everything and everyone, and God help them if she caught any of the servants wasting time talking or playing with me!

For the first few months after my Mother's death my Father tried to make up for her loss. He did pay more attention to me than he had when my Mother still lived, and I often told him how Aunt Elizabeth made everyone sad and fearful, but I think that he, too, was intimidated by her, and it made life easier for him to let her have control of the Manor house.

We lived too far from London to be knowledgeable about the momentous events that were taking place there, but the reverberations of the plot to kill the King and blow up the Parliament which happened in November in the year that my Mother died, eventually reached us by Christmastide, and our home was drawn out of mourning. The bells of St. Peter's rang out long and loud to celebrate the safe survival of King James and the capture of the miscreants. Father Thomas preached one of his long sermons, this time all about the evil plans and actions of the Catholic anti-Christs. The wicked band of traitors were all found guilty and my young ears were protected by an edict of my Father that no one in Thornhill or Thornton village was to tell me the details of their executions. But much was whispered abroad and soon began to hear people describing to each other the fearful fate, the hangings, drawings, and quarterings of the would-be King killers, in hushed and horrified tones. I was a young maid still missing the warmth and comfort of my Mother's love, and it was not long I began to have nightmares of her being killed in such a way. Only Bessie knew how to hold me and calm my frights and fears.

One day when I was out in the snows of early spring, my Cousin Christopher sprang out upon me, having silently followed my trail from the gardens to the woodland just beyond.

33

"So here is the little frightened rabbit who cries at night into Bessie's fat paps!" He jeered at me. "Was it Master Fawkes or was it your Mother who was hanged from Tyburn, cut down while still alive and then chopped, chopped and chopped into little pieces?"

He was making hanged man faces with his tongue hanging out, and then making chopping actions. His face then changed to become a wicked, leering grin. I screamed at him to go away and ran as fast as I could back to the safety of Bessie. I tried to tell my Father about Christopher, but he had no patience to understand my childish, crying babble and he would not listen to me.

~~~

As I grew older my childhood prettiness did not develop into any great beauty. I was small boned and slight and had become quite plain apart from my large dark eyes and my hair which was dark and glossy and grew down below my waist. But I did show that I could be quite clever, and my Father was pleased and surprised at my willingness to learn. So each day I spent some time with him in his library improving my reading and lettering; and he even began to teach me a little French and Latin. I was very fortunate because, unusually for a maid, my Father also taught me numbers and accounting. And it was through the account books that I learnt, little by little, all about the tenant farms, and businesses held by my Father; which ones easily brought in good profits and which ones needed help and good management to prosper. My Father kept careful note of all these profits in his Journals, and kept a goodly amount of gold and silver coins in his oak coffer. This chest, which had a domed lid, was but half the size of my Chest. The whole of the coffer was heavily bound with iron bands, and it was kept locked and safe in his private room, next to the library.

But even with the extra attention my Father was giving to me, I was terribly lonely, and I was continually afraid of Christopher. I spent as many hours as possible with my Bessie who, although she was only a few years older than me, at the age of nearly thirteen, was almost grown up. Bessie became my only real friend, a confidante and a second Mother to me. She had grown tall, she now had a full woman's figure and she had already started her monthly bleeding. It was she who taught me about womanhood, and many things about life and the outside world. For some reason Aunt Elizabeth was unable to cower or frighten Bessie as she did everyone else. She did not try to change Bessie's work or take her away from me, and I would shield myself behind Bessie's strength and good humour.

One day, when Bessie was brushing my hair, and helping me to dress for the day, she was telling me that she would like to marry young Godfrey Haydock, and she told me all about what wives and husbands did together. I was horrified that such a thing would happen between me and Christopher! "But have no fear, sweet Mary, although Godfrey has asked me twice already, I shall not be leaving you all alone with Christopher and your Aunt Elizabeth!"

I started to cry. "Oh, Bessie," I said. "You may want to be married, but I do not. Christopher has lived here now for three years, and I still hate him, and I am still afraid of him. You know how horrible he is, and I know that he would not be gentle as you described – he would want to dominate and hurt me. Would you ever want him for a Husband?"

"Oh, goodness, young Mary!" she exclaimed, "You know that I hate him almost as much as you do! He has improved in his looks since he came here, but no one likes him. Only yesterday he hit Peter, the stable boy, across the face with his riding crop, and he did bleed terribly. He said Peter was not holding his horse still enough for him to mount!"

"I know," I said. "I saw poor Peter standing in the courtyard, by the well. His Mother was holding a cleaning rag to his face, trying to stop the blood. Whatever am I going to do, Bessie?"

It was then, as we talking about Christopher, that I decided to show Bessie the secret drawer in my Bridal Chest. I struggled to find the right place to push, and eventually I managed to open it. Bessie gasped with surprise. Then I took out the pearl ring that my Mother had given to me on my fourth birthday. It was still wrapped in her green muslin handkerchief which I held to my nose, and I sighed as I breathed in the lingering, well loved fragrance of her body. After a moment I took from the main body of the Chest her pearl necklace, a string of beautiful matching lustrous pearls with a large oversized one in the centre, which my Father had given to me after her death. I wrapped it in one of my own handkerchiefs and put that, too, in the secret drawer. I sighed. How my Mother had loved pearls!

Bessie was now nearest person I had to a Mother, and I wished that there be no secrets between us.

"Well, my dear", she said, when she had recovered from her surprise. "I think that it is very fortunate for you that you have somewhere to hide things from Christopher. Things that he will never know about. You must ensure that whatever happens between you and Christopher, you never tell him about that secret drawer. Then if you are ever in need to keep anything from him, he will not be able to find it, or take it from you. You know that I will never tell anyone else your secret. Not even Godfrey, if I ever marry him!"

We laughed together, but how true her words were to become!

Since that momentous fourth birthday, and until my Mother's death, I had all but forgotten the secret drawer. In the main part of the Chest I had stored away things for my future that my Mother had given me while she was still alive, mostly bed linen and a little silk. I had also put in there all my own little 'treasures' that I had made or found or had been given as presents. To me, the Chest had become a treasure trove; a remembrance of my Mother, and a reflection of myself and all that I valued in life. I kept the Chest locked and at all times I kept the heavy iron key attached to my girdle, like a little chatelaine of a great castle!

Christopher had improved in his looks as he grew older. As he reached manhood he grew tall and strong. He became a good rider, galloping and jumping hedges and gates with fearless ease. He lost his childhood fat and his horse riding ability helped him to develop a lean and well defined body with broad shoulders and slim hips. Unlike me, the de Courtsey characteristics favoured him, and his dark eyes, strong aquiline nose and a mass of dark hair curling to his shoulders gave him the look of a fine and handsome young man.

His character, however, did not make a similar change for the better! He no longer pulled the wings off flies or threw stones at the dogs and children, but his bullying developed a quiet subtleness and nastiness. In public he showed a graceful, if arrogant, charm; but in private, amongst his family, the bully in him remained in total control. He grew taller than his Father and as he grew older I could see that he followed his Mother's lead and learned to despise and dominate his Father while basking in the glowing praise and blind love of his Mother.

When away from home Christopher had always with an eye for a pretty woman, and I heard the whisper of stories about his manner with the serving women at a local tavern, especially if any were very young and unschooled in the ways of men. By his drinking and other pleasures he did render himself very unpleasant to all. He would speak tenderly, and touch the curl on the neck of a young girl who brought his food and wine, and she would be flattered by the attention of someone so handsome and so far above her station. He always took what he wanted, and he never allowed resistance as an answer. He did not care for anyone or how he was regarded by anyone.

I had witnessed some of this behaviour in our own dairy, and washrooms, even in the cowsheds, indeed, in any of the Manors' outbuildings where a young servant could be found. He always behaved in such a fashion when he was away from the eyes of my Father and his, who were both kind Masters and Honest Gentlemen.

In spite of stories and rumours that my Father must had heard about his behaviour abroad, at home Christopher was rapidly becoming the favourite son of the household. Beloved and Idolised by his Mother, admired by his Father, and preferred above me, his own Daughter, by my Father. But instead of my growing to admire Christopher, my childhood fear and dislike of my cousin increased as I grew older. And now the care and protection of my loving Mother was replaced by the condescending control of my Aunt Elizabeth.

It was she who had the control of the household purses, and it was she who was the Mistress of the seamstress, a young woman called Catherine Beckett. If I chose a pretty piece of muslin, silk or even velvet to be made into a new dress, in shades of blue and rose that suited my colouring, Aunt Elizabeth would go against my wishes, and order bright oranges and greens that made my skin look pallid and sickly. If the travelling hawker came with his barrow of pots and pans, shoes and stockings, fabrics and silks, salt and spices, it was she, and she alone, who made the choices for the Manor. I no longer spent many happy hours, as I had with my Mother, going through all his wares. There was never a pretty ribbon or a new doll for me now.

Aunt Elizabeth also did the best she could to interrupt my precious studies with my Father, the only real time that we spent together, by finding little tasks that must be done at once, or others that had not been completed to her satisfaction. Why did not my father stand up to her? It was he, after all, and not she, who was Sir John, and Lord of the Manor!

And while Aunt Elizabeth was doing all she could to undermine my closeness with my Father, Christopher quietly and slyly did his best to do the same too. He slowly dripped poisonous falsehoods about me into my Father's ear, until my Father began to believe everything that Christopher said of me. Daily he made up untruths about me. On one occasion he stole a purse full of silver that had not yet been locked in my Father's coffer and told him that it was I who had taken it. It was he, it must have been him, who hid one of the coins in my workbasket, and then made a great show of 'discovering' it there. All my denials and shows of independence of spirit were crushed as waywardness or obstinacy. And when I protested my innocence or made any counter accusations, it was I who was punished by my Father for telling falsehoods. On these occasions I lost my lessons for the day and was sent to my bedchamber to remain, without Bessie, for the remainder of the day.

Christopher was always mightily pleased!

~~~

Christopher first violated me, his betrothed and his bride-to-be when I was only eight years old.

At the age of eighteen Christopher was powerful, strong and confident. The trouble started, as it often did, with his teasing me. One day he found me alone in my old nursery, and to discomfort me, he snatched at the iron key of my Chest that dangled, as usual, from my waistband.

"So, come on Little Mary", he said with a dangerous smile upon his face. "What do you keep in that precious Chest of yours?" The smile disappeared, and was replaced by a look that I knew well. "I want to see. Give me the key," he demanded.

"No you cannot have it. It is mine, and it is private. And you should not be up here in this part of the house. Go away!" I said as I tried to stand up to him. I was mightily afeared because I knew what Christopher could be like if his wishes were thwarted. I wanted to run away to the protection of my Father or my Uncle Raymond, but Christopher anticipated my intention and barred my way.

His mood changed, and he became angry. "Nothing you do or have is ever private from me," he said in a low and dangerous voice. "I shall soon be in charge of everywhere in this house, and everything in it, including you! Just you remember that."

He let me leave the room, and then quietly followed me when, foolishly, instead of running to my Father, I went to my bedchamber where I kept my Chest at the foot of my bed. Creeping in behind me, he shut fast the heavy door, closing it with the gentleness of a maidservant. Then, silently, he advanced upon me and wrested the key from my girdle. I was too frightened to scream and I watched as he knelt down and opened the Chest.

Then I saw his face fall with disappointment. In hast to discover my secrets he flung all my treasures about the chamber. These treasures that I valued so much were little more than a few pieces of linen, two bolts of fabric – one of silk and the other of damask. After my Mother's death I also added some trinkets and two of her dresses, the peacock blue and yellow silk dress that she had worn on my fourth birthday and her dark blue velvet winter robe that she kept for the Christmas season. I also had her beautiful and ancient Book of Hours, which was in fact the only item of real value I kept in the main body of the Chest. (Christopher knew nothing of the secret drawer, that still held my Mother's ring, and her pearl necklace).

There were also little things that meant nothing to him or anyone else: my favourite doll, the feather from a barn owl that I had found in the woodland, some pretty round stones and a book of pressed flowers; flowers that I had gathered from my Mother's memorial garden.

"What is all this rubbish?" Christopher roared at me. "Where are all the gold coins that your Father has given you?"

I was trembling with fear. "Please leave me alone, and get out of my room," I said and started to cry. I was greatly afeared now. "I have no gold coins. If my father has put by any for me, then they will be in his coffer. Please go away," I sobbed. I will never know how I was able to keep quiet about the secret drawer!

His disappointment made him vicious. He turned to me, and seeing a little maid attempting to stand up to him, a little maid near to tears and cringing in fear of him, must have caused a flood of sexual arousal to add to his anger. My Father, his parents, Bessie and the servants were all engaged elsewhere, so, without hesitation, he attacked me in the most vicious way possible. I did not know what he was about to do, when he lifted me and pushed me down onto my bed. He pushed aside my dress without damaging it, held me down, and parted my legs, with what I realised later, was the expertise born of much experience. I was truly terrified by then, and before I could scream out loud he roughly clamped his large hand over my mouth to prevent my screams from being heard. With the other hand he managed to undo his own lower garments. Then with one quick movement he forced his way into me and ravaged me again and again until he was spent. I tried to scream in my terror and pain, but his hand was pressed so hard upon my mouth that I all but lost my senses. I did not even possess the wit to bite. Yet through it all I was sensible of piercing pain as though I was being rent asunder. I felt my senses leaving me and I felt desperate to breathe so I stopped struggling and I quietened down.

Then he let go of me, a sobbing, bleeding child, and thrust into my hand a kerchief to wipe myself clean! He shouted at me. "You are a wanton and a slut. This was all your fault and I had to punish you for your disobedience."

As he readjusted his breeches he continued. "If you ever tell anyone; not your Father, my Mother or Father, not even your nursemaid, I shall do it again – and next time I will kill you," he hissed at me, and stood over me menacingly as I lay on the bed in confusion, pain and misery.

I was stunned, shocked and crying. I did not know what had

happened to me, except that it hurt more than anything than I had ever experienced. I was frightened at the blood which was still oozing from where he had so hurt me. Never had I ever known such fear of anyone, and this was my Cousin, the wonderful, handsome Christopher, to whom I was pledged to marry!

I had no knowledge of what a wanton or a slut might be, but I was prepared to believe that I was both, and that I had done something wicked that deserved punishment. I felt that there was no doubt that he would kill me if I related to anyone about what had happened. In mortal dread that Christopher would hurt me again, I sobbingly agreed to everything that he wanted, and he left the chamber, leaving me alone with my scattered treasures, my pain, my blood and my confusion.

Christopher must even frightened himself a little at what he had done, and what might be the consequences if I were to tell my Father, for he made no attempt to follow me or trap me for many weeks, but the heightened sexual pleasure that he enjoyed from ravaging and hurting a terrified maid ensured that he would take the risk and do it again whenever the opportunity arose. But eventually, whenever he entrapped me, I learned to accept his attacks with docility as it became clear that any resistance by me only increased his lust and the roughness of his violations.

From that time onwards I lost all my spirit and withdrew into myself. I was now completely terrified of my Cousin and tried to keep away from him at all times, hardly leaving my room if I knew that Christopher was at home.

But occasionally he caught me, sometimes in the house, and at other times when I was out unsuspecting and unattended in the gardens or woodlands, away from any view from the Manor, and he repeated his violation of me. There was no way I could match his strength. I could not fight him off, and I was forced to submit to him every time.

My deep fear and terror of my Cousin made me unable to tell my Father what had been happening to me, knowing how much he admired and even loved Christopher, I knew that he would disbelieve me. I had now lost the Father I loved, who had sworn to love and protect me when my Mother died. Although he continued to tutor me, it was the only closeness we now shared together. He now preferred his charming nephew's company to mine and his amiable manner contrasted with the lacklustre, disobedient and unsociable maid that I had become. My Father took no account of my open dislike of my Cousin thinking that it was jealousy of the time and attention everyone gave Christopher, that made me so disagreeable.

I did not even tell Bessie what was happening to me, although she had been puzzled and had questioned me about the blood she had discovered on the coverlet. She knew I was frightened and questioned me often about this new deep displeasure that she found in me. She guessed that it was about Christopher, but she thought that it was my fear of being married to him. I did not dare to speak of my violations or of Christopher's continued attacks on me.

Our Contract for Marriage was not only a family union, but a business union too. My Father often told me that I was extremely fortunate to have such a wonderful and handsome young man to marry. He would tell me that he could have married me to Sir James Walden, who lived twenty miles distance and was even older than my Father. I do not know whether this was true, or to make me feel better about marrying Christopher. By the time that Christopher had persuaded him that I would be of marriageable age when I was just twelve years old, all my Father's promises to my Mother that I would not be Married until I reached the age of fourteen, and that I would share future ownership of Thornhill Manor, and the family lands and monies with my Husband, were no longer considered.

My Father drew up a new Will to celebrate our Marriage, in which he took away everything from me apart from the small amount gold coins that had been put aside for my adult usage. After his death, everything would belong to Christopher – including myself.

4th April 1611

My wedding day! Christopher de Courtsey and I, Mary de Courtsey were married by Father Thomas in St. Peter's Church six weeks before my twelfth birthday.

I tried to be content for the day, and I chose to wear my Mother's peacock blue silk dress, and her pearl ring and necklace, which I had retrieved from the secret drawer in my Chest. The dress was overlarge and too long for me, so Mistress Beckett altered it beautifully to fit my young body. I even had a large piece of the blue silk remaining for me to fashion it into something else.

Bessie washed and brushed my hair until it shone, and she wove for me a pretty headdress of spring flowers, including the white narcissi that my Mother had so loved. Even I thought I that I looked quite lovely, and all the reminders of my Mother gave me courage.

Christopher dressed in new fashionable clothing, looked even more handsome that usual, and I knew that a stranger looking at us might think that I was, indeed, a fortunate maid to be wedded to such a man. As we stood before God's altar, right next to my Mother's tomb, exchanging our vows, I knew then that I was losing forever any power of choice that remained to me.

Forced sexual relations between marriage partners are not considered a violation, but that is what it was to become. Although I had been repeatedly ravaged by this man since the age of eight, I was yet a maid, with a maid's body, and now Christopher could take me, legally, at any time that he wanted to. And this he wanted almost every day. He had developed a strong desire for young and immature women. He was not faithful to me and, when he could, he found opportunities to indulge his Lust elsewhere. In the privacy of our bedchamber, which was now on the other side of the house, far away from Bessie and my father, his wicked treatment of me was probably also a way of taking revenge on me. He had always been envious that while we were both growing up, that I, a mere maid had 'stolen' his expected inheritance, and had had a higher status than him. He had thought of me as Mistress Mary, the beloved daughter of the High and Mighty Sir John and Lady Edwina! Treated like a queen, spoiled by everyone and personally tutored by her Father.

Although I continued to work on the ledgers and have occasional lessons in French and Latin with my Father, after our marriage I was completely in Christopher's power. He had already manipulated my Father so that I was no longer his special and beloved daughter. Now as my Husband he had full control of my every movement. Publicly he was smiling and polite to me, but privately he was wicked and cruel. On most nights, when he did not render himself incapable from drink, he forced himself upon me violently. Often he did bite me on my budding breasts, sometimes until they would bleed, and he did beat me around my legs and body, whether I showed resistance or not. He was a shrewd man. He had not lost all sense of right and wrong, but he knew that my fear of him would make me keep his secret, and he made sure that the bleeding and bruising did not show above my clothing.

I was, indeed, so afeared of him that I did not dare to say anything to anyone about what was happening to me in my marriage bed for fear of even worse treatment. Bessie, who was no longer my nursemaid, but now my ladies' maid, was the only one who knew that I was being attacked at night, but any hesitant approaches that she made to my Father, to make him aware of the situation, were dismissed by him. As far as he was concerned his unattractive and surly daughter was now the property of her Husband, and any Husband had every right to chastise his Wife and to expect her to submit to him!

Christopher's sexual demands were so regular that I did not even know when I had become a woman. At thirteen, without my even having my first bleeding, I found myself with child. Christopher was mightily pleased at his prowess, and even became a little kinder to me. My Father, my Uncle Raymond and my Aunt Elizabeth were delighted, and they too, began to treat me with much more kindness and consideration.

1st June 1613

I will not describe the tortures that I suffered in childbirth. I will only say that with the help of Bessie and Goodwife Mendelson, brought all the way from Chelmsford, my Son was delivered on the 1st June 1613, less than a month after my fourteenth birthday. He was a beautiful baby, with deep blue eyes, a healthy body and a lusty cry, and in spite of his humiliating and unloving conception, I loved him from the moment he was born. After my confinement my baby was baptised by Father Thomas, and we named him John Raymond for his two Grandfathers.

Christopher was much angered when I dismissed the idea of a wet nurse, and decided that I would nurse baby John myself. This also meant that I kept my baby in a crib beside our bed, and it made it difficult for my Husband to mistreat me during the night. I knew that I would have to pay later for this little triumph, but the joy and love I experienced from the closeness of holding and feeding my child rose above any fear I had of later retribution. I was content for the first time since my Mother had died, and I prayed to God that she was looking down at me and baby John from Heaven. I prayed for her continued love and protection for us both.

I was also content to let Aunt Elizabeth continue her role as Mistress of the Manor without any comment or question by me, and Bessie and I passed our days nursing and playing with my baby. He grew big and strong becoming the very image of his Father, his eyes darkening to a deep hazel colour. Like his Father too, he developed a loud and demanding voice to make sure that everyone, even Christopher, paid proper attention to him!

When John was just three months old I resumed my studies with my Father, and my work on the ledgers, although the lessons were so often interrupted by my Father's delight and playfulness with his Grandson. I could scarce believe that my industrious and stern Father could laugh and play and crawl about the floor as he did! John almost became my Father's own deeply longed for son and heir, and I was blessed by him for producing such a marvel. I was as happy as I had ever been with a child that I adored and my Father once more returning my love.

By the time John was crawling it was deep winter outside, not too much snow, but continual rain and a very cold east wind. I feared for him catching a winter sickness, so Bessie and I kept him wrapped up warm. We only carried him outside when it most necessary, or on an occasional warm and sunny day, just to take the air. Within the Manor we played with him in the Great Hall. Benjamin Haydock had made him several wooden toys. There were building blocks which he demanded that I or

Bessie should build so that he could knock it all down again, and many animals with wheels, which to his great delight, we would push across the stone floor where it was warmed in front of the roaring fire. But John's favourite game was to climb the intricately carved oak staircase that led from the Great Hall to the upper floors, and on reaching the top he would clap his little hands together in merriment, and then howl for me or Bessie to bring him safely down again!

But this domestic contentment did not last long. Ten months after John's birth, my Father developed a cancer in his stomach. He did not, at first, complain of the strange lump that grew almost daily, but by harvest time he was unable to conceal his discomfort and pain, and he began to decline rapidly.

The Christmas season that year was most difficult for everyone. I was heavy hearted and very sad about my Father's failing health. It was obvious to me that he was dying, but we still had to be merry and cheerful for John, who was far too young to understand sickness and death. By springtime I was passing most of my time in my Mother's old bedchamber, so that I could remain close to my Father's bedside to attend him day or night as he needed. He began to look old and wizened. His flesh left his body and he started to look like a living skeleton. But in spite of his looks and his great pain I knew that the Father I had loved of old had returned to me.

Now was the time when we were able to love one another once again. Forgiven and forgotten was my Father's harsh and unfair treatment of me. In his final months I as nursed him tenderly, he realised at last, and too late, how he had been duped by Christopher and Aunt Elizabeth to think badly of me and to sign away my birthright.

In the final days of his life he had only a few lucid moments between bouts of intolerable pain. He told me of his desire to change his Will once more, but there was no time to summon the legal clerk from Colchester, so he called for Uncle Raymond and for Christopher to tell them his final wishes.

It was summertime again, and just two years after young John had been born, his Grandfather lay dying in my arms. I told him how much I had always loved him. He kissed me gently and said how proud he was of me, and how content he was that I was again with child, and was expecting to be confined in the autumn.

"My sweet and loving Mary," he said, "you have become my most beloved. Will you ever be able to forgive this foolish old man for all the wrong I have done to you? I know that you are but sixteen years old, but you are a grown woman now, and I see that you are more content now with Christopher. Although I have not written any changes to my Will, Christopher and Raymond have both sworn, with their right hands on the Lord's Bible that after my death you will be given outright ownership of Thornhill Manor, its gardens, parkland and woodlands, and a fair portion of our monies. Christopher will have the rest of the lands, and hold them in trust for baby John. And he has promised that in future he will continue to be kind to you, and cherish and protect you always. Perhaps you will grow to love each other, even as your Mother and I did, and you know how she loved us both".

"Thank you, dear Father," I said, while tears were falling fast from my eyes. "All will be well for us. Do not fret for me." But I was not telling him the truth, for although Christopher had been kinder to me since the birth of our Son, he had recently begun once again to mistreat me in the privacy of our bedchamber, whenever I was not attending my father.

John had slept in the nursery with Bessie since he was weaned, and I no longer had the 'protection' of my Son asleep in his crib beside my bed. Just a few weeks after John's birth Christopher had resumed his almost nightly demands of intimate relations, and now he was once more taking pleasure in beating and wounding me, especially when he was sexually aroused, and in spite of my being once again with child.

But I had related nothing of this to my dying Father. "When I am gone" he said, "Raymond will inherit my title and continue his ownership of the Grange and its farming lands. The rest, apart from your portion, will go to Christopher. The title will, in due course, pass on to Christopher and then to John. I have also made Christopher promise that you shall continue to look after the books and ledgers to help to keep all in profit. So with your own share of the family wealth and profits, and your own power to use it as you will, you will always be secure. Here take the key of my coffer. The gold coins that I have already put away for you lie within, and I have a special treasure here to give you right now, into your safekeeping."

I took the key and added it to my girdle where the key to my Chest still remained attached. Together they were most heavy! Then my Father pointed to the book on his prie-dieu. It was one of the newly printed versions of the Bible, revised by our own King James. Huge, very thick and heavy, and a treasure indeed, written in the most beautiful English prose, and under the authority and title of the King himself.

When he first obtained his copy of the new Bible, my Father had told me the history of its printing. How one hundred years earlier William Tyndale had been the first Englishman to translate the Bible from Latin into English, and how these translations had been treated as heresy, and the Bibles had been publicly burnt whenever copies were found. William Tyndale himself had been forced to flee to the Low Countries where assassins sent by the Pope had eventually caught up with him, and strangled him.

"King James," said my Father, "is a learned man and he had studied the Latin Bible with his friends in Scotland while the Old Queen was still alive, and he had been only the King of Scotland. That was before you were born."

"It was the Old Queen," he continued, "who wanted the Bible preached in English in every church in the land. But by then there were so many different versions of the Bible written in English, that churchmen from Bishop to local priest, began to argue about which one was right."

"So how did the King get to write this one?" I had asked.

"Well," said my father, "soon after he was crowned King James the First of England, the King decided that he wanted a Bible that would please all Protestants, and especially his new subjects. This new Bible would be the one to be preached from all pulpits throughout the land. The King did not write this new Bible himself. No, no, no! He asked many scholars, fifty-four of them, I believe, to re-write it, using William Tyndale's translation as the main model."

"So, although William Tyndale was a killed as a heretic by the Papists, he triumphed in the end," I said, "and King James is awarded all the recognition for the work of William Tyndale's and the fifty-two scholars!"

"I suppose that is how it will be seen in future," laughed my Father. "But you should not say that abroad in public, it might be considered as treason!"

And, with that, my Father and I had had a rare time of laughter together. I remembered that occasion then as I picked up the weighty book, and held it close to my breast.

"Oh, my Father!" I gasped, once more with tears in my eyes. "I will treasure it always, and I will teach my children to read in their own language from it, when they are old enough to do so."

"Take the Bible away with you now, and put it in your Chest," said my Father. "Things will alter swiftly when I have gone to God."

"Do not speak so," I said. I was now crying softly. "I need you at my side even now."

"No, no, my child," he whispered. "I am ready to go, and I am mightily content to leave this world of pain and suffering behind, and to be rejoining your Mother. Let me kiss you and give you my last love and Blessing, take the Bible to your chamber, then go and bring to me my Brother and my Nephew." He shut his eyes, but before I left the chamber he spoke again. "One last thing. I have asked the gardeners to collect and dry summer flowers again so that at Christmastide you will have reminders of your Mother and me once more."

8th August 1615

Within a few hours it was all over, and I quickly understood what my Father had meant by change happening swiftly. Even before my Father was laid in his tomb, my Husband wrested the key of my Father's coffer from me, and abjured his sworn avowal to my Father and his Will. He overruled his own Father, took charge of the coffer and moved himself into the main Hall, forcing the new Sir Raymond, Lord of the Manor to remain in the smaller quarters of the west wing. Our child and his nurse were also left in the west wing, and I, most reluctantly, found myself moved into my recently deceased Father's bedchamber.

Christopher did, however, allow me to have the servants bring my Chest and I had it placed in my Mother's chamber, which I now used as often as I could get away from Christopher. He was very dismissive as he allowed me continued ownership of both the Chest and the key. He still knew nothing of the secret drawer, but I had not yet started to keep anything in it other than my Mother's pearls. The contents in the main body of my Chest that Christopher did have knowledge of, held nothing of value to him. Not even my Father's expensive Bible, but everything in there was still a treasure to me. The contents now included my Son's Christening gown as well as the Bible and my Mother's Book of Hours. Those things that I kept in my Chest were all I was ever allowed to call my own. You may be assured that I was never was given ownership of the Manor, never had the control of my Father's coffer, or the use of a single coin, either gold or silver.

Christopher had always despised my education and he had been envious of my ability to manage the Thornhill lands through accounting. Although he had been taught to read and write he had no understanding of numbers or reckoning. Because of this he would not allow me to demonstrate his own ignorance. The account books were abandoned and I was no longer allowed to have any more say in how the family lands, some of which were rightly mine, were used or ordered.

With Aunt Elizabeth's support, Uncle Raymond's objections to the abandonment of the accounts ledgers were overruled. Rents continued to be collected and wool, farm produce and livestock sold at market, but most receipts went into the deep pockets of my Husband and his Mother, leaving barely sufficient reserves put by for wages, purchases and everyday expenses.

It was just six weeks after the death of my Father, as we were preparing ourselves for bed that I did the most foolish thing that I had ever done. I really do not know why I was so foolish, but I was remembering my Father, and I was angry at the broken promises made to him. Promises that Christopher had sworn on the Holy Bible to a dying man. I questioned Christopher about my rights and those Sacred Promises. I even asked him if I was ever to have any of the gold coins that my Father had been putting aside for me in his coffer since I was a little maid.

For the first time I was showing my anger at Christopher's arrogance and particularly at his treatment of me. My anger mounted. I did not even stop when the look of rage that I knew so well, crossed his face. I continued. "You are unfair and unjust." I was almost shouting at him. "You must know that you are doing wrong in taking control of everything. You have even debased and disgraced your own Father, Sir Raymond, who I need not remind you, is now the rightful Lord of the Manor. All you have left him is his title, and..."

I got no further. Christopher flew into the rage that I should have known was coming. He beat me to the floor, shouting, "do not ever dare to question me, woman. I am Lord and Master of you and everyone here!"

He then commenced kicking me, at first on my back as I cowered on the floor trying to protect my belly and my unborn child. Then he kicked me again and again in my belly, hurting the child within.

I was screaming, but Aunt Elizabeth prevented Uncle Raymond and Bessie from entering our bedchamber saying that they had no right to interfere between Husband and Wife. No one dared to push past her to come to my rescue until Christopher left the bedchamber. I find this so difficult to write; but as a result of his viciousness he killed our child which was due to be born in only seven weeks time.

I was so badly injured that I nearly died too. Aunt Elizabeth sent for a physician to be brought from Chelmsford, who was needed to deliver the dead child, the little Daughter that I had prayed for, and to save my life. This time Christopher could not hide what he had done; and he was even shocked and a little afraid of the consequences of his violence.

But his mother, the new Lady Elizabeth, was ever ready to cover for him, and let it be known to everyone that Mary de Courtsey had fallen down the stairs of the Great Hall. I do not think that the physician really believed the falsehoods told to him, but he did his work well and was rewarded with a fine purse of gold.

20th October 1615

For my nursing and slow recovery I have retired to the chamber that used to be my Mother's private withdrawing room. Bessie and John have joined me on this side of the house, and they are now close to me again, in my old childhood bedchamber.

And here, in the room which is full of memories for me of my dear Mother, when I have not been crying over the loss of my Daughter, whom I would have named Susan, I have been recording into one of my father's accounting Journals all that I can remember of what has happened in my life since I was four years old.

And since Christopher has no knowledge of the secret drawer in my Chest, I shall store it there. It will be a testament for my Son John to read when he is old enough to understand the relationship between his Father and me.

Christopher did not dare to object when I insisted that our Son and Bessie be allowed to move to the adjoining room, and it seems that he will leave me alone to recover, with his Mother acting as sometime nurse, and I'm sure, sometime spy. I think that he is afraid that I will accuse him of attempting to murder me.

Bessie knows that I have started this Journal, and she runs to hide it in my Chest as soon as we hear Aunt Elizabeth's footsteps. It is not always replaced it in the secret drawer. Most often I just wrap it in the remaining piece of my mother's blue silk dress, and Bessie puts it in the main body of the Chest.

To make sure that Aunt Elizabeth does not engage in suspicions about my writings, I have also started to write little daily notes about John's progress, and I leave them in my bedchamber where she can peruse them if it pleases her. This means that I have no need to hide the quills and ink, or to hurriedly clean my stained fingers whenever she approaches.

Christmas 1615

I am almost recovered now. With Bessie's help I can climb up and down the stairs to the Great Hall, and when the weather is clement I can even walk abroad a little. Most often I go to sit and reflect on the bench in my Mother's memorial Garden. Bessie has been wonderful. She has stayed with me the whole time, and nursed and cleansed me tenderly when I was unable to leave my bed. She hardly leaves my side both day and night.

Bessie has grown to be a strong and handsome woman, and like Aunt Elizabeth, I think that Christopher is perhaps not frightened of her, but he is certainly in awe of her. He never tries to command her, and he knows that she is loyal only to me and John.

She is still enamoured of Godfrey Haydock, but even though I have often promoted that she should marry him, she will not leave my side. Quite selfishly and privately I thank God every day for her determination to be my protector.

Last week Bessie told me that Christopher has found himself a young mistress, Edith Young the Daughter of the Thornton village thatcher, who is willing to submit to his brutal way of love-making. I have no objection if it keeps him away from me. He has allowed me to remain in my Mother's withdrawing chamber. Her private bed chamber between this and Christopher's bedchamber are now our Son's nursery and schoolroom. Now he no longer has access to me during the night. If I spend any night with Christopher in our marriage bed, it is with my consent, and I do so to keep an atmosphere of peace and calmness between us.

Christopher has never told me that he regrets what he has done to me, but he has become quite attentive and warmer towards me than he has ever been before, and this Christmastide he has been surprisingly pleasant to everyone, even to the servants. There have been several falls of snow this year, and outside there are many deep snowdrifts, which make it difficult for all necessary work to be completed on the Manor farms. All the tenants can do for the present time is to make sure that all the animals and fed and watered, and to keep warm the best that they can.

The Yule Log has been dragged into the Great Hall and the Manor has been festively decorated with fragrant dried herbs and spiced fruit. The great garland of dried flowers, which has not been made ever since my Mother's death so many years ago, and my Father's last wish, has been reproduced. There are baskets of apples from our own orchards, which have been stored in one of the barns since they were harvested in the autumn. There are also a few rare and expensive oranges which were shipped from Spain to the port of London, and have been conveyed to Chelmsford by merchants. Some of these exotic fruits Bessie and I have pierced with even more exotic and expensive cloves which have travelled from the other side of the world to reach the shores of England. The scent is wonderful, and it mixes well with the wood burning smells that come from the huge Yule logs that burn day and night in the fireplace, keeping everything bright, merry and warm. I am not merry, but I am content.

Christmas 1620

I open my Journal this Christmas Day in the Year of Our Lord 1620, and I am astonished to find that it is now five years since I last wrote.

My Angel Mother and Beloved Father, I have kneeled at your tomb in St. Peter's Church and prayed to you each and every Sunday after the service. How I miss you both and my memory of your beloved faces now fade and merge with the images of the effigies on your tomb. But you were never stone faced as they are. I still remember the soft warmth of your smile, Mother, how it used to make the whole world a safe and happy place for me. And Father, I remember your concerned, yet loving look, especially in the days before you left me to return to my Mother in Heaven. Life is calmer for me now, but I still feel the desire of your watchful Blessings from Heaven.

To my great content Christopher and I have entered a state of harmony between us. I have kept the peace by voicing no opinions or taking any part in the management of Thornhill Manor, and its farms and lands.

Instead I have been happily engrossed with the raising and education of little John Raymond. He is my life and my joy. I can hardly believe that he is only seven years of age. He is so tall and strong, and is a most handsome and intelligent boy. In looks he is so very like his Father, but because of his horse riding and training with his fencing master he does not carry the fat upon his body that his Father had as a child. I am most pleased that from me he has a will to study and learn. He already reads and writes better than I did as a maid, and now I have started to teach him reckoning. His little fingers fly over his abacus and he has a correct answer almost at once. But most of all I love the time we spend walking in the gardens and woodlands, sitting quietly to espy a baby fox or fawn with its mother, or a barn owl on its evening flight to hunt for mice.

I have had very few hostile encounters with Aunt Elizabeth as I leave her to order the household as she pleases. She is still self absorbed and cares for none but herself and Christopher.

During these past five years, contrary to my expectations, my Husband has been industrious with the management of our lands and the tenant farms. He and I are most calm with each other, and I am content to write that he now shows genuine pleasure when he plays with his Son. Occasionally I find myself laughing out in merriment when Christopher goes down on his knees in the Great Hall, and John sits astride his back. He spurs his Father on like a great stallion and rider! My Husband now finds much of his evening entertainment outside the walls of Thornhill Manor with other wealthy young men, in drinking, gambling and womanising. That troubles me not at all as it keeps him in good humour and away from my bed.

Until this year crops and harvests have been abundant and profitable, and my Husband's pockets have been full of good silver to pay for this entertainment, but because we have had such a wet summer, this year's harvest has been very poor. We have sufficient corn to feed the Manor household and the tenant farmers, but there has been no surplus to sell in the market. Fortunately our wool yield was good so we will survive the winter well, but the poor harvests everywhere means that bread is expensive and there are many beggars abroad.

In past times of poor harvests my Mother and Father would always give extra alms to the church to feed the sick and hungry, and they would never turn away beggars at the gate without giving them bread. Sometimes they were even offered shelter in the barns and old clothing to keep them warm.

At the commencement of December Aunt Elizabeth objected to the preparations of the great garland, and she complained to Christopher about the expense of inviting the tenants to our Christmas feast in the Great Hall, she wished to cancel it for this season. Then she did say, "ten beggars I have turned away this week alone. They dare to come to our very gate to beg for food. Do they all think that we have bread and meat to give to every lazy itinerant?"

"Mother, we will and must have our Christmas feast and festivities as usual. Even more so because of the poor harvest which affects everyone," my Husband replied, "and do not be too harsh on the beggars. There is much hunger and sickness abroad. You do not have to welcome them into the Manor with the other guests, but I am sure that we can spare some silver to give to Father Thomas for him to give alms."

"Tut. Good silver for beggars," she muttered. "What will they want next, the very clothes from our backs?" And she walked away, muttering to herself all the while.

And here I write of great tidings. Yesterday, on Christmas Eve, my dear Bessie was married to her long time love Godfrey Haydock. Now that my life with Christopher has become easier, Bessie has, at last, given in to Godfrey's pleas to marry him. She considers herself an old maid now, at nearly twenty nine (Godfrey is thirty-three), but they still love each other, and they are well suited. During these past few years Bessie deferred her marriage time after time, in spite of the pleading from Godfrey, because she always wished to protect me from Christopher. But now, at last, I have persuaded her that Christopher's rages are almost a thing of the past, and that she must now think of her own contentment.

Like Christopher and me, Bessie and Godfrey were married in St. Peter's church in Thornton village, and I tried not to let memories of my own marriage there spoil the day. Father Thomas, who is now an old man, is still our resident pastor, and gave again one of his long and tedious sermons. He is very proud of the part he played in Godfrey's life by teaching him to read, write and to use numbers, and I think that he feels quite fatherly towards him.

Bessie looked so content and pretty in the creamy yellow damask gown that I had Mistress Beckett make for her. Somehow I also persuaded my Husband to give her a small purse of silver to start her married life. She will now live with the Haydock brothers in their cottage, which lies just across the courtyard from the Manor House, so she will not be far away, and she will continue to spend her days with me and John.

John and I shall miss the feeling of security that we have when Bessie was so close to us at night, but as the terror that I once felt from Christopher is no more, it was not just for me to let Bessie delay her marriage any longer.

21st November 1621

Today Aunt Elizabeth died after a short illness. At forty-six she was of a fair age. I have been nursing her day and night for three months and I am exhausted. Christopher is laid low with sadness. He came to my bedchamber where I was resting before attending her funeral. He sat on my bed and gripped my hand tightly. "Whatever am I to do without her?" he cried out in his pain. "She is the only woman that I have ever loved."

I took no offence at his words. I know that he has never loved me, but I do feel his sorrow. "My dear Husband," I said very gently, "I am mightily saddened for your loss, and I promise you that John and I will do our best to comfort you. Uncle Raymond will need our love and comfort too. Perhaps you and your Father can help each other." Christopher sat for a while longer, and then he left without saying another word, but I do believe that he was comforted.

I feel no sorrow that Aunt Elizabeth is no longer with us, indeed all I feel is relief, and I think that, secretly, Uncle Raymond is also relieved. I cannot pretend that I felt any love for her and I am mightily content at last to become the Mistress in my home, and of the Manor servants. But I shall make no great changes, and I shall give my Husband time to adjust to the loss of his Mother.

I am a mature woman of twenty-two now. As I have grown older Christopher no longer finds my adult body as arousing as he did when I was an undeveloped maid, so he makes fewer and fewer demands on me, and invites me to his bedchamber only rarely. For my part, I am relieved that my Husband no longer wants to share a bed with me regularly, and on those rare occasions when he wants to do so, I am compliant and even inviting, keeping his temper appeased and our relations harmonious in the hope that he no longer has the desire to hurt and abuse me.

12th January 1622

Christmastide was rather subdued because of Aunt Elizabeth's death, and we were very solemn during the Christmas mass at St. Peter's. But after mass John Raymond was very merry opening his Christmas gifts, and enjoyed sharing the festivities with Bessie and the servants. John was delighted with my gift of a fine rocking-horse, a dapple grey mare complete with saddle and stirrups, and Christopher, who now takes real pleasure in his Son's company, bought John a real pony. When he saw the pony, who he has named Falstaff, in the stables John clapped his hands in merriment. It pleasures me greatly to see him and his Father together, Christopher on his fine stallion and John and his pony, as they ride off to inspect a pasture together. John is helping Christopher with his grief over his Mother's death.

20th March 1622

I am overwhelmed with sorrow. I have to write of another death in the family. On 3rd March my Uncle Raymond died suddenly, after a fall from his horse. Christopher and I were both mightily shaken this time. This unfortunate deed has happened only four months after the death of Aunt Elizabeth. My Husband can hardly believe that both his Mother and Father have now gone to God. In the years since the death of my Father I had come to love my Uncle Raymond. He and I drew near to each other, especially as we were both thrust aside by Christopher and his Mother. Indeed, since Aunt Elizabeth's death, Uncle Raymond had begun to find a voice of his own for the first time in many, many years, and I thought that recently he had begun to look more content than I have ever seen him.

Whatever the quarrels and differences between all of the adults, little John Raymond loved his Grandparents, and he will miss them both sorely.

However, Christopher, who is now in the prime of life, has now inherited the title of Sir Christopher. It has made him grow in stature, and he fills his new role with glee and confidence. And with the title and status he is also now the legal owner of all the de Courtsey lands and monies. My status too has changed. I have become Lady Mary de Courtsey, Lady of the Manor; but that will make no difference to the way Christopher treats me. I will still have no say, power or rights in the lands and property that should, by rights, be shared equally between us.

16th May 1622

It is a fine day again and I am twenty three today!

This morning I was sitting on the bench in my Mother's memorial garden, enjoying the warm spring sunshine, listening to a bold cuckoo calling in the distant woodlands and looking at the lovely spring flowers as they tossed their heads in the morning breeze, when my Husband came to me. I thought, at first, that it was to offer me birthday greetings that he came. But it was tidings of a different nature which, unusually for him, he wished to share with me.

"I have news that may make a difference to us at Thornhill Manor," he said excitedly. "Have you heard tell of the man they call the 'favourite' of our King James?"

I shook my head. I know nothing of the King or his Court. Christopher sat down on the bench beside me.

"Well." He said. "King James's 'favourite' is called George Villiers, who the King has made the Marquis of Buckingham, and it seems that he and his Wife, the Marchioness Katherine, are the people who bought New Hall. The renovations to the old palace are now complete and they are about to become our new neighbours! I also hear tell that they paid an enormous sum for it; £30,000."

I gasped with astonishment. £30.000. That sum of money could almost buy the whole county! I knew that New Hall was once a country palace owned by King Henry VIII, and then by Queen Elizabeth. She gave it to her 'favourite', the Earl of Sussex, and now it seems that it will belong to another 'favourite'!

The palace lies some four miles to the north of Thornhill Manor, nearer to Chelmsford. It has many acres of land, some of which adjoin ours. Christopher has often desired to purchase some of the New Hall parkland to add to his own lands, but the cost was always beyond his reach.

"I wonder if we will meet them," I mused. "I remember seeing New Hall once when it lay empty. It was when I was but a little maid, and my Father and I went trespassing in the grounds out of curiosity. We rode our horses through a gap in the boundary, and spent an hour or two riding through the overgrown gardens and parkland. I thought the mansion looked huge and quite overwhelming. I much preferred our own Manor House."

Christopher scowled. "You were fortunate that your Father was then the Lord of the Manor. You were given too many privileges when you were a maid."

I lowered my eyes and said nothing more. But he was not angered. He jumped up, smiling, and with a look of determination upon his face. He continued with his discourse, "I desire to meet this George Villiers as soon as it seems fit," he said. "I'm sure that he will soon be riding out to explore his property and, as our lands adjoin his, I consider that it would be polite for me, as his nearest neighbour, to greet him and welcome him to our neighbourhood!" He patted my hand and left me to my solitude.

3rd June 1622

I have been having discourse with Father Thomas, who spoke to his Bishop about our illustrious new neighbour! George Villiers is twenty-eight three years younger than Christopher, and like Christopher, he is the son of a country Knight. (Just like us, but with a lot more land and wealth!) His Father took him to the Court of King James when he was a youth, and he became friends with the King's younger son, Prince Charles. When Prince Charles' older brother, Henry, Prince of Wales, died of a sudden of typhoid fever ten years ago, Prince Charles became the most important child in the land, and his friend and adviser, George Villiers, was introduced into the inner circle of the King's family. Then King James took a fancy to him too. So George Villiers, already the friend and companion to the Prince of Wales, is now also the King's 'favourite'. Christopher thinks that George Villiers must be, or will become soon, one of the most powerful men in the land. And it must surely be of benefit to him to befriend the King's 'favourite'!

1?th July 1622

Two weeks ago while Christopher was out riding, he found a way to meet and introduce himself to the Marquis of Buckingham, and he welcomed him as our new neighbour. He has now met the Marquis, George as he calls him, several times, and I do believe that they are becoming friends! I do not know what it will mean for us at Thornhill Manor. We cannot possible match our household with his, so I do not know where this 'friendship' will lead, but next week Christopher and I have been invited for an informal lunch with the Marquis and the Marchioness!

19th July 1622.

We have been to New Hall, and what an occasion it was! What powerful people, far above anyone that I have ever known before! New Hall is indeed a palace! It is even more overwhelming on the inside than it is from the outside, and so beautifully furnished!

It was an unusually cold and wet day for July, so we were driven to New Hall in our covered coach by John Newbold, the stable master. Christopher was wearing a new, all black doublet and hose, which has, as its only decoration, a double line of seed pearls around each cuff. And I was wearing a new satin dress in pale rose, with a high collar made of silk lace, and also decorated with seed pearls. And we were both wrapped in warm velvet lined cloaks to keep out the dampness of the dull summer's day.

Young John was not a little angered, (he does look so like his Father when he is displeased), at being left behind. He thinks that now he is nine years old that he is quite grown, and should also have been invited!

I think that both Christopher and I were nervous at the prospect of this, supposedly informal meeting with the Marquis and Marchioness Katherine.

"You know well that I have not been introduced to either of them. Are you sure that we are expected to be informal? How do we address them?" I asked Christopher.

"George has insisted that we call them George and Katherine," he replied. "Although I am comfortable with George, I have not been introduced to the Marchioness either."

Soon we were approaching the house through a long and handsome avenue of beech trees. New Hall was much larger than I remembered. It is indeed a palace, and it must be at least four times larger than our simple Manor House. From the outside the building looked light and airy with so many windows. And so grand! The weed tangled gardens were full of men making them beautiful after so many years of neglect.

And what can I relate of George Villiers?

He is such a handsome man! It is no wonder that Christopher says the Marquis is described at Court as the most handsome man in the realm. He has a fine face and dark hair. Christopher, who is also a handsome man, really looks like a country bumpkin compared with the elegant Marquis of Buckingham. He is tall and slim, with a most elegant figure; and he displayed his shapely legs by wearing white silk stockings and shoes bearing diamond buckles! I found him very attractive and, at first, I had much envy for the Marchioness Katherine.

She has less height than her Husband, but she is his equal in elegance with her dark hair coiffured high upon her head. She was wearing a splendid dress in dark green satin, which suited her complexion and green eyes perfectly. And I am sure that they were real emeralds, and not paste, decorating the lace of her high ruff collar. I felt very ordinary beside her obvious wealth and elegance, and she quite took my breath away. And this was a 'simple occasion between friends!' But in spite of her grandeur the Marchioness is quite charming, and she greeted us very warmly as she welcomed us to her home!

I could see at once that Christopher and the Marquis, with such a similarity in family backgrounds, really like one another. For all the beauty and charm and his splendid home and Court life, I think that at heart, the Marquis misses the simple life that he once lived. He and Christopher are most agreeable together, it is if they have known each other for years! I always knew that my Husband could display a distinguished air, but yesterday he surpassed himself!

We were ushered through a long and handsome portrait gallery, into the private dining room. The room was flooded with light on one side from tall windows that reached from the floor to the ceiling, and the walls either side of a very grand fireplace were hung with two rich tapestries. On the far wall hung a full length portrait of a lady whom I knew to be of our last queen, Queen Elizabeth. The painting, so expertly painted that I almost believed that she was standing there, showed the richness of her clothing, covered all over with jewels, and a high collar of very fine lace edged with hundreds of pearls, a double row of huge pearls hung to her waist and she appeared to be caressing them lovingly. The artist had painted the gleaming jewels and lustrous pearls in such a way that they looked as though I could just reach out to take them into my own hand. The Queen's eyes had the most piercing and direct regard. No wonder it was reported that her subjects had always been in awe of her.

A handsomely dressed servant in a livery of red and black showed us to our places at the table which was laid with the finest white linen, silver plates, silver gilt dishes, and crystal glasses. I gasped at splendour such as I have never encountered before, but I did see that my host and hostess were most comfortable and natural in their magnificent surroundings. Both the Marquis and Marchioness insisted that we call them George and Katherine. I felt quite humble and awed as I said to the Marchioness, "What a magnificent chamber. I have never seen one so beautiful! And the light from those windows – it makes our own Manor house have the appearance of a dungeon!"

Marchioness Katherine laughed. "I am sure that your home is quite splendid, Mary. As you may well know, we have had much building work done to renovate the house in the last few months, and this and many other chambers are now likened to the house of the late Countess of Shrewsbury, who used to be called Bess of Hardwick. Do you know of Hardwick Hall in Derbyshire?"

I shook my head and my cheeks reddened. I felt just like a country bumpkin. I did not even know where Derbyshire was, let alone Hardwick Hall!

During our 'simple' meal, which was more splendid than a banquet at Thornhill Manor, George talked about his life at Court. He had such vibrant expressions on his face that I soon forgot my embarrassment and I laughed in great merriment all the while he was talking.

"King James is mightily clever," he said, "but he is also quite kind-hearted, and he loves his wife and family. But, in my opinion, he is a most unattractive man. He has very thin and crooked legs, and his tongue is too large for his mouth, which makes him drool and unclear in his speech." George demonstrated this, and, over exaggerating I am certain, he slobbered like a village idiot.

Once more we all laughed, but now I was beginning to feel uncomfortable. I was sure that this discourse must be treasonable, but George and Christopher were smiling in merriment! The Marquis continued, quite unabashed, saying "King James is completely infatuated with me, and he slobbers over me and kisses me all the time." Then, quite casually he said, "You must know that I am the King's lover!"

This time I was not only uncomfortable, I was horrified and disgusted. Again my cheeks reddened with embarrassment and my attraction to him deserted me all at once and completely. Inwardly I thanked God that we had not brought our Son with us! I looked over to Marchioness Katherine, but her face revealed nothing!

Full of confidence and without any discomfort, George continued his discourse about King James, about being the King's adviser, and the leader of the King's Council. All this discourse took place quite openly in front of the many servants that were in attendance. I quickly came to the opinion that he has taken advantage of the King's infatuation to gain wealth and power. He boastfully listed for us all the advancements that he has made since his introduction to King James: "First he made me a Gentleman of the Bedchamber, then Master of the Horse, Lord Admiral, a Viscount, an Earl, and now the Marquis of Buckingham. And I am sure that it will not be long before you will have the pleasure of talking to a Duke!"

Each of these posts has brought the Marquis increasing wealth, and now he has used some of that great wealth to purchase New Hall in order have a home near London fit to invite the King and the Royal Family for visits.

I was mightily content to leave, and that we did not stay on after our meal to look over New Hall. Thence we came home and on our return to Thornhill I asked Christopher what he had thought about the visit.

"Oh!" he said. "George behaves like that all the time. That is what I so admire about him. I have no doubt that he will be made a Duke someday"

I said nothing. I wanted never more to see him again!

9th November 1622

So much has occurred during the past three months that all at Thornhill has been completely changed. Before George Villiers entered into our lives I was simply Lady Mary de Courtsey, who had no say in anything about Thornhill Manor, or how any of the businesses of its entailed estate, lands and farms were conducted. In the past I was often scolded or beaten if I offered any opinion, so I learned to say nothing and spent my days raising my Son. Only since the death of Aunt Elizabeth last year have I been also Mistress of the Manor House and its servants as well.

But the greatest change in my life commenced when my Husband wished to impress his new friend George Villiers. At first as he spent our silver lavishly to purchase new clothing for himself and expensive wines for their entertainment. I became concerned that he would soon drain our coffer of all the gold and silver that is needed for Thornhill to survive the unprofitable winter months.

But I can see that a real bond has developed between Christopher and George, so much so, that when the Marquis returned to Court two months ago, with very little discourse between us, Christopher went with him. He also took with him all the profits of this year's harvests, and left me alone in Thornhill, to manage the winter season as best as I can with the rapidly depleting family fortune. I have heard nothing from him yet, but I am sure that he will send a message soon demanding yet more monies!

For myself, I am most content about this new development in our lives. It appears that for the first time since we were married Christopher needs me. As much as he hates to rely upon me, he has commanded that I manage Thornhill profitably in order to fund monies for his new lifestyle. Of course he has given me very direct instructions on everything that I must do, but, at last, at the age of twenty-three, I shall have freedom such as I have never had before!

12th November 1622

Finally a letter from Christopher (the first one that I have ever received) containing a little news. Its main purpose is to demand for yet more silver, and the messenger is waiting to return as soon as he and his horse are refreshed.

> *Dear Wife*
> *The King's Court at Whitehall is likened unto a city. A multitude of people live here. I have not yet met the King and Queen. They have all around them their close circle of attendants – many Lords and Ladies, Bishops and Clerics, who also have their own attendants. And then there is a host of servants to cook, clean and serve for all who attend the Court.*
> *I share a bedchamber with others in the far end of the palace. I see George but little. His time is occupied by the Royal Family.*
> *I have heard it said by many at Court that George is most*

important to the King and Prince Charles, but he is much disliked for it by all his rivals for the Kings attention; the Nobles, the Kings Chancellor, the Clerics and the lesser Knights.

I am in need of more funds to pay my way until I can, via George, secure a well-paid post, and so I am instructing you to send £20 with my messenger.

Your Husband
Christopher.

That is all. No message for me or John. As long as there is silver to fill his pockets we are forgotten. £20 is all the profit we have made from the autumn market sale of mutton and beef. I am afeared that all this foolishness is going to lead the Manor into danger, and I feel that there is a danger for Christopher too, if he clings too close to the Marquis.

I have the purse of silver and must hurry to give it to the messenger.

22nd November 1622

Another letter from Christopher today, delivered by a most disagreeable muddy and tired messenger. He has ridden overnight without stopping from the Palace of Whitehall to Thornhill, and my generous Husband has promised that I should give him a gold coin if it was delivered the next day!

Dear Wife,
I continue to share a small chamber here in the cramped quarters for lower Courtiers. It is as busy as a city with strangers coming and going day and night, and we all live close. Much of it is also dirty and smells like a midden.

To my regret George has little time for me. He passes most of his days in the preferential quarters of the Palace with King James, and Prince Charles. I have not yet been allowed access to any of these grand chambers and I have not been presented to any one of the Royal Family.

George finds himself in the difficult position of dividing his time, diplomatically, between the King and Prince Charles, therefore he has very little time to visit or go abroad with me.

I have passed a few short hours in George's very spacious and grand apartment, an apartment to which the King visits often. I have not seen the Marchioness Katherine here at Whitehall, and I think that she must be either with her parents, the Earl and Countess of Rutland, or at another of George's homes.

It angers me not a little to find myself only on the fringes or Court life. That I am a friend of the Marquis of Buckingham means nothing. All manner of persons around me jostle for position, and they all appear to be suspicious and envious of everyone else. All are very envious of George, who has received countless favours, gifts, titles and grants of land. George is in a magnificent position of power, but I have heard it is said that he wastes it by giving the King foolish council, advancing costly expenditure and wars which result in high tax demands from gentlemen of all ranks. He is daily becoming hated by most taxpaying Englishmen. But still at Court, he is envied by everyone. They all desire advancement – as do I!

Because of this constant rivalry, and envy of George, I find that I have been unable to make any friends at Court. Because he is disliked, I am also disliked! However, this does not make me want to take to my heels and return home.

On the contrary, I have other plans. This small chamber is useful as a convenience for me, because I am able to meet with George somewhere at Court for a few moments daily, but I would like to have some private space for the few occasions that George has any lengthy spare time to spend with me, and to get away from all the intrigues and jealousies of the Court. So I have decided that I need to have my own separate private residence away from Court. I have already found a small house near the Aldgate within the City of London, and I plan to buy it at once.

As soon as you receive this letter I bid you to call in Sir Thomas Smallwood, the lawyer from Chelmsford, and give him the enclosed letter. I am instructing him to sell The Grange, and all its lands to Anthony Buckshore.

As you well know, I have rented The Grange for many years to Mr. Buckshore, and he has often said that he desires of me to sell the house and lands to him. I have now decided to do so, and with the proceeds I shall buy the house near the Aldgate. I have chosen this house because it is well away from the Palace of Whitehall. It is also well positioned for me being situated near the entry gate to the City where I can rest, refresh and change my clothes after the future journeys I shall be taking from here to Thornhill.

I demand that you obey these instructions without delay;
Your Husband, Christopher de Courtsey

At first I was astonished. Had my Husband totally lost his wits? Then I became angry. Very angry. How dare he? How dare he not only take away a large part of our income, but also our capital? But I knew that I had to obey. Although life is more harmonious between us, more harmonious than it has ever been since we have been married, Christopher still would not hesitate to beat me if I were ever to disobey or argue with him. The Grange and the attached lands and farms have never belonged to me. They have been rightfully owned by Christopher since the death of his Father. No matter that he had taken ownership of my lands and property, The Grange is his to do with as he wishes. I had no choice or say in the matter. I sent for Sir Thomas Smallwood and Mr Anthony Buckshore, and together they made an agreement. Within one week contracts were signed and sealed, and The Grange was sold. The next day £2,000 in gold was on its way to Christopher via his messenger who was accompanied by an armed servant.

1st January 1623

A new year and a complete new start for me and everyone here at Thornhill. Christopher remained at court for the Christmas and Yuletide season. His messenger brought me and John a brief note with seasonal greetings, and telling me that he has kept his chamber at Court, but he has also established himself in his new home. I have not missed his presence, but John has missed his Father.

In the last few months since George Villiers entered our lives, Christopher has all but ignored John. I have attempted to fill the gap by introducing pleasure into his studies. I sometimes go riding with him, but I have never been a proficient horsewoman, and it saddens me when I see John sad and lonely on his pony. My first task this New Year is to find him a companion for outside sports.

20th January 1623

Last week Bessie's twelve year old Nephew Alfred Blackstone came to stay with her. He is very like Bessie, sturdy as an oak, and has a mop of light brown hair that constantly falls over his blue eyes. I sometimes wonder if he can see at all! I have seen him out riding and he is a very able horseman. Bessie brought him to me when I was at my desk in the library. I did speak to him, saying, "I am pleased that you have come to Thornfield Manor. Does your family live in Thornton?"

He nodded shyly, looking down at the floor.

Bessie said. "Alfred is my Sister's boy. Her husband works with my Father in the Blacksmith's shop. Alfred started to learn smithying, but he broke his arm last October, and it is not yet strong enough for him to return to the forge."

"Would it please you to spend some time here with my son? I asked Alfred. "His name is John, and he is nine years old. He's not as big and strong as you, but he does like to ride his pony. Would you like to ride with him?"

Bessie nudged him. "Please Mistress. Yes Mistress," he muttered, still not daring to look at me. His cheeks were as red as a cockerel's coxcomb!

"Well Bessie," I said. "Why don't you take Alfred to the kitchen to see if Mistress Tadworth has any of that nice apple pie left? I am sure that he looks as though he could eat some." This time Alfred looked at me and grinned. I continued. "I think that John is in the kitchen too. You could introduce them to each other."

I had no wish to force a friendship, but it will please me mightily to see John with rosy cheeks from a good canter in the frosty air, and with his eyes glowing with merriment again. I pray that Alfred and

John enjoy each others company, and develop a great friendship just as Bessie and I have done.

Bessie is most content in her marriage with Godfrey, her only sadness is that she has not yet been able to conceive a child. Last week I employed Godfrey as estate manager. He can now read and write almost as well as I do, and he will also be able to work with me on the accounts ledgers. With his help and that of the new bailiff, Adam Fulbright, who I have also employed, I am learning how the farms, lands and businesses can become more efficient and profitable to make up for the loss of the Grange.

It has been difficult for me to re-establish the ledgers after so many years of no entries. Many of the amounts that I have entered here had, of necessity, to be approximates rather than exact, but I hope all will be corrected in the next few months as the financial position becomes clearer. I shall also be able to judge the effect on our finances caused by the selling The Grange, with the loss of rent and our share of the harvest from the farms.

Since her marriage my faithful Bessie has continued to come to the Manor daily to take care of me and all my personal needs. She will always be my best friend and confidante. She is such a competent woman that I have asked her to become the housekeeper for Thornhill, with responsibility for all the housemaids, cooks and cleaners. So I now have as much time as I need to work on the Manor's accounts.

1st February 1623

I realise now that ever since Christopher became so involved with George, Marquis of Buckingham, I am most content, and my daily life has become interesting and fulfilling. Even in the cold of winter I wake up in the morning as though spring has arrived, and I feel good about starting a new day! I enjoy my work of looking after the estate. It is now essential as my Husband has not yet succeeded in securing a handsomely paid post, and has need of a great deal of monies to fund his new lifestyle, and as long as silver is plentiful he stays away. Although he will expect me to give full account of everything I have done while he has been absent, he is not able to question me daily on how I am running the estate or how it is managed.

Winter shows no sign of easing, and it has been a very hard one this year, I have been abroad with Adam Fulbright, making it known to all the tenants that he and I will be there not just as landlord and Masters, but as reliable Masters who will help them improve their yields to the benefit of all. All the tenants, save the Taylors at Crossover farm, are most industrious and self sufficient. The Taylors have mainly pigs to rear but even this easy task sometimes seems to be beyond their capabilities! Adam Fulbright will have to be very strict with Robert Taylor, who is slovenly and lazy. I do not like to see evictions on the Thornhill estate, especially during a harsh winter, but perhaps he will need to threaten Master Taylor. There are now many beggars abroad, many of them unprofitable farmers evicted by harsh landowners. We will have to see if the Taylors can increase the production and improve the care of their animals with more competent management.

I like in particular the Ropers of Willow Farm, who are mainly sheep farmers. Mistress Roper is fat and jolly, and has a swarm of merry children running around her, no doubt being useful shepherding and tending their fields of vegetables too. At present her Husband, Tom Roper, has with him their two eldest boys. They are up on the hill in one of the lambing shelters with the first of the ewes about to lamb this year. Keeping the sheep safe, fed and watered during the last weeks of frost and snow has been so very difficult. After Easter, Emily, the Roper's nine year old Daughter, will be joining Mistress Wagstaff in the Thornhill dairy.

20th February 1623

Another letter from Christopher, dated 14th February, with a surprise announcement. I know not whether to be content or fearful!

> *Dear Wife*
> *I have now officially joined George's personal entourage, and I have even secured a small paid post as aide and assistant to the Marquis. I expected to return to Thornhill at the commencement of the year, but I have not yet found the time as I have been*

preparing myself for a long journey overseas. If the winds drop and the sea conditions improve, in a few days time I shall be joining George as we set off for France, on what he calls a 'dashing adventure'. It is somewhat secret so I cannot give you much detail, except to say that I, and a handful of soldiers, are about to accompany the Marquis and Prince of Wales, who will be travelling incognito, on a journey through France and Spain in order to arrange a marriage between Prince Charles and the Spanish Princess Maria. I expect to be away for some months.

I regret that I am unable to come back to ensure that all is in order before I leave the country, but I trust that you will continue to follow my orders as far as the administration of Thornhill is concerned. If you have done as I have instructed there should be no problems. I expect to be back by harvest time.

Please tell my Son that I wish that he was old enough to accompany me, and that I look forward to riding with him again soon.

Your Husband Christopher

What a turn this attachment for the great Marquis is taking! Six months he expects to be gone! And gone away with very few thoughts for John, and without a kind word to me! I do not know if I am fearful or not, but I shall await his return with interest!

As for his 'orders'. His orders were to not change anything without his direct approval. But the estate will fail if we do nothing. Failure will mean starvation for all the dependents of Thornhill, and I cannot risk the lives of everyone here, just so that Christopher can continue his detached life away from us.

Meanwhile I have commenced with the improvements that I consider to be necessary. Geoffrey Haydock and I have identified what needs to be done to improve the profitability of the whole of the Thornhill estate. As well as good silver going to Christopher, there is everyone to feed and high taxes to be paid. All the more since these 'adventures' of the Marquis and Prince Charles have to be paid for by taxes from everyone – rich or poor.

Young John is willing to take his part in learning what he will need to know as the next Master of Thornhill. He is already beginning to understand the mathematics and logic of the ledgers. I have also asked the new bailiff, Adam Fulbright, to take John on his rounds so that he will get to know the tenants, and understand how well the farms and other business are run. In his leisure time he is very happy to ride and explore the countryside with Bessie's nephew Alfred.

I am very hopeful that things here will be so much better when Christopher finally returns that he will be astonished at the improvements that we have all made, and thus I will avoid his anger for disobeying his orders.

16th May 1623

I am twenty-four today! After a long, cold and difficult winter for many, spring has arrived at last. The skies are blue and all the birds are a-twittering as they seek food to feed their young. As I look from my window at the flowers tossing their heads in my Mother's memorial garden, and pretty cherry trees in full blossom, I can hardly believe how much has happened, and how life has changed for me since my last birthday when my Husband told me of our new neighbours. Can that have been only a year ago?

It is now seven months since Christopher left Thornhill to join his friend George, the Marquis of B. Just three letters from him, and I expect to hear nothing more until he returns to England at the end of the summer!

As for us, we are all in good health, and the changes we have made for the improvement of the Thornhill estate, so far seem to have been for the better. The fields and orchards are in fine growth, new lambs were more than we have ever recorded before, and now most of the cows have already produced healthy calves.

Bessie, Alfred, John and I are to forget work for the day and we will be enjoying the warmth of the spring sunshine. John Newbold is to drive us to the Market in Chelmsford. Then we will go to St. Mary's church in Chelmsford for a springtime Thanksgiving Service before we return to Thornhill. I shall be asking God to let the progress that we have made continue, so that I can record good harvests and profits to show Christopher when he returns.

1st June 1623

John is ten today. He knows that his Father is away from England, but he is still disappointed to have no word or birthday greetings from him. I have given him a fine mare to replace his pony, Falstaff, which he has now out grown, but will keep as a companion for his new horse. He has decided to call her Sunset because of her russet colour, and I know that John will take great care of her. He is very kind with animals, and takes delight, if he finds a wounded animal or bird, in nursing the creature back to full health. John even has a tame fox, whose leg he mended when it was a cub. The fox he calls Jethro, and he answers to John's call each evening, accepting food from his hand, but he is afeared of everyone else. Yesterday evening Jethro came as usual and he brought with him a vixen and four cubs. It seems that John is so trusted that a whole family of foxes will now come a-calling!

John has grown well in the last two years. He is the same height as me now and I am sure that he will very soon be as tall as his Father. But unlike his Father at that age, he is a pleasure to be with and he is admired by all. He is very healthy and he loves to be active all the time. John and Alfred, who is now a delightful young man, have become firm friends. Alfred did not return to work in the Thornton forge, and he has now joined Adam Fulbright in his work as bailiff, and I am so proud of John when I see him join Adam and Alfred on their rounds of inspection.

Christopher and I have been married for more than twelve years now and I wonder that the years have passed so fast. After the terrible start of our marriage, I have come to accept it. My Husband and I do not love each other. He has justified his past behaviour towards me by saying that he had no choice in who he married either; although I know he took great pleasure in my body when I was but a flat breasted maid. However, now, as long as I keep his wants supplied, he too accepts things as they are.

I wonder when he is coming home. He did say harvest time in that last letter. Could it be that I miss him?

It would be nice for John if his Father were here today to spend a few days with his Son. No doubt he would check what I have been doing with the estate, and I would be scolded for going against his wishes even though all is now profitable again. But we will both be eager to hear his tell stories of his adventures. Some, I am sure, will be exaggerated to excite young John, to make him admire his Father.

22nd October 1623

Well, Christopher came home at last. He stayed for ten days, and has now returned to 'his good friend George', who King James made Duke of Buckingham while they were away! He did, indeed, foretell the future that one day he would be made a Duke!

Christopher is most changed for his months of travel. He seems to me to be much more of a solid man, and he has grown a full beard! The privations of being on the road and living on his wits for months on end have hardened him. Do I prefer him now, I cannot tell? I did admit to him that I had missed him, and we spent many nights together. To my delight and amazement he handled me gently. Perhaps we will grow to love each other after all!

Naturally I have been scolded for my disobedience and criticised for my management of the farms and land, and for the employment of Geoffrey Haydock, Adam Fulbright and young Alfred, but we had a really fine harvest, the barns are full and as Christopher left with his pockets full of gold, he did not seek to undo what I have done.

Apart from the general complaints about the household during the daytime, in the evenings Christopher did amuse us exceedingly with his exciting stories. John sat giving rapt attention to every word that his Father uttered who was chuckling as he spoke. "During our journey to Spain Prince Charles needed to go forward unrecognised and unchallenged as we crossed France, so we all travelled as country squires, riding fast over dusty roads on strong horses and carrying our own baggage. At night we stayed at inns and travelling lodges. The Prince and George thought it all a great adventure, never before had the Prince ever experienced anything of life as a commoner. The evenings that we spent together in lowly taverns were so different to life in a grand palace that the Prince could hardly believe that it was real life for most people. But flagons of good wines flowed each night and all was merriment while many a cup was drunk between us."

During his discourse he disclosed that the grand venture to Spain did not result in success, because the Marquis annoyed or upset the Spanish Royal Court. With his wine goblet in his hand Christopher sat back and laughed in merriment. "So what do you think about my friend the Marquis, now becoming a Duke? Even when he makes errors he remains the King's most favourite, and now he is the Duke of Buckingham! Did you ever think that I would move in such elevated circles?"

"But does he remain the same person?" I asked. "Has he changed? Now he has the ear of the highest in the land, I wonder that he has time for a mere country landowner!"

"He is exactly as he was the day that you met him." Christopher replied. "I do not know why he has taken to me, and I count myself very fortunate to have such a pleasant and powerful companion."

Christopher appears to be most content with his new life, and he has great hopes of a good promotion in the Dukes' service, especially now that he has found favour in the eyes of the Prince of Wales. His contentment with his present life makes him so much nicer in his way than I have ever known him to be, and, to my surprise, I found that I was saddened when he left. I wished him Godspeed, soon to return!

6th January 1624

Christmas and New Year has come and gone, and Christopher turned his back to the Royal Court and celebrated with us at Thornhill. I cannot quite believe this new Christopher. I keep looking at him when he is unaware of my regard, and I wonder if this is the same man who, only eight years ago, nearly killed me with his temper, and did kill our unborn child.

What has happened to him? Is it the influence of the Duke? To my great content I have never seen him so merry and cheerful to all. After the Christmas Mass, Christopher invited Father Thomas to join us all for a family Christmas feast in the Great Hall, which was festively decorated once more with a great garland and Yule log burning in the grate. Afterwards he disappeared for a while, and returned with gifts for everyone. A glittering ruby necklace for me, and a wonderful, highly polished Moorish sword and a Spanish spaniel puppy for John. Even Bessie, who Christopher has never really liked, was given a pearl broach. Father Thomas' gift was a pair of Spanish leather boots and a fat purse of silver to give as Christmas alms for the poor.

John was so merry that he danced around the Great Hall, and had fierce pretend sword fights with his Father. We all laughed and were very merry. John decided to call his puppy Wolf, although no dog could ever be found to be less wolf-like. He loves his dog and takes him everywhere he goes. Unlike the other Thornhill hounds which are exercised with the horses and are kennelled near the stables, John keeps Wolf inside the Manor, and he even takes him to his bedchamber at night!

Christopher and I even had several nights of gentle loving again!

I pray to God that the changes He has wrought in my Husband are permanent.

1st June 1624

It is John's birthday again, and he is eleven today. He is almost as tall as Christopher now, and he is developing into a fine young man. He has the good looks and charm of his Father, and from me, I think, his love of learning and his sensitive and caring nature. The puppy, Wolf, is becoming a very handsome dog. He still clings to John, and is always to be found at John's heels.

Christopher has only visited us once since Christmas. He arrived the day after my birthday, and stayed for but two days. He was not in such a fine temper as he had been for the previous two visits, and I was bitterly disappointed. I did not argue with him and just accepted all the usual criticisms without comment or quarrel. He even quarrelled with our Son calling him a Mother's Boy, and derided John's developing sense of duty towards the tenants and workers on the estate.

I believe that he only came home for more gold, and to prepare me and himself for yet another adventure with his wonderful Duke! I dare not say anything critical about the Duke to Christopher, but I do not think that the Duke so wonderful. It was he who persuaded King James to make war with Spain. Just another adventure for him, an excuse to go off warring, and Christopher will follow him just like John's little dog does, trailing at his Master's heel!

1st April 1625

I have not seen my Husband for since my birthday last year, and I have had only a few short letters asking for me to send silver with his messenger. In his last letter he told me to expect him for a week or so for my next birthday in six weeks time. But today I have heard from Father Thomas that King James collapsed and died on March 27th. The Court must be in turmoil, and I expect that Christopher will be unable to leave.

Charles, Prince of Wales, is now King Charles. He is only twenty-four years old, he is totally inexperienced, and from all that Christopher has told me, he will be relying greatly on his trusted friend and advisor, the Duke of Buckingham. God help us all! Already there are growing murmurs amongst the landowners in the countryside against the Duke who has been encouraging King Charles to marry a Catholic Princess. The Duke also promotes costly wars in Europe which require more taxes to be raised from everyone.

Last year Christopher related to me that Prince Charles has been well tutored by his Father on the power of the monarchy, and what he called 'the Divine Right of Kings'. As a new King, Charles will not want to harken to other advisors, and he will dislike being told what he can or cannot do by Parliament, especially when he will want more taxes. Buckingham (and Christopher) must be delighted at the turn of events.

I surprise myself to find that I am looking forward to Christopher's next visit. However I expect that it will be well after King James's funeral and the new King has settled on his Throne!

13th September 1625

My Husband has come and gone again after spending only five days at home. I am saddened. Both John and I had thought that Christopher had rekindled an interest in us, and we were both anticipating his return with great pleasure. After the King James' death I did not expect him to return for my birthday in May, but I had hoped for a letter, and then John's 12th birthday in June, and still no word.

And this week, at last, Christopher did return to us. He barely greeted us, his Wife and Son. His discourse was all of our new King Charles, and how important the Duke has become. I could determine that he no longer has any interest in Thornhill other than a source of monies to enable him to keep up with the Duke of Buckingham. I do not know why he loves the Duke so; all I can see is danger ahead. Here in the countryside the muttering against the Duke gets stronger by the day, and I am sure that Christopher, as a close associate of the Duke, will become hated too. Christopher himself has often spoken to me of the Duke's enemies at Court and in the Parliament, but he just laughs it off!

The three of us were walking in the orchards inspecting and tasting the delicious apples which are many, and ready for harvest in the next few days, when John turned to Christopher and said. "Father, you always talk about the time you spend at Court, and how you address the King, and how important the Duke is. Do you ever talk to them about us? Do you even remember that you have a Wife and Son? Do you ever ask my Mother if she would like to visit the Court and meet the King? I know that I would like so to do."

I looked at my Husband, and then I turned my face so that he could not see my look of apprehension. Was he going to reply with anger?

To my surprise he laughed again."My dear Son," he said. "How could I ever introduce your Mother to Court? She is no more than a country bumpkin. No, excuse me Madam." He turned to me and bowed elegantly. "You are an English country rose, and you would stifle and wither in the foulness of the Court. And as for you, Young Sir," he turned to John and continued. "You are yet a child, and it would be dangerous there for you. I promise you that I will take you when you are older."

I said nothing, but John was angered. "How dare you call my Mother a 'country bumpkin'. She is beautiful, and she is very clever. It is you who keep us here, hidden away in this backwater. I think that you are ashamed of us!" He turned and walked off with Wolf at his heels, leaving us both quite taken aback.

Christopher turned to me, with a smile on his face, and said. "Well Wife, I can see that you are raising my Son to be your defender against the world. Would you really like to be introduced at Court?"

I reddened and shook my head.

Christopher continued, "If you really wanted to I would take you, but I know that you would hate it. The King's Court is really like a human cess pit, with everyone, even the Duke, struggling against each other to rise to the surface, and to stay there once having achieved their aims. I will admit that I do find it exceedingly exciting too, especially as I consider myself a friend of His Majesty's 'favourite'. But I am also industrious in my efforts to win wider favour, even with the King himself, so that I, too, can earn wealth and maybe a title or two!"

Then Christopher actually held my arm as we returned to the Manor. He told me more of his plans with his Duke, who is about to go on an 'adventure' again. It seems that the Duke wants to regain prestige for himself and the King by repeating what Sir Francis Drake, the Old Queen's pirate adventurer, did, by setting fire to the Spanish fleet in the port of Cadiz. Christopher gave no more details and he told me not to repeat his news to anyone. But I fear that land owners and merchants will soon know of this new 'adventure' when they will be asked for yet more taxes to pay for it. Then came the important part of the story, the reason why he was home in good humour, and wanting my co-operation – Christopher is going with the Duke again, he will be away from England for a few months, and wants as much gold as we hold in the coffer!

I do have to accept that, after all, all Christopher wants from me and Thornhill is gold. He does not like giving me the power to do things as I wish. He does not like my employment of Godfrey Haydock and Adam Fulbright, but he finds himself having to accept what I do in order to keep gold flowing into the coffer for him.

But at least while the gold is coming in I have smiles and occasional gentle ways, and not harsh words and beatings. The love that I thought was beginning to grow between us is all an illusion!

It will be his own 36th birthday next week, but he will not be returning! John is even more disappointed than I am. He is growing into a confident and clever young man now. I am so, so proud of him.

18th December 1625

Dear Wife

We are returned. The expedition to Cadiz was a complete disaster. This adventure was an embarrassing failure for the Duke, but for me the months away from England, away from the King and the Court, were the finest that I have had with George.

We were very close, and we shared the rough privations of a soldier's life on a warship. I was his close friend and companion. We were even sleeping partners in the master cabin which we shared.

I thought that as the Duke became ever more important as the King's favourite and chief advisor, that he would need me to help him with his work. I had fully expected to be promoted to an important and highly lucrative post at Court on our return to England, even though the expedition had been a failure.

But no! He has betrayed me. I cannot believe how the Duke, who I have seen as my greatest friend, betrayed me. Once we were back at Court I was shamed and humiliated by George in front of the King and his friends, the high Lords and Ladies of the land. It seemed as though our friendship and intimacy were completely forgotten and I was treated by the Duke as no more than the lowest of his aides, with no promotion in prospect. And I was once more, just one of the many courtiers in the Duke's entourage. I am so angered that I am determined to leave George and the Court forever.

I desire to be with you and John for Christmas, but first I need to face George for an explanation of his treatment of me.

Your Husband Christopher

10ᵗʰ February 1626

With much trepidation and fear of the changes which would inevitably be wrought if my Husband were to abandon his ambitions and return to Thornhill, I made preparations for his return home. But then I heard no more. No letters from him, no Christmas greetings, or elaborate Christmas gifts from him, not even for John.

I hoped that it meant that Christopher had changed his mind, and I resolved to make it a merry time at Thornhill, except that John missed the presence of his Father. Risking that he was not on his way home, together Bessie and I recreated the Thornhill of Christmases past when my parents received all the tenants and farm workers after the Christmas Mass and blessings. John was most content and quite the Little Master as he gave everyone of them a small silver coin. Then we offered them and hot punch to drink in the Great Hall, and Christmas sweetmeats to take home for the children.

We have waited until now for Christopher to return. Finally, in mid February, he is home with no advance warning, and the worst time to travel on muddy winter roads. How long he will stay I do not know, he says nothing about George and the Court. And he is in a bad, angry mood. I have already suffered a few blows for wasting good silver on the 'peasants'. He said nothing of his bitter feelings towards the Duke.

Yesterday we were sitting in our small parlour after supper, and Christopher was mellow with wine. I summoned the courage to question him. "How is it," I asked, "that you still desire to be at the Duke's side when he treats you so badly? You said in your last letter that you were determined to abandon the Duke and Court life, and return to Thornhill. Do you not prefer to be here with your Son, than amongst the intrigues of Court?"

Christopher leaned back in his chair, took a deep draft of wine, and smiled, more to himself that at me. "Oh," he said, "I am returned to George's favour now. His treatment of me was all an endeavour to protect me."

I was astonished. "Protect you?" I queried.

"Yes. George told me that the King had shown great displeasure at being neglected for so long, even though George was abroad and unable to be at the King's side. He said that he had had to show me no favouritism when we returned from Cadiz because some of the Duke's enemies had told King Charles of our close friendship aboard ship. The King had been angry, and George had been forced to deny everything and to distance himself from me, to save me. It had been prudent of him to treat me in an offhand manner to avoid me being arrested on false charges. I could have ended up in the Tower of London!"

I was aghast! "The Tower of London? Is that not where traitors are taken?" I asked.

"Indeed, yes. It could have ended very badly for me," replied Christopher. "For the present I am to remain just as the Duke's aide; but he has promised me that as soon as he is able, and it must be without further annoyance to King Charles, he has a well paid position to offer me. And he said that he will present me with gifts of land that are at his disposal."

I was relieved. I did not love my husband, but the thought of him being locked up in the Tower gave filled me with great terror.

"I am most pleased that you were not sent to the Tower," I said, "but does this now mean that you will have to give up your hopes for a title?"

"Oh! The King can sometimes be most changeable," he replied. "I'm sure that now that Buckingham is at his side once more he will forget all about his jealousy of me. I will be most humble and courteous when I return to Court, and I am sure that the King will soon smile upon me again."

He said no more, and the next day he received a message from his Duke. He was delighted to be needed again and, having filled his pockets with monies from my Father's great coffer, he left Thornhill with hardly a goodbye to either his Wife or his Son, for whom life now reverts to peace and contentment.

I had been thinking of that last letter to me, and I had not dared to make further enquiries about the closeness and intimacy that Christopher and the Duke had shared on board ship. I think that the answer might have revolted me! And I was most content that during this recent visit Christopher had not invited me to share his bed!

13th February 1626

Now that Christopher has returned to Court I can all feel more at ease. Although I am saddened that he spends so little time with his Son who at thirteen is growing rapidly, and needs his Father to teach him to become a man. For my part, I have taught John all that I can. He reads and writes exceedingly well in both English and Latin. For the first time in John's life, when he was with us, Christopher exclaimed pride in his Son, and he showed great pleasure in taking John, who is now a capable young horseman, out riding, hunting and training with the dogs.

But before they had a chance to develop a strong Father and Son bond, the messenger arrived and, like a faithful dog, Christopher responded and returned to Court and his Duke.

I have always found it difficult to adjust when Christopher returns home and I have to explain and justify what I have been doing in my running of the estate. I am forced to accept my Husbands' inevitable rebukes and alterations to what I have ordered to be done. I realise now that I was really content during the long months that Christopher was away on campaign.

Apart from the death of King James which I heard from Father Thomas, I never know the details, other than some things that Christopher tells me, of the great events in London and overseas that are happening far away from my everyday domestic life. I am more interested in the health of the crops and the animals, the markets and the price of wool. I am only really concerned and affected by the outside world when my Husband comes back home.

Christopher, too, when he returns from London, finds it difficult to adjust from a world of action and Court intrigue to becoming just a country landowner, even if he is Sir Christopher and Lord of the Manor.

Events following August 23rd 1628, written in London in October 1628

I have not written in my journal for more than two years. It had been all but abandoned it as life at Thornhill Manor seemed to go on in a set pattern without much to report upon. For the past six years, while my Husband's life has been so entwined with that of the Duke of Buckingham, I have been most content at being left behind to continue my life as a loving Mother to my John. And while he has been away from the Manor, although he never intended it to happen, he also gave me the opportunity to become the successful business woman that I have strived to be ever since I was a little maid and my Father took the unusual step to educate me. Contentment for me when he is away, and more difficult times for a few weeks when he returned home!

But disaster has now visited me. My life now has been turned upside-down, and for John's sake I must record the upheaval in my life, and resume my entries in my Journal.

23rd August 1628

The dramatic change for me and everyone at in Thornhill happened when the Duke of Buckingham was fatally stabbed on this day in far away Portsmouth. It was not until three days later that I discovered, from Robert, Christopher's manservant, all that had taken place. My Husband was attending the Duke as they both were about to board a warship which was preparing to set sail for the port of La Rochelle in France. For a second time an attempt was to be made to effect the relief of the Huguenots from the siege of land based French Catholic forces which surround the town on all sides.

The Duke's attacker was John Felton, an army officer who had been wounded in the previous failed attempt to relieve La Rochelle and who, along with most English people, blamed Buckingham for this and many other ill-judged and disastrous military campaigns. Even to those of us living in the countryside it was well known that the Duke of Buckingham had become the most hated man in the country, and many had expressed the desire that he be killed!

How many times had I warned Christopher that it was dangerous for him to continue his close attachment to the Duke? But it seemed that he was most besotted by him, or the wealth and power that he had at his command. And he was always assured that that very power would always protect both of them if there were to be any trouble.

Robert was nearby when the stabbing happened. There was chaos all around as the Duke sank to the ground in a pool of blood, but Christopher was not amongst those that tried to save the dying man. He prevented Robert from offering assistance to the Duke and took the forward rush of others who were there as his opportunity, and together they disappeared into the crowd. Christopher was shocked, horrified and devastated. Of course he well knew how hated the Duke of Buckingham had become, and he knew that he was not safe in Portsmouth. Walking as inconspicuously and as fast as they could he and Robert went to the naval stables where Christopher commandeered two of the best horses.

Together they rode away as quickly as was possible, but it was not until after midnight that they arrived at his home in the City of London. Overnight Christopher had to assess his situation and to decide what to do before general knowledge of the Duke's death reached London and King Charles. He knew that his life at the Royal Court was at an end and, with it, all his plans for wealth and advancement.

Even though he was relatively unimportant, my Husband thought that as a friend and constant companion of the Duke, now that the Duke was dead, he would be in great danger from the Duke's powerful and revengeful enemies if he remained in London. Panic overtook him once he reached the relative safety of his home at the Aldgate. He had almost lost his wits with distress, shock and panic as he gathered up essential papers and belongings. He did not dare to delay so after only a few hours rest they set off at the break of day for Thornhill Manor.

24th August 1628

The ride had been hot and exhausting under a cloudless sky, and Christopher was in a very dark and angry mood, his cloak, hose and breeches covered with a thick layer of dust from the road when he arrived at Thornhill in the late morning.

At the time I knew nothing of the momentous events that had taken place in the last few hours. I had already taken refuge from the heat of the day, and I was sitting at my desk in the library doing the accounts with Godfrey Haydock. We were discussing the improvement in farming that Robert Taylor has made in the past few years, and I did not hear the horse's hooves pounding into the courtyard, or the commotion of Christopher's arrival.

All of a sudden he burst into the chamber, and seeing Godfrey and me seated together he shouted, "Get out, Haydock. You are dismissed!"

Godfrey looked at me; he was as startled as I was.

"Christopher!" I exclaimed, "Whatever has happened? I thought that you were about to go on campaign again. You look as if you have been riding hard for days."

Christopher looked at me with hate in his eyes, such as I have never seen in all the years that I have known him, even during those terrible times of molestation and rapine. Then he looked at Godfrey again. "Get out," he repeated, and advanced menacingly towards both of us.

I was alarmed and not a little afraid. I tried to calm the oncoming storm, and I said quietly and calmly, "Godfrey, just go to Bessie in the kitchen, and I will speak to you later." Godfrey saw the look of menace in Christopher's eyes, and he got up quickly and left, shutting the door gently behind him.

I left my chair, walked over to Christopher and laid my hand upon his arm. I tried to be as calm as I could, and I asked again in a very soothing and gentle voice, "Christopher, whatever is the matter? What has happened? Let me call the servants to take your travelling cloak and bring you some cooling ale."

By then, in spite of his weariness, Christopher's energy returned and his rage mounted up. "Godfrey, you call him. Godfrey. You slut!

You whore! I caught you. You and your lover together. You whore!" He ended shouting it directly in my face.

I recoiled. I could not believe what I was hearing, but I knew that I had to try to stop the coming storm. "Christopher, calm down," I said gently and quietly, and trying not to show my fear. "Let us sit down together and you can tell me what has happened. You know that I have no lover, and that Godfrey is Bessie's Husband. Don't be foolish..."

I heard his intake of breath and I looked up at his face. I knew at once that I had said the wrong thing!

Foolish, am I? Foolish! We will see who is the foolish one!" Then he lunged at me, and before I could turn away he punched me in my face with his full force, and then threw me to the floor. There he kicked me viciously until I lost consciousness, and without considering that there were servants in earshot, he tore at my garments and ravaged me, there and then on the floor.

By the time I had recovered my senses Christopher had recovered himself too. But he was still aroused, his anger was undiminished, and he attacked me once again. This time took me from the rear, like the dog that he is, and forced his way into my back passage, all the time shouting, "you hateful whore! I shall treat you like a whore! You will see who the Master is in this house!" He then got up and began to kick me again, until I lost consciousness once more.

This time, as I regained my senses, from the floor I could see my husband above me about to strike again. But as he aimed his foot once more at my head, Bessie and Benjamin Haydock summoned up enough courage to enter into the chamber. Benjamin was fifty years old by then, but still had his powerful shoulders and carpenter's strength. Bessie ran to me and Benjamin went to Christopher and held his arms, "Stop Master. Stop," he said quietly, "you will kill the Mistress. Stop Master. Let Bessie take her away."

Christopher shrugged Benjamin off, and pushed him away. "Take her away?" He said, suddenly collapsing in complete weariness, and exhausted emotion. "Yes, take her away. You can take her right away. And I want all you Haydocks gone, out of my cottage and off my land by morning. And you can take your whore of a Mistress with you!" Then he departed.

Bessie picked me up. She saw from my torn clothing what had happened to me. I was sorely hurt and weeping quietly. She and Benjamin helped me climb the stairs to my bedchamber, each step sending a piercing pain throughout my body.

My eyes were already turning black and my nose was a a swollen lump upon my face. "Don't put me to bed," I said to Bessie. "I will not stay here with my Husband another night. Just let me rest for a moment and bring me a draft of ale to steady myself. Then get my travelling clothes, and put some dresses and other things that I will be needing into my Chest." Then I whispered to her, "and make sure that my Journal is in the secret drawer."

While Bessie was fetching the ale, I spoke to Benjamin, "Please get your brother to take my Chest to your cottage, and I shall go to speak to my Husband. I am so sorry about what has happened. I cannot think at the moment about what will be our future, but will you and your family stay with me?"

Bessie came back with Godfrey, and it was decided between us that I would stay the night in their cottage, and that we would all leave Thornhill in the morning.

I drank down the ale that had been brought to me in one long swallow and then, with great difficulty and in great pain, I left my chamber and made my way back down the stairs and to the stables where Christopher was sitting slumped on a bale of hay with his head in his hands, and I am sure that he had been weeping. I had seen John was just returning with Adam Fulbright and Alfred from their rounds of the Thornhill tenants, and they would soon come into the stables too.

I had to say what I had determined before John came in. "Christopher," I said to him quietly, "I do not know what has happened. There must have been some disaster, but you have no right to treat me this way. You want me to leave the home that is rightfully mine. And although I love it, I shall do so because I can no longer accept you for my Husband. I shall take our Son, and remove us to your house in London. You have my home and John and I and shall take yours."

Christopher still had some strength left in him. He got up and faced me menacingly, and hissed, "You will do no such thing, you filthy whore. You can leave as soon as you wish, and you can go and live in London if you wish, but you will not be taking my Son with you." He took hold of John, who had just entered the stable, and held him fast.

"Father!" exclaimed John. "When did you arrive?" Then I saw the horrified look upon his face when he turned to look at me. He saw my bruised and bloodied face and torn clothes.

"What is happening?" he asked. "Whatever has happened to Mother?"

"I caught your mother with her lover, and she is leaving," said Christopher.

"That's not true. Mother has no lover!" John exclaimed again. "Mother, you cannot leave. This is your home," he said.

"John, I have to leave. Look what your father has done to me. If I do not leave your Father will beat me again, maybe until he finally kills me," I said. I was desperately sad. "I am going to your Father's house in London. It appears that, for the present at least, I am forced to exchange my lovely home here for your Father's home there. You are nearly a man now. I think that perhaps you had better stay here with your Father, and help to keep Thornhill running properly, as you have been taught. But I hope that you will come to see me as soon as I have settled in London." I turned to leave, tears running down my face.

"Mother, don't go," John called out, and made to run after me. But his Father now held him firmly with both arms, and prevented him from making any move towards me.

"You will do as I say now," said Christopher. "No more 'Mother's Boy'. You will stay here and learn to be Master of Thornhill. Master! Not friends with the servants and peasants. Master! And you will start by dismissing Fulbright."

Adam Fulbright had been standing by in shocked astonishment

at what had taken place before his eyes between the Master and the Mistress. He had not known that he and his Wife and family were about to be evicted from their cottage, and that their comfortable life on Thornhill Manor was about to end.

<center>~~~</center>

All that night I prayed to Jesus that John would come and talk to me. I prayed that we would find some way to stop this disaster happening and become a family once more. I cried and cried with the desire to hold my Son in my arms once more, and to make everything right with him. The thought of leaving Thornhill was dreadful, but even more terrible was the thought of leaving John behind.

I was still crying when the dawn broke, and nothing had changed. My Chest, filled to the brim with as many of my belongings, linen and clothes that Bessie could fit in it, was all I took with me. The secret drawer not only held my Journal, but there was also room for a few items of my mother's jewellery, including the ring and necklace that I had worn on my wedding day, and the ruby necklace that Christopher had brought back from Spain and given to me when all was happiness between us. Was that only just four years ago? Just the look of it now makes me shudder and remember Christopher's viciousness. I had also squeezed into the drawer a purse of silver, which I hoped would keep us from hunger until we knew what life had in store for us all. How I wished that I had, from time to time, taken the opportunity when Christopher was away to put in there some of the gold coins that were rightly mine. And now it was too late. With the passing of the years, and the harmony that had developed between me and my Husband, I had never dreamt that such a thing as this could ever happen, and I had never thought to put by some coins for myself for future need.

Bessie, Godfrey and Benjamin were also in the same position. Their lives too were changed forever. We hoped that we would have no need of furnishings for Christopher's house, so they, too, brought only their personal possessions and workday tools. But they were heavy hearted to leave behind all the pieces of furniture that Benjamin had crafted since he was a young man. My Chest and everything that the others could gather together in such a short time, was loaded on our travelling wagon.

It was time to be leaving. With Robert to guide us, Benjamin, Godfrey, Bessie and I, slowly made our way to London. As we drove down the avenue and away from Thornhill I turned back and gave one last long look at the Manor house, full of memories of my parents, my childhood, and my Son, and the only home I had ever known. I could hardly make out John who was standing by the door to the Great Hall so blinded was I by my tears.

2nd November 1628

With gentle care and nursing from Bessie, it has taken two months for me to recover from the attack by my Husband, and to settle into what has become my new home at the Aldgate, in London. Although the house is large by London standards, having several chambers, stables and a stable yard with a well, and a pleasant enclosed garden, it seems small and cramped compared with my lovely family home. I miss Thornhill Manor so much, my beautiful gardens, the woodlands, the orchards and all the green land and space all around. And the wonderful air to breathe! I do not know if I will ever be content living here. I feel so enclosed, with people living all one on top of another, the continuous noise outside of the traders and travellers in the street, and the hideous stench and filth running down the street in open sewers. Why do people want to live like this? Our tenant's pig yards were not as noisome as the London streets!

The house itself is warm and well furnished, and fortunately there is no feeling of Christopher here. I believe that he spent very little time here, hardly a home, and nothing like the comfort of Thornhill Manor. My lovely lost home!

But more than my home, I miss my Son, the only real joy in my life. My John, with whom I have spent every day of the last fourteen years nurturing, teaching, and loving. How I miss him. Much as I love Bessie, I cannot fill my time with only her and the Haydock brothers.

Old Benjamin is now living above the stables, and he is converting one of the stables into a workshop so that he can earn a living with his carpentry. Bessie and her husband Godfrey fit comfortably into the second chamber upstairs. She has taken charge of the kitchen, and it is well that she brought with us her pots and pans as I do not think that Christopher's servant has ever cooked here. We have sufficient pewter plates and dishes and goblets for our needs. There is even a goodly supply of wines in the cellar.

Benjamin and Godfrey have agreed that while Bessie will stay close by to look after me and the house, Benjamin will find work as a carpenter and Godfrey will seek work in the City, where he was told that he might find employment at the Royal Exchange. Robert has returned to the King's Court to see if he can find a placement there. We have decided to keep the horse, but Godfrey is arranging to sell the wagon, he will also seek out a jeweller or goldsmith to whom I can sell my ruby necklace.

28th November 1628

It is very cold now and today Bessie and I were sitting by the fire in the large downstairs chamber where Bessie was mending my clothes. She was re-sewing some of the embroidery on the pretty fine lawn nightdress that was the last work of Mistress Beckett before she died last spring – before all the evil days came upon us. I was worried about the cost and supply of logs; with trees all around us when we were living at Thornhill, it was something that we did not even have to think about. "Oh, Bessie," I sighed, "whatever are we going to do? I have not yet had any news from Thornhill. I have been praying that John would come to visit me soon, and that he will bring us monies to see us through the winter. My purse of silver will not last for more than a few weeks. I suppose that I must accept the miserable amount that Master Erskine the jeweller has offered me for the rubies. He says that they are of poor quality and mounted in low grade gold. I should have known that Christopher would never have bought me any costly gift!"

"My dear Mistress," she said, "you really should not worry about money. Now that Godfrey has succeeded in finding work as a clerk in the Royal Exchange, I'm sure that we will be able to manage."

"But Bessie," I cried, "I cannot let Godfrey and Benjamin support me. I have been working on my account books, and trying to assess how I am going to be able to support myself in future. I was hoping that John would be able to persuade his Father that I shall need money from Thornhill to support myself here in London, as I did when he lived here." I sighed. I was worried, and I did not like my new life at all. "I do miss my Son so much. Please God that he will come to see me soon," I sighed again. "If silver does not come from Thornhill soon I must consider what I can do. I am younger than you all, I am healthy, and I was well taught by my Father; I must be able to do something to contribute too. Perhaps I could earn money by tutoring a child? There must be many a merchant in London who wants his son educated, but cannot afford a private live-in tutor."

"I am sure that there is no need for you to worry. Godfrey and Benjamin think that it is their duty to look after you; and you know that I will never leave you in want," said Bessie. "But if you feel that you would be happier if you had a child to teach and look after, perhaps Godfrey can ask amongst the traders and merchants if there is one who has such a need."

30th November 1628

I cannot believe it! Yet I know all the symptoms and I know that I am still of childbearing age. I have even felt the child quicken within my womb. This is the result of Christopher's attack on me. Whatever shall I do? I have barely enough silver left to survive here as we are now, even if I do find a child or young man to educate, how will I manage? I must talk to Bessie.

1st December 1628

Bessie is wonderful. The best friend that I could ever have! Contrary to my fears she is even excited at the thought of another child to help to bring into the world, and to nurture. She has longed for a child of her own for years but she has never conceived; so this new babe of mine will be almost as real to her as mothering one of her own. For the present time I will not tell Christopher that I am once more with child. He already calls me 'whore', so I am sure that he will not believe that the child is his. I shall wait until the child is born, and then decide upon my discourse with Christopher.

How I miss my Son. Every day I pray to Jesus that he will send John to me. How can I face the season of the birth of the Son of God without my own Son at my side?

27th December 1628

What Joy! Without any prior warning John has found his way here through winter cold and mud, and arrived two days after the saddest Christmas I had ever spent.

How I missed the contented and smiling faces of the servants and tenants of Thornhill. This year I am sure that my Husband gave them no gifts of silver. Because I am no longer there, they will have had no Christmas foodstuffs and clothing from the Lady of the Manor; no family feast to attend, no great garland and no huge Yule log in the fireplace of the Great Hall to bring warmth and contentment for the season.

Here in London on Christmas Eve there came a deep fall of snow, which covered much of the filth in the streets of London, and, taking no joy in the prettiness of it all, Bessie, Godfrey, Benjamin and I trudged glumly through it to attend the Christmas Mass in the church of St. Botolph in Aldgate. There I tried to find inner peace as I welcomed the Blessed Child, whilst enduring the fear of want and hunger for all of us, and my own child to come. This fear was somewhat alleviated by the warmth and generosity of Bessie, Godfrey and Benjamin who all did of their best to calm my fears and to promote a feeling of Family and Feast. Godfrey even struggled through the snow and brought home a huge Christmas goose from the Meat Market at Smithfield.

Bessie, for all her clumsy fingers, gave me a gift of a beautiful lace cap that she made for me, and some clothes for the child to come. I used a little of the remaining silver to buy a few oranges which a trader brought from Covent Garden Market. I also bought from him some tobacco for Benjamin and pencils for Godfrey. To Bessie I gave a silver ring, given to me many years ago by my Uncle Raymond.

And now my sadness had turned to Joy! Two days after Christmas, John has arrived. At last my beloved and sorely missed Son has found me.

I had heard a horse stamping and whinnying as he came into our courtyard, and I thought that it might be Benjamin coming back from the blacksmith. I turned towards the door as it opened, and there was my darling Boy!

"John, John, John," I cried out as I saw him, and I rushed to gather him into my arms. "Oh, my dearest, I am so happy to see you. Come! Let me take that wet cloak. Come! Warm yourself by the fire. Then you can tell me all about what has been happening to you and Thornhill."

"Oh Mother! How I, and everyone at Thornhill, miss you!" he exclaimed as he held me tight. Bessie took his cloak and then he sat beside me on the cushioned bench in front of the fire. "Father does not know that I have ridden to London. He went off with some of the fellows to roister in Colchester for the season of New Year. He says that he will not be returning to the King's Court, at least until he knows that he will be safe from the Duke's enemies. Even though the Duke is dead, he heard from some of the servants who remain at New Hall, that there is still quarrelling amongst the King's friends as to whom is to be a replacement 'Buckingham'."

While warming himself at the fireside John was talking non-stop! "Although Father continues to blacken your name to all at Thornhill, he is, nevertheless, following the new regimes for using the estate to make the best profits that you and Godfrey devised. I am fortunate that he did not dismiss Alfred who remains in at Thornhill, and I continue to work closely with him. Father, rather grudgingly, joins us in our surveys of the farms and businesses."

Bessie was mightily pleased and happy to hear that her nephew was well and still working at Thornhill, and that strangers had not been moved into her old home. But how I laughed! "Do you know just how much your Father despised and ridiculed my bookkeeping and land management?" I asked John. I paused as I was thinking of my lost home. Then I asked John, "and has anyone replaced Bessie to manage the household and look after you?"

John made a grimace as he replied. "Father has brought to Thornhill a new housekeeper called Lucy. She lives and works in the Manor house and her mother, who accompanied Lucy, assists Mistress Tadworth in the kitchen. Mistress Tadworth is a sad woman now. Gone are all her merry chuckles. Every time I go to the kitchens she talks about the wonderful Lady of the Manor, and how she wishes that you would come home; as does everyone at Thornhill I may add! It is hardly the same place without you there." John paused, and looked at me. I could see that we were both wishing the same thing. I sighed and he carried on talking.

"Lucy is rather saucy and has tried to 'mother' me, but I do not like it, or her! And I do believe that she visits Father in his bedroom at night!"

John was quiet for a moment, and he stood again to rub his hands together in front of the flames. He looked directly at me and said, "I have asked and even begged Father to ask you to return home, but he will not. If ever I speak your name he is angered. He continues to call you a slut and a whore, even though I have told him again and again that he wrongs you. I know that ever since Father started dancing to the attendance of the Duke of Buckingham, you have never done anything other than work hard to improve the life for everyone on who depends on Thornhill, and that included him the most! But he will never listen to me."

He sighed and I held him close when he sat again. I was not surprised or even angry about Lucy, and I did not want John to feel that he had to defend me. "It matters no more," I said. "All I need now to make me content, is to see you and hold you in my arms like this."

John kissed me on the cheek, and then stood up again, this time to warm his back at the fire. "I am only here for a day or two," he said, "because Father is to return to Thornhill quite soon, and I do not want him to find that I am away from the Manor and am wondering abroad. He left me in the 'care' of Lucy and her mother, but I dare say that they will be reporting back to him that I was gone for a few days." He laughed. Then he continued, "but I do not care what punishments he will give me, it is worth it to see you again."

My expression did not change, but I felt sick in my stomach as I took a moment to assess all the news that John had delivered. Then it was my turn to throw questions at John. They came all at once, giving him little chance to reply.

"And what about you and your Father? Do you want to stay with him and make a life there? Is he kind to you? Do you and your Father ride together? Do you still ride for pleasure with Alfred? Have you any other friends of your own to be with?"

"Yes, Mother, yes," he said. "All is well for me apart from missing you. I still desire that you return home. I can see that you are comfortable here in this house, but it is not really your home. What can I do or say to Father to make him bring you home? Perhaps, now that I am here, I should stay?"

"Listen to me my darling Son," I replied. "You saw what he did to me. Your Father has beaten me many times during our Marriage, and twice he has beaten me so wickedly that I thought I might die. I cannot go back to him. If I did he might well succeed in killing me. Much as I love you and miss you every day of my life, you must return. Thornhill is your inheritance. It is your inheritance not just from your Father, but mainly from me and my Father. If you and your Father maintain peace between you, it is for the best that you remain there to safeguard that inheritance."

"Master John?" asked Bessie hesitantly. "Can you tell me what has happened to our cottage? Is our furniture still there? Has your Father put anyone else in it?"

"No, Bessie," he replied. "Alfred still sleeps there, and he takes his food in the Manor. Everything in the cottage is as you left it."

Bessie was trembling when she asked. "I am pleased that Alfred is still living there, and there are no strangers rummaging through the things we were not able to bring here, but do you think that it would be possible for my bed and chest of drawers to be conveyed here by wagon when the roads improve? Benjamin made them for Godfrey and me when were married, and I do so miss them."

She turned to look at me as her cheeks reddened. "I am sorry, Mistress. I am comfortable here, but I do miss my own bed," she said.

"Bessie, of course you miss and desire your own furnishings," I said. "It is I who am sorry that, because of me, you have been forced to leave your home too."

John smiled at Bessie. "I will do my very best to have all the things that you desire from your cottage carried here, perhaps in the springtime when the roads will improve. Do you think that you can wait until then?" He asked.

Bessie clapped her hands in delight. Then John sighed, and all of us, John, Bessie and I, and Godfrey, and Benjamin, who had joined us, spent the rest of the day together talking about Thornhill and all the people we all knew there. It appears that, in spite of his treatment of me, Christopher does have some real affection for his Son, for which I am gratified. If John is to make his life there, and away from me, it is my greatest wish that he should be content.

31st December 1628

New Year's Eve and John has returned to Thornhill. We spent such a wonderful two days just talking, talking, talking about Thornhill and everyone there, and about the past – his babyhood, his childhood, his Grandparents and his Father. He had to return and whilst my heart is heavy, I know that it is the right thing for him do. He is a child no longer and his future lies in Thornhill, and becoming the next Sir John. I decided not to tell him that I am with child. If John were to tell Christopher, his Father would never believe that the child is his, and he will certainly be convinced that I am indeed a whore! Then he will justify to everyone, including John, his vile treatment of me.

I did tell John of my sore need of monies, and he said that now he knows the way to my home here in London, that he will do his best to return at Eastertide, and bring me some silver too.

I know that by then I will no longer be able to hide my condition, but I will leave the explanation until then!

29th May 1629

I was saddened when Easter came and went with no sign of John, or Bessie's furniture. Perhaps it is better that he did not see me with my swollen belly. I think that it may be easier to explain about the baby when he does return.

My second Son was born on May 16th. It was a more difficult birth than John's, and we had to find monies to pay for a midwife to assist me, but I have now recovered after resting well under Bessie's tender care during my confinement. I was somewhat disappointed that the child is a boy and not the girl that I was hoping for, but Baby Edwin, (I have named him for my mother Edwina), is a perfect baby, and he is almost identical in looks to John as a baby. Is spite of the terrible circumstances of his conception, he is already looking to be a handsome child, just like his Father and his Brother.

Benjamin has made for him a beautiful little cradle which is almost a miniature of my Chest, which he made for me so many years ago. It has carvings around the sides just like those on the Chest, and instead of a lid, it has a little hood and rockers. It pleases me greatly!

Baby Edwin cries very little, and I am sure that I even saw a smile today! As always, Bessie had been wonderful and she already adores baby Edwin. I do not know what I would do without her.

10th July 1629

I am continually horrified at the cost of living here in London. Bread, milk, butter, fruit, vegetables, meat, ale and even firewood have prices that I do not recognise. Previously all these things were freely available at Thornhill. I never considered the cost of anything that was just growing or being produced on the estate, although I was aware of the good husbandry that was needed to keep it all in production.

We have been so seriously short of monies that after Easter, when there was no word from John, we sold the horse, and although it tore my heart to do so, I also sold my Mother's precious Book of Hours. Now, since the arrival of Edwin, things are not much better, and I have considered selling the one valuable treasure that remains – my Father's Bible. After the sadness of parting with my Mother's treasured Book, just the thought of selling my Father's Bible has made me feel sick.

It was on an unusually cold and grey summer's day last week that I left baby Edwin with Bessie, and Godfrey and I braved the filthy streets and the beggars of London. Godfrey had told me of a merchant of books and documents called Elias Fogge, whose shop is near the Fleet, and we made our way there. The entrance is three steps down into a dark and gloomy space, the only light coming in from the doorway. I looked around for Master Fogge, but I could only see shelf after shelf filled with large leather bound books and a dusty table full of maps and papers rolled up and secured with red cords and ribbons.

Master Fogge appeared from the depths of his gloomy shop and I showed him my Father's Bible. I told him that I was a widow, Mistress de Courtsey, and I explained to him some of the reasons why I needed to sell such a well loved treasure. His dark skin and hair, together with his large, hooked nose told me that he was a Jew, and I could see that it worried him not a little to buy a Christian Bible.

Although Jews have been banned from England for hundreds of years, I know that there are many who live unobtrusively in London, and I believe that Elias Fogge is one of them. But I have no fears of Jews, even if they are not Christians, they can be good men too.

"You see", I said to Master Fogge, "This wonderful edition of the Bible was given to me by my Father, and I am loath to sell it. Not only is it all I have left of my Father, but I used it to teach Son to read in English, and I shall want to do the same for my baby when he is old enough."

"If that is the case you cannot sell your Father's Bible," he said most quickly. I could see that he was relieved to find a good reason not to buy it. "But," he continued, "you must be a very able woman not only to read, but to teach too," said Master Fogge. "Have you taught your elder Son to write as well?"

"Oh, yes," I said. "And I have also taught him Latin and account ledgers too. Indeed, I will soon be looking for someone else's child to tutor. I am in sore need of monies."

"Well l if I do not buy your Father's Bible, I have another idea. Would you consider teaching my Son, Toby? It is his eighth birthday next week, and my Wife and I think that it is time that he began to learn to read and write. This may be a very opportune coincidence. Would you like to meet Mistress Fogge and Toby?"

"I would be delighted," I replied with inner excitement. "Are they here? It would pleasure me greatly to meet them."

At once Master Fogge left the shop, and returned some minutes later with a short, dark lady and a little boy.

They were delightful. Toby was as different to John at that age as any child could be. He is small, with dark skin and large blue eyes. He seemed to be very timid. I was completely charmed by him.

"Toby," said his Father. "Let me introduce you to this lady. Her name is Mistress de Courtsey, and she has agreed to teach you to read and write."

"Good day, Mistress de Courtsey," said young Toby, in a most polite and nervous manner. "I am pleased to meet you."

He seems to be a very sweet child, and I am sure that we will suit each other splendidly, and I told his parents so! In order to confirm our newly agreed arrangement Elias Fogge advanced me three shillings in silver, and with that and the earnings that Benjamin and Godfrey bring in we will be able to survive until I commence my teaching with young Toby, who is to join us here in this household in the next week or so. It will good to have a child in the home again, and with little Toby we shall feel like a family household again.

28th August 1629

A full year has passed since I was forced to leave Thornhill, and although I still have many sleepless nights when I long for my home and my Son, I have become used to living here in London. Edwin is a happy and healthy baby in spite of the fetid air that we breathe and all the mess and filth which surround us in the streets. I try not to think about the open space and sweet air of Thornhill, and the times I spent with John as a baby walking in the gardens of my lost home.

Bessie continues to be my Guardian Angel, as usual. She not only takes care of baby Edwin, she also nurses and cherishes little Toby, who joined us six weeks ago.

Toby is a delightful child. To begin with he was very timid, afeared of saying or doing anything. But with every day that passes he is growing more confident, and I am sure that he already loves Bessie like a second mother! He abides here with us from Saturday to Thursday evening when Godfrey returns him to his parents. I know little about the Jewish religion, and, although we do not discuss it, I am sure that they celebrate the Sabbath quietly at home. It would be dangerous for them to do it openly, and, for their safety, they also attend a Christian church on Sundays.

Toby, who is very Jewish in his looks, with his blue eyes, curly black hair, and, for a little boy, an over large nose! To make his race and religion less obtrusive, while Toby lives with us he joins us on Sundays when we attend the Christian mass. His Father has no objection to me teaching Toby from my Bible, as long as I teach from the Old Testament. Toby is a quick learner, and he even recognises some of the Holy Scriptures that the priest reads on Sundays!

Everything has now improved with the increase in our income. Godfrey earns well enough from the account work that he does for the Royal Exchange, but sadly Benjamin is now ailing, his strength has all but gone, and he has been unable to work for many weeks now.

I have had no tidings from John since Christmas. Alas.

21st September 1629

I can hardly bring myself to write this. I am heartbroken. I have lost John completely to his Father, and I do not think that I will ever see my darling child again.

After months of waiting for him to come, with no forewarning, he arrived last Tuesday. I was in the parlour nursing baby Edwin at my breast, when I heard Bessie exclaim as she opened the door to the stable yard. And before I was able to rearrange my clothing and set baby Edwin down in his crib, the parlour door opened and in came John.

I saw the expectant look on his face change to surprise as he saw me nursing a baby.

"John," I exclaimed, "it is so good to see you!"

At the same moment he also exclaimed, "Mother. What is this? A baby! Whose is it?" I could see his manner changing and hardening as he spoke. His face then became the living image of Christopher's face when he was angered and about to attack me.

"I never believed it before, but everything that Father has said about you is true. You are a whore!"

I took a step forward towards him, and he stepped back, away from me. "Oh! No, John, no," I cried. "This is your baby Brother. His name is Edwin. Let me explain it to you."

He would not wait for any explanation.

"My Brother!" He almost spat at me. "He cannot be my Brother.

Before last August it was almost two years that Father had been home, and bedded you, and that child is no older than six months. Even I know how long a woman carries a child from conception to birth!"

I was stunned, shaken and I started to cry. "John. John. John!" I called out to him. "Do you not remember that I left Thornhill that day last August when your Father attacked me? How could I tell you this before? You saw the results of the attach on me. You saw my torn and blooded clothing. His attack was not only brutal to my body, he ravaged me too. And the result of that attack is little baby Edwin that you see here. He was born on the 16th of May, just nine months after I left Thornhill. Look at him. He looks just like you did as a baby, and you both look just like your Father!"

He did not look at Edwin, and he turned his back upon me.

"Mother!" he said disgustedly. "I am ashamed to call you Mother. Every word you say is a falsehood. Father has been telling me about your whoreish ways, and I did not believe him. But I do now. You are no longer my Mother!"

With that he walked out of the room. I ran after him calling out "John, do not leave. I am telling you no falsehoods."

He turned, and when I tried to put my arms about him, he thrust me away with a pure look of disgust upon his face. "You whore!" he almost snarled at me. I can only believe that the shock of seeing me nurse Baby Edwin at my breast made him react with such violence. Was there never such a reminder to me of me of his Father? Please God he will reflect and return. I will write him a letter to explain all to him, and find a messenger who will take it to Thornhill. How I regret not telling him that I was with child when came at Christmas this time last year!

~~~

16th May 1639

Today is Edwin's tenth birthday! So many things have happened since I last wrote in this journal. I should have continued, but after my last heart crushing parting with my dearest Son John, I have been too often sad or afeared to write. Bitter things I can remember I find I am unable to write about.

But I must now write about John. Even now it grieves me sorely to write about him. My beloved Son has never returned to see me again in all these years, he never replied to any of my letters, and I have never dared to return to Thornhill. That terrible last visit six months after Edwin was born was the last I saw of him. He must have told his Father about Edwin, and I am sure that his Father, taking the opportunity to break John's tie with me, denied his violation of me. Poor John must have come to believe his Father's assertions that I am indeed a whore.

I am also saddened to write about old Benjamin who died in April of 1630, and he lies buried in the churchyard of St. Botolph in Aldgate, so far away from all his family. But Bessie and Geoffrey still remain with me. Dear old Bessie, still looking after me after all these years. Still my best friend and the person in this world whom I trust the most.

Toby Fogge lived with us for six years and became almost a big brother to Edwin. I taught him all that I know, and we were saddened when he left here to become an apprentice clerk to a lawyer in Grey's Inn. He is doing well I hear, from his father Elias, who I call in to see if ever I pass his shop. After Toby I taught Stephen, the delightful Son of Andrew Caldwell, a Scottish wool merchant, who was introduced to me by Elias. Stephen was a funny little boy with a shock of red hair. He often made me laugh with merriment at his comical expressions and his use of unusual Scottish words. He would look at me, his teacher, and say in a very serious voice, and in an exaggerated Scottish accent, "do you not know what that means Mistress de Courtsey? Shall I have to explain it to you?" Three years of merriment and laughter we had with Stephen until he left us only recently to join his Father's business down at the London docks.

Then, of course, there is dear Edwin himself. He has grown to become a most wonderful and caring Son, just like John at the same age. For his tender age he is tall and slender and so good looking. He has the exact look of his Father, especially when something displeases him. If only John would come and visit us again, I know that he would see Edwin's likeness to himself and Christopher. And know the truth, that he is indeed Christopher's Son and John's full Brother. Much as I love my Edwin, I still desperately miss my elder Son, my John.

Edwin regards me as I write.

"What is that book that you are writing in, Mother?" he asks.

I laughed at him and said, "I am writing all my secrets in my secret Journal!"

Edwin laughed too, and said, "I do not believe that you have any secrets."

I just smiled and said no more. The Journal is getting quite full now, and I wonder if I shall have to buy another one, perhaps I will just have to squeeze in my entries from now on. Although there is now no real need to hide it because I know that Edwin would never take anything out of my Chest, but still, out of habit, I keep it in the secret drawer.

23^h October 1642

John, Oh! My dearest Son! Now lost and gone from me forever! Killed fighting for King Charles! And that wicked Christopher is to blame. Here in London Bessie, Edwin and I have weathered all the storms brewing in the City caused by the struggle between the King and Parliament. All around us people take sides, but we prefer not to. We do not voice our opinions abroad and we keep safe!

Christopher not only took the King's side, as I had expected, but he also took up arms to defend his old Master. And he induced, no, I'm sure that he forced John, to take up arms too.

John is, was, only twenty-six, and he should have let Christopher go off warring on his own. He should have stayed at home to be the Master of Thornhill. But Christopher, that evil Husband of mine, joined the Royalists and took my John to war. My darling John was killed in the very first battle against the Parliamentarians at Edgehill in Warwickshire, on the 16th of October. Christopher wrote to me telling me about the cruelty of my Son's death. I did not keep the letter, because I tore it into a hundred pieces, wishing with each tear that he had written falsehoods, or that it had been a letter from John telling me that it was Christopher who had been killed. I am certain that the letter was not written just to tell me about John, but to hurt me in the worst way that he could, more than anything he has ever done to me. More than any physical attacks he has made on me. More than any violations. He always knew how much I loved John, how special he was to me, and as soon as I left Thornhill, Christopher must have worked hard to make John despise me and hate me. And he succeeded.

Oh! John. John. Now I will never be able to show you the truth about Edwin, and make peace between us. I will never be able to hold you in my arms again. John. My baby. God bless you, my darling, and take you to Paradise.

1st September 1650

After all these years a letter from Christopher!

> *Dear Wife*
> *Life has not been good to me since we lost our John. After I brought him home to be buried in St. Peter's, I returned to Thornhill, and for six years I remained there and did not return to fight for the King. But in June of 1648 I was in Chelmsford when a riotous crowd took the Essex County Parliamentary Committee and declared themselves for the King, and I was forced by them to choose where my loyalties lay. When Sir George Lisle and Sir Charles Lucas joined the rebels, I decided to rearm myself and rejoin the King's forces. All is well documented about our march to Colchester and the siege which followed, wherein I was trapped for eleven weeks. It was the most piteous and dreadful campaign. Not only the troops but all the citizens of Colchester suffered in the extreme. The city suffered extreme mortality, and we who survived were all starving and were reduced to eating rats, cats, dogs and horses. The Parliamentarian Lord General Fairfax and his armies stood firm against the town, and it was only after the Royalist defeat in Preston at the end of August that Sir George Lisle, Sir Charles Lucas and the other leaders surrendered to Fairfax. They were captured and executed.*
>
> *I managed to escape, thence I came home to Thornhill, but to my great horror and anguish I found that during the siege it had been confiscated and occupied by Fairfax and his Parliamentary*

...rces. They remained there for four months. When they left they set fire to and destroyed the Manor house, and the whole of our lands remain confiscated. I have never recovered from Colchester and its aftermath. The King's murder last year by that wicked Oliver Cromwell has also laid me low, and for the past two years I have been living secretly and quietly in my childhood home, The Grange, which is still owned by the family of Anthony Buckshore.

But at the end of this month I am forced leave here, and I have no other home to go to other than the one I still own I in London.

Although we have been apart these many years, you remain my Wife, and you are duty bound to respect and honour my commands. I desire that you take me and the few possessions that remain to me, to my home in Aldgate.

I shall send a carriage to bring you here.

Your Husband Christopher.

I could scarce believe what I was reading. I knew that many properties and lands of Royalists had been confiscated during these last terrible years, but this was my home – and it was now destroyed! I let the letter fall as I sat in tears and disbelief. I thought of all the wicked things that had been wrought by that hateful Husband of mine. He had killed my girl baby, he had killed my Son, and now he had lost my home. Yet he commanded me to bring him into my life again, to bring him here? This was a command that I would never obey!

2nd **September 1650**

I showed the letter to Edwin.

"Mother," he said. "We must go. Even if you decide not to allow my Father to return with us, I desire above all to meet him. All my life I have heard discourse between you, Bessie and Godfrey about Thornhill. Remember it should be my inheritance now, and even if the lands remain confiscated, I do desire to see them too."

So, I am persuaded. I remain most reluctant, but I shall go. Although I know that my heart will break, I shall have the opportunity to visit John's tomb, my parents tomb, and have one last look at my lost home.

13th September 1650

Well now! He's dead! Christopher is dead too, and I killed him! One more secret to bury in my Chest, along with my letters, my Journal recording all that he has done to me, my account books, and now this Confession too!

Christopher sent a carriage to bring me back home, but before we went to St. Peter's in Thornton, we went first to The Grange. I do not know why I agreed to stay there with Christopher until his tenancy expired the following week, but I did want Edwin to meet and get to know his Father. I was already ill tempered as I followed Christopher into the central hall, and I stared at him in disbelief; the handsome man who had been my Husband was now shabby, and stumbling with drink.

Edwin is now a man of twenty-one years and this was the first time ever that he saw his Father. They both looked hard at each other, and without acknowledging or speaking to Edwin, Christopher asked of me, "Why did you never tell me directly that I have another Son?"

That was his only greeting after twenty-two years!

"Because he was born of your violation of me," I cried, my anger suddenly arising. "You called me a whore. John must have told you that I had another child. You made no effort to find the truth or to visit me, and you let my Son believe that his Mother was a whore. He died never knowing the truth! I have never hated anyone as I hate you!"

Edwin stared at me and his Father in disbelief! Never in his life had he heard me raise my voice, or express my hatred of his Father. "I will have discourse with my Father later. I shall first discover the church at Thornton," he said, and then he fled the house leaving us together.

Christopher, looking most haggard and old, advanced towards me as if he were about to embrace me. I jumped backwards to avoid any contact with him. I could hardly bear to look at him.

"Mary," he said, "You are still my Wife, and the house in London still belongs to me. All I am asking, not demanding, is that you allow me to join you and Edwin when you return."

My anger heightened and I became as angry as I have ever been. "How dare you bring me here just to beg for shelter? You have never accepted Edwin as your Son, in spite of Edwin being the very image of you as a young man. Even you can see that." I think that Christopher was about to acknowledge Edwin, but having had the courage at last to face Christopher, I continued. "And you still call me a whore! No word of 'sorry' for all the ill you have brought to me over the past forty-two years! No begging for forgiveness for the death of John and the loss and ruin of Thornhill Manor and its lands."

Christopher bridled at these accusations and I could see him getting stronger. "Our troubles were as much your fault as mine," he said. "I had no desire to marry you. I had no choice in who was to be my Wife. I forced to marry you by my parents and yours."

I did not back down. "Yes," I said, "but our parents did not force you to be cruel to me, and to steal from me everything that I ever owned. All you ever left for me was my Chest". I started to rage at him. "And do I have to remind you that you were obviously so repulsed by me that you violated me again and again from the time I was only eight years old?"

Now he dared to stand up to me. There was no real humbleness or contrition in him. All I could see before me was a drunken, broken man, who in his foolishness in supporting a stubborn and reckless King, had caused the death of my beloved Son John and had lost everything he owned – I owned. Now here he was, desiring of me to take him back to my home in London, which he even dared to say, still belonged to him!

Edwin was praying in St. Peter's when it happened. This time it was I who rendered myself unto my temper. It was I who struck the first blow. And it was I who picked up the fire-iron from hearth and belaboured him about the head as he begged me, not for forgiveness, but for me to give him a home. He rose up and lunged towards me as I backed away. My back was hard pressed against the door of the wine cellar, and I thought that he would reach me, forcefully taking the fire-iron from my shaking hands. Then he stumbled over the rush matting and fell at my feet. Before I could gather my wits I hit him once more. He groaned loudly and he lay still at my feet. I was terrified while I waited to see if he would regain his senses, then I opened the cellar door. With all my remaining strength I managed to drag his senseless body to the cellar. Then I rolled him down the steep stone steps and he lay still at the bottom. With my heart pounding, once more I waited for a minute or two, and when he did not move I found the courage to go down. I took the steps very slowly and carefully, one at a time, avoiding the blood splatters on the way and expecting him to rise up again at any moment. I was shaking when I reached the bottom and I stood over him. Then, very cautiously, I bent low to examine him, still afeared that he might awake and take hold of me. But he was no longer breathing, and I could see from the way his head was twisted that he must have broken his neck in his fall. He was dead!

I was stunned at what I had done. Now that my temper had cooled I was also mightily afeared. All I desired was to beg Christopher for forgiveness, but I realized that I could not undo the evil that I had done. So for Edwin's sake I decided to cover my evil deed with a simple lie. His Father's neck had been broken in the fall and the blood on the stone steps could account for the injuries on his head.

I left Christopher's body where it lay, and in a daze I remounted the steps, cleaned and replaced the fire-iron, and wiped away some small spots of blood from the hearth and the stone floor. The blood on my skirt I could account for by saying that I had tried to revive him after his fall. Then I sat and waited for Edwin's return.

He could scarce believe his eyes when I showed him his Father's body and gave account of what had taken place. He did not know or love his Father but he had just met him for the very first time that day and he had wanted to know him and demand of him the reason for his neglect of his second Son. Now that was no longer possible.

I was amazed how everyone, including Edwin and the local magistrate, who was brought in by Edwin, was willing to accept the lie. I told them all that Christopher and I had been reconciled and that he was getting his last bottle of vintage wine to celebrate our agreement. I told them that Christopher had already rendered himself incapable with wine. I told them that I had wanted to make that agreement without that last bottle, but that Christopher had insisted. I told them that Christopher had reached the top of the cellar steps when he tripped and fell, hitting his head and breaking his neck at the bottom. Together they looked at the blood on the stone steps and

Christopher's twisted body at the bottom. They agreed that his head wounds must have happened during his fall, and Edwin confirmed to the magistrate that when he had left us together, his Father had already taken too much wine.

I stayed at The Grange until Christopher's funeral and burial at St Peter's, a hurried and unhappy affair that only Edwin and I attended. Silently I prayed for my dead Husband's forgiveness. Memories of my youth, of Father Thomas, of my beloved Mother and Father, my Marriage and my Son John, swirled around my head as I kneeled before my parent's tomb. I prayed and asked for theirs and God's forgiveness. I prayed before John's tomb too, asking for his forgiveness too.

After leaving the church, with the heaviest of hearts, I walked slowly up the hill to see the remains of my lovely home. Thornhill Manor was no more! Burnt to the ground! All that remained was a blacken ruin. Even the cottages, the stables and the dairy were destroyed. And Bessie's cottage containing her beloved furniture which never was carried to our home at the Aldwich. My heart cried out in pain. Verily, I could scarce believe my eyes, and then I felt renewed anger for Christopher that his folly had allowed this to happen. I had asked for forgiveness for my Great Sin, but I was not sorry that he was dead.

And so, after I returned to London, I add this Confession to my Journal, and put it for you, Edwin, to discover when I have gone to confess all my Sins to my Maker. I shall continue to pray daily for Christopher's soul. And may God forgive me my Great Sin.

For years I have kept this old Journal in the body of my Chest with no fear that Edwin, or anyone else, would seek to discover whatever I have placed therein. But now, with Confession included in my Journal, I shall return it to the secret drawer, no matter how my old knees will complain when I reach for the release knob.

One day soon I will tell Edwin all about the secret drawer, and ask him to swear that he will not open it until after I have gone to God.

The Confession of Lady Mary de Courtsey.

Mea culpa, mea culpa, mea maxima culpa.
My fault, my fault, my most grievous fault.
Forgive me Father, for I have sinned.
Our Father, which art in Heaven, and knows whereof all Our Sins of the Flesh and of the Heart, I make this my Confession unto Thee.
After many years of Violence and Violation given unto me by my Husband Sir Christopher de Courtsey, and the death of my precious Son John caused by him, I have Committed a Great Sin. I have Killed my Husband.
It was not an act of planned revenge, but an action taken on an instance, and promoted by the Devil.
I do daily penances and say many Hail Marys, and, although it is now forbidden, I shall soon make a pilgrimage to the shrine of Saint Thomas Becket in Canterbury, to again confess my Great Sin, and I beg Forgiveness for my Soul.
Mea culpa, mea culpa, mea maxima culpa.
My fault, my fault, my most grievous fault.

Mary de Courtsey
30th September 1650

~~~

5th September 1666

Edwin came in to find his mother collapsed on her Chest.

"Mother," he called. "Oh Mother. Everything will be all right. The fire is under control and our home is safe. You should never have tried to move that heavy Chest. Come; let me take you to your chamber to rest."

Mary roused herself a little. "Is that you, John?", she asked weakly.

"No, mother, John has gone, it is your other son Edwin", he said as he lifted her gently. He realised as he carried her, that his beloved mother was dying.

"Oh! Baby Edwin, I was just thinking about you and John", she breathed.

Edwin was a full grown man of thirty-seven, but now he began to weep like a baby as he carried Mary to her room, and laid the old lady on her bed.

"Oh yes", Mary thought to herself. "Yes John had gone, fighting for King Charles back in 1642. And she, herself had killed Christopher eight years later. He had become a drunkard, stripped of his wealth, and living back in his childhood home, The Grange.

They were all gone now. Mother and Father, John. Christopher. King Charles, and his murderer, Oliver Cromwell. And dear old Jessie and the Haydock brothers. And Thornhill Manor, confiscated and ravaged by the victorious and hateful Parliamentarians. After Christopher's death I never saw my lovely childhood home again or received so much as a silver penny in compensation for its loss after the Restoration, all that remains is my Chest, my Father's Bible, and my Journal and all the secrets held within."

She breathed a long, deep breath. "Edwin", she whispered, her eyes still closed. "Edwin. Are you still with me? I never told you about the secret .." she paused, "please don't go away..." Mary seemed to lapse into sleep as Edwin held her hand, with tears running down his cheeks. This was not the moment to ask about secrets.

"Mother," he said, "do not worry about secrets. Just rest awhile."

Now Susan, Edwin's daughter, and Mary's only granddaughter

came quietly into the room. Mary seemed to be aware of Susan at the side of her bed.

"Edwin," Mary whispered again. "My Chest. I want you to have everything inside my Chest. Look in the drawer. But I want Susan to have the Chest Itself. Her Bridal Chest". She slept again, and this time she did not wake up.

Secrets of the Chest
Part Two

Maria Rochester
1791–1836

Miriam Rosen
1878–?

18th October 1891

It was still dark outside when, with her father and her step-mother asleep in their bedroom upstairs, twelve year old Miriam crept downstairs to the parlour. Even the housemaid, Daisy, was still abed, and last night's fire had not yet been renewed, but the red glow from the embers led her directly to the fireplace and the heavily decorated mantelpiece above. Fumbling in the gloom Miriam found the heavy iron key which was half hidden behind the clock. She lit the oil lamp on the side table, and then went over to the Chest where it rested on the far side of the room. Although her step-mother had placed her own things into it, Miriam knew that the Chest really belonged to her; a last gift from her mother Jessica, who had run away from her and her father three years earlier.

Jessica was the daughter of Michael Jacobs, who was her father's partner in the Rosenberg Gallery, and they were both stunned and horrified at Jessica's betrayal. She was immediately disowned by both of them, and her father started divorce proceedings without delay. Jessica's name was never mentioned again in their home, or between the partners in the Rosenberg, and poor, timid little Miriam was left motherless without any clear explanation. She was only nine when it had happened, and she had been so wrapped up in her own unhappiness after her mother's abandonment, that she had been mostly unaware of the subsequent scandal of her parent's divorce.

All Miriam ever learned about her mother's actions was from part of a conversation that she had overheard last year when her father was talking to Esther, who was soon to become her step-mother. Miriam had been sitting on the stairs of the upper landing and the door of the parlour below was open. Her father's raised and angry voice had drifted up towards her.

"I just do not understand how that woman, I will not call her my wife, could ever think to leave my home. I am, after all, Abraham Rosen. I am famous as an art dealer and I own the Rosenberg Gallery. I am a man of wealth and position in this City. I gave her everything that she could ever have wanted! How could she go off with a person of no consequence? The man is nothing but a fiddle-player who plays in the city orchestra, and travels around the country like a gypsy!"

Miriam heard no more because before Esther could reply the parlour door had been shut from inside with sharp force.

Abraham had remarried just over two years after her mother went away, and during those two years Miriam felt as though her father, who had never been warm and affectionate towards her, now positively disliked her. Perhaps it was her blond hair and the fragile looks of her mother that reminded him of her mother's betrayal. She felt unloved and unwanted, almost as if she had lost both parents instead of just her mother. Only Jacob, her grandfather, remained affectionate towards her, and Miriam tried to be with him as often as she could.

Her new stepmother, Esther, was the widow of Abraham's friend Gabriel. She was kind, warm and friendly to Miriam, and tried to make up for Jessica's abandonment of her daughter. But Miriam was sad and confused, and she did not want to be comforted or mothered by Esther. She longed for her own mother's return, and she often wished that Jessica had taken her too when she had run away.

To add to her unhappiness, Miriam was also discomforted by her new stepbrothers, twins Leon and Daniel, who had been boisterous fourteen year-olds when her father remarried, and now, at the age of sixteen, teased her unmercifully whenever her father and her stepmother were not watching. They did not really mean to be unkind, but she was just a girl, and they did not like sharing their mother with either Miriam or her father. They were subdued and respectful with Abraham, but with Miriam they could sometimes be quite spiteful, and they absolutely refused to call her their sister. They were much bigger and stronger than Miriam, and they would hide her things to annoy her, and call her 'goyim', and 'not a proper Jew', because her mother was not a Jewess. Miriam had begun to turn away whenever she was left alone with them.

Although, after her mother had left, the Chest was supposed to be hers, Miriam's father had not allowed her to use it. And now it had been given to her stepmother for her own use. Miriam was told by her other not to open it or rummage through it because Esther had placed some of her own private possessions in it. But on that early morning Miriam lifted the lid, looked only briefly at the inscription carved into the underside of it, and started her search. She knew what she was looking for was right at the bottom. It was an old book that had fallen out of the pocket of the dress that Esther had removed and discarded. Miriam had spotted it there as her stepmother was putting in her old patchwork quilt.

Miriam was sad about the old dress being thrown away; she had protested and said that she would keep it in her room, but as usual, her protests were ignored. That dress was one of her happy memories of childhood and of playing with her mother. Miriam had often dressed up in it when she was a little girl. The size of the dress had swamped her, but she had loved to pretend that she was a witch or a fairy and the enveloping folds of the dress held much powerful magic. But she did not remember a book in the pocket when she had worn it, but it was so small perhaps she had forgotten it. Perhaps her mother had put it there later? But when Esther had taken out the dress Miriam had seen the book fall out and into the dark corner of the Chest, directly below the candle tray and hidden out of sight. Now once again it was buried underneath her stepmother's quilt and set of bone china serving dishes.

The mystery of the little book intrigued Miriam, so she had decided to rescue it as soon as she could. After all, she told herself, the Chest and everything that had been in it before Esther took it over, really belonged to her!

So that morning, while everyone was still asleep, after silently creeping downstairs, Miriam had unlocked and opened up the Chest. Very carefully she took out the chinaware and put it on the floor beside her. Then, trying not to alter the position of anything else, she felt under the quilt and other things until her fingers found and retrieved the book. She put back everything as carefully as she could, and hoping that Esther would not notice any disturbance of her possessions, she re-locked the Chest, and put the key back on the mantelpiece.

Taking the oil lamp with her, she went over to settle herself on the window seat of the parlour where she was half hidden by some heavy velvet curtains. (She imagined herself to be just like Jane, the heroine from her favourite book 'Jane Eyre', hiding behind curtains to avoid detection by the older children of the family, who all despised her!)

Miriam quickly discovered that the 'book' that she had rescued was hardly a book at all. It was a little dairy, which had lost its outer cover, and was loosely stitched together in a soft binding, which itself, was rapidly falling to pieces. When she opened it a letter fell out onto the floor. She picked it up and looked at it curiously, and then decided to read the book first. So she put the letter at the back of her window seat amongst the cushions, and carefully opening the first page of the diary. The first thing that she saw was that it was written nearly one hundred years ago in a large bold hand, and the writer was a girl just a few years older than herself, named Maria Rochester. What a strange co-incidence, she thought, Rochester was the name of Jane Eyre's great love! She was soon enthralled as she read on…

Diary of Maria Rochester, age 15.

23rd March 1806

Today I am quite grown up. At last I have reached the great age of fifteen!

One of my gifts from my father is this little book. From the time my brothers were just babies I have made up short stories to amuse them, and ever since I could write I have recorded some of these stories, as well as some poems, on to scraps of paper which I have stored in a box in my bedroom. On occasions have even written stories on blank pages in my father's legal note books if they were scarce used.

"Here!" said my father, with a laugh. "I am giving you your very own note book to use as you like, so you will no longer need to thieve mine. You bad girl!"

I love my father, and I knew that he was not angered by me. We often talk to each other in an affectionate and mock fierce day. We enjoy much fun and pleasure in each other's company – much to the displeasure of my mother!

I was about to make up a completely new story to start this book, when I decided that the story that I know best is my own. So I shall write about me and my family. Perhaps it will turn out to be a diary of sorts. So here I will start with the time that my parents first met.

It was a pity that my mother is so prim and proper, because my father, although he can be very serious when he needs to be, was, when he first encountered my mother, always full of fun, laughter and silliness.

That day, the day when they first met, the wind was blowing hard just before an oncoming storm and my father, Master Henry Rochester, Attorney at Law, had just dropped his legal papers in the city high street. When gathering them up as quickly as he could before they were blown away or could be trampled by any passing horse and carriage, he came across what he thought was probably a very trim and fetching ankle which was covered up with a high buttoned boot!

The boot, and indeed the ankle, were holding down the top page of his brief – the matter of Henry, 3rd Duke of .... v. Caroline, the Dowager Duchess of ....

Having retrieved the title page from the foot, the boot, and the ankle, my father lifted his eyes to the sleek silk skirt, the very trim waist, the delectable bosom, the long neck, and, at last, his eyes came upon the most perfect face that he had ever seen.

At least this is how he later told it all to me. This was his first encounter of that faultless being who was later to become my mother

"Was it love at first sight? Was she pleased to have helped you?" I had asked, with all the curiosity of an eight year old child.

"Indeed it was, on my behalf", my father had replied. "But it took much longer for your mother to love me in return. No, at the time, she just scolded me for being so careless and treating the Duke's legal matter with such disrespect. She did, at least tell me her name."

It turned out that my mother was a Stanford, Sarah

Stanford, and she is a distant relative of the Duke whose name she recognised immediately on the scattered documents. She also knew the Duke himself because she lived with her parents in a cottage on his estate.

It was the day following her eighteenth birthday when my mother met father. After that fateful encounter, my father made sure that, on each of his regular visits to the Duke, he also called upon my mother's family to pay his respects and to enquire about their daughter, Sarah.

It is my grandfather, Edward Stanford, who is the 'poor relation' of the Duke. The Duke's grandmother had been the younger sister of my grandfather's great grandmother. So many, 'grands' and 'greats', but I think that I have it right. And most those 'grands' and 'greats' were unimportant females, which makes me hardly related to the Duke at all!

My grandfather still thinks of the Duke as 'family', even though he and my grandmother, Elizabeth, have very little intercourse with him or his family. But my grandparents were pleased to get to know my father, who, as the Duke's legal advisor, had so much more contact with the Duke than they did.

My father and the Duke spent many hours in each other's company and they were quickly becoming friends. The legal matter involved the Duke claiming back from the his stepmother, now the Dowager Duchess, many valuable antiques, paintings and silver that he considered belonged to him and the titled estate. The Dowager Duchess had removed them when the old Duke had died the previous year. The court case was really about inheritance and the interpretation of the late Duke's will. It became the most important brief that my father had handled. Winning it had given him high prestige in the town of Alderham, where he lived, and more lucrative work from the Duke.

I believe that my beautiful, but haughty mother was also impressed by my father's success. Slowly she thawed towards him and eventually accepted his pleadings to become his wife. And thus I was born on 23rd March 1791, some sixteen months after their marriage.

I am sure that my mother has grown to love my father, but she is never happy with the lightness of his nature. She does not

think that he takes his profession seriously enough, and at home
he disapproved of the way he played and fooled around with
me when I was a child, and then later with my two younger
brothers.

Whilst I have inherited my mother's looks, her lithe figure,
her bright auburn hair and her green eyes, I have my father's
happy and friendly nature. Frivolous and empty headed, my
mother calls me. My two brothers, unfortunately, have grown
up to be exactly like our mother. They are humourless, serious,
ambitious, alert to any risk in body, or, more seriously, in
reputation.

After my parents' marriage they lived in my father's home
in Alderham, where I, and then my brothers, were born. It is a
pleasant house, but when my brothers are home from boarding
school we all live so close together in it that I often feel that I
am crushed. My father, who is now a very successful lawyer in
Alderham since he won the Duke's property lawsuit, is my only
friend and support at home. He is still a happy creature, but a
lot of the fun that I used to have with him when I was a little girl
has disappeared, I think it is because my mother so disapproves
of him when he is in a light and playful mood. In the few hours
that I get to spend alone with my father, we sometimes just sit at
home reading, or on fine days, walk to the park to feed the ducks.
We have no pets at home because my mother's eyes always
became red and weepy whenever she is near or touches a cat or
a dog.

Apart from that, I have always been happier when I am away
from the criticisms and quarrels that I have with my mother and
my two brothers. My brothers, Thomas and William, are three
years and five years younger than me, but they both think that
they are more important than me, because I am only a girl!

I loved my brothers when they were babies, and I was such a
happy little girl when I helped our nursemaid, Matilda, to bath,
feed and dress them. I was even allowed to hold them on my lap
if I was sitting down in the big leather armchair that we had in
the nursery. It was when they were quite small that I started to
make up bedtime stories for them. But as we all grew older they
began to lose interest in me and my world of fairies and dragons,

especially when I wanted to make them laugh or join in my games. They were so serious, just like our mother. They acted like little grown-ups, and they seemed to prefer their own humourless company to mine.

We had all been taught our letters and numbers in the nursery by Matilda. She was plump and jolly and, along with my father, she encouraged me in my story telling. But when Thomas was seven he was sent to the Highcliff boarding school for his education. He loved it there and when he came home once a month, he hated all the 'mother fuss' that he was made to endure. He much preferred to be with the other fellows at school! William was most envious of his elder brother, and he longed to be seven too, so that he could join him at Highcliff. To satisfy William, and because I wanted to be taught too, my father asked his clerk, John Matthews, to teach us both once a week, on Saturday mornings.

John Matthews is a Welshman. He was then about forty-five, short, thin as a rake, but he had the most beautiful and melodic voice that could charm the birds from the trees! I was so happy at last to be learning more than music, embroidery and painting – the ladylike skills that every growing girl from a good home is forced to learn in order to make her marriageable! While William was set to learn the alphabet and numbers, I now took flight on the wings of stories. It was really history and geography lessons, but for me it was story after story about people's lives, kings and queens, soldiers, explorers, inventors, their triumphs and their failures, and their lusts for power, riches, domination and adventure! I also learned how to read and write properly, and the three years that Master Matthews filled my life with his magical voice and tales of adventure were the best I have ever spent.

Then William also went off to boarding school and my lessons came to an abrupt end. Mother insisted that at twelve years old, I should return my attention to domestic training to prepare myself for my future as a wife and mother. Then I longed for coming of the summer months when I could return to the home of my grandparents.

I had started to stay with my grandparents, who still live in their cottage on the Duke's estate, soon after Thomas was born.

To begin with my stay was for an occasional week at a time, and for two or three weeks at the height of the summer. Then after William's birth the weeks I spent away from our family home in Alderham were extended until It became a regular thing for me to spend every summer from June to September with my grandparents.

When I was seven years old my father bought for me a lovely pony, who I called Jupiter. I still have him and he lives at my grandparents' home – my grandfather looks after him, and my new mare Sally, most of the time. When I was little as well as my summertime visits, I used to climb up on my father's horse every time that he went on business to see the Duke, and I would spend a few days with my grandparents and Jupiter. My father's own horses and carriage were kept at livery stables near our home in Alderham.

How I love my wonderful grandparents Edward and Elizabeth Stanford! I sometimes wonder how they managed to produce such a strict and humourless daughter as my mother. They are both such happy people who are completely content with their lot in life. They are not at all envious of the Duke and his family in their grand Palladian mansion. (I have been inside the great house a few times, and although there are parts of it that are very beautiful indeed, I find it cold and uncomfortable.)

My grandparents' cottage has its own driveway with a separate entrance on the main highway. It sits on the far side of the great lake, hidden from view from the Duke's mansion by a small group of trees. So although my grandparents live very near the Duke and his family, they keep to their side of the lake. They hardly ever meet anyone from the great house apart from some of the groundsmen, gamekeepers and gardeners.

The cottage itself is much smaller that our house in Alderham. It has just three bedrooms upstairs and two rooms and a kitchen downstairs, with a great big oak Chest, all but filling the hallway. But I find it warm, cosy and friendly, and apart from my Saturday morning lessons with Master Matthews, I have always been much happier when I am staying with my grandparents than I am at home. My grandmother, Elizabeth, often tells me stories of her family, who have lived in these parts for more than two hundred years. I don't know how many of these stories are true, but one she told me when I was about twelve years old, was of a girl who hated her wealthy husband so much that she ran away to London, taking only the old oak Chest with her.

"How did it get here?" I asked.

"Well", my grandmother had replied, "my own great-grandmother told me that this Chest has always belonged to the daughters and grand-daughters in our family, and that the grand-daughter of the one who ran away to live in London, decided to leave London and come to live here in Alderham, and she brought the Chest with her."

She took me into the hall and opened up the lid of the Chest, (which I could see was full of her best bed and table linen). "See here," she said, and she pointed to some writing that was carved into the underside of the lid. "Can you read it?" she asked.

"I think that it says 'Mary de Courtsey'," I said. "That sounds like a French name to me. Was she French, Grandmother?"

"I don't know, my Sweeting," she replied. "She could have been. The Chest is a very nicely made of good English oak, and I think that Mary de Courtsey, whoever she was, probably had a rich father or husband to have had this made for her. Perhaps they were local landowners, although I have never heard of a Thornhill Manor in these parts."

"What do those letters under Thornhill Manor mean?" I asked.

"They are Latin numbers which show the year 1599. It could be when Mary de Courtsey was born, or perhaps when this Chest was made," she said. "This Chest is more than 200 years old! I often wonder how many of our grandmothers and great-grandmothers have owned it!"

"Can you read Latin numbers?" I asked. "How do you work them out?"

"Well, my Sweeting," said my grandmother, "I couldn't work them out myself, but I knew that some of the tombs in St. Augustine's church have letters written on them instead of numbers, so I copied the letters from the Chest onto a piece paper and I took it to Father Taylor at the Church, and he explained how to work it out."

"Is it easy? Can you show me too?" I asked.

"Well," said my grandmother, pointing again to the carving, "that group of letters MDIC is one number, and each separate letter has a different value. The first two letters are easy to explain. M is one thousand, D is five hundred, but the last two are more complicated. C means one hundred, but because there is an I in front of the C then that one has to be taken away from the hundred, which makes it ninety-nine. So MDIC is 1599."

"That is very complicated, Grandmother. Why do they do it when it is so much easier to write numbers?" I asked.

"I really don't know, my Sweeting," replied my grandmother. "I asked that very same question to Father Taylor, but he didn't know either!"

30th April 1806

Those are some of the memories I have of my childhood, but my diary will really start from today, because I have been told that tomorrow I am to join my parents for a special May Day performance of 'A Mid-Summer's Night Dream' by the famous playwright William Shakespeare. I am very excited. I have often asked my father if I could go to the theatre with them, and this is the first time that they have agreed. I wonder what I shall wear?

2nd May 1806

The play was wonderful! Although I had a little trouble understanding all the words, the action explained everything. Maybe I should try to write a play. It really does bring a story to life.

We were all wearing our best clothes. Mother looked stunning in her shimmering daffodil yellow silk dress, fashioned in the popular Empire line style. And I saw that she wore a new diamond gem which sparkled at her throat. I could see also that there were many heads which turned towards her as we climbed the richly carpeted stairs to the auditorium. I believe that I too looked at my best and my father was as proud as a peacock to have a beautiful woman and a pretty young daughter to grace each arm.

After the performance we met, and were introduced to Master Richard Rawson, his wife and their son James. That was an 'interesting' occasion! Master Rawson is a merchant of fine wines, and he is a client of my father. His son James, a rather spotty and diffident young man, is just completing his third year of training to become a doctor. The adults all talked together congenially, and James and I were left in an awkward silence.

He reddened and stuttered, "I hear th...that you are re... related to the D...Duke of .... Is th...that so?"

"Oh!" I replied. "My mother is a distant cousin, but we don't really know them at all."

He continued to stutter. "D...d...d...did you like the play?" I replied civilly, but I did not feel at all comfortable with this young man, and I did not want to continue a conversation with him. I was wondering to myself how quickly I could escape his attention, and get away with my parents. It was not until we were in our carriage taking us home, and my parents were praising the Rawsons, and in particular their spotty son, soon to become Dr. Rawson, that I deduced that the meeting with the Rawsons had not been accidental. Were my parents starting to introduce me to 'suitable' young men? Surely they are not seeking out a husband for me already! I trembled at the thought of telling my mother that I had no desire to meet 'suitable' young men, and that when I was ready to be married I would seek my own 'suitable' young man for myself! As I was preparing myself for bed I promised myself that I would confront my father when the moment was right. Surely he would speak to my mother.

6th May 1806

I have decided that I was mistaken in my parents' intentions, and that the Rawsons just happened to attend the play at the same time as us. At home there has been no more mention of them, or their son James, so I will say nothing either. I certainly do not want to put ideas into my mother's mind!

1st June 1806

I am happy. Today I have returned to my grandparents' home. I can forget all about confrontations at home, and enjoy the freedom of my life here. I will take again my wild, dashing rides on my horse Sally to escape the constraints of my life in Alderham, and to put aside all thought of men and marriage!

16th June 1806

Oh! How soon I have changed my mind! How wrong I was when I wrote the last entry, because today is a day I shall remember forever! A day when childhood friendship blossomed into adult love!

Because it was today that I fell in love with George. George is the Duke's son. In two weeks time he will be twenty-four years old. He is a man but the nine years between us makes me still a child to him. But I shall do everything that I can to show him that he is mistaken, and that I am a child no longer. I have seen him only occasionally during the last seven years because when George was just seventeen he joined the King's Hussars as an Officer of the Brigade of Light Horse in the English army. He is now promoted Captain, and he has been given extended leave to recover from a severe wound in his leg. For years he has often been in serious danger fighting the forces of Napoleon of France. England has been at war with Napoleon for years and years; it all started even before I was born.

George, who was named after good old King George III, has been my friend since I was a small child. It was here, whilst I staying with my grandparents, that I first started my childhood friendship with George. He was then a mischievous boy of twelve, and I was a baby of not yet four. The day I first came across him he jumped out at me to scare me when I was sitting in the reeds on the far side of the lake, trying to catch tadpoles in my net. That is the far side of the lake from the grand house, but only a little walk through the woods from the cottage for me!

At first all George wanted to do was to frighten me, or show me how clever he was at riding or climbing trees; but soon he started to take an interest in me, and he would show me things *like how to catch a frog, or how to make a dam in the little stream that fed the pond. I had a little puppy, called Rex, who lived at my grandparent's home, and George showed me how to teach Rex to fetch sticks and to sit and beg. He never took me to play in 'the big house', as he called it, so I hardly ever saw or talked to his parents, the Duke and Duchess. During those happy summer months of my childhood I looked upon George as a big brother, so much nicer and more fun than my own brothers. And until he left for the Army, my memories are of, many, many days of sunshine every summer, playing together in the parkland and meadows of his father's estate. I wonder why it is that I never remember the rain?*

The relationship between his family and mine has always remained amicable, but we are not at all intimate. Although no one encouraged our childhood friendship, no one had forbidden it either. George's father, the Duke, and my father are still friends, but there has always been an element of master and servant in their friendship.

So when George and I met yesterday in the parkland, while he was out riding a splendid thoroughbred stallion, at first for me, it was the recognition of our childhood friendship. But then I looked again at him and saw him as a man, and my heart started beating fast! He looked so handsome. He is tall, slim and upright, with the bluest eyes I have seen. He was wearing his officer's uniform covered with so much gold braiding all across his chest that it almost obscured the front of his bright red jacket, and from the way he controlled his horse, even with a wounded leg, I could also see that he has developed into a superb horseman. He pulled up his horse in front of me.

"Hello. Who is this?" He inquired. "Are you not my little Maria? Do you still stay with your grandparents in the little cottage over there?

"Yes," I said. "Every year I come to spend the summers with them. And I am not so little either, I am fifteen now!"

"Are you indeed?" he said, laughing. His handsome eyes were sparkling, and his smile made my heart leap! "And do you still ride that piebald pony of yours?"

"No, he is much too small for me now," I replied. I started to

tremble, and my nervousness made me talk in a flurry. I wanted to show him that I was much too grown up to still be riding a pony. "Last year, for my birthday, my grandfather bought me a lovely grey mare. I have called her Sally, and she is stabled at the cottage. I have still kept my pony, Jupiter, do you remember Jupiter? He keeps Sally company when I am not here to ride her. Sally is a sweet and gentle horse, but she likes to run too, and I come here to ride her as often as I can. I use the side saddle only occasionally, I much prefer to sit astride my horse, and I love it when we canter over the meadows to the wood on the hilltop."

"Good for you," said George, giving me a real quizzical look. "You look like a very capable young lady, but you must have kept your hoydenish ways to ride using a man's saddle! Perhaps we will meet again when we are both out on our horses." He gave me what I thought was a real flirtatious smile, and, with a wave of his gloved hand and a flick of his whip, he rode off.

My heart was racing as I walked slowly back to my grandparent's cottage, and I am sure that I was blushing like a little girl. But I will be out on Sally tomorrow, and I will make sure that we meet again. Then I will show him how well I ride! And I will show him that I am grown up too!

So here am I, a pretty girl looking for adventure and fun like the old days, and there is George, a dashing Captain of the Hussars. I will be so happy when he, at last, sees me as a child no longer, but an attractive young woman. Is this what it feels like to be in love?

28th June 1806

It is George's 24th birthday today, and it has happened at last!... We have kissed...

At first the attraction was all mine, he was still seeing me as just a little girl. But during the last three weeks I have been making sure that I just 'happen' to be out riding exactly where he would be taking his morning rides. And today, at last, he leaned over from his horse, pulled me as close as he could, and whispered in my ear. "You have grown to be a beauty. I love your shining red hair and your bright green eyes." And then he kissed me! I was not sure, at first, how to return his kiss, but George was very gentle with me and it only took a moment or two for me to respond to him. It was my first kiss and it was not only was it wonderful, it made me feel that I want so much more!

I hope that he remembers this birthday gift forever!

10th July 1806

We have been meeting almost every day since his birthday, and he kisses me all the time. I love him, and although he has not said anything to me, I'm sure that he loves me too. Mostly we gallop up to the woodland at the top of the hill together, then we dismount. He helps me down from Sally and holds me close to kiss me. My insides melt at his touch and we kiss, and kiss and kiss. George. George. How I love to say his name! I love him, but I do not dare to tell him!

14th July 1806

I have allowed, no, encouraged, George, to make love to me! For weeks now we have been kissing and holding each other close whenever we meet.

And now we are in love! It is summertime, and the meadows are flowering in colours of the rainbow. Today we dismounted our horses and George tethered them to a gate post. Together we walked hand in hand through the near waist high grasses and flowers. He stopped to pull me to his chest and we kissed. Then, I don't know just how it happened, but we just sank down amongst the flowers, and he taught me how a man and a woman make love.

After the initial fear, discomfort and, I must admit, a not inconsiderable amount of pain...it was wonderful...Apart from his poor injured leg, his body is so beautiful, so manly. And his thing!...When he pushed it into me it made me feel as though I wanted it to go on forever...

At first, after the world stopped spinning, I was powerfully aware of the smell of crushed flowers and grass. Then I opened my eyes. It was not a dream, George was still there, nuzzling at my neck.

"Little Maria. My lovely Maria" he whispered in my ear. "Are you all right? That was the first time for you, wasn't it?"

I could not speak, I was trembling so, but I was so happy. I just smiled and nodded my head.

Again he whispered. "You are so beautiful. You are my special girl now. I could do this again and again with you."

We both know that it is wrong, and that a liaison, let alone a marriage, would not be accepted by anyone. Neither his parents, the Duke and Duchess of .... , nor mine, simple attorney at law, Master Henry Rochester and his wife Mistress Rochester, would approved of what we are doing, so we have agreed to keep it to ourselves.

But even as I write this my insides are still throbbing and I am longing to be with him again tomorrow, to touch him all over, and for him to make love to me again!!

George. George. George. How I love to write his name!

25th August 1806

Life is wonderful! We have been meeting in the flower meadow whenever George is free and unobserved by his parents. And we make love. Most days, when the sun has been shining and we are glowing with warmth, we undress completely. We lie on the blanket that George brings with him, and he and I make love with our whole bodies. I tremble with pleasure and anticipation when he kisses me on my breasts and all over my stomach. Then he touches me in my private place making me cry out for fulfilment, and I almost feint with pleasure when it happens. I do not like it so much when he wants me to hold his 'thing'!!!

When the weather is not so good, or George needs to be elsewhere, we just loosen our clothing and make love as best we can. Not so nice!

I must make sure that this diary is kept hidden. It would be disaster if anyone, especially my mother, were to find it and read it!!!

1st October 1806

The summertime is over. George's leg is now healed and he has gone back to rejoin his Regiment, and I must go back to my family in Alderham.

I am so unhappy. George seemed almost glad to be going away again. He says that I must not write to him because his Regiment will be on the move, probably going to the Continent quite soon, and letters may not reach him. Even if I do write and my letters reach him he will not be able to reply because there would be questions from my family if I were to receive a letter from him!

The last time we made love was already four days ago, and my body is aching for his. Afterwards he took me in his arms and kissed me gently. "You know that I have to go back to my Regiment," he said. "I do not know when we will be able to meet again, but I want you to believe that I will miss you too."

"Do you love me? I found the courage to whisper as we were dressing.

"You know full well that I do," he replied. And then he mounted his horse and was gone.

21st March 1807

I am sixteen today, and at last I am really grown up. But I am not excited. I spend most of my days longing for George's return to his family. I have heard nothing from him since the day he left seven months ago.

Since then life for me has returned to normal. Only nothing is normal for me now. Family life in Alderham goes on in the same usual way. Last week Father said that I looked unhappy and asked me if anything was the matter, but he knows nothing of my love for George, and I dare not tell even him my secret.

12th May 1807

At last! News of George. Father has heard from the Duke that George has been overseas fighting the French, but that he will be back sometime in early June to visit his family. They hope that he will be able to stay until his 25th birthday on the 28th.

I must get Father to let me go to stay with my grandparents earlier than usual for my summer stay with them. I must be there when George comes home. I will tell Father that Sally needs proper attention from me, and not just the occasional visit. I cannot wait until I see George again. Will he still love me? Will he still want to go riding with me again? Will we make love again in the meadow?

1st July 1807

I have been waiting here at my grandparents for nearly a month now, and a month has never been so long! But George is back at last! And he still loves me!

He came back last week to celebrate another birthday. I can hardly believe that it has been a whole year since we first kissed and made love.

We went 'riding' again yesterday. He told me that I look beautiful and exciting and that he wants to make love to me day, after day, after day!!

My grandmother now knows that I am meeting George. She has not told anyone else, but she has warned me to be careful. I do already know how ladies have babies, and my grandmother told me what to do to avoid that happening.

8th July 1807

The weather is hot and the meadow is in full bloom again, and I feel wonderful! I love him. I LOVE HIM. And he says that HE LOVES ME!!

21st August 1807

It has been raining for almost two weeks now. We have met for brief kisses under the trees, and in one of the follies in the parkland, but we have not been able to use our favourite place in the meadow.

23rd August 1807

George has gone again. He says that he had to go back to his Regiment sooner than expected, and he left yesterday. It will be months until I see him again. How can I wait so long? Again he said that he cannot write, not even send letters to me at my grandparents home. I cannot bear it.

1st January 1810

I have heard nothing from George for over two years now. I think that he has forgotten all about me.

21st March 1810

My 19th birthday, and still no news from George. I still love him, and I want to be with him, and only him. My parents are beginning to find it strange that I make no progress with any of the young men that are introduced to me. I was right, after all, about James Rawson. He is a Doctor now, and is a junior partner to old Dr. Catchpole, or own family doctor. My mother invites James to tea on Sundays with boring regularity. Cannot she see that I am not interested in him?

My father, too, has joined the conspiracy against me and regularly brings his partner, Jeremiah Langton, home after work. James is at least a young man. His complexion has improved, but he still stutters whenever he tries to speak to me. But Jeremiah Langton is quite old. He must be at least thirty-five! I cannot wait until I escape to my grandparent's home again.

18th June 1810

I have been here since the end of May, and daily I have prayed for George's return, and now he is back! But only for ten days, as his Regiment is on manoeuvres again.

The War with France continues relentlessly and every report I heard in the last few months of the few triumphs of the English Army glorifies our soldiers, but very little is said about all the young men who have been killed. Every morning I have woken up

...th the fear that George has become one of them. Napoleon is getting stronger and stronger. Everyone is afraid that he intends, once again, to try to invade England, so the Navy and all the Army Regiments must be at attention at all times.

But for now at least George is safe! Will he come to see me? Does he even want to see me again? Is he too much of a soldier to care about anything more that his career?

I hope to see him again tomorrow when I go out riding in our usual place. Please, George, please, PLEASE BE THERE.

It is getting more difficult for us to meet now. His mother, the Duchess Henriette, has become aware that George and I are sometime lovers and she disapproves. I am no longer allowed anywhere near the big house and its immediate gardens, although she has not forbidden me to come to the ducal estate to visit my grandparents.

As George is the Duke's only surviving son and heir, his parents are continually promoting 'suitable' females, usually heiresses, to him. So far George has rejected them all. Earlier this year, at Eastertide, the Duke invited his friend's daughter, the Lady L......... to stay with them. She is an old maid of thirty-eight! Poor George, he is still a very handsome young man of twenty-nine! How could he possibly want a woman so much older than he is? I do not even think that she would be able to give the Duke and Duchess the grandchild that they long for! I am praying that nothing comes of the 'Lady's' visit!

The last time that I saw George he said that he loved me. I wonder if that is still true. I suspect that I am not the only woman in his life. I was still a child when I started to write this diary. Now, as a woman, I read it back and I see that it is full of my childish longing for George. But, no matter that I am a woman, I still feel exactly the same. The same longing! The same excitement when he comes home! The same joy in his body, and fulfilment when we make love! And the same dread when he goes away that he will either cease to love me, or that he will give in to his parents and choose a 'suitable' wife! I dare not even think of the possibility that he will be dreadfully injured or even killed in this terrible war.

28th June 1810

Wonderful! Wonderful! Oh my darling George. He does love me, and only me he says!!!

We have managed to snatch several stolen moments together, and yesterday we spent the whole of the afternoon in our favourite meadow. Of course we made love again, and it is still wonderful. I love him so, and I hope that one day when he is able to make his own choice of wife, he will choose me. He says that it is only me who he wants.

But although it is his birthday today I must say goodbye to him yet once more. I do not know when he will be returning again. Even if he returns at Christmas, I doubt that I will be able to see him. And if we could meet it would not be possible for us to have a secret rendezvous in the cold barren meadow, or even in the folly!

There is to be a great ball to be held in his honour at Christmastide. Of course, I shall not be invited.

4th September 1810

I cannot believe it! Whatever shall I do? I have been sick for six mornings in a row and I believe that I am with child. Whether he likes it or no, I must write to George. What will he do? Will he come to me? Will he defy his parents and marry me?

5th September 1810

I have written to George thus;

My dearest George
I know that it has long been your wish that I should not write to you, or indeed, communicate with you in any way, but this is an emergency.

I am in great trouble. I am sure that I am with child.
I know that after these three years had passed and I never quickened, in spite of all the wonderful occasions when we have made love together, I thought, indeed we both thought, that I must be barren, which in our situation, was good fortune.

But I am fertile after all. I am with child, and I am afraid.

I do not know what to do. I have not yet told my family, but my situation will become evident to everyone soon.

Please help me. Surely now must be the moment to face your family, and declare your love for me. You have so often told me that you love me. That at least is true, is it not? I have long wished that you were in a situation where you might choose your own wife, and not have to accept that a wife should be chosen for you by your parents (particularly your mother!) Could you not do so now?

Your father may think that I am unsuitable to become his daughter-in-law, but he does not dislike me. He may be disappointed in you, but he would never disown you or disinherit you. And I sure that the disapproval of your mother would lessen when she has a grandchild in her arms!

If I am carrying a boy child, he could, in time, become the Duke of... .....

I am being fanciful now, but I am so afraid. Please write, or better still, get leave to come home so we can talk about this together.

Your loving Maria

I have sent the letter by stage coach today, and I must be patient as it will take at least ten days for my letter to reach George at the barracks at Hounslow in Middlesex, and for his reply, if he does reply, to reach me. Perhaps he will come directly. Please God, let him come!

20th September 1810

No reply. No reply. No reply. Whatever shall I do?

10th October 1810

Nothing. If he has received my letter, then he does not care for me. All his avowing that he loves me is lies. He must have received the letter or surely it would have been returned.

1st November 1810

I do not know what to do. Shall I tell my father? I am sure that he will not be angry, but he will have tell my mother, and I do fear her scorn and rage. I am getting fat too, and I have loosened all my skirts and dresses.

Fat and ugly. No wonder no one wants me.

12th November 1810

I have had to tell my father. He found me being sick in the frost covered vegetable patch in the garden. He looked at me directly and asked, "my dearest daughter, is it possible that you are with child?"

I ran to his arms, crying."Oh, Father," I cried. "I am so sorry to let you down. I am carrying George's child. I've written to him, but there has been no reply. What am I to do? Please do not tell mother."

"Are you absolutely sure, my darling?" he asked gently, rocking me in his arms.

"I am sure," I replied. "I have even felt strange movements, like having a butterfly flutter within me. It must be the child who is growing. Whatever am I to do?"

"I am sorry my darling, but we cannot keep this from your mother," said my father. "Let us both go in together and we will all talk about what is to be done."

The conversations were not good. My mother called me a slut. My brothers called me a whore! They are all ashamed of me, and no one, not even my father, thinks that George will marry me.

"I will go and talk to the Duke," said my father. "I do not think that it will do much good. But he will have to know about it, and I am sure that, at least, the Duke will be kind."

18th November 1810

Still no word from George!
Father has spoken to the Duke and Duchess. They are not at all pleased as there are already arrangements in hand for George to become engaged with an 'acceptable' person at

Christmastide. This 'situation' as they call it might well upset these arrangements. Good!

It has been agreed that I shall remove myself from our home in Alderham to live with my grandparents. Not to be nearer to George, who, I've been told is away on campaign, but to hide my shame and to be away from view of the good and respectable people of Alderham, and thus shame my mother and brothers to the general public! At least the latest military campaign has forced the cancellation of the Christmas Ball in honour of George, at the big house.

Christmas 1810

Still no word from George. But father tells me that his Regiment of Light Horse is fighting against the French out in Spain. God keep him safe and bring him home to me soon.

My grandmother and grandfather are being very good to me. They have not scolded me at all, and say that I and the child, who I think must be born in the spring, can live with them as long as we may wish. How I love them, and wish that my own mother was more comforting and forgiving. She came to see me here yesterday, and in spite of my grandparents begging her to be kind to me, she was as harsh as ever, still calling me a slut, and saying that I am unwelcome, and unwanted at home. My brothers refuse to see or speak to me at all.

10th February 1811

At last. A message for me. Delivered by a servant from the big house. It was from the Duke.

He says; 'We hope that you are keeping healthy, and have no other problems. If you have any need for medical assistance, you may get word to the major domo here, who will see to your needs.

The Lieutenant Colonel is safe and well and will be returning from the Peninsular within the next few weeks.'

Lieutenant Colonel! George has been promoted again! He has surely been bold and brave in this most recent action against

Napoleon's soldiers. Thank God! Thank God he is safe! Does this note mean that the Duke and Duchess are relenting? Please, please, please let them accept me. Perhaps they are waiting to see whether the child will be a boy or a girl.

March 1st 1811

Still no word from George. I feel that his child will be born in the next few days. Will it be before his father comes home?

March 22nd 1811

My baby was born during an unexpected snow storm, in the early hours of March 11th.

Fortunately my delivery was reasonably straight forward, I am told! To me it was extremely painful and exhausting. The midwife from Alderham was unable to travel because of the snow, but my wonderful Grandmother acted as my midwife, and my daughter was delivered safe, healthy at half past three in the morning, shouting for her father! (As was I!)

I have received just a short acknowledgement from the Duke. They are pleased with the safe delivery of the child, (not 'our grandchild', I note) and they hope that we are both doing well. They are probably pleased and relieved that the child is a girl, and not a boy with a possible claim on the title and property! Still I want nothing from them.

The snow has all but melted away now, and my father and mother have been to see me. Father was soft and loving as usual, and said that my daughter looks just as I did as a baby. My mother was her usual self, but I do detect a little softening in her attitude towards me. She did pick up the child and cooed at her for a moment or two!

I have decided to call her Elizabeth after my Grandmother.

May 11th 1811

Elizabeth is two months old today. Already I see a lot of George in her, especially in the shape of her head. She is a healthy and happy child, she gurgles all day long, and she is beginning to sleep longer at night time. I am so proud of her, and I love her deeply already. I have not been allowed to take her to visit her or her grandparents, the Duke and Duchess, but my father is to do so this afternoon. That will be interesting!

My mother has warmed slightly, and if Elizabeth is well received by the Duke, I think that she will finally accept what has happened.

May 12th 1811

Elizabeth is acknowledged by the Duke and Duchess, but will not be accepted into their family. My father reported that they appeared to be much taken by their granddaughter, but they were reluctant to make a great display of welcome. They told father that George and his Regiment were Reviewed two days ago by the new Prince Regent, on Wimbledon Common in London. He will be back for his birthday in June, after a second Review, which takes place on 17th June, at Hounslow Heath, where the Regiment has its barracks.

To my great joy the Duke told father that he will not prevent George from visiting his daughter, however he will stop any attempt that he might make to offer marriage to me. The Duke and the Duchess will accept me as his mistress, but they will continue to promote suitable women of independent wealth and title.

But he will, after all, be twenty-nine years old on the 28th of June, and I hope that he is by now man enough to stand up for his own desires.

I went yesterday to St. Augustine's, the parish church close by the main entrance of the Duke's estate. I usually attend there on Sundays when I am living with my grandparents, and yesterday as I sat amongst the grand tombs and effigies of George's ancestors and the simple ones of his little brothers, I prayed that George will come home soon and agree to marry me. I know that it would be against his father's wishes, but I have a strong and healthy daughter, and there should be no reason why we cannot produce a healthy son!

Seeing the little tombs of his dead brothers made me realise *just how important a grandson and future heir is to the Duke. George is his third son. I read the dates on the tombs; Henry his first child, died aged only two, some years before George was born, and Robert died at the age of five, when George was just six months old. These little tombs of his brothers saddened me, and now as a mother, myself, at last I feel a connection to and sorrow for Duchess Henriette.*

June 21st 1811

George has been to visit me and his daughter at long last! He said that it was the War prevented him from replying to my letter or getting any message through to me. How do I feel about his visit? It has been nearly a year since I saw him last. I am still very aware of his attraction to me and mine to him. I do love him, but I feel that he does not return my love as deeply as he did before. He was very taken with his daughter and held her for some time.

My grandparents gave us some privacy and we made love in a bed for the very first time! It was wonderful for me, but I felt that George became anxious to leave us quite soon afterwards. And he left with no word of commitment, marriage or even love. But he did say that he would return soon.

June 28th 1811

George has been back and we made love again in my bed. Still wonderful. Afterwards he sat with me and Elizabeth, and he talked to me properly for the first time since Elizabeth was born.

He looked very serious, and I was frightened at what I surmised he was about to say.

"My dear Maria," he said, "first of all I want to tell you that I am very happy to have Baby Elizabeth as my child. I will acknowledge her as my own, but I now agree with my father that ours would be an unsuitable marriage."

I started to cry, and he put his arms about me, and he also had tears in his own eyes. "My darling," he continued. "I still love you, and I want to continue to be your lover, and a father to Elizabeth. I am very happy that you will continue to live here with your grandparents, where I can visit you and the baby whenever I am at home."

"That is not fair on me." I cried. "You want me as a mistress, and you will also want to marry someone else. Someone more suitable' than me! How can you say that you love me?"

"I do love you, but you know now that is impossible for us to be married. My father just will not accept it. I cannot help being the only living son of a Duke, and I have to fulfil my father's expectation for me."

He then told me that he will be resigning his commission in his Regiment by Christmas, so that he can start to take over the management of his father's estate (and his inheritance), now that his father is aging. My father told me three weeks ago that the Duke has a serious problem with his breathing, and he thinks that he will not live to be an old man.

So it appears that I just as George will be returning home for good, when I could see him almost daily, I must accept the position as his mistress and not his wife. I think that deep down I had realised this when I had no word from him directly for all those months from the time I wrote to him and he knew of my desperation. If he had really loved me, even if he felt that he could not marry me, he would surely have sent word.

12th November 1811

Baby Elizabeth was Christened on Sunday. At eight months old she continues to grow well and is in excellent health. She is also very bright and inquisitive, and she always laughs and reaches out to take hold of anything that is dangled in front of her. I am very pleased that she sleeps through the night. She is now sitting up, and she has two tiny front teeth which show delightfully when she smiles – which she does all the time. A smile so very much like her father's. She looked very, very pretty in the white silk Christening gown, which is embroidered all over with tiny white flowers. That Christening gown was a surprise gift to her by her grandmother the Duchess Henriette.

It was a very cold morning, and we were all wrapped up

warmly against a biting wind. The Christening took place after the morning service, in St. Augustine's. Elizabeth's Christening gown was all but covered in a beautiful white wool shawl that my grandmother had knitted, and George, taking his part reluctantly, fumbled and nearly dropped her in the font as he was trying to loosen her clothes. The Duke and Duchess took no direct part in the ceremony, but they remained in their family pew to observe the proceedings. My father and mother and my grandparents were there, but my two brothers are still too proud to acknowledge that their sister has a child born out of wedlock.

After the baptism my father and the Duke stood together outside the church, and seemed to have a comfortable and pleasant conversation.

I do believe the Duke and Duchess are warming towards me. Duchess Henriette even smiled in my direction once or twice. However it would appear that as the Duke and Duchess are beginning to melt, so George is beginning to freeze on me.

He still visits us quite regularly, when he is at home, to see Elizabeth, he says, I think that it is mainly to make love to me, but there is very little mention of him loving me. Indeed I have heard from my father that George has taken up with the set around the Prince Regent, and he has been seen in gaming houses and ....

~~~

Miriam stopped reading as her two step-brothers, Leon and Daniel, burst into the parlour seeking breakfast. In the light shed from the oil lamp on the windowsill, they immediately spotted Miriam sitting snugly in the window seat. She jumped up and quickly attempted to hide the book from their prying eyes.

"What's the little goyim girl up to?" asked Leon.

"I think that she is up to no good," replied his brother.

Whereupon they encircled her and Daniel snatched at the small book. The fragile bindings gave away, and Daniel tore away part of the diary from her hands.

Holding tightly on the last few pages that were left, Miriam called out to Daniel "Give that back to me; it's mine."

"We're just looking at your ragged book. Aren't we?" said Daniel, looking at his brother. Leon tried to snatch it from his brother, and in doing so, the rest of the bindings gave way and the fragile diary became individual pieces of paper, which flew about the room.

"Don't, don't, don't," called Miriam. "You are wicked beasts. You spoil everything." She ran about the room trying to retrieve the loose pages, but the boys were quicker.

They gathered them up in handfuls and then Leon said, "Let's stoke up the fire!" He put several pages on the glowing embers, and in a flash they caught fire and were burned up, the brightness lighting up the room.

Miriam screamed this time. "Don't! Oh! Please don't burn my book." She was able to rescue a few more loose pages, and held them close to her body together with the part of the diary that she had been able to hold on to. But it was no good, both the boys danced around her, tormenting and tantalising her by holding so many of the pages just out of her reach, and then screwing up page after page and tossing them on the rekindled fire.

"Whatever is going on?" called a deep voice from the doorway. All three children looked around to see Miriam's father standing in the doorway, in his nightclothes.

Miriam ran to him crying, "Oh father! Those horrid boys have burned my book." The horrid boys in question quickly shuffled out of the room and disappeared.

"Don't you cry my pretty little daughter," said Abraham, giving Miriam a hug. "I will buy you another one."

"You cannot," sobbed Miriam. "It is not a printed book. It is a handwritten diary, and it was left for me by my mother. I think that it was written by her great grandmother."

At the very mention of the words 'my mother' Abraham stopped listening to his daughter, and became very angry. With unexpected forced he pushed Miriam away from him, and she stumbled backwards.

"Your mother is a strumpet, I told you never to mention her to me again. She is no longer your mother."

Miriam sat in a heap on the floor and her face reddened. Her father said no more, and after giving his daughter another angry look, he returned to his bedroom.

Miriam was still crying as she picked up the last un-burnt page. Fortunately the letter that had fallen out of the diary had remained undiscovered by her step-brothers, so she took it and all the pages that had survived their sabotage to her bedroom where she sat down on the bed. She looked at the papers in her lap, and she saw that the few pages that she had saved were the final part of the diary. The beginning that she had read, and the middle part that she had not read, was now lost forever. She was too upset to read any more that morning so she tucked what remained of Maria's diary, and the letter, into the back of her Atlas, which had been the last present her mother had given her before she had left home.

Miriam looked at the inscription on the first page. It read;

'Happy 9th Birthday, my sweet Miriam.
I hope that one day you will be able to spread your wings and fly away to discover the world.
But before then perhaps you could pretend to disappear down a rabbit hole like Alice.
When you are old enough I recommend that you take down Alice in Wonderland from the top shelf in the nursery.
Your loving Mother, Jessica Rosen. 1st September 1894

It had been some time since Miriam had last read her mother's message in her Atlas book, and she puzzled over it. Alice in Wonderland was a book that Miriam thought she outgrown a long time ago. Her tears dried as curiosity got hold of her again. The nursery was now the twins' bedroom, and all her old books from the nursery were stacked at the bottom of the wardrobe in her bedroom. She went to it and rummaged for a while, then she discovered Alice and pulled it out. Why had her mother mentioned this book? What had she meant by 'being old enough' when it was a book they had read together when she was eight?

It was a thick book full of delightful drawings, and some coloured ones in the middle. Miriam turned at once to her favourite centre pages, but they were no longer there. The coloured plates had been removed and in their place, so that it was hidden and disguised within the book, was a letter addressed to Miriam!

What? She said to herself, was this strange day about to become ever more strange? 'Curiouser and curiouser'. She looked around, almost expecting to see the White Rabbit. Perhaps she was in her own rabbit hole! Opening the envelope Miriam felt as if she had indeed stepped into Wonderland.

The letter was also dated 1st September 1887

My dearest Miriam, my own baby girl
It breaks my heart to write this letter. Even though you are so very young I must try and get you understand the reasons why I have left you. It is not you who I am leaving, it is your father. I cannot any longer bear to live with him, and I can stay here no longer. It would be my dearest wish to take you with me, but I know that your father would not allow it. He would never allow any of his 'possessions' to be taken from him. And that is just what I am to him. His possession, not his wife!

I have at last found love and an escape to freedom, and I have to take the chance that one day you and I will be re-united.

You were too young for me to explain much about the relationship I have with your father, but I will try now and hope that you will find this letter when you are old enough to understand.

I am the only child of your father's business partner, Michael Jacobs, and my mother, your grandmother Rosemary, died when I was only eight years old. My mother had not been a Jewess, which, in the eyes of Jewish tradition, meant that I (and you) are not a Jewess either. Our family, although nominally Jewish, followed very few of the Jewish laws apart from not eating pork, and celebrating the main Jewish festivals of Passover, the Jewish New Year, and Yom Kippur, the Day of Atonement. These were the only times that I was taken to the local synagogue.

All that I had to remind myself of my mother, was her old oak Chest, which had once belonged to her grandmother and great grandmother, neither of whom I had ever known. Inside the Chest I found a pretty silver brooch and a silver hat pin in the candle drawer that had been fitted at the top on the left hand side, just below the lid. In the body of the Chest I found some old books, two delicate oil paintings of vases of flowers, several sets of bed linen, and an old fashioned dress (perhaps belonging to my grandmother?). Inside the pocket I found a diary, which I believe was my great-grandmother's. I know that her name was Maria.

During the next few years as I was growing up, gradually most of these things had been used up, lost or given away, except for the old dress and the diary which remained in the Chest, and the two paintings which I hung on my bedroom wall. The Chest itself I hardly used at all.

My father never remarried, and for the following eight years he tried to fill the gap in my life by showering me with gifts and beautiful clothes. But he was a busy man and I grew friendless and lonely. I was just sixteen when your father, who is almost twenty years my senior, first started to pay me special attention. I had known him since I was a little girl, and since my mother's death I had often spent time with him and my father in the Rosenberg where they sold valuable antiques as well as paintings. Sometimes I helped them with their displays, but more often I had to sit quietly by myself reading a book.

Just a week after my seventeenth birthday, and with my father's full approval, your father started to court me seriously. I was lonely for attention and I quickly imagined myself in love. Without my mother to advise me, I agreed to marry your father within a few months. I thought that being a married woman would give me freedom and a chance to out into society and make friends. My father had not warned me, and I myself did not realised, that your father is a very private man who rarely invited company into his home or went out to seek the company of others. I very soon discovered that he was also an Orthodox Jew who took his religion very seriously. Both your father and mine thought that the marriage had been an ideal way of strengthening their partnership, and keeping the business 'in the family', while not really thinking that little Jessica would one day grow up and perhaps want to choose a life of her own.

You were born on 13th September 1878, just a year after our marriage. Your father was disappointed that you were not the son and heir that he wanted. But how I loved you, my special baby! But after only a few months your father brought in a nanny who took over all the care of your daily needs, and I was allowed very little time to have you to myself. My vision of going out into society to mix with other married ladies of my social standing was crushed by your father almost as soon as I had been married, and now I felt enclosed and suffocated, just another of your father's possessions to be dressed like a doll and sit around looking pretty. Every inch the mistress of the home and wife of a rich and important man. I was not allowed to soil my hands with anything like baby care or cooking.

From the time that you were born I went to the Gallery only occasionally to help with exhibitions and displays, and during the following nine years I lived with the burden of strict Jewish law and rituals imposed upon me by a husband, who was continually disappointed with me for not producing a son. He also controlled most of my everyday movements, and made all my decisions for me, making me long for freedom.

Twice a year at the Rosenberg Gallery, they would hold a reception to promote a new exhibition, and it was at the Autumn Showing that I first met a violinist called Alfred Manson. He was the leader of a string quartet, which was entertaining the invited guests. I had been so happy at the prospect of meeting new people and having a little pleasure for the evening. I dressed in my favourite dress of maroon silk made with a tight corseted top and a full skirt without a bustle, which showed off perfectly the fine lines of my slim body. I also wore my mother's sparkling ruby pendant, given to me by my father on my wedding day, and it accentuated my bosom which was daringly displayed in the low cut dress. I knew that your father disapproved of my attire, but it was the fashion, and most of the invited ladies would be wearing similar dresses.

My happy mood made my vivacious, and I attracted Alfred Mansor's attention as soon as he saw me. Although I did not realise my feelings immediately, I too was similarly attracted to Alfred Manson. He was a good looking young man, only a few years older than me, and he had long, wavy, light brown hair which matched his hazel eyes. And such a happy personality! This time I really fell in love! It had happened almost in an instant while I and Mr. Manson were talking together during a break in the music. As well as being attracted to him, I quickly recognised in Mr. Manson characteristics which were quite the opposite to those of your father, who is so earnest and hard to please. Mr. Manson said such funny things, and I found myself laughing out loud, something that I had not done for many months.

From the other side of the Gallery your father recognised my laughter, and he was immediately displeased. He excused himself politely from his guests and crossed the room. "Jessica, my dear," he said with a smile that I recognised. A smile which betrayed underlying disapproval. "You must not let this gentleman monopolise your time. Our guests are waiting for you to entertain them."

"Yes, indeed, Abraham," I replied, "but first I would like you to meet Mr. Manson, he is the first violinist with the City Orchestra."

"Mr. Rosen," Alfred said, giving your father a deep bow. "I am so pleased to meet you, and I am also honoured that you have asked my quartet to play at your reception."

Before your father had a chance to reply he continued. "I would be honoured and delighted if you and your charming wife would attend, as my guests, the concert to be held next week in the City Hall. The world famous pianist Oliver Bruer is to play Beethoven's Emperor Concerto."

"Yes, yes, Mr. Manson. Delighted. Delighted," your father replied as he hurriedly ushered me away. He hissed quietly into my ear. "Now go and make apologies for your lack of courtesy and attention to the wives of my guests."

There was an icy silence between us in the carriage as we were driven home after the reception. This continued after we reached home, and the manservant had taken our outer clothing, but as soon as the parlour door had closed behind us your father lost his temper completely.

"You are an absolute disgrace," he shouted at me. "How dare you show me up like that in front of all my important business clients. You are dressed like an 'actress', you ignored my guests; and, right in front of them, you were talking and laughing out loud like a common fishwife, and with a mere hireling! Don't you ever, ever, behave like that again, and I absolutely forbid you to have any association with that 'lowborn itinerant'. And Madam, in case there lingers any question in your silly little head, we will certainly not be going to any concert at the City Hall or anywhere else!"

He turned on his heels, opened the door and left the room, slamming the door behind him. Then he hastened to his dressing room, where he bedded himself for the night on the chaise longue he had in there.

I was stunned. I had not even had the chance to respond. Your father has often lost his temper with me, but I had never seen him quite so angry. I thought that I had been nothing more than a charming hostess at the reception, and I knew that his clients and their wives had not been at all offended either in my dress or my cheerful friendliness. Indeed at the end of the soirée my father had congratulated me on the way that I had brightened up the evening and had helped to enhance the profile of the Rosenberg Gallery.

It was at that moment, when the door was slammed into my face, that my defiance was born. Until then I had never even thought of disobeying your father, but his unjust anger and accusations, together with the thoughts of Alfred's smiles and laughter which echoed in my memory, gave me strength of purpose.

The next day I sent a note to Mr. Manson saying that my husband and I greatly regretted that we would not be able to attend his next concert. I also managed to include, in my innocent and informal style of writing, the information that I occasionally took afternoon tea in the Bluebell Tea Rooms in the High Street.

It was hardly discreet, but if I did happen to come across Mr. Manson in my favourite Tea Rooms, would it not be churlish of me to ignore him? And if Abraham were to find out, I would explain that we had met by chance. It was quite remarkable how that 'chance' had happened only three days after my note was received, and how the 'chance' meetings took place again and again! So in spite of me being a respectable wife and mother, for the following six months I enjoyed regular and secret liaisons, *but nothing of an improper nature, with Alfred Manson. We both declared our love for one another, and I knew that if I wanted happiness in my life I would have to simply pack my bags and leave, even though it would break my heart to leave you.*

Please believe that if there is any way possible for me to come back for you, I will.

I leave you, my dearest Miriam, with undying love
Mother

Miriam was stunned to read about her mother's life. "Mother," she whispered. "Mother. I'm still waiting for you. Do you really love him more than you love me? Will you ever come back for me?"

As she read the letter again two fat tears ran in parallel lines down her cheeks and she wondered if her mother was still happy 'discovering her own world'. She missed her sorely. It was fortunate for her that the letter had not been discovered when her nursery had been emptied. She thought that her Atlas was probably the best place to keep it along with the last pages of Maria's diary and the curious letter which she would read later. For now she decided to hide the Atlas and its new contents in her room until she could be sure that she could read them without the boys bursting in on her. She hoped that the day would come soon when she could reclaim her Chest for her own.

Then perhaps she could keep the Atlas, her own secrets and her most precious belongings safe from those horrible boys!

Secrets of the Chest
Part Three

Marie Beauville
1944–2008

November 1993

Marie had lived with her father since her divorce ten years ago. During that time he had been slowly deteriorating with dementia. It was not easy for her at first because of the strained and uneasy relationship that they had had for most of the forty nine years of her life. But for some time now their relationship had become comfortable and warm, even loving. Sadly, in the last few months her father had also developed a throat cancer caused by his long years of chain smoking. Marie had been nursing him as gently as she could and as she looked at the fragile and wasted body of this eighty-seven year old man she remembered, with sadness, the virile and handsome father of her youth.

His adjustable bed, which faced the window, was raised just high enough for him to be able to look out onto the sea. Today the sea was bleak and grey. Even now he still loved to watch the sea in all its moods – from the foaming rage which, at high tide, would half drown anyone who dared to walk on the lower promenade, to the rare occasions when, with clear blue skies, it became a startling azure blue which could rival any Mediterranean sea, reminding him of his youth and adventures with his brother in long forgotten, far away Constantinople.

Whilst he knew that she was Marie, his daughter, more and more often during the last few months, in his confusion he thought that she was his second wife, Marie's mother, Susan. But Susan had died nearly fifty years ago. Marie had tried to make him understand that she was not his wife Susan, but his and Susan's daughter, Marie. But he had been so convinced that, sometimes, it was easier to let him think that she was Susan.

It was on that last morning, when she knew that he was quietly slipping away, that he looked up at her and said, "I keep telling you Suzie, the divorce will come through soon." Then he said no more, but looked up at the seagulls which had started to whirl and screech in front of the bedroom window.

Marie ignored the birds. What divorce? She asked herself. His? Hers? Although she knew that he had been married and divorced before he met her mother, she had never heard him talk about his divorce before. Was there another mystery in his past life that he never talked about?

For years Marie had longed to know about her own past, especially the beginning of her life, but he had never answered any of her questions, and he had never talked to her about her mother and their life together before she was born. Marie had always found it difficult to accept that the first thing she had done in her own life was to cause her mother's death. No wonder that her father had found it so difficult to love her.

This much Marie had been told about her birth; she had been born in Bangor, North Wales just before midnight on 9th September 1944. Her mother, Susan Beauville, who was already the mother of her three little brothers, had been evacuated for safety from the family home in London to Bangor, during the Second World War when the bombing raids on London had resumed in June of that year. Her mother Susan, who was only twenty-seven years old, had died of a childbirth haemorrhage in the early hours of the 10th September 1944, just a few hours after giving birth to Marie.

Marie had often thought how difficult it must have been for her mother to be expecting another child so soon after the boys were born. She must have been terrified at the knowledge of yet another hungry mouth to feed with very little money coming in, and all the additional work a fourth child would involve. Let alone another delivery so far away from home, and without the help and support of her regular doctor and her husband.

Her brother Edwin had been little more than a baby himself, being only seventeen months old at the time, and still in nappies. Marie imagined the work involved with two babies in cloth nappies – no disposables then! No fridges, washing machines, tumble dryers and dish washers in the 1940s for most women to help with their housework, not even running hot water in the tap! What a nightmare managing a family home must have been, especially in wartime when housewives who lived in the big towns and cities already spent hours queuing for what little food they could buy with their measly ration vouchers!

Her half French/half English father, Jean-Pierre Beauville, had stayed in London to earn a living. He had lost his job as a school teacher, teaching French in a private school when, for safety, the school relocated out of London. He still taught in evening classes, did some French/English translations for the Ministry of Information and he did voluntary work as an Air Raid Protection (ARP) ambulance driver. Marie vaguely remembered, years ago, seeing an old photograph of him washing an ARP car.

When the family arrived in Bangor, Marie's two elder brothers – Ray, who was five, and John, who was just two and a half, were billeted out in a foster home. Baby Edwin was put into a nursery. Their mother, Susan, who was very unwell in this her fourth pregnancy in five years, was sent backwards and forwards between a billet and a maternity home, where there were no doctors or senior medical officers in residence. It was there that Marie was born, and where her mother died, all alone with none of her beloved family at her side.

While she was musing about her birth her father spoke again. "You were so young and pretty."

Me? Pretty? Susan? She asked herself. No. It must be Susan he is talking to. He has never told me that I am pretty.

Her father continued to talk to her as if she were Susan. This time she did not correct him. "I have always loved you. Those other women meant nothing to me. I had my needs..." He paused and then he continued. "You know. When you couldn't..." He trailed off.

Other women? She knew that he had been unfaithful to her stepmother, Betty. Was he also unfaithful when he was married to her mother, the love of his life? She could hardly believe her ears. She had learned all about the other women he had had when she was a teenager. She knew, and saw for herself exactly what Mum had had to put up with. Why Mum had tolerated his continual infidelities she never knew.

This time she looked at her father. "What about Mum? Betty?" she asked.

"Betty? Betty?"Was he genuinely puzzled, or was he choosing not to talk about the wife with whom he had lived for nearly forty years?

After a moment he went on again. "You know that it was always you that I loved. You are forever my special darling. But you were not there." He paused again. "Betty? Didn't she stay here to look after the children?"

Marie was quite shocked. Had he forgotten all the years he was married to Mum? Did he only marry her as a stand in for her mother? Had he known Mum before her mother had died? Was he unfaithful to Susan with Mum?

Mum had once told her that she and her father had met when she went to learn French in an evening class, and that she had fallen in love with him. But she had never said that they were lovers before her mother's death.

Marie knew that her father had married her Mum when she was just six months old, only six months after Susan had died, but he had needed to remarry because he was not able to work and look after four young children too. He had solved the immediate problem of looking after a newborn baby by asking his young cousin Francine to take care of baby Marie for a while. Francine, too, had moved to England from Paris. She lived in Harwich, and was married to an English sailor who spent many months each year at sea. She was childless and very lonely when her husband was away, and she had longed for a baby. Francine agreed at once to look after Marie and she travelled to Bangor with her cousin to collect the baby when Marie was just two weeks old. Jean-Pierre had told her that it was to be only a temporary arrangement. He was desperate to get his whole family back together as soon as he could manage it.

Marie remembered nothing about Francine. She did not even know what Francine looked like, but she did know that Francine had loved her desperately and had wanted to adopt her, but her father would not agree to that. And so, to Francine's deep distress, when Marie was fourteen months old her father took her back from his cousin, the only mother that Marie had known, to be brought up with her father, her step-mother Betty, and her three young brothers.

Poor Francine was broken-hearted to give up the baby she had thought of as her own, and she was very angry with her cousin. She and his family never met again and the following year she returned to France. Apart from these bare facts, Marie grew up knowing almost nothing else about her foster mother or her real mother. Susan's and Francine's names were hardly ever mentioned when Marie was a child, and she had never seen a photograph of either of them.

Perhaps this was the moment for her to find out why her father had never talked about Susan, and why he had been so hard on her when she was growing up, but before she could phrase the right question in her mind, he started to talk to her again as if she were Susan. "You were the best mother. How those little boys loved you. You loved us all so much."

At last Marie dared to ask the question she had always wanted to ask. This might be her last chance. She took a deep breath and quietly asked, "And what about Marie?"

There was no response. She thought that, perhaps, he had not heard. She held her breath. Her father turned his head to look out at the sea, and it was quite a while before he spoke again. "Marie? There is something bad about Marie. She's pretty like you, but there is something wrong about her. I don't remember. I don't remember."

Something bad about Marie? Did he really dislike her right from the start? Why had he not left her with Francine to be adopted by her? Marie was shocked. Could it really be true? Knowing that her mother had died on the night that she was born, she had not only felt guilty herself, but she had always felt that her father had blamed her for her mother's death. Her birthdays had never been celebrated as happy occasions, no gifts when she was a little girl. Yes, the family had been very poor then, but still…?

"Did you ever love Marie?" she asked very gently, very quietly.

Now he looked her straight in the eye. "Marie? I lost you because of her. I found it hard to love her at first. Then she grew up to look just like you." He sighed. "But, yes, she is part of you and I do love her. I have always loved her."

Tears were running down Marie's face as she said, "Thank you," and she leant over to kiss him gently on the forehead. She sat beside his bed holding his hand. That hand that used to be so strong and vital, was now just bones covered with blotched, paper thin skin. It was news to her that she looked like her mother as a young woman! She did not have time to wonder about that for more than a moment, because, as Susan, she had to ask her most important question.

"If you loved Marie so much," she held her breath for a moment, and then continued to whisper, "why were you always so hard on her when she was growing up?"

But it was too late. His eyes were closed and he gave no answer. Perhaps he did not hear. Perhaps he could no longer take in the question or make a reply. Marie continued to sit with him quietly, still holding his hand for another half hour.

Then before her father lapsed into his final coma, he roused himself again, and registered that she was Marie, and not Susan. "Marie," he said. "Take that." He pointed to a well sealed envelope which was on his bedside table. "Open it after I have gone," he whispered. "And don't be sad, be happy for me. I am going to be with your mother again." Perhaps there was an echo of his last conversation with her lingering in his mind, because he continued. "Remember that I have always loved you, even though I often found it difficult at times to show it. I have always loved you; and your brothers too. Au revoir, ma chérie. You have been such a good girl to me!"

Through a veil of tears Marie reached for the envelope as she leaned forward to kiss her father for the last time. Finally, he had been a good father, but it was not until he became the grandfather to her children that she had been able to let go of the pain he had caused her during her harsh and troubled teenage years. Taking the envelope with her she went downstairs and telephoned her brother, Ray.

"He's going now," she said. "You'd better come quickly if you want to say goodbye to him. Will you bring John and Edwin too?"

"Is he peaceful now?" asked Ray. "I cannot bear it to see him in so much pain."

"Yes. The diamorphine that Dr. Feeley gave him last night has taken all his pain away. He has been talking to me a little this morning and he is now sleeping. I think that he may not wake up again," she replied. "He gave me an envelope to open after he has gone. It's quite heavy, but I don't think that there is much in it. I think that it probably contains the key to his antique chest."

Marie was talking about the old iron key that, cumbersome as it was, their father had always kept attached by a chain to his belt. No one had ever been allowed to look into his old oak chest. It was where he kept all his private papers, bank statements and personal things.

He had told Marie long ago that the chest had once belonged to her mother, and that it had been handed down through the daughters of her mother's family for generations. A real family heirloom, and the only thing that his children had to remind them that they had once had another mother; and one day it would be hers.

Ray, John and Edwin all lived with their families, within thirty minutes' drive of Eastbourne. Ray the eldest, who was married to Andrea, always knew his position in the family. At fifty-five he was a stout and rather pompous man. His curly dark hair, just like their father's when he was younger, was now very thin on top, giving him a look of Friar Tuck, the legendary monk and friend of Robin Hood. Ray was a well known and respected solicitor whose large legal practice was not only in Eastbourne, but also had branches in Seaford, Lewes and Hastings too. But in spite of his pomposity Ray was a very kind man and he had always remained close to his brothers and sister.

John was fifty-two, and was a school teacher, head of the maths department at the local comprehensive school. His wife Christine was a teacher too and taught art in the same school. John was tall and fair haired, the one who looked most like Marie, and he had her temperament too. He was loving, very impulsive, and for a mathematician – very artistic. He had a shed-cum-studio at the bottom of his garden where he loved to dabble in oils, and his paintings of the Downs and of his wife and family were impressionistic, very colourful, but still very recognisable.

At fifty, Edwin was the youngest of Marie's three brothers. He had had many a girlfriend, but he had always avoided marriage and was still the little boy who had never grown up! By training and education he was an architect, but at heart he was a clown! In looks he was very like his elder brother Ray, but was quite the opposite in his ways. His passion was cars, and in the barn in the courtyard of his house he had a collection of what other people called 'old bangers', but which he insisted he would restore one day. He was never down and unhappy, hardly ever serious, and always saw the lighter side of every situation. But occasionally, in quieter moments, he remained the little boy who, long ago, had lost his Mummy.

The three brothers arrived together within an hour after Marie's 'phone call, and even on this saddest of days Edwin greeted his sister with cheery smile and a warm hug.

As a group they climbed the stairs and gathered mournfully and silently around their father's bedside, and one by one they bent over him to kiss him and say goodbye. He opened his eyes long enough to see them all, smiled and then died just as he had wanted to; at home, with all of his children standing around his bed.

When all that was necessary to be done immediately was completed; Dr. Feeley who came and wrote out the death certificate, and the undertakers who took their father's body to the chapel of rest, the four children sat around the kitchen table drinking tea and talking sadly about their father, and having a few laughs too at old family stories that were retold. It was late in the afternoon when Marie picked up the envelope again.

"Shall I open this now?" she asked her brothers. "Or shall we wait until all the arrangements have been finalised?"

"No. Do it now," they said in unison.

John went on "There may be something important that we need to know about for the funeral arrangements."

Marie opened the envelope. It was indeed the old key, and a single sheet of paper wrapped around it. It was a will, of sorts, and it had been written five years previously. She reached for her glasses and read the letter to her brothers.

My Dear Children,
'I shall be going soon to re-join your blessed mother, Susan. You are all grown up now and no longer need me to guide you on

your paths in life. You have all been good children, and I know that your mother would have been proud of you. I talked of her so little over the years because I was always distressed whenever I thought about her, and of our great loss, and I did not want your step-mother Betty to feel uncomfortable. But I have kept as much as I could of your mother's memories, and they are stored in her chest.

Marie, by right of her mother's inheritance, is to have the chest and those things to do with your mother, but of course, all of you may all read the letters and diaries that you will find there.

I also want Marie to have my violin and the house that has been her home for the last few years, along with all the furnishings (apart from my paintings and antique furniture). She has dutifully looked after me, without complaint, since Betty died.

I shall also be rejoining Betty too, and I think that after all the years that she looked after you, and loved you when you were young, your mother in heaven, will have forgiven her, and have come to love her too.'

Marie broke off, and looked at her brothers with a puzzled frown. "Forgiven Mum? What's that all about?" she asked. Then she remembered the last conversation that she had had with their father, just a few hours ago. For the present she kept her suspicions about Mum to herself. She looked at Ray and said. "You're the oldest Ray, and you just about remember our real mother. Do you know what 'forgiven' means?"

"All I know," said Ray," is that Dad married Mum when you were just a tiny baby, and I don't think any of us ever really thought about the how, when and why? I was only six, and I can't remember much about their relationship. My childhood memories go back to when I was about three, after John was born, and all I remember clearly was having a mother who was sick and expecting a baby most of the time. When Mum came into the family a sort of calm... normality... came into our lives.

Of course you, Marie, did not live with us for another year, so in the early days of their marriage Mum's time wasn't taken up with dealing with a small, crying baby, (and how you did cry!), and we able to settle in as a new family."

Ray paused, thinking of his own childhood, and then he went on.

"Like all of you I just accepted that Mummy Betty, as we called her at first, was there to look after us. I suppose that for her, there must have been the ghost of our mother around for a long while. I remember, quite soon after they were married, going to Wales with Dad to visit our mother's grave. I remember being quite overcome at his passionate crying. He said over and over again how much he loved her, and how she had been the best of mothers. It was strange to go back home to Mummy Betty afterwards."

Ray paused again, and Marie had to dig deep to remember the little secret conversations that had gone on between the four of them when they were little. They had often talked about their 'real mother' and about those journeys to Wales that Ray, and sometimes John, had taken. They had questioned where their 'real mother' had gone and whether Mummy Betty was really their mother now. But within a few years they had stopped talking about Susan, and they had all accepted Mummy Betty, who became just Mum. Edwin did not remember Susan, only his feelings of loss, and Marie had never known her at all.

Ray's voice brought Marie back to the present. "Mum never said anything to me, or to any of you, I suppose, about the circumstances of their marriage. Did she?" he asked. They all shook their heads. "Maybe", he continued, "there are secrets to be revealed in those letters and diaries that Dad was talking about."

"Secrets? How intriguing," said John.

"How exciting," said Edwin, always the impetuous one. "Let's dig 'em out and have a look!" With a dramatic gesture he took hold of the old key, and was about to go to the chest.

"Hang on!" Marie called out, snatching the key back from him. "Let's read the rest of Dad's letter, and make the arrangements for his funeral before we go delving into his past and his secrets." She then took a deep breath and carried on reading aloud.

There is an old atlas and also some historical documents relating to your mother's family that go back to the time that the chest was first made, that you Marie, with your interest in history, may find particularly interesting.

Now my rugs, paintings and antiques. I want you, John, to have the Mark II, and my collection of modern art paintings. Edwin is to have the E-type. I hope that you both will look after the cars well. I know that you, Ray, will already have the latest model of the BMW cars that you so admire, so I hope that you will not feel disregarded, especially as I give you my two 18th century seascape paintings, and the antique walnut desk and matching paper cabinet of mine that I know you long admired.

For the rest, I want you all to have equal shares in the investments, savings and bank accounts. You will find the papers and documents for these also in the chest. They are in good order, and there should remain about £800,000 in all to be shared equally between all four of you.

Please remember that I always did my best to keep us together as a family after your mother died, and that I have always loved you all.

Your loving Dad.

They were all stunned, not just at the thought of the family documents to be discovered, and perhaps their past to be revealed at last, but also at the substantial amount that their father had left.

"Wow!" exclaimed Edwin. "I knew that he had saved some money when he sold the business, even after he bought this house at the posh end of the sea front. But I never guessed that he had put by that much! And his E-type; I shall be the envy of everyone when I drive that!"

"£200,000!" said John, practical as ever. "I will be able to pay off my mortgage."

Ray, the professional lawyer, came to the fore. He always felt that he should be in charge of family decisions, and now he held up his hand to stop the flow of excitement and speculation. "Let's hold on a minute," he said. "First we need to finalise arrangements for Dad's funeral. Then we will need to register his death, sort out his bank accounts and see if that letter is acceptable as a will for probate. And remember that the letter was written five years ago, so the amount of his savings could be considerably altered by now. There could be more than £800,000, or there could be less!"

They all went to the back room where their father kept his office. All the box files containing the old documents relating to their father's business, the European College, and its sale were kept on two large shelves. The chest was in its usual place under the window, its lid covered with piles of books and papers, and his old violin in its battered case. These were quickly removed and put on the desk, and they all knelt down to open up the chest.

Notwithstanding that their father had only passed away a few hours before, they were all excited, and Marie's hand trembled when she fitted in the key and turned the lock. She found it well oiled, and in spite of its age, easy to turn. The lid also lifted without so much as a squeak! They all peered inside. If they expected immediately to see anything that looked as though it was full of age or interest, they were to be disappointed. There was actually not a great deal in the chest. To one side there were four bank folders, containing statements of their father's various accounts and savings, together with a box file, which, when opened, revealed a bundle of share certificates and national savings bonds.

Ray lifted all these out, and said, "Shall I take charge of these and sort them out? We will need to take Dad's death certificate to the bank, and send copies to all these share companies and the National Savings HQ."

"Let's have a look at them first," said John, "and see if the total is anything like the £800,000 that Dad thinks…thought he had."

"Yes, but that might take a while," said Marie. She looked at her oldest brother. "Ray, you're the solicitor. I think that it will be great if you would take on the job of registering Dad's death and sorting out all the finance. Why don't you take the files and papers home and have a quick assessment, and tell us all what's what when you all come back? Is that OK by you two?" she asked, looking at John and Edwin.

"Fine by me, and I'll go with Ray to the Registry Office if you like" said John. Ray nodded in agreement.

"And that's fine by me too," said Edwin. He was more than happy to sit back and let his two brothers sort out all the legalities.

Marie continued. "And there will be probate to sort out. There may well be some death duties to pay too. Would you do it all for us for us please Ray? That really is your speciality." she paused, and then went on, "I suppose that there must also be the deeds of this house in the chest too. Are you all happy with the fact that Dad has left the house to me?"

Her three brothers agreed at once, after all it was their Dad's expressed wish, and they all had houses of their own.

"We already knew that Dad was going to leave this house to you, Marie," said Ray. "It's only fair after all that you have done for him. And I will get the deeds transferred into your name after probate has been granted."

Edwin and Marie pulled out more of the contents of the chest. In the other half there was a metal box containing the house deeds, and underneath it were several large brown envelopes and an old chocolate box.

"Ah ha!" said Edwin dramatically. "Are these envelopes wherein all the family secrets lie?"

"Don't play the fool, Edwin," Marie scolded him, gently. "I think that they might reveal things and histories more important that just 'family secrets'." She turned towards Ray and John. "Would you three please allow me to look through these envelopes and the box quietly on my own after you have gone? I've a strange feeling that what I will find here will change everything for me."

Marie's brothers looked at her, and saw that she was trembling. Edwin put his arms around her and said. "Of course, Sis. We'll push off now, and come back in a couple of days to talk about Dad's funeral, if that's OK by you two. Just give me a ring if you want to talk before then." He looked at Ray and John, who both nodded in agreement. Edwin continued. "I wasn't making fun about family secrets, you know Sis. I'm very interested about our mother, too, and what really happened when we were babies. And I shall look forward to hearing all your news when we see you again."

"I'm sure that there will be so much to tell you all by then," she said. "And please bring Andrea and Christine. Dad loved them too, and they may want to add their ideas about the funeral service."

~~~

The day had turned quite chilly and after Marie's brothers had gone. She turned up the central heating and went into the sitting room where she sat quietly in her favourite armchair. Then she called her little dog, Misha, to come and sit on her lap. She wanted a pause to reflect on her father's death before plunging into the mysteries of the past. Her thoughts lingered on her own past; her babyhood, her childhood, playing with her older brothers, her father's tempers when they were young, and her difficult teenage years.

She thought about the obsession that her father had developed about keeping her away from boys, restricting and restraining her to an extent that she was never allowed to go anywhere unsupervised where there might be other boys; not to simple children's parties, not even junior school swimming lessons because the boys went too. How sad that this destructive obsession had eventually led to her not being allowed to go to university like her brothers, or to develop her longed for ambition to work in art and design.

Marie wondered what was it about her father that had made him the way he was? Was she about to find the answer? Before she opened up any of the envelopes and packages she reviewed some bald facts of her father's life history that she knew of. Things that had happened in his life before she was born:

His name was Jean-Pierre Beauville.

He was brought up French speaking, but he was British.

He was born in London in 1906, to a French mother and an English/French father, and he was taken to France as a baby when his father took over the family business, a large hotel in the centre of Paris.

That hotel was a great success for more than twenty years, and the family became very wealthy. Then the business began to lose customers and started to fail as the Second World War approached.

He had been married to, and divorced from a French woman when he lived in Paris.

In 1936, he left Paris, and because he had kept his British citizenship, he was able to move to London. He had very little money, and no belongings other than what he carried in his suitcase, and his violin. He was a semi-professional violinist.

He met her mother, Susan Harrison, who was a trained concert pianist, at a musical soirée in London, and they fell in love. Her mother was just twenty at the time, and her father was thirty one. They were married and lived in London where all the boys were born, starting with Ray who was born in May 1939, just a few months before the War started.

Her mother gave up her music to become a wife and mother, and her father became a French teacher in a residential private school.

The only thing that her mother brought from her family home was her chest. She did not bring her piano.

During the War her father lost his job when, in order to keep the children safe, the private school moved out of London.

The family became very poor, and had to make do with the earnings her father made from teaching evening classes, and some translations he did for the Ministry of Information.

She was born and Susan died in Bangor, Wales on 9th/10th September 1944.

So here, possibly, was Marie's chance, at last to find out more about her background. And perhaps, she would find the answer as to why her father had hurt and disregarded her so, when she was young. Was it because she looked like her mother? Wasn't that what he had said just before he had died? But her father had loved her mother, so why did looking like her mother make him treat her badly? Were some of these answers about to be revealed?

When she had summoned up the courage to look Marie took a deep breath, gathered the remaining contents of the chest and took them through to the kitchen table, where, having made herself a large mug of hot sweet tea, she sat and readjusted her glasses. She took two sips of the tea and, with shaking hands, she picked up and opened the first large and bulky envelope. This contained an old atlas and several pages of what appeared to be some entries into an old diary, and two letters in old and faded envelopes. The loose pages were very old, yellowing and had brown spots all over. The handwriting was large and bold, very feminine. Attached to the front of these pages was a note, written in blue ink, in a different small and very neat handwriting.

> 'At the very bottom of the chest, I found these few pages of a diary of a woman called Maria Johnston, and a letter from her father. They were folded together and tucked into the back of an old atlas book which belonged to a Miriam Rosen at the end of the last century. There was also a letter from Miriam's mother Jessica tucked inside the atlas. When I was a girl I used to hear my mother talking about her own mother who was called Miriam, so I am sure that she must have been my grandmother, and Jessica my great grandmother! If I am right, then it would appear that we have Jewish blood in us too!
>
> This chest is the only thing that I have inherited from my mother, Edwina, who died last month. Being in disgrace and virtually shunned by the rest of my family, I suppose that I am indeed lucky to have been given the chest at all. I was never allowed to keep my beloved piano, but it appears to be an ancient and unbroken tradition in my family that this old chest is passed down through the female line via the eldest daughter. So my mother could not deny at least this, my inheritance from my foremothers.
>
> I am so tied up with trying to earn some money, looking after my husband and child and trying to get some rest, with the new baby due in the next couple of weeks. But when this baby born and I get back to normal again (and when this damn war is over), I want to do some digging into the stories of my ancestors to see if I can find out any more about any of them. Reading these few pages I am already asking myself who was Maria Johnston? Was she related to Miriam Rosen? Was she an ancestor too? And the chest itself which once belonged to Mary de Courtsey, is hundreds of years old. Where would I start to look for Mary de Courtsey, and Thornhill Manor? All these

names, versions of Mary; is that a family tradition too? Perhaps I should keep it up if I have a girl. Marie would be a nice name, and it's Frenchified too, so I'm sure that Jean-Pierre would approve!

I think that tracing ancestors could be a very difficult task to take on, and the trail will be difficult to follow, especially because the family name through the female line has always changed from generation to generation. But I mean to try!
26th October 1941

Marie put down the tea, and was immediately wide awake. Was this written by her mother? It must have been. This was her mother's handwriting! My real mother! She thought. Am I finding her at last? She brushed her fingers over the writing and looked hard at it. Did she expect it to look like her own handwriting? Of course it didn't, but it gave her butterflies in her stomach just to hold the note that her mother had written. Had she chosen her name so long ago? Perhaps she had wanted to have a girl after her first boy. She was writing about the chest and her family. Was it her mother, Marie's grandmother, who was named Edwina? Was that where her brother's unusual name of Edwin came from? He had always wondered about that. Just wait 'til she told him! This was fascinating!

While only momentarily pausing to wonder who Mary de Courtsey was, and what sort of disgrace her mother had been in, Marie picked up the pages attached to her mother's note. They were quite fragile, and some of the edges were stuck together, but, very carefully, she managed to prise them apart. Marie saw the first date at once – 1819. This was written over one hundred and seventy years ago! She started to read:

"......and because of that George, who is now the new Duke, comes to see me and Elizabeth less and less.

1st October 1819

Now that it is settled that he is to be married at Christmastide, Duke George has agreed, with his new wife to be, that he will no longer keep his mistress and his bastard daughter close by. I knew that he was reluctant to dismiss us, so before he summoned up the courage to pension me off it was I who decided to make the first move, and I asked him to provide us with a new home far away from this estate!

I shall be very sorry to leave this pretty little cottage with all its memories of my grandparents, but I must admit to not being at all heartbroken to be leaving the Duke. In fact during the past year or so our relationship has stagnated, and for me it will be a relief to have to submit no longer to his 'panting pleasures'! For years and years I loved him with all my heart, and longed to be his wife. But now I want him no longer, and she is welcome to him!

How is it that a young man, a King's soldier no less, who was so strong and beautiful in physique, has become so fat and ruddy in complexion in just a few years? The change in him started around the time when Elizabeth was born; when he became a drinking companion of the Prince Regent! But I must remember that he was not mine then any more than he is now. If he had persuaded his parents that I was a suitable woman to marry, we would have worked together to create a perfect family and he would have had little time to spend carousing with the Prince Regent.

It is no good me dreaming of what might have been, I must live in the present, and start to think about uprooting myself and Elizabeth from everything and everyone we love, and what we will want to take with us when we leave.

16th November 1819

George came to visit us yesterday with news about our future. He looked very grand in his new scarlet jacket and white breeches, but I did not encourage him to aspire for any intimacy – I just gave him a simple peck on his cheek. With a deep sigh he sat down and told me that our new home will belong entirely to me, and will be in the village of Chelsea, which is near London. I shall be expected to present myself to my new neighbours as a widow woman of modest means. Mistress Maria Rochester, Yes I shall retain my maiden name, especially as Elizabeth has always been called Elizabeth Rochester. My (our) daughter Elizabeth will no longer be tutored at home, but is to attend the village school.

My darling Elizabeth, I can hardly believe that she is eight already! She is such a beautiful child, with her big brown eyes, her long dark ringlets and rosy cheeks. She is also clever, pleasant and placid, and I adore her. Now that George, the 'important Duke', wants a legitimate son and heir, he all but ignores his daughter, but for me, she is the best thing to have come out of my years of love and passion with him.

Elizabeth has always thought that I was a widow, and that her father had died when she was a baby. She has accepted the irregular attention that her real father paid her during the passing years as just the interest of a benevolent benefactor, and I think that she will miss him even less than I will.

George has indeed been generous and once more and I shall be provided with all our needs from clothing, linen and furniture to pots and pans for the kitchen. And with a fixed annuity of £40 per year I shall be able to manage very well, and will no longer feel like a 'kept woman'.

But I shall be glad to take with me the one thing that is really mine – my oak chest, which is now being filled with my most precious belongings, including my grandmother's linen and chinaware, Elizabeth's christening gown, shawl and baby clothes, and of course this diary which I shall one day give to Elizabeth to read. But I will have to make sure that she is old enough to understand, and to learn about her parents and the strength of our love for each other when we were young.

My lovely old chest and all its contents will eventually belong to Elizabeth, with instructions that it must be handed down, in turn, to her eldest daughter, following the family tradition since it was first made for my many times great grandmother Mary de Courtsey.

I can still make out her name carved into the underside of the chest lid –'Mary de Courtsey, Thornhill Manor' and a date 'MDIC' (which I believe to be 1599). This date may have been when she was born, when the chest was made, or even when it was given to her, but it is surely as old as the date suggests."

Marie put the papers down and ran to the chest, opened the lid and peered inside. Sure enough, the inscription was still there, faint now with the ingrained dust and grime of four hundred years all but obscuring the carving, but still just legible. Another Mary! If her mother was right their names too, have been handed down in various forms from one generation to another. Mary, Maria, Miriam, and her own, Marie. Or was it just a coincidence? She went back to the kitchen and the pages from the diary.

"I looked again at that carving yesterday when I was packing my chest, and I wondered about my ancestor Mary. What was she like? Was she an adventurer like me? Had she been a happy woman? Did she have many daughters, and were any of them bastards like my poor Elizabeth?

No! I must not turn my thought to unhappiness and turn them instead to thinking about our next adventure in Chelsea. I'm sure that we will be happy there. Perhaps I will even meet a pleasant man, a widower maybe, who would be pleased to have a new wife with a pretty, readymade daughter. If not, I shall be quite happy to keep my independence, with no need for a man to support me!

10ᵗʰ January 1820

I have just spent my last Christmas in this lovely little cottage which is always so cosy and pleasant, and I can hardly believe that I may never see it again. It is so full of happy memories for me of my childhood and my dearest grandparents, who I still miss every day. I can hardly believe that it is now three years since they both passed away.

My father and mother came for afternoon tea the day after Christmas, (Boxing Day the servants up at the Duke's home call it.) But not Thomas and William, who are still ashamed of having an older sister who had a child out of wedlock, even if she is acknowledged by her other grandfather, the Duke.

Father was, as always, full of warmth, happiness and goodwill towards me, and we will miss each other sorely when I leave for Chelsea. As for Mother, she has still not forgiven me, but at last she is now warm and loving towards her grand-

daughter, and I believe that she will miss her. I wonder if she would have been warmer if I had named my daughter Sarah, after her, rather than after her mother, my loving grandmother Elizabeth. Mother even cried a little when she and my father left to return home. As a Stanford she was always proud that her father was a distant cousin of the Duke, but she could never forgive George for ruining her daughter.

George also came to say goodbye to us and my heart started beating fast as I took him in my arms for the last time. We looked deeply into each other's eyes but said nothing more as Elizabeth was standing by to receive her parting gift.

In spite of how our relationship has disintegrated since Elizabeth was born, I recalled all the friendship and love that has passed between us since I was a four year old child. Uncontrolled tears ran down my cheeks when we said our final farewells, and I swear that I saw tears glistening in his eyes too. Then he mounted his horse and was gone away from us forever!

George's gift to his daughter is a very fine and delicate porcelain dolls' tea set. It is quite beautifully decorated with prettily painted flowers all over it, almost too good for a child to play with. Elizabeth is delighted with it, and I am sure that she will take good care of it.

Now it is all packed away, along with all her dolls and other toys. It is quite heart wrenching to be leaving everything that I have loved, even George! Although I no longer love him, he has been my only love and part of my life for so long, I know that I shall miss him deeply.

The driver is even now taking my chest and the last of my belongings out to fit onto the back of the carriage (the furniture and six boxes containing our clothing and other belongings have already left on another wagon). He says that although it is bitingly cold, he is sure that it will not snow today. The roads are in a good condition, so our journey should take only three hours. Elizabeth is already settled in the carriage with her Mimi to keep her warm. As a King Charles spaniel, Mimi should be keeping Elizabeth's feet warm, but they both much prefer it when Mimi snuggles under the blanket on Elizabeth's lap. So now it is time to say goodbye to my home and my memories. Time to start again, and so I shall put away my diary and make sure that my own foot warmer is in the carriage. Then I will make a new entry when we are settled in Chelsea waiting for a new adventure to start.

January 20th 1820

We have arrived safely and are settled in our fine new home, but I am too heartsick and homesick to write more.

March 11th 1820

Elizabeth is nine today, her first birthday here, and I know that she is happier now than I have seen her since my grandparents died. It is cold and wet today. I am happy that her father did not forget her birthday; she was so excited when she discovered the handsome dolls' perambulator that he had sent for her. She has made friends with Olivia, who is the daughter of my new friend Emily Johnston, and, in spite of the rain, they had a very pleasant day together playing in the parlour with their dolls and the new perambulator, and how I laughed to see Mimi with a doll's dress on her, sitting within! My gift, which gave her much pleasure too, is a set of colourful reading books, and two pretty muslin dresses which she will enjoy wearing when the weather gets a little warmer.

Elizabeth is very happy going to the village school, and she is learning fast. It has been a strange experience for her to be sitting in a class of twenty girls and boys but she has taken to it like a duck to water! She reads and writes well, and is also very good at her numbers (much better than I have ever been!). As well as Olivia, she has other new playmates that she has found at school. I had not realised until now quite how lonely she had been before.

It will be my own birthday in twelve days time. I shall be twenty-nine years old!

October 15th 1820

We have been in Chelsea for ten months now, ten months of adjustments to the big changes in our lives, and we are now fully settled into our new home. I cannot believe just how much I missed George to begin with. For the first five months I found myself crying almost every night, and I told myself that I am stupid, that he does not love me, and that I do not love him! I have adjusted now, but, nevertheless, I do still occasionally miss him, not the lover, but the lifelong friend. The only person in the world who really knows me! I have fought against these feelings of loss, and have tried my best, for Elizabeth's sake, to accept this change in my life. He was thirty-eight last June. The 28th of June was always such a special day for us both. Yes, it was on his twenty-fourth birthday that we had our first kiss, when I was just fifteen! I wonder if he thought of me this time as he celebrated his birthday.

October 20th 1820

Chelsea is indeed a pretty village, but it is a lot bigger than I expected it to be, and very busy with people and traders for London coming and going, many of them by river barge. We are happy in this comfortable house which is so near the river that we see and hear the boatmen call out as they pass one another. On these autumn days when the river fog is thick, the boats and boatmen are like ghosts that suddenly appear and then just as suddenly disappear into the gloom, their calls to each other lingering on in the foggy air.

Our rooms are very much larger than those of my grandparent's cottage and my furniture and belongings fit in well, and are not cramped together as they were before. My chest has pride of place under the window in the drawing room.

I, too, have made new friends in the village. I like especially Olivia's mother, Emily Johnston, who is the Doctor's wife. She is about my age, very pretty, and a real chatterbox who tells me all the local gossip. My other friend is Mrs. Annabel Smith who is very different from Emily. Annabel is the very prim and quiet wife of the vicar of St. John's Church, Reverend Anthony Smith and she and I sometimes have very serious talks about God and nature. Though I do not know if either of them would be my friend if they knew that I have never been married! How shocked *they would be. I might even be shunned in the village, so I am very well advised to keep my secret.*

Emily says that she has a widowed brother-in-law called Edward (the same name as my beloved grandfather), a banker, who has a home in London, and who will be coming to visit them next week. She is very anxious to introduce me to this mysterious brother-in-law, and seems to think that we could be a good match. So I have an official invitation for me and my daughter, to take tea with Dr. and Mrs Johnston next Thursday afternoon at 3p.m. and..."

There the pages ended. What a pity thought Marie. There was one last page, all but empty except for a few words:

18th November 1835

I am so sick now, and I thank God daily for giving me my sweet Edward who has cared for me so tenderly. I know that he loves and will always look after my Elizabeth. This will be my last entry... Maria Johnston.

Marie was frustrated. She had become immersed in the story of Maria Johnston and wanted to know more. Did the first part of the diary describe Maria's passion for George? Where were all the other pages of the diary? What happened to Maria and Elizabeth during those fifteen years? How soon did Maria marry the 'mysterious' Edward Johnston? She must have done so, as Johnston became her name. Marie thought that perhaps one day she could go to St. John's Church in Chelsea and see if she could find a mention of their marriage in the parish records. Was it a happy marriage? Did she ever tell him that she was not a widow, but a 'scarlet woman'? Were there other pages of Maria's diary hidden in the Chest somewhere? Marie hoped that she might come across them amongst the other documents.

Then she very carefully opened the first letter, which was also attached to the diary pages and her mother's note. The quality of the paper was richer and thicker than that of the diary and it was beginning to crack where it had been folded in the envelope. It was also yellowing with age and some of the edges were torn away, but there was enough for Marie to be able to read it. The script was very flowery and handsome and she saw at once from the embossed heading that it was from Elizabeth's father, the Duke, and written to her for her twenty-first birthday. It said:

1th March 1832

My Dearest Elizabeth,
First of all I want to congratulate you on reaching your 21st birthday, and then I want to tell you a little about myself and my side of the history between me and your mother.

To begin with, whatever your mother has told you about me over the past few years is probably all true. She is a decent and honest woman, and I truly loved her when we were young, even from the time when she was but a child, and all through the years leading to your birth, and then for many years afterwards.

I know that it was a shock to you when we met briefly on your 12th birthday, and it was revealed that I am indeed your father, and I am very sorry for all the pain and confusion that you have subsequently suffered.

I do not want to make excuses for myself, and for how I treated your mother, but I do want you to understand that I did not act with purely selfish motives.

As the only son of the 5th Duke of ...., I was raised with the full expectations of doing my duty not only to King and Country, but also to my family. In fact my whole life plan was laid out for me by my parents from the day that I was born. I had very little choice in how I was to live my life or who I would marry.

I was trained to succeed my father in both his position as the Duke, and his role as a leader in the British army and a defender of the King. Although England and George 3rd lost the fight to keep the American colonies, as a young man himself, my father, like me, had more than twenty years service in the British army, and he played a gallant and heroic part in defending Boston, leading his men and saving them from complete massacre at the Battle of Bunkers Hill in 1775, when more than 1,000 British soldiers lost their lives. And during my own service in the defence of the realm, I had the honour of serving with

Lord Wellington when we finally defeated Napoleon in June of 1815.

My love for your mother resulted in many years of stalemate and disagreement between myself and my father as he tried to force me to fulfil my duty to the family, to marry a lady of suitable birth and produce an heir to the dukedom.

The fact that my parents not only tolerated but even admired your mother and her family, especially your grandfather, Henry Rochester, who was their lawyer and legal adviser, delayed their ambitions to have me suitably married until you were 9 years old – and I was 36!

However, that is all now in the past. Your mother was very brave to make the decision for both of us, and move both of you to your home in Chelsea. For these 12 years past I have been watching from afar to see you grow up to become the beautiful and well educated young lady that you are today. I have corresponded with your mother in recent years to confirm my continued support of you both, and with the full agreement of your excellent and charming stepfather, Edward Johnston. Indeed it was with my full blessing and approval that he formally adopted you and gave you his family name, a name which I know that you honour.

Now that you have reached your age of maturity I am gifting to you a small acreage of land from my estate which includes the cottage in which you were born and lived the first years of your life with your mother and your great grandparents. You may sell it if you wish, but the Duchess and I both hope that you will stay there from time to time and get to know your half-brothers George and William.

In addition to the land and cottage I have made arrangements with my lawyer (your uncle, William Rochester) to settle upon you £60 per year for life, so that you will not feel like a 'poor relation' when you start to go out into society.

I trust that you will be pleased with these arrangements, and I hope that you will take up my offer to re-introduce yourself into our Family.

Your father
George, 4th Duke of ....

What an interesting letter! Marie was pleased that Maria seemed to have had not only a successful marriage with Edward Johnston, but that she had also had a reconciliation with the Duke which, on the face of his letter to their daughter Elizabeth, also suggested that father and daughter were reconciled too. As the last few pages of Maria's diary and the letter had survived, Elizabeth probably had read the whole of the diary. She must have learned the secrets of the love that her mother had had for her father. Marie thought about that triangle of relationships for a moment, and decided that whatever the father's faults, he was a product of his age, background and upbringing, and maybe he had been worthy of understanding and forgiveness by all his womenfolk. She put the letter back in its envelope hoping that she might come across more of the mysterious diary. No! No more diary, but there was a second letter. This was much younger – only a hundred years old.

It was from Jessica the mother of Miriam Rosen to her daughter, the owner of the atlas that Marie was holding. A sad letter to a sad and lonely child. It was probably the only reminder to Miriam that she still had a mother. Marie wondered if she ever saw her mother again.

While she was pleased to have a little more history of the chest, Marie thought about men. What was it with them? Why do so many of them want complete control over their wives and daughters? She put the diary and letters back into the atlas and she opened up the next of her father's envelopes. This contained a few postcards, and some trinkets that must have belonged to her mother.

Marie completely forgot about the diary and letter she had just read. This was real. This was her own long lost mother! She felt very emotional as she handled a small gold brooch in the shape of a flower, with a little pearl in the centre. Was this her only piece of jewellery, or was it her favourite? There was also a silver propelling pencil, a mother of pearl powder compact, and a folded sheet of piano music; Für Elise by Beethoven; had that been her mother's favourite piece? Marie picked it up and out fell a plain gold ring.

Her mother's wedding ring! She put down the music sheet, picked up the ring and rubbed it gently. "I think that I would like to wear it myself." Marie did not even realise that she was talking out loud. She was lost in wonder and speculation. She put the ring on, and was immediately sure that she felt a buzz inside, a connection to her mother. The ring was a little big, so she put one of her own rings on next to it to keep it on. She did not realise that she was crying until she felt a tear running down her cheek as she looked at these few treasured possessions – had her mother had so very little?

She wiped away her tears and then she turned to the postcards, while still looking at the ring. They were all old black and white ones: the Arc de Triomphe in Paris, the Trevi Fountain and the Coliseum in Rome. Why did her father keep these? There was nothing written on the back of them, but there must have had a significant reason for him to keep them all these years, and…what's this? She was looking at a picture of an ancient country church…Thornton. That name rings a bell, she thought wonderingly. She turned the postcard over and there was a little note attached to it, and there was that handwriting again. The same hand as the note attached to the journal pages, this time written in pencil, fading slightly, but still legible. Her mother's handwriting!

June 1942

I can't believe it! I've found the de Courtseys – when I wasn't really looking for them! They're here in this old church. An effigy of a Knight and his Lady – Sir John de Courtsey, 2nd November 1557 – 8th August 1615, and Lady Edwina de Courtsey, 4th April 1565 – 26th May 1605. (Edwina! My mother's name! Did her name somehow pass through the generations to my mother?) Were Sir John and Lady Edwina Mary's parents? If so, her mother died only two years after the chest was made. There is no tomb in the church for Mary de Courtsey, but she probably moved away and was married into another family. But there are other de Courtseys here. They must have been the main family here in the 17th century.

There is a tombstone let into the floor for Sir Raymond de

Courtsey, 21st July 1570 – 3rd March 1622, and his wife Lady Elzabeth de Courtsey 3rd June 1565 – 21st November 1621. (She was older than he was!) Then there is a plaque on the wall for John de Courtsey, born 1st June 1613 who died fighting for his King at the Battle of Edgehill 23rd October 1642. Erected in his memory by his father, Sir Christopher de Courtsey. (No mention of John's mother). The Battle of Edgehill was in the English Civil War, so the family were Cavaliers. I wonder what happened to their lands when Cromwell and the Roundheads won?

There was a separate tomb in the floor for Sir Christopher, 20th September 1589 – 13th September 1650. No mention again of a wife for Sir Christopher, so where was the mother of the John of Edgehill? And was Christopher Sir John's son or Sir Raymond's son?

Another little mystery for me to solve. And who was Mary de Courtsey? She surely was part of this family! Was she Christopher's sister? Was she his cousin? Could she have even been his wife? I must come and visit my sister in Colchester again, and see if I can get to see some of the ancient record books. Would they still be kept in the church archive? I must find out.

That was it. Marie was bemused. All those names! Her mother must have taken them to use for her sons. But wait, she thought, Ray was born before their mother had found the church. Was that just a coincidence? John was there, and Edwin, well, he must have been named for our grandmother Edwina, but where did she get her name from?

Then another thought struck her. Her mother had had a sister who lived in Colchester. This was exciting – she had, or had had an aunt! She might even have some cousins she knew nothing about. Before Marie went back to her present task she resolved that she would try to find out more about the Harrisons, her mother's family. Perhaps there was a trail she could discover in Colchester?

So who was Mary de Courtsey? Was she the first owner of the chest, and why did she matter so to our mother? Did she ever find out what had happened to her? Maybe she would have to go to Colchester and find out about Thornton and Thornhill, as well as search for records of her aunt Harrison.

Then Marie looked again at the old postcards of Paris and Rome! What was the significance of them she wondered? Why did her father keep them?

Those thoughts and questions were put by when she opened the third envelope, and out came even smaller envelopes, numbered from one to six. Marie's tea was unfinished and stone cold by now, but she did not care. She spread the six envelopes over the kitchen table and sat and looked at them for a minute or two. Then she took a deep breath and decided to open them in order – it must have been what her father had wanted her to do.

1. The first envelope had two pictures in it. The first was an old, postcard-sized sepia photograph of a huge old-fashioned sports car, with a young man in the driving seat. Marie turned it over. On the back was printed 'Lassere et Fils, 116 Le Grand Rue de Pera', and hand written in faded ink 'Jean-Pierre avec sa nouvelle Bugatti 1922'.

Wow! she thought. That must have been Dad at sixteen. He owned a car, and an expensive one at that! Marie was no expert in vintage cars, but even she knew the name Bugatti, and she was sure that those cars cost a small fortune. She looked at the picture again. The face of the young man was too small for her to recognise or pick out any features.

She thought about her father and his love for motor cars. He had rarely spent money on himself, buying only what clothes he felt were necessary to keep him looking respectably clean and tidy. His one indulgence, even when he was struggling financially, was motor cars. The excuse was always that they were needed for the business. Marie remembered the first one that he had bought soon after their move to Eastbourne. It was an old black Rover saloon. The glass in all of the windows was beginning to become opaque, and if it was driven up a steep hill, like the one to Beachy Head, everyone had to get out and walk to the top! She even remembered the number-plate – DY 7686, and her father was the only person who owned a car along that part of the Eastbourne seafront.

Even now after all these years of sickness her Dad had still not wanted to sell his old cars. He had two of them, both Jaguars, both in pristine condition, now left to Edwin and John. His first love for years had been the 1958 E-type painted bright yellow which Marie and her brothers had christened 'the flying banana'! The Mark II was just like the one driven by Inspector Morse on the TV, only her Dad's one was painted in a dark metallic grey – it was the leather upholstery that was scarlet!

Marie she looked at the old photograph again, then she peered at the background. It showed a stretch of water and an old wooden bridge. And what was that on the far side of the bridge? She looked closely and was sure that she was looking at a mosque with many tall minarets. Funny! she thought. I've been to Paris quite a few times, and I did not remember ever seeing this view.

Marie put the photograph down and picked up the second one. It was one that she vaguely remembered as having seen before. Yes, it was one taken during the War, and it was of her father washing a large black car with an ARP ambulance sign attached to the front of it. She did see this photograph as a child, and she remembered laughing to see her Dad with a beard! He had never worn one since.

2. The second envelope had four photographs in it. They were also ones that Marie remembered seeing before. They had been taken in a London park on a sunny day before they had all moved to Eastbourne. It must have been spring time because the flower beds were full of daffodils in bloom, and she must have been about eighteen months old. Perhaps it was the first family outing after she had returned to the family after living with Francine.

Marie peered closely at the photograph. Here she was sitting on Mummy Betty's lap, studying a Kodak Brownie camera box, and with a whole head full of tightly curled blond hair! How young and pretty and happy Mum looked as she smiled directly at the camera! Marie remembered that blond hair of hers. It got darker and straighter as she grew older, until when she was a teenager all that remained was flyaway straight hair with a broad blond streak at the front. How many times had her father shouted at her, accusing her of 'peroxidising' her hair like a slut!

The other photos of the family taken that day showed Ray and John playing on a swing, and Edwin kicking a large ball, almost as big as he was! And there was a picture of her father sitting on the grass with all four of his children around him. Betty must have taken the photo. Marie looked again at the one with herself holding the Kodak box, perhaps it had been a new camera being used for the first time that day.

> 3. More photographs that Marie remembered having seen a long time ago. These were a set of pictures taken in the back garden of their home in London. She was about thee by then. They were the best photographs that had been taken of the Beauville family when they lived in London.

There was one with Mum, sitting, with Marie on her lap, and Ray, John and Edwin grouped around her. Mum was about twenty-five then, and she was stunningly beautiful. She had long dark hair curling about her shoulders, a hip-hugging skirt which showed her slim waist, a white blouse and a string of pearls. Then a photograph each of Ray and John together, and of Edwin and Marie together, and a family group with their father, holding Marie, Mum holding Edwin's hand and Ray and John either side of their parents. All of the children were dressed in what looked like hand-me down clothes. The boys wore grey shorts that looked too big, the waists so large and distorted that the trousers needed braces to hold them up. Their jumpers were ragged too and had holes in them, but they were all polished, clean and tidy, with their hair slicked down with water, or perhaps it was Brylcreem! (Yuk! That was the horrid stuff the boys used for years to look smart.) Marie was wearing a summer dress that looked several sizes too big, or maybe it was covering a huge nappy, and she had a ribbon tied in a big bow in her hair. Everyone looked so happy, a real family photo session! Marie wondered who had taken that photo? She also wondered when her father had stored them away in the chest, and why? Perhaps it was when they moved to Eastbourne – perhaps they were packed away in the chest and had just stayed there.

Marie reflected on the many happy times in that London home. Sometimes her father would pretend to be a monster, chasing them around the house and garden until they screamed in delighted terror. There were regular trips to various parks, and occasional full day outings to Southend in Essex, or to Box Hill in Surrey.

But as Marie was growing up she also remembered the other times when he really was a monster with an evil temper. She did not know then about the deepening depression with which her father was suffering, all she remembered was the anger, the shouting, his fist thumping the table, and the bamboo cane he used to beat his children with when they were naughty. Punishment could be for being too noisy at play, climbing trees in the garden, or simply for disagreeing with him. "I will not have answering back!" He would always shout at them. And there was Mum standing by, never butting in, never saying anything, unable to protect them, but always ready to comfort them when the storm was over.

Her Mum had never been able to exert any authority over her step-children. Marie remembered her father so often shouting at Mum when they were all quite small, "I am their father, and I know what is best for my family. They will do as I want. And I shall be obeyed!"

~~~

Marie sat there at the kitchen table and thought about her young childhood. The old photographs had taken her back. Apart from these, her first real memories were more of feelings than of pictures. She did not remember Francine, but she did remember growing up feeling unhappy and unwanted by everyone. Mummy Betty, as the children called her at first, was too busy to pay attention to Marie for long, and her brothers were always calling her 'cry-baby', and did not want to play with her.

When she was growing up they had often told her that she had cried almost without stopping for two years after she had been returned to the family. How she must have missed the love and attention that Francine had given her. There were no psychologists then to explain about the trauma she must have been experiencing because of her separation from Francine. I was not a naughty crybaby, Marie thought, I had simply been a broken-hearted baby!

It was not until years later, when Marie talked to her Mum that she learned just how inexperienced Mum had been as a mother. Marie was twenty-four, and she had just had her own first baby, and her Mum had come to visit her, without her father in tow. While her Mum was cuddling baby David, Marie suddenly took the opportunity to ask questions that she had not dared to ask when her father was around.

"Mum," she had asked, "you've never spoken about your marriage to Dad. How did you first meet him, why did you marry him, and how did you cope with four babies? I sometimes struggle to look after just that one!"

She was so surprised when her Mum had replied, because Mum hardly ever talked about the past. But that day it was as if Marie had pressed all the right buttons, and floodgates had opened; Mum told her more about herself and her father than she had ever done before.

Her Mum had heaved a big sigh before she spoke. "I met your father during the War," she replied. "I had been working as a typist in a factory that had made silk dresses before the War, and now made silk parachutes for the Royal Air Force. I had wanted to get a better job in a nice clean and smart office, so to improve my employment prospects I decided to attend evening school. On Mondays I went to bookkeeping classes. The teacher was a fussy old maid of about ninety, and the two hours dragged on forever. But the best was Thursdays. On Thursdays I went to learn French. It was there, in the French class, that I first met your father, and within weeks I had fallen head over heels in love with him. He was so good looking then. Not very tall. Only an inch or so taller than me! But he had dark curly hair, a very handsome face and such a sexy foreign accent. I fell for him at once! He was fifteen years older than me, and I thought that he was such a real man. So distinguished and charming. Just like a movie star. My English boyfriends seemed just like country clods in comparison to him."

Her Mum had looked at Marie straight in the eye as she continued. "It took me a few weeks before I dared to ask him to join me for a cup of coffee after a lesson, and I was surprised when he agreed. I did not known, at first, that he was married, or that he had several children." She had paused, took another deep breath, and then spoke about what had happened when I was born. "He was crying the day when he told me that your mother had died. He broke down completely asking, 'how will I be able to look after my children?' and it was then that I offered to help him.

"He went off to Wales to bury her." she continued, "and then he came back with your three brothers. You, the newborn baby, had already gone off to be looked after by his cousin, but I was still shocked to see just how young little Edwin was. Little more than a baby himself. But I was so in love with your father that I disregarded convention, and offered to move in with him. And we were married six months later, just a few days before the end of the War in Europe."

She paused again and then continued once more. "I know that you have sometimes seen us angry and fighting, but it was different then. How I loved him. How I wanted him. And if I had to have his children too, then so be it!"

"How did you cope with your instant, ready made family?" Marie had asked.

"I must have been mad. What did I know about children? I had hardly ever held a baby, let alone looked after one." She looked down at my baby in her arms, and continued. "Just my sister's baby a few times when I was a girl. My sister was ten years older than me, and she and her family emigrated to Australia before the War so I was never a real aunt as the baby grew up. When I moved in with your father I was overwhelmed with having three young children to look after, and I looked to your father for advice. That's when the rot set in, and, without knowing it, I set up a pattern for the future. He made it clear that they were his children and that he would make all the decisions; and I had to go along with what he wanted. It was even harder when you were brought back into the family. I then had three youngsters and a baby to look after, and a difficult and demanding husband, too. No wonder I didn't have as much time for you as Francine had had with only you to look after. And how you cried and cried! Sometimes it was more than I could bear."

"Why didn't you put your foot down with Dad?" Marie had asked. "You were doing all the hard work of looking after us, why didn't you insist in sharing the family decision making? You could have threatened to leave Dad years ago. Why didn't you? He would not have been able to cope without you." Marie had been thinking of the temper tantrums, the fist pounding on the table, the insistence on 'These are my children!' and 'I will be obeyed' scenes.

"Oh. Well!" Her Mum had exclaimed. "By the time that I had had enough of him and his moods and tempers, I had already begun to love you lot, and I couldn't have left you. You were all my children by then. And besides I felt that owed it to your mother." Then she stopped talking, clamed up tight, and said no more that day.

Marie returned her thoughts to the present and recalled what her father had said about Mum just a few hours ago, before he died. She was sure that she was right! He did have more than just a friendship with her while her heavily pregnant mother was away in Wales, perhaps even before she had left for Bangor. Marie now realised that it must have been guilt over having the affair with her Dad while his wife was living and dying in Wales that made Mum say that she owed it to their mother. No wonder her Mum had clammed up. She must have thought that she had said too much. Marie asked herself if this knowledge make any difference to the way she felt about Mum? No. Not really. Mum had always done the best that she could for all of us children. For me and my brothers, Mummy Betty had become just Mum. We all had loved her, and she had been a loving mother to us all, until she had died ten years ago.

On to the next envelope.

4. Here Marie found two photographs of the family in the back garden again, this time with two other well remembered and loved people – Dad's mother, Grandmama Anna, and his sister, Auntie Mariette. (Until now she had always thought that her first name was for her aunt.) She was only three when they came from Paris, to live with them, but Marie remembered them well, and enormous difference their coming had made to the family.

It was 1947. After the hotel in Paris had failed at the start of the War, her aunt had moved to Athens, Greece with her new Greek husband who she had met and married in Paris, taking her mother with her. All three of them had lived together there for six years or so, but Aunt Mariette and her husband had separated during the Greek civil war and she and Grandmama Anna. who also had British passports, had sought refuge with her father in London. That was all that was ever said about their past. They never spoke of Paris or Athens, and the children were too small to ask any questions of that sort. After a most terrible winter when deep snow fell for weeks and the whole of the country was frozen – even the coal mines – all of a sudden the freezing little terraced house in London became filled with people. Her Mum, who up till then had had no help with raising her four stepchildren, suddenly had two willing, loving and somewhat interfering in-laws! And Marie, 'the poor motherless child' as they called her; suddenly had two new Mothers!

Everyone felt warmer and happier. Her new Grandmama and Auntie were both of a completely different temperament to her Mum. They just loved small children, and especially babies, and they played with and cuddled the children, especially Marie and Edwin, all the time. Marie was picturing her grandmother, a short, cuddly woman, with soft skin and grey hair which was always done up in a bun. She also remembered that she had never seen her Grandmama dressed in anything but black. She wore long black flowing skirts, and Marie used to run and hide behind those skirts whenever her father was angry with her. He never dared to cross his mother so Marie always knew that she would be safe with her. Grandmama Anna never learned to speak English, so in order to speak to and understand her all the children began to learn French, and learned it in a natural, oral form. Auntie Mariette was taught English by her brother and it was not long before she became proficient enough in the language to get herself a job as a supervisor in a large branch of Marks and Spencer, and begin to bring in some much needed cash to help support the family.

As for Marie, she was so happy, deeply happy for the first since she had been taken from Francine. She went from being the extra one needing care, to being continually cuddled and petted. Years later her Mum told her a typical story of her three "mothers" each worrying in the winter time that she was too cold when sitting on the stone floor of the kitchen, and each one of them putting an extra pair of panties on her until Marie had protested, "no fee, four, five!"

The new expanded household was very busy and loving. There were no quarrels or conflicts between her Mum and her Grandmother and Aunt over the management of the household. They all loved all four children, and for two years or so they all enjoyed the extra loving and attention that they got from their new relations.

But for their father it was an extra busy time. After the War he had recommenced daytime classes teaching French in the private school that had returned to London, and now he was also teaching evening classes again, in order to earn enough money to feed everyone. He had never recovered from his depression which had started when Susan died, and now it was taking a strong hold on him again.

Marie made her thoughts turn away from those times which were difficult for everyone in the family, and she opened the next envelope.

5. Here she found four photographs and an old British passport.
Three of photos were of a young woman.

"What's this?" she asked, speaking out loud. This time Marie was astounded. "I can't believe this. This must be our mother, Susan!" She had been certain that she would at last find photographs of her mother in the chest, but, even so, she was still shocked when she saw them. Marie adjusted her glasses and brought the photos up close to her face. She was looking at the small figure standing outside a terraced house, proudly holding a baby. She did not know that she had started to cry again until the image became all blurred. She pushed her glasses aside and wiped her eyes with the back of her hand, and then turned the first picture over. On the back was written 'Raymond. June 1939'. Ray! As a baby! The next picture was also of Ray, this time in a huge pram, with huge wheels, and Susan was crouched down looking at him. Then there was her father holding baby Ray, and finally a close up of Susan holding Ray. Marie peered at this last one closely to see if I could recognise in her mother any features that had come out in her children. The pictures were all a bit too small to really distinguish her mother's face in detail. She does look a little bit like me, though, Marie. Or should I say that I look a little bit like her. All four photos were taken at the same time, just a couple of months before the World War II had started.

Marie found that her hand was shaking as she reached for the passport. She opened it, and this time she gasped with astonishment. This too was her mother's, and the two inch square passport photograph was clear as any picture could be. Was it her mother, or was it herself that she was looking at? Marie with an old fashioned wavy perm hair style?

Taking the passport with her, Marie ran upstairs to her bedroom, and reached up to the high shelf of her wardrobe. There she found what she was groping for – an old chocolate box filled with various pictures of herself, taken when she was younger. Yes, there was the one she was looking for. Her hands were shaking as she looked at it. A studio portrait taken of herself when she was twenty-two. Marie stared at it; herself aged twenty-two, and then she looked at the passport photograph; Susan, taken when she was twenty-two. Apart from the hairstyles, the two women in the two pictures were almost identical!

Marie stared and stared at the two photographs. She could hardly believe her eyes. At that age she had been the spitting image of her mother. She had grown up to be almost identical in looks, yet her father not only had said nothing to her about the resemblance, he had been restrictive and unkind to her. Yet he was supposed to have dearly loved her mother, and had been heartbroken when she died. Marie shook her head in disbelief, she just did not understand!

Marie had had nothing to eat or drink since her brothers had left and she felt in great need of a sandwich and a hot and sweet cup of tea to calm her shock. She made both, and sat eating the ham sandwich without really tasting it, while thinking back on her difficult relationship with her father. She scalded her mouth taking a sip of the tea, and putting the cup down, she thought about her childhood. Her father had treated her brothers so much better than herself. Maybe it was not just because she was a girl as she had always thought; perhaps it was because she had reminded him too much of Susan. But then why hadn't he loved her? Then she remembered his last words. "There's something bad about Marie." She put her head in her hands and her tears overwhelmed her.

~~~

Marie was determined to continue with her task, so, when she had recovered a little she opened the sixth and final envelope, resisting the temptation to open up the small box, another chocolate box, which was under the last envelope. She realised that her father had put all these old papers and photographs in a specific order for her to make sense of her discoveries, knowing that she needed to know the real story of her past, and to lead her into it gradually, and in stages.

> 6. This, too, contained photographs. At first all she could see were publicity photographs that had been taken of the College. The family business. There was the double front of the two buildings joined together, a class room full of girls busy studying, a bedroom with four neat single beds, the dining room with six tables laid up for six places each, and the sitting room with its comfortable armchairs, TV and record player.

Most of her childhood and teenage memories were of being brought up in the Guest House that became a College.

As a little girl Marie had not realised her father's suffering with deep depression, and when she was four years old, his doctor had told him to go for a holiday by the seaside to help his recovery. And it was while her father was in Eastbourne in Sussex, that he had seen a small guest house for sale at the far end of the sea front. Her father had thought about his family hotel in Paris, and he was interested at once. She was just five when her grandmother and aunt moved to a rented flat and father sold their house in London. The whole family moved to Eastbourne. Her father had taken a gamble, taken on a huge mortgage, and bought the little guest house, which he renamed 'The Hotel de Paris'.

It wasn't very big. Only eight guest bedrooms on the first floor and two double rooms on the top floor where the family slept. Marie's parents had one room, and the four children shared the second room, all four of them sleeping top to tail in a metal framed double bed. Later their father had this room divided so that Marie had her own small space apart from her brothers. But in the first few years their parents were so desperate to make enough money to pay the bills that they let out all the rooms at the height of the summer season. All of June, July and August.

Marie remembered the first few summers when all the family, the children as well as their parents, made their beds at night wherever they could. Ray's was in the storeroom at the back of the kitchen; John and Edwin's slept in the downstairs cloakroom, and in that first year, Marie had climbed into a large wicker laundry basket and slept in the kitchen! Their poor parents had only a mattress that they put down on the floor in the sitting room. They could only do that after the last guest had gone to bed at night, and then they had to get up and clear the room before any of them got up in the morning.

Nights were short for them and their parents were always exhausted. Her father dealt with the guests, did the bookings, the accounts and the cooking, and Mum did everything else; all the housekeeping and all the cleaning, including the bedrooms and the kitchen. Her father loved doing the cooking, and he was very good at it. He introduced the family to continental cooking; pasta, aubergines, garlic and rice. This was in the 1950s – long before they became part of the English diet! On top of all the housework Marie's Mum still had the four children to care for and look after, but because she was so busy, they enjoyed many hours of freedom each day. They had a very strange mixture of strong discipline and punishments at home, and complete freedom to do whatever they liked when they were out. As long as they all stayed together, with Ray always in charge, for the most part at weekends and in their summer holidays, as long as they had done their chores, they were able to go out to play.

What fun and freedom they had too! Freedom such that no child is given today. As children, summers always seem to be remembered as long hot and sunny, and Marie thought about the long days that the four of them had they spent on the beach, on the pier, walking the South Downs to Beachy Head, taking only a sandwich and an apple for lunch, and not returning until the evening meal was being served to the guests. Of course there were rainy days too, and Marie remembered playing card games, canasta was the favourite, reading, and making model balsa wood aeroplanes with John. He was always the artistic one and he had the patience to help Marie when she got into difficulties with cutting the balsa wood to fit the scale plan.

The autumn and winter seasons were much quieter. Then they were able to live again as a family. Their Mum did most of the work for the few guests that still came for the 'off season', and because they didn't make enough money to cover all the bills, their father found extra work, once more teaching both daytime and evening French classes in the local College.

Then their father had an idea which was to change their lives once again. With his contacts in France, he decided that he could make more money by turning the Hotel into a residential finishing school for young French girls who would come for a whole school year from October to the end of May. It started with their father giving the girls daily lessons in English. By then he was perfect in his spoken and written English, and he also hired a part-time teacher for secretarial training. Her name was Mrs. Wilson, and she was a fussy little woman who had retired from teaching some months previously, and had no conversation other than her many dogs! Marie had always thought it strange that the girls liked her, and they were all happy to sit and work hard with their old fashioned typewriters which her father had bought as a cheap job lot at a local auction house. After a while, with the help of agents abroad, there were girls coming Italy, Spain and other European countries too.

For four months in the summertime, June to September, boys also came to the School for four to six weeks at a time. They were mostly French, Germans, Spanish and Italians. They were housed as bed and breakfast guests with local families, and they had their meals and lessons, together with the summertime girls, in the School. Extra teachers were employed and classes expanded to include the hiring of a couple of local church halls. The business was then making good money and life became a lot easier when her father employed a cook, a kitchen hand and a chambermaid.

Then the hotel next door came up for sale and their father took another gamble and bought that too. The building was the reverse duplicate of the one that he already owned, with their main entrances at the side, and facing each other, and so he employed builders to join both buildings together with a covered walkway. Marie, who was always fascinated by building design and how things worked, remembered how her father had so often told her off when he saw her talking to the builders – old or young, it did not matter – she was not to talk to men!

It took six months to convert the new building into a proper school, with classrooms, toilets, office, a kitchen and dining hall, and a sitting room with a T.V. and a music centre. Then all the rooms of the original hotel, including the sitting room, dining room and office, were converted into dormitories with two to five beds in each room. The kitchen became a communal shower and bathroom, and the back storage room became a washroom. Now the school was able to take up to thirty girls at a time, mixed European and even a few from the Middle East and her father renamed it 'The European College'.

During the years while their father was developing his business from Guest House to Girls School to the College, bit by bit, and year by year, Marie's brothers found their independence and their own friends until, one by one, they went off to University, and by the time she was twelve there was only herself and Edwin left at home. And even Edwin, before he went to University, no longer wanted his little sister tagging along, and then all Marie was left with for friends and company were the college students. Marie was allowed to mix with the students, the summertime boys as well as the girls; but this was only within the College or in students groups for outings, and always under her father's supervision.

Marie became very resentful and unhappy, especially after she left her junior school and progressed to the Grammar School for Girls.

She soon found that she was never allowed to play with school friends after school or go to their homes, meet up with them at the weekends, or bring any of them back to the College. Her school friends, on the other hand, were envious of her because she 'lived with' all those exciting and handsome foreign boys! The freedom that she had had as a young girl was gone and the only friendships that she was able to make were transitory ones with the female students.

They still lived as a family on the top floor of the old building, with the attic converted to make a small private sitting room and an extra bedroom and bathroom for her parents. Marie then moved into her parent's old bedroom and her small bedroom became another bathroom, but they had no kitchen and they all ate their meals with the students in the dining hall. Marie spent most evenings not being private with her family, but sharing the main sitting room with the girls, and with some of the boys in the summertime, she even did her school homework there. From the time that Marie was a teenager she did not have any real privacy; everything she did has always been under the ever watchful eye of the 'Big Brother' supervision of her father. Via his office switchboard he had listened in to all her incoming telephone calls, and he had opened and read all her incoming letters.

Amongst all her feelings of frustration and injustice there were burned into Marie's memory two occasions when her Dad had hurt and humiliated her so much that even now, when she recalled them her cheeks flushed and all that hurt and humiliation returned. The first had happened at the beginning of a new term in October, just after her thirteenth birthday. Unknown to her, she had received a letter from one of the summer students, a girl called Marie-Joelle, who had returned to France. As usual her father had opened the letter and had read it. Then he had called Marie into his office.

"What's this?" he had shouted. "I told you what I would do if you went out with boys".

Marie did not know what he was talking about and she protested her innocence when he had shoved the letter into her face and read out the offending sentence.

"I didn't do anything. I didn't go to the cinema with any boys!" Marie had protested, but her father had not believed her. He had slapped her around her face and started raging at her. Grabbing at the letter Marie ran from the office to her Mum, who was in the kitchen talking to the cook. In floods of tears she had showed it to her Mum. "I didn't do anything." She had protested again. "I don't understand this letter."

Marie-Joelle had said in a sentence in the letter 'do you remember the day when we went to see the film with.........?' then she had written two French boys' names.

"Why! These are the names of two French film stars!" Mum had exclaimed. "They were in that old film 'Les Enfants Terribles'. Dad and I went to see it ourselves!"

"Film stars!" Marie had been astonished. She felt vindicated and unjustly treated. "I knew that I hadn't gone to the cinema with boys" she said, "but Dad would not believe me!"

She then took the letter back to her father. "They were not boyfriends. I didn't lie." She had said triumphantly. "It was a French film called 'Les Enfants Terribles' that we went to see, and those two so called 'boyfriends' of ours were the two stars of the film. You saw the film with Mum!"

Marie had expected her father to say sorry, and to comfort her, but all he said was. "Just you make sure that you don't go to the cinema with boys. That's a lesson on what to expect!" She had left his office dumbfounded and feeling bitterly angry at the injustice of her treatment.

The second occasion, which had happened the following summer, was much worse. In order to be accepted as one of them, and not be treated suspiciously for being the headmaster's daughter, Marie always sought to make friends with the students, the only young people with whom she had contact. Apart from their English lessons, she joined in all their activities both in the College and outside from going in groups to the beach, rambling on the Downs or accompanying them on outings to London and nearby tourist sites, She spoke French and Italian all the time, and tried to melt in the general background to become just one of the crowd.

It was during the morning coffee break at the College on a wet

August day when, instead of gathering outside on the seafront as was their usual custom, most of the students, and Marie too, were crowded into the into the sitting room. All the seats were quickly taken, and the rest of the students were standing around, chatting to friends. That morning Marie had joined two other girls, who, instead of standing, sat perched on the very edge of the knees of three of the boys who were sitting on a bench. Everyone was talking and laughing together in a relaxed manner when her father had walked into the room.

Before Marie could jump up he rounded on her and slapped her face so hard that she was knocked to the floor, all the time shouting at her in uncontrolled rage and at the top of his voice. In front of everyone in the room he called her 'putain', which she knew was the French word for prostitute! Before she could get up properly, and before the astonished eyes of the collective students who stared at what was going on in shocked silence, her father had dragged her out of the sitting room and to his office. He ignored her cries and tears whilst repeating his vile words of abuse.

"You are nothing but a filthy slut, a whore!" He shouted at her. "Only a slut would sit on a boy's lap and let his filthy hands touch your body and go up your legs!"

"I wasn't, I didn't," she cried. "I was only sitting on the edge of his knees, not in his lap. He wasn't even holding me there. He wasn't touching me." Marie had sobbed and sobbed while her father had just glared at her.

There were teachers and staff, all within the hearing, who had opened their classroom doors to see what was going on, and became witnesses to her shame and humiliation.

Marie stopped herself thinking about what had happened next, but the memory of her humiliation remained and her cheeks burned as she picked up the smaller photographs that were under the promotional ones. She was jolted again. There were her parents standing in front of the College with two lovely Italian girls, aged about eighteen. She looked at the back 'Gabriella and Francesca. Summer 1956. She had been twelve then, a year before the 'Marie-Joelle letter', and it was the first time that Marie had realised that her father was being more than friendly with some of the students. How had her Mum put up with it?

The next picture really disturbed her, and she began to shake in anger. It was a group photo of all the College teachers and office staff taken in 1962, with her father in the centre and his secretary Emily, standing next to him.

Emily. That was not just a fleeting romance of a student passing through. That was a full blown affair that lasted for years. Marie had always wondered what her father had seen in the bitch! She was such a nondescript person. The picture was a true image. Average height and body shape, brown shoulder length straight hair, blotchy complexion which was always covered in thick make-up. Emily, who had devastated her Mum. Emily, who had spied on Marie and reported back to her father, especially when there were any of the boys were around. Emily, who made sure that all her private mail continued to go to her father first. Emily, who had later prevented Marie from taking any position in the College management, in spite of her fluency in French and Italian. And Emily, who had probably advised her father not to let her go to university when she wanted to study Art and Design. All that 'free love' going on in London in the sixties!

And that was it. Marie had not been allowed to work in the College and she was not allowed to go to university, like her three brothers had done. She left school at sixteen and had never completed her education. For many years she had felt less worthy than her brothers, all of whom had professional careers, and all because her father did not want her to have the opportunity to be free to mix with, or go out with any young man. He had never wanted her to be free of his direct control. It had not been that he was jealous and wanted to keep his little daughter all to himself. No. It had always seemed to Marie that he didn't really want to be with her, love her, or take any interest in her other than to protect her virginity at all costs.

Marie could not bear it. In tears once again she tore the photograph up into small pieces, and threw them on the floor in disgust.

~~~

Slowly Marie put the photographs back into the last envelope. She felt wrung out. It was late now, and she had not eaten properly since breakfast time. Did she have the strength to open the last item at the bottom of the chest? A Cadbury's Milk Chocolate box? Yes, she said to herself. I must do it. Finish it, before I go to bed.

She made herself another sandwich and another cup of tea, and took the chocolate box to the sitting room. It was a pity, she thought, that there were no chocolates in the box! Even a soft centre would have been welcome at that moment!

As Marie plopped down into her comfortable leather chair, and invited Misha to join her, she wondered what new rollercoaster ride she would be taking when she opened this up. Whilst readjusting her glasses she had a feeling that this box held the most important documents of all.

There were only two things were in it. First there was what looked like an old autograph book, about six inches by four inches, which had multi-coloured thick card pages. The second was another plain brown envelope.

With much trepidation, Marie picked up the book, opened it and read:

1st September 1945

This is dedicated to my beloved children Raymond, John, Edwin and Marie, in memory of Susan their ever regretted mother. I wish never to forget her supreme sacrifice and her life dedicated to loving us.
  Jean-Pierre Beauville

Although it was an autograph book, her father had used it as a journal!

When I first met your mother (in 1936), my children, she was a lively young girl of 20. Her gentleness and charm conquered my heart. Her smile had a sweetness that moved all who knew her.
  At that time I was 30 years old. I was married but life had not been very kind to me. I was struggling hard to make a living in a country which was foreign to me. This all Susan knew too well, but she was not afraid. She was also prepared to forget

my stormy youth and she came to me with love and tenderness. I had never been so happy as at the time when she was my sweetheart.

We travelled a little in France and in the Mediterranean and finally settled for a new life.

The beginning was difficult. We had no money and as my earnings were very meagre, my beloved Susan went to work too, as a receptionist at the BBC. She never complained and faithfully helped things going, still cheerful, still smiling. In the evenings she played the piano for more money, while I was giving lessons for money.

We loved each other very much and she knew what she represented for me: a lovely wife, a tender and devoted companion whose youth and courage were a constant source of stimulation to me. I ignored everyone. I had only one soul to care for me: my Susan. She embodied everything a human being could desire and I know now that had she turned me down, my life was finished.

Yet never, in her real modesty, would she claim anything but the monotony of a life with me, a life devoid of any pleasures, except an occasional outing. Though I knew of this I took it for granted. What a fool I was! Anybody could have envied me and I wish my sons to find a wife like her. In 1938 we went on a cruise and it was happiness for us too.

The postcards of Paris and Rome!

Then when we came back, my darling Susan conceived. On the 1st May 1939 Raymond was born. Two months before her confinement Susan was still carrying on with her job. She resumed work two months later and went on working for another three months.

By that time my situation had slightly improved and Susan could devote her time to her duties as wife and mother. Oh! What a wonderful mother she was! Raymond was a very lucky child to have a mother like this.

We were all very happy. Then at the beginning of September 1939 we saw the outbreak of war. I lost my job and things once again became more difficult. I went into the Civil Defence as an ambulance driver. Susan sustained my courage and my faith in the future.

She had developed into a lovely young woman with striking beauty and great charm. Yet her modesty was still as great as before. Devotion, love and faithfulness were her motto. Raymond was proving to be a bright child and we were both very proud of him.

Raymond was growing fine; he was healthy and putting on weight. Remember, he was just a baby, and we were extremely proud of him.

Then Susan went to see her sister again while I worked away. Days went by and at last a month, which to me had seemed unending, was over. I came back to fetch Susan and Raymond from Colchester and take them back to London. What a reunion this was! I felt 21 again. I shall never forget the moment I had my divine Susan in my arms again. What love I saw in her eyes, and what a kisses she gave me! Oh my Susan, how much I loved you! I thought I was going to die with happiness!

Raymond had grown during that month of my absence beyond recognition. He failed to recognise me, but was soon on my neck bubbling away. Yes! We were a happy picture.

Yet, I was without work once more and with most schools evacuated the prospects were not bright. My application letters remained all unanswered. I was furious and miserable. My bad temper would have disheartened anyone but my adorable companion. Despair? No, had I not a lovely child to fight for; had I not a wife who deserved all my care and perseverance?

Then in September 1940, the blitz against London began. It was terror and death every minute. Never did my courageous wife think of her life, never did she show a sign of fear. People were evacuating London: we could not move. I had no money to assure the safety of my dear ones.

People were losing their lives all around us and still Susan never complained, never lost her nerve, never frightened our Raymond. In my spare time I was working with the ARP as an ambulance driver. I was dealing daily with the horrible results of homes being bombed and the bodies of people scattered all around. Trying to save the lives of some of the people that were pulled out from their wrecked homes. Homes and families just like ours. And I was frightened all the time for the safety of my Susan and Raymond. But she was admirable my Susan, as admirable and brave as I expected her to be. She was an inspiration, a model.

Then in October 1940 I started work in a factory and I could then, oh what a relief, send Susan and Raymond to safety at Burnham Bucks. They left one evening and that splendid woman found billets in Burnham that very day.

I visited them once a week until February 1941, when I managed to get a job in a factory in Burnham itself. Then we found a bungalow to let and we lived happily once more. My work was new to me and it was tiring and dirty. I was not always in a very good mood. Often I made my Susan cry; but she knew I was never meaning to hurt her. She knew I loved her as before; she knew I admired her courage. She knew I appreciated all she was doing for us. And she was so effaced, so tender, so consoling. She soothed my feelings and helped me back to my self assurance.

In October 1941, I returned to teaching. I took a job Ealing, in London. This work suited me. I had regular hours and a clean work once more. It also meant respectability. It meant peace at home.

It was complete happiness once again. Susan was expecting another child. She was cheerful and conscious of her responsibilities. She knew we would both have to make sacrifices to help bringing two children up. As usual, she never complained and was waiting the new arrival with calm and confidence.

John was born on the 10th November 1941. The birth occurred in our home in London and poor Susan had a difficult time. John was a hefty boy and soon showed signs of an excellent constitution. Susan looked after him as affectionately as she had nursed Raymond and both children were very happy.

In February 1942, we took residence at Ealing Common as this was convenient to my work. We were having periods of calm, exempt from bombs. As I had not much money, I took a four-roomed flat. Unfortunately, the two basement rooms were *very damp and the kitchen in an awful state with water pouring straight through the skylight and the old windows.*

As usual, my sweet Susan did her best to make a comfortable home for us and although so many things were missing, she never complained. By now I had started taking evening classes in the county's schools and money was easier.

There was, of course, no room for luxury in our existence, but we had a relative comfort.

In June 1942 I went for work to Scotland and Susan and Raymond and baby John went stay with her sister, Monica, in Colchester.

This was when her mother had found the de Courtseys! And her aunt's name was Monica. That must make it easier for me to trace her, thought Marie.

I was very miserable about this separation, the object of which was to help make more money. Susan and I exchanged passionate letters which revealed how deeply in love we were with each other. We were longing for the day when I would come back.

Late in that year Raymond began to go to school. John was a funny baby who made me often laugh. But Raymond and John were in excellent health and looked much bigger that their actual age.

Time went in happiness. On the 25th April 1943 Edwin was born. Susan was very ill, but the doctors from our Hospital, where she was admitted, never told me how dangerous her condition was. Yet we nearly lost her then.

She recovered very well and quickly and that contributed into deceiving us into believing that nothing was wrong with her. Edwin was not as strong as Raymond and John, yet he was healthy and very happy. His mummy adored him. At his birth, John and Raymond had gone to a nursery in the country. I fetched them back by the end of May. We had a very happy day at home and as money was more plentiful we were making plans for the future.

Unfortunately by the end of the year the air raids began again, and Susan was expecting another child. Things were terribly difficult for my poor Susan. Three children to look after, shopping and queuing, a home to keep tidy, and in addition she had to contend with the tiredness of her condition and the depressing effect of the bombing. To make thing even worse, in June 1944 began the attacks by the flying bombs, and I was asked to return to the ARP.

We decided Susan and the children should be evacuated and they left by the end of June. I stayed to finish the school session, but when my holiday came, I stayed in town to take some private lessons.

What a fool I was, but how was I to know what a tragedy was to befall on us?

Susan and the children were sent to Bangor in Wales. The travel was exhausting in an overcrowded train. Susan was sick when she arrived. Then they walked her to find billets. They had finally to admit her into a nursing home. Raymond and John were taken to a nice family; Edwin was admitted to a baby's nursery.

At the beginning of August I spent four days in Bangor, and my heart broke to see that everything was not satisfactory. Still, nothing in Susan's condition was causing any worry, except, the poor soul, that she had very swollen ankles.

I came back to London. We wrote to each other almost every day. On the 6th September she wrote to say that she was expecting to have the child the day after. The 9th in the night, I received a telegram saying that my wife was very ill and my presence was required in Bangor. I took the first train which reached Bangor at 2.30 pm the next day, but my poor darling had died during the night. I was thunderstruck – my Susan dead, dead at 27! It was too cruel to be true!

Yes it was true and with our little Marie born a few hours before our Susan's death during that night of the 9th – 10th September. I had now four children who had suffered the hardest blow in life; the loss of their beloved mother.

Oh! What a mother they had lost! And they were so young! Raymond the eldest was only 5 years and 5 months old. Their mother who had given them their life had given her own, and would not be here to see them grow!

Oh! Poor Susan and criminal doctors who let her die through negligence and through not telling me that she should have abstained from having further children!

I took the children back to London in November 1944 and I was lucky enough in finding in Betty, a good girl, who would look after my children with devotion and affection.

Marie is now with us. 1945 is for us a new life. I do not know how it will all end. I hope that my Betty, whom I love tenderly, will be worthy of our attachment to her. One thing I know. I shall give her all my faithfulness and continue to make her happy. I shall expect my children, who are hers now, to love and cherish her for all she gives them.

But I want my children to remember that their mother's name should be constantly in their minds, for they owe her more than their lives; they owe her what she has made them and what she has given them. They owe her more, they owe her what she would have given them, had she survived, her love and protection for her whole existence.

In my heart, her place will stay hers for ever. Let my children never forget that I am not the only one to whom they owe what they are. Susan's name is blessed now, that must be written in golden letters in their hearts.

I want my Betty to know that in all this she is not forgotten, her name is as sacred in my heart as Susan's. I want my children to remember this too. And I bless them all in anticipation for all the love that they give and will give her, all the comfort in later years they will assure her.

This must be a happy family. It is and must remain united in the strongest bonds of parentage and brotherhood.

Remember my children that so long as you are all for one, and one for all, you have nothing to fear from life and our name will not perish. You owe to the memory of your darling mother who made no exception amongst you, to perpetuate the spirit of love which she taught us with her example.

Life is short and often cruel. It will lighten your burden if you know that through your good heart and your harmony you have continued to deserve the love of all of us. If I happen to close my eyes before I have fulfilled my mission to bring you up, remember and keep these words of mine alive in your hearts. When I have gone, there will still be your loving mummy Betty with you.

Love and respect her. I know she will carry the torch. Do not fail her; she will not fail you. As for me, I want all of you to give me this reward as to think of me as a father who loved you dearly and gave his life's thoughts to work for happiness.

I have made mistakes in my life but I never forgot for a minute what you are entitled to expect from me.

If I have succeeded in making you happy, if I have succeeded in giving you a good education, I shall thank the providence for having given a chance of being a good father. I thank you for being good children.

If I have been a good man and a good husband, I thank my Susan for having taught me how to be such, and my Betty for helping me to remain such. In my various misfortunes of heart I have been lucky to have met such wives.

That is why I want all our names to go on in a loving circle. Happiness is ours on this condition and so will be consolation for those of us that survive the loss of one of us, and Eternal Peace for any who may depart this Earth before the others.

Perhaps life may allow me to add another chapter to the journal one day. I hope I can and it with the word happiness.

10th September 1945

This is to be the first of the visits we, in our family, will pay annually to our mummy's resting place.

This year, I came with Raymond. All of you others are so young that it would not be fair to you to take you along and show you such a depressing place as a cemetery. But, my beloved ones, sooner or later you will come to learn that life is not eternal. Death is an awful law which calls on all of us. Yet, though I despise that teaching full of lies and inventions called religion, I do believe that the principle of life is eternal; that is to say that life continues after death. I do not profess to know how or in what form. But all intelligent human beings feel that it would be senseless to live such a short existence, in worries and grief's, if there was nothing beyond it.

Because it in our nature to thrust for an unknown ideal which may compensate for the too materialistic ways of our earthly life, rather than giving yourselves to a deceiving and interested religion, oh! my beloved ones, cultivate the love and respect of your dead.

Now, we have my Susan in that frightful unknown. Whether she is at rest or not, who knows? But you may be sure that she must feel happier to know you do not forget her. If I am wrong and life is a meaningless thing, you would have done nothing wrong in paying her your regular visits. But think of what these visits will mean to her and to you, my children, if, as I feel sure, she can see you, feel you near her.

Yes, as you grow, you will know more and more what it means to have lost her. Let her remain the link between you so that our family is never broken to pieces. She will protect you as much as she is allowed by that unknown law. The more she will be in your minds, the more you will be in hers. If you betray her memory, my children, you will loose a powerful key to Happiness.

Oh! She would forgive you if you were to forget your duty, but you would have lost that spirit of faith, that was unselfishness, which is the remedy against the shocking aridity of material life.

You see, if I were to wait to tell you these words, you may think, as all people do, that I am an old man speaking a language which is old fashioned. Darlings, generations follow generations and always the elder people are right because they have learned the science of life through experience of life.

As you grow and learn the wonderful lessons of science, you will get increasingly the feeling that you know more than the other fellow next door. But our knowledge compared in years of schooling and reading is negligible when faced to the unaccountable depths of the Secrets that surround us.

I, your father, who watches and supervises your studies, am bound, in any case, to know a lot more than you do. Trust my love for you, my children, my only aim is your happiness and this, I assure you, you will attain if you listen to my guidance.

If you have the hard luck to lose me as well, one day, never forget my words.

For, though the miserable nature that is ours is, you will often come into conflicts between yourselves and if you were to let your pride impair the patching up of your quarrels, you will feel alone in this inhospitable world.

Mummy is our link and in her we shall find the good spirit that will keep us united and happy. Think of her who has loved you so much and who gave her life for you. Let her memory be blessed in our hearts Forever.

And here are the thoughts that came to me over her tomb on this 10th September 1945.

Susan, my darling, we have no choice other than accepting the fate decided for each of us. Yours, so far, is the most tragic. But rest assured, my darling, that your memory will be present in our minds for ever. Whilst placing everyone under your protection we pray that you enjoy a perfect and happy peace, we pray that you may be forgiven whatever your actions that might have ever been considered a sin in your mortal life.

For us, your husband and children, we are proud of you and are determined to be worthy of your love. Darling, we all love you and shall never forget you, your smile and your golden heart.

Au Revoir, darling.

I have passed in front of the house in Bangor where she lived a few weeks before being admitted to the maternity home. I have seen again the scenery to which she had got used. Seen also other places we went to together and the people who had been so good for us: the Bishops, Matthews, Doyle, Hewett and families. Susan is not forgotten. Strangers do not forget her; will you my children? I am sure you won't.

1st November 1945

Raymond as he was on the 1st November 1945. Very healthy, tall and well developed, weight very much above his age. He is only 6 years and 6 months and looks easily 8. He has chestnut hair, grey eyes, lovely teeth. His hair has gone straight now. He is very proud and sensitive, is good hearted and very intelligent and *strong willed. I would like him to become a doctor, for I know he can do it; he likes studying and with his character he will not have any difficulty. This will be a career and a protection for him when he will be a young man and will have face the vicissitudes of life. He owes this to me. I want him to remember that I have placed a great responsibility on his young shoulders as he is my eldest and the one who is my natural lieutenant.*

There is John, nearly 4 on this 1st November 1945. He is very big and good looking. He has an adorable nature, very loving and very attached, but he is not very determined, as Raymond is. I want him to develop fighting qualities and not to become a dreamer. His looks will give him personality and success, but these will prove fallacious if he does not use his advantage to make first a career. Architect, I suggest. or civil engineer, but I would like him ,too, to be rather a doctor, surgeon or specialist. This would suit his good heart and charm. Perhaps Raymond and John could then work in partnership. He has fair hair, green eyes, very deep and smiling, long lashes and splendid teeth. Really a beautiful child.

Edwin is 2 years 6 months. Not so well developed as Raymond and John, but seems extraordinarily intelligent. Is very amusing and very attached. The passing away of Susan when he was only 16 months has impeded him from learning to speak early. Betty and I have spoiled him a little to compensate his loss. He may be later in taking a career. But then again, so long as it is a career, he may choose anything. He has got the stuff to make anything a success. I want him to remember he was the last youngest of his mother who simply adored him. I say the last youngest because she had no time to give this title to her little daughter Maria. So Edwin owes to her memory to be worthy of her and of all of us. He has very blue eyes, a charming smile, brow and forehead. Fair hair. He is a fool, a gymnast.

Marie is 1 and 2 months on this 1 November 1945.

Marie gasped and took a deep breath. Here she was as the baby that no one else had ever talked about.

She has been very weak but is doing better. She is a "Beauty" and she is the pleasantest and quietest baby I have ever known. She has been looked after by my cousin Francine from her birth up to her first year. We all adore her and the tragedy of her birth makes her the more beloved to us.

Was that true? If so, what had changed?

Because she may be spoiled either by us or those who like her she may think that life is easy so I say now, Marie take a career

What career without a university degree?

and be free: do not rely on anything or anybody. If you do, you will be hurt and the more so if you like those who betray your faith. You have only real friends in your family, and mainly me. Darling, away from offices and shop. Learn music as a professional concertist or take another career. I shall be there to guide you. She has blue eyes, long black lashes, fair curly hair, beautifully made ears and what a smile!

Marie was crying now. If her father had loved her so much, and was her main friend and protector, what happened to make him abandon these aims? She wasn't even allowed to have piano lessons like her brothers did, let alone go to university.

This last picture is the link between a past, which shall always be sacred to us, and the future which I hope to be happy. Remember my children that you are fortunate in having such a good mummy to replace your darling mother. Both have given you their love and so far you have deserved it. I hope you will always do.

10th September 1946

Raymond, John and Dad have paid their yearly visit of love and regret to their unforgettable Susan. Kneeling down on the stone they addressed her with this fervent promise and homage.

Mummy Susan darling, we come here to tell you that we love you and do not forget you. We know how much you loved us all; we know that you have sacrificed yourself to see us growing as you had wished; we know that you have given your life in your uncertaking to grow a happy family.

We shall never forget all this. We promise to follow the sacred example you have given us. We promise to love each other and be united in you; we promise to become the worthy children of an incomparable mother; we promise to give our daddy and mummy Betty our best love and respect.

We also promise to be all united and protect each other in our hour of trial. We are determined to come and see you every year at this date and ask you to give us your blessing and inspiration.

Please, mother dear, help us to follow the right path as you wish. Extend your blessing hand over all those we love. We then will do all we can to alleviate your trial in the other world and contribute to your eternal happiness. We hope then, when our time will have come, to join you and live, once more, and forever in your beloved company.

Darling Susan, we love you and shall always do.

Au Revoir

Ray was right about the visits to her grave. He and John must have been seven and four. Poor boys. It must have been hard for them, especially Ray who would have been old enough to understand what was going on. And that prayer to their Mummy, Marie was sure that it was what her father had said for them over the grave, but the boys must surely have been traumatised standing next to their deeply depressed and weeping father. Marie was quite shocked at her late understanding of what her brothers had endured on these graveside vigils.

10th September 1947

I wrote my usual journal on independent pages.

Marie searched but she did not find these pages, they must have been lost.

10th September 1948.

I neglected this little task, but did not fail to visit the tomb, but I went alone

With her tears flowing thick and fast Marie also came to the realisation as to why her birthdays had been so awful when she was a little girl. She had not remembered her father being so sad at her birthday time. She did not remember him going away or taking her brothers with him. She did not remember her brothers talking about what had happened in Wales when they had gone off with their dad. All she remembered were those little secret conversations that the children had had together. She must have been at least five to remember them but that all stopped when they left London.

10th September 1949

My Susan Darling
Five years have passed by. For you we can only pray in our hearts that you should be given Peace and Happiness in your Spiritual Life.

My adorable Susan, you know that I never forget to address this prayer to After Life daily. We are a miserable lot, we human beings, not to know what happens after our death and if there is anything that takes care of our soul.

Yet I feel sure that whatever the case you will manage to see and hear me. It is very hard to do what is right. I admit failure and mistakes but I can say with sincerity and without false modesty that I am a better man. I am sure, I owe to your spiritual influence, my darling, for life being eternal your spirit with us mingles with the present and the future.

Perfect material beings, as they all are, our children will only let themselves to be guided by material impressions. When comparing you to me, they will only grasp the fact that I am in the present and therefore deserve from them love and respect to me as the living one. They are too young to know. Too young to see that I have enjoyed the gift of material life longer than you, who have only had to accept the bitter sacrifice of death.

I implore our children to think again, for if you were sacred of their origins, you are also the Final Destiny who waits for them. We all belong to each other, and to forget it would be a crime.

You brought in my life, my Susan, the treasures of love and kindness. These I try to transmit to our children. When they

> know how much your spiritual happiness depends on their good behaviour and on the loving memory they strive to keep of you, they will do, I feel sure, their utmost to improve their ways and worship everything that was or is you. They are doing all right so far.
>
> Raymond is developing into a charming young man. Many of his features remind me of you, my Susan. Though he does not put his intellect to very good use yet, he has good material and shows it by developing into an excellent pianist, just as you were, my darling Susan. At ten he still looks older than his age. He was disappointed with his school results, but I hope he will do better next year.

"Why," Marie asked herself, "was he never interested in my school results?"

> John is a loveable little boy. He has his moments of temper, and at times, he has to defend himself. But he is all right and will be a fine and successful man, for in addition to his good manners, he is handsome and well built little boy. His looks still remind me of you. He is improving at school and he has even surprised me by suddenly developing talents at the piano.
>
> Edwin still remains my Baby. He is amusing and charming. He is the Baby who slept at my side that night when I was crying because of your death. He is alert and strong, though slightly built.
>
> Marie is the very reproduction of you now, my darling. Same hair, same eyes, same mouth, same ears, same chin, same nose. She is an extremely intelligent child, and a beauty, so everyone spoils her, except I her father, who wants her to develop into a useful member of the community. I think that she will be all right, especially when she has found that her old father loves her more than anyone will ever do.

Marie gasped again. Here it was, in his own hand. 'The very reproduction of you.' She had been a copy of her mother even as a little girl, just five when this was written. And what did that mean, 'everyone spoils her, except I her father'? Was he deliberately harder on me? But the very next sentence he says that 'her old father loves her more than anyone will ever do.'

Marie sat and sobbed for a full five minutes before she felt strong enough to carry on reading.

> I am about to start a new venture. I have been sometimes ill and discouraged since last year, that I want start working on my own, possibly exploiting a guest house. I shall need your Blessing and your Protection, my darling. Do not let me down, for my mission has not been achieved yet.
>
> I did not take the children because they are still too young to grasp the seriousness of the pilgrimage to your tomb. I shall try again next year. The day will come when they do not need to be reminded of this.
>
> Rest in Peace, my darling.

Ah! The boys did not go with him that time.

> Nothing will separate us. Pray for me as our children and I pray for you. Protect also Betty, who can no longer be considered a stranger to you. Love, Trust and Remembrance will also be the motto of the Beauville family.
> Your Jean-Pierre

Eastbourne 10ᵗʰ September 1953.

> Four more years have passed and the memory of our darling Susan is still alive. Circumstances have prevented me from continuing my Pilgrimage to Bangor.

He stopped going to visit her grave! That must have been when we children stopped talking about her amongst ourselves.

> First of all my nervous breakdown left me in a constant state of tension, and I had to fight any possible causes of morbidity. If I had to live long enough to see you all, my children and my beloved Betty, safe from the insecurity I felt that I had to relieve my mind from further sorrow.
>
> I know now I was right in this, for my mind is pacified. I have done what I know was my duty as a father and a loyal husband.
>
> My dear Children, it was very difficult keep the cult of our deceased Susan, as I had to give all my affection and care to the

admirable woman who took so well over the task of giving you, my children, the love and care of a mother. We have succeeded in making a happy family and I felt all the time we had in this our Susan's blessing.

Money was short and anxiety reigned in our household for many years, but Mummy Betty kept cheerful. She worked hard for all of us and today we fell that there are better times in store for all of us.

Betty watched your steps and saw to it that you grew sensible and good children. You owe her an eternal debt of gratitude. The continuity of the family as assured through her. And I can say today that I have known that I have been eternally lucky, more that I deserved to be. My love for Betty is therefore as everlasting as my love for Susan. I ask you all to forgive my failings and remember that I am always devoted to you.

10th September 1987

Years have flown by and I am now an old man of 81. My nervous breakdown and the overbearing occupation that, in the end, brought success changed the course of our lives. I could not find the courage to continue my pilgrimage to Bangor. And, yet, the memory of Susan has never died in my heart.

Life is never what we thought it would be for us. We all want so much out of it and our hopes are often disappointed. But let us be satisfied with our achievements. You, my children have not done too badly. You all have good children to continue our family line.

You are successful in your careers, and at least, you are not likely to go through the appalling difficulties that your parents have known.

Let you, therefore, be happy and try to remember that the key of success was the love that we, your parents have striven to develop towards our family and between each other of you. And then, when the time has come for me to depart this cruel world, I hope you will remember that my sins were my own way of survival, a survival that was needed in the pursuance of my mission.

> *My task is now done and I hope that I have deserved your forgiveness and your lasting love.*
>
> *Your mother Betty was generous to me. She knew, deep down, that I was good husband to her. She also knew that we needed each other's love to survive and fulfil our parental obligations when you were little children.*
>
> *She, too, had much to forgive me for, but she knew that I loved her as much as she loved me. She has now gone to join Susan, and together I am sure that they are looking down from heaven forever to watch over you all.*
>
> *So altogether let us carry on the good work and remain for ever a good family united by love and generosity.*
>
> *Jean-Pierre, your Dad.*

Marie cried and cried after reading her father's deepest thoughts of lost love and raising his family. The 'letters' within the journal were addressed to all of his children, so he did mean, at some future time for them to read them, even as he wrote them some fifty years ago!! Maria could hardly believe this emotional and loving journal was written by her father, her father who, while writing those words, had shown so very little of that love and emotion towards the very children he was writing about. By now Marie was completely shattered emotionally. For half an hour or so she sat in a daze. She read and re-read many of the entries, especially those describing herself as a baby and a growing child. But she did not want to wallow in the pain and disturbed memories of her childhood, and determined to continue with her task before she went to bed, so she strengthened herself and doggedly carried on to the final envelope.

It contained some letters, written faintly in pencil, but still legible, and clipped together with a red plastic paper clip. There was also a small bundle of Birth, Marriage and Death Certificates this time clipped together with a large rusting metal paper clip.

Marie recognised the hand writing in the letters immediately. It was her mother's. So her father had kept her letters, too, all these years.

The first one here had the first page missing, but it must have been written shortly after her mother's arrival in Bangor. So it would have been about

June/July 1944,

... you would bring the red jumper for Edwin as he has no proper coat and the sea breezes can be very chilly here at times.

I had to get a taxi from the station to here as my case was too heavy to carry to and from the bus. It cost me 8/6d, and to pay for it I sold the remainder of my clothing coupons not used to a fellow evacuee for 10/- and very glad she was of them.

You had better send me one book of coupons in case Mrs. B needs to get anything for the children or me. As for the matter of billeting etc. I will talk it over with you when I see you; also you yourself can see the billeting officer here; it may carry some weight.

I quite realise you're wanting me back home especially when you return to work; also I am not looking forward to a winter up here if it can possibly be avoided; and having to live in someone else's home with a new baby; still all this must wait; the main thing is to have my baby and get fit as soon as possible before returning. Must close now as it is dinner time.

Love & kisses
Susan
P.T.O.
Send me Dr. Smith's address in next letter.

Mrs. B. has received your letter and written in reply

The Evacuation officer has just been to see me and informs me that you are liable for a charge of 10/6d. per week for Edwin, payable in advance. As I said in my previous letter the matron at the home did not deal with money charges and left it to the Evacuation authorities. She (the Evac. Officer) is calling next Tuesday if by then I have the money (£1.1.0.), and calls each week after for it. She also said that out of the allowance allotted to Mrs. B. you are liable for 6/- for each child but this is dealt with in Ealing. As they have not contacted you about this perhaps you might make enquiries. We do not want a

> whole lot of arrears to be piling up as we have enough to worry
> about without that. You can of course appeal on the grounds of
> hardship and see what they say. It means already that a month
> @ 12/- per week is due for Raymond and John.

My mother obviously had had to account for every penny she spent, just like Mum had to do, thought Marie. But she was surprised at the high charges of billeting for evacuees. She had always assumed that the government had covered these costs.

> I wish these people would state all this at the beginning instead
> of telling you a whole lot of nonsense. That's the worst of all these
> W.V.S. and voluntary workers, they don't know half the details
> that are most essential.
>
> I feel so worried about it all that for two pins I would
> come home and have the baby in W. Middlesex, raids or no
> raids, rather than be harried with the thought that it is all too
> expensive.
>
> This pregnancy is causing far too much trouble; I didn't
> want it in the first place and I want it still less now. <u>Never, never
> again</u>; whatever it is, I do not want to live through another
> period like this. No wonder we get nervous and irritable with
> a constant sword of Damocles held over us. I would consent to
> anything rather than go through this again, and the worst is yet
> to come.
>
> Anyway, find out what's what and let me know.

~~~

Marie was shocked to read that her mother had not wanted her, and she was afraid of her oncoming labour. Written from the nursing home – ? August 1944 – Again the first page was missing.

> ...I have written to Mrs Compton, and will write to Dr. Smith
> when you send his address.
>
> What do you think about the news? We do not get any papers
> unless someone happens to bring one in – and no wireless, so
> I rather lose contact with the outside world. Perhaps it will be
> all finished by next month and we can come back to peace and
> quiet.

I hope you're managing all right for food, we could do with a bit more here; they certainly don't overfeed you, but Mrs. B. is bringing me some fruit and tomatoes on Sat. if she can get some.

Bye, bye for now darling; waiting for your next letter.

Love & kisses Susan

PS.

Some poor devil's going through it next door. Good job it isn't my first or I should be out of the window by now.

~~~

57 Brook Street
Bangor
14.8.44
JP Darling (She called him JP!)
Just a line before I go to the nursing home. I asked Mrs. B. about putting you up, and a friend in the street will gladly do so for a few days. Also we have been told that under the evacuation scheme your fare will be about £1. I'm leaving my things at no. 43; also Mrs. B. has promised to come and see me to do my personal washing as I don't think that the hospital does this. I also meant to tell you that the nurse is seeing to Edwin's immunisation. And that he is happy and content there. In fact the nurse said that she hadn't heard him cry yet! I'm, just going to say goodbye to Raymond and John & to tell them that you're coming soon. Bye bye darling.

Love & kisses
Susan

~~~

St. Katherine's Nursing Home
Bangor
17.8.44
J P Darling,
Have just received your letter of yesterday. I am looking forward to seeing you on the 25th or there abouts.

Perhaps the excitement will do the trick; as I am getting tired of waiting.

I am still by myself though in a different room which looks out over the promenade and boating pool, so it is not so shut in *as the others. I can also get up for a bit & and go and talk to the other patients. They are nearly all Londoners in here; some real East Enders; and a number of girls from the Forces who have been unlucky.*

I'm feeling better now, and a real good night last night and in consequence not so depressed and irritable.

(the rest of this letter is missing)

~~~

St. Katherines Nuring Home
Bangor
31.8.44
Dear J P,
I was not a great deal surprised to receive your letter of 28th inst.
I knew and felt that something would have to settled between us but unfortunately the lack of opportunity and lack of privacy prevented it.
You accuse me of arguing, rebelling and having a lack of understanding when for most of the time by your constant criticism you have made me nervous, uncertain of myself, afraid to say what I feel and think for fear of causing an upset; in fact given me an acute inferiority complex.

Marie, who had been ready to drop off, was suddenly wide awake. What had happened? Did they have a fight when he went to visit her?

You do not seem to realise what is at the bottom of all this. For three years I have been subjected to a great physical strain, plus the nervous stress of war, raids etc. For three years I have had nothing but babies, babies, babies, with no break, and no respite. I definitely did not want anymore children after Edwin. He is enough baby for me and I love him dearly, he is still so small. I have no affection for the one who is coming; it was forced upon me. It could have been avoided; and I resent bitterly the misery I have had to and still endure for something I had forced upon me. If as you say, there will be no more then that could have been done nine months ago; it would then not have been necessary to separate the children and I. You would not prevent it and would do nothing to help me abort it. Perhaps it was your

> *idea of a subtle revenge, knowing that in any case, the heavier burden came on my shoulders.*

Marie was stunned and horrified. Not only had Susan not wanted her, she had wanted to abort her too! It took her several minutes before she could return to the letter.

> *If you have to take precautions with other women (as I know you must do or let them do so) surely it is not asking too much if I, already the mother of 3 children, should have the same right. I know about the one you meet after night school. My friend saw you both together.*

When Marie understood the implications of these last sentences she was too horrified to continue for a while. No wonder her Mum felt she had to stay and look after us when she could have left, she thought. Then she continued reading...

> *It has made our sexual relations a nightmare to me instead of a pleasure; I cannot relax for thinking of possible consequences; and you seem to take it for granted as a mere physical convenience for you. I tell you frankly that I dread the resumption of sexual relations between us unless something can be done. It puts me in a state bordering on hysteria; and then you wonder I snap and am irritable and impatient.*
>
> *If it were not such a big problem for us it would not cause such a disturbance in our living; but we are both passionate by nature and where this relationship is upset, it reflects upon our ordinary domestic life.*
>
> *It is always there at the back of my mind, and whether I wish it or not it shows itself in a hundred different ways.*
>
> *You remember how it was at first when I gave myself gladly and with delight; indeed it was often I who invited; but when I found that all this was taken for granted; that you could get exactly the same satisfaction and gratification from others I was bitterly hurt; it put me on a level with any other casual encounter, by whom you might have had children without any intention of doing so, I felt degraded and humiliated.*
>
> *You know that I love the children; I do not regret having had*

> them; but it would have been better for them and for us to have
> penned them; not for them to be born when I was not in a fit
> state to care for them so I have felt them a burden instead of a
> pleasure.
>
> Again I repeat that I do not think that you realise just
> how great a strain it has been upon me; I am not complaining
> unjustly; you yourself will admit that I was just about all in
> before I came away.
>
> Even now, when I can have a rest, I worry myself sick
> about this and that; my vitality is sapped away: I have fits of
> depression when I don't care whether I live or die, or anything
> about the baby.
>
> Perhaps I shall feel different after it comes; but at the
> moment I can only think of the extra work, the extra money
> needed, the thousand and one problems to be faced when and if
> I come back. I am a coward as regards physical pain and though
> I try not to dwell on it, I dread the thought of the coming event.
> It haunts me night and day; I ask myself why, why?, when it is
> unnecessary; it seems so unfair one is caught like a rat in a trap
> and cannot break free.

She did not want me! She felt like a rat in a trap!

> I hope that I have been able to convey to you some of the things
> I've been feeling and thinking for so long, but have hesitated to
> express for fear of giving you offence. If only you will be a little
> kinder and understand that I am of a different temperament;
> that I am young and wish to enjoy a little play as well as work. I
> do not question your authority as head of the family; but I resent
> being ordered and shouted at as I were something you'd bought.
>
> You say that you might have had some rich girl and so on;
> the same might have been said for me; you were not the only one
> to sacrifice things. I have done my share; I have to all intents
> and purposes broken with my family (being just about on
> speaking terms).

Why? What happened there? Did her mother's family not like her father? Did she tell them of his infidelities and the bullying and shouting?

> *I have had no time or opportunity to cultivate friends; you practically forbid me any interests beyond the house and children. I do not see why it should be considered a crime in these days when there are so many things to interest one; you cannot exist with a horizon bounded by four walls. You have your work and your children come as a relaxation; they are my work and I need some relaxation to appreciate them.*

He was controlling with her too. His great love.

> *I, no more than you, would like to see the home broken up; for the children's sake if not our own; they need both father and mother; if you will help I will try and do as you ask; I cannot promise miracles; I can only do my best and no more.*

Of all the documents she had read and all the photographs she had seen, it was this letter that upset Maria the most. She read it again and again trying to absorb all the awful implications of what her mother had written. She must have been in such emotional pain when she wrote it. And there it was, written loud and clear. In just a few short sentences Marie's mother had described the way she had been forced to live, without friends, not being allowed out in any free time to enjoy her life, and living an enclosed life with only Marie's three little brothers for company, and without any adult conversation or stimulation.

Having known all her life that her birth had caused her mother's death, Marie now had the added pain of knowing just how much her mother had not wanted her, and how afraid she was of her oncoming delivery, not caring if she lived or died.

Her father's culpability in her mother's death was also plain to see. Why? Why? Why, had her father kept such a damning letter. Marie gave way to her pain in uncontrollable sobs.

After a while she decided that she could read no more. It was now past midnight, and she was physically and emotionally exhausted. She just had to rest. She could not even face reading the remainder of the letter, and she took herself off to bed to try to get some sleep before she would have to work it all out again. But peaceful and calming sleep would not come and as she lay down all Maria could think about was that letter. Her mother had got her fear and unhappiness off her chest, maybe she had been able to write in that letter, things that she would never have the courage to say to her husband face to face. But the shocking implications of what she had written were plain to see.

Firstly: she had wanted to abort Marie, which in 1944 was illegal and extremely dangerous. Her mother had not wanted more children, and this one was 'forced' upon her, almost as if she were the victim of rape! Marie also suspected that her mother had realised that her health and strength would be damaged, even if she had not realised that this was to be a fatal pregnancy.

Secondly: She knew that her husband was seeing one of his adult students after night school – Betty!

Thirdly: he had bullied and controlled Susan as much as he had both herself and Mum. And finally; her mother had contemplated leaving her father, possibly divorcing him, an action only very rarely considered in the 1940s.

Eventually Marie did manage to get a few hours of fitful sleep, and when she woke up again a few minutes after 5.30a.m. her immediate thoughts were of her three parents, and of everything that she had and learned about them the previous day. She went to the bathroom and looked at herself in the mirror. "Oh God!" she exclaimed out loud. "I look as though I have been crying all night".

She got herself up gradually and had a long bath to revive herself, thinking all the time of all the revelations that she had uncovered the day before. Was it was only yesterday that her dad had died? She had been so immersed in the past that she had almost forgotten that he was gone!

It was a beautiful day outside, sunny and cloudless with a light wind blowing, so after a small breakfast of a piece of toast and a hot cup of strong coffee, Marie went for short walk with her dog to clear her head. They crossed the road and then she let Misha off her lead to run down the twisty path on the cliff face to the lower promenade. After a ten minute walk Marie sat for a short while on a bench, her brain mindlessly watching the waves, which were sparkling in the early morning sunlight as they gently lapped the shore, whilst her emotions were still digesting her father's death, his journal and her mother's damming letter. The fresh air and the blue sea restored her somewhat and she walked slowly home with Misha trotting at her heels. She now felt that she had the strength to finish reading through the remainder of the letters and last of the documents that her father had left for her.

Sitting once more in her favourite armchair it was with trembling hands that Maria returned to her mother's fateful letter. She decided that it would unloose her resolve to not cry again if she were to start it from the beginning once more, so she started where she had left off the night before. It was most strange, almost as if it were a different letter. After getting all her pain and emotions off her chest, her mother had simply returned to everyday mundane matters.

> *When I saw the evacuation officer on Tuesday she told me that the charge for Edwin had been reduced to the minimum. That is 6/- per week. I paid her 28/-, which is one week here at 16/- and 2 weeks for him. Next Tuesday I shall pay £2.4.0. to bring us straight, with a week in hand. After that it will be 22/- per week for both of us until I go into hospital when only the 6/- per week is payable for him. I cannot give you an exact sum for the billets as it depends on when I go into hospital. I have about 12/6 left, having bought the wool and buttons for Edwin's suit, stamps etc. So will get the material for his coat when you send my money.*

Back again to accounting for every penny spent!

> *I have finished John's jacket, it looks very nice; I will give it to Mrs. B. when she comes. I've also seen about the hospital fees, but it is nothing to do with them, it concerns the Public Health authorities here, so will send them. Will close now as I have to go to bed and sleep if I can.*
>   *Love & kisses*
>   *Susan*

It took Marie back to read about hospital fees. She was so used to the NHS being totally free that she had forgotten that it only came into being after the War, in 1946. In 1944 everyone had to pay for doctors and hospitals. Had her mother considered the cost and not seen a doctor regularly during this dangerous pregnancy?

~~~

St Katherine's Nursing Home
7th September 1944
J – Darling
Thank you for your lovely letter. I'm so glad that you weren't too angry when you got mine, and that we have cleared the air between us. I must admit that after it had been posted, I wished that I hadn't sent it. But maybe it will result in things being better between us.

I hope that you will keep to your promise to stop seeing other women. I know that you feel that you must have sex regularly to sustain yourself, but please be patient and wait for me to get back to normal. <u>And use a condom in future</u>. I have been so ill this time, I don't think that I would survive another pregnancy.

I love you so much, and I can't wait for us all to be back at home together. After I have recovered from having this one, I am determined to come home, bombs or no bombs.

Love and kisses, Susan.

P.S. Here are some names to think about.

Girls: (please let it be a girl this time!) Marie or Maria, Rosemary, Anna (after your mother), Elizabeth.

Boys: Peter, Ivor (A nice Welsh name), Julian, David.

Here the letters ended, and Marie was gladdened to read of their reconciliation, but, of course, she knew what had happened next. She had been born two days later, and her mother had never recovered and had bled to death. Did her mother ever know that she had had her longed for daughter? Maria hoped that at least her mother had been able to hold her! And here I am now, she thought – Marie Susan, named after her mother's first choice and her for mother herself. She just felt so sad and empty.

There were no more letters so Marie went on to examine the final package, the collection of Birth and Marriage Certificates. She wondered if there was anything more she could possibly learn about her extraordinary family. So with renewed curiosity she unclipped them.

1. Susan's Birth Certificate – born 16th October 1916. In Walthamstow, London. Father – James Harrison, piano salesman. Mother – Edwina Harrison nee Marchant, housewife.

It only just dawned on her that she had never even known her mother's date of birth. That was sad too. And here were some details to try to trace her aunt Monica. She must have been younger than Susan (because the chest was always passed onto the eldest daughter), and she may well have been born in Walthamstow too,

2. Susan's Death Certificate – died 10th September 1944, St. Katherine's Nursing Home, Bangor Wales.

How pitifully young she had been. What a sad death and a waste of life!

3. Her parent's Marriage Certificate – Married in Maidenhead Registry Office on 16th September 1941. Jean-Pierre Beauville. 35. Divorced. Susan Harrison. 26. Single. Both of 23 High Street, Burnham, Buckinghamshire.

Hang on a moment, thought Marie. She was suddenly quite alert again. 16th September 1941 was eighteen months after Raymond was born!

She looked at the certificate again to make sure that she had seen right Yes! And the address shown was the same for both of them.

So Raymond was born before they were married, and they were living together 'in sin'. That must be why her mother's parents had 'all but disowned her'. But since they loved each other so, why had they waited so long to get married? Then Marie remembered the line at the beginning of her Dad's journal 'I was married and life had not been too kind to me.'

4. Divorce papers. A marriage between Jean-Pierre Beauville and Monique Dinan which had taken place in Paris on 1st January 1928 (His 22nd birthday!) was dissolved at the Wandsworth Court in London, 12th September 1941. Both parties admitted adultery.

Marie knew that he had been married in France, but she had always assumed that he had divorced there too. He had remained married for thirteen years. He had left France in 1936 so he must have lived with this Monique for at least seven of those years. And they had both had other lovers. Did she take a lover because of his infidelities? Had he always chased after other women? Marie wondered when he had started divorce proceedings and why it had taken so long to finalise. Perhaps it was because they were both Catholic?

So in the years between 1938 and 1942, in an era in England when any extra marital behaviour was highly frowned upon, and 'living in sin' was thought to be totally immoral, Susan was having an affair with a married man, had moved in with Marie's father, and then had had a baby! No wonder that her upright and very moral family had 'all but shunned her'. No wonder Susan had been allowed to take nothing from her family home except the old chest, which was hers by right and tradition!

And poor, proud, pompous Raymond; he's illegitimate – a bastard! How Marie laughed to herself, the first laugh she had had since her brothers had left yesterday morning. How he would have hated that years ago, but now, when so many children were born to couples who were not married but just living together, it did not matter at all. Marie hoped that he, too, would feel that way when he found out the truth of his birth.

Just wait until I tell them everything!" She exclaimed out loud. And she laughed again as she was imagining the look on Ray's face. Then she continued to look at the final three documents. Surely there could not possibly be any more surprises!

4. Betty's Birth Certificate (Short Version) – Elizabeth born 28th June 1921. Father Eric Ramsey. Mother Louisa Ramsey

5. Dad and Betty's Marriage Certificate – Jean-Pierre Beauville (Widower) married on 20th April 1945 to Elizabeth Ramsey (Spinster)

6. Betty's Death Certificate – Elizabeth Beauville died 7th July 1982. Eastbourne District General Hospital.

7. Then Marie opened the final piece of paper. It looked like a birth certificate, but not like any she had seen before It was her father's!

Jean-Pierre Beauville, born 1 Jan 1906 in Constantinople, Turkey, and registered at the British Embassy. Father – Phillippe Beauville, a Maltese/British subject, and a Shipping Agent in Constantinople. Mother – Anna Beauville, nee Giradet, nationality French.

This time Marie was totally bemused. After all the revelations that she had absorbed in the previous twenty-four hours, this new one was the most surprising. What did this final secret mean? Was her dad Turkish? Surely not. A British subject born of a Maltese father, Philippe Beauville, and a French mother Anna Beauville. What were they doing in Constantinople? That's now called Istanbul, isn't it? How did they get to Paris?

Marie was intrigued. This was a puzzle that she promised herself that she would follow up after her father's funeral. As far as Marie knew, his birth and babyhood had had no direct effect on the lives of her brothers and herself, so she put the birth certificate aside and went back to her contemplation of her parent's complicated love lives.

~~~

She thought how extraordinary were their lives for the period in which they all lived. Her father had been married three times in sixteen years. He lived with, and had a child with his second wife, her mother Susan, before his divorce from his first wife, Monique. His second wife lived with him and had a child with him before she could be married to him. He had an affair with his third wife, Betty, before the death of his second, and most cherished wife. He married his third wife only six months after the death of his second wife. And his third wife had had an affair with him, a married man with three children and went to live with him before they were married.

Marie shook my head. She had always thought that everyone lived such prim and proper lives until the wild times of the sixties! No wonder her father had not wanted her to follow the examples that they had all set!

What a story Marie would have to tell her brothers when she saw them again! But, she thought, life will not be empty for me now that my father has gone. Not only do I have my mother's sister, Monica Harrison to trace in Colchester, I also have the Thornton church with all the de Courtsey's to find. And now I have my father's final puzzle and adventure to follow. I will soon make plans to go to Istanbul with a big, fat notebook to see and record all that I can discover about the Beauville family in Turkey!

~~~

14th April 1994
Istanbul

I am only here in Istanbul for three days so I must make the most of my time. My appointment at the British Consulate is at 2pm, so I decide to spend my first morning in Istanbul playing the tourist! It is as warm as a summer's day at home and the very air smells of excitement and adventure. The buzz in the air is not of bees but the multilingual chattering voices of the crowds visiting the Hagia Sophia and the Blue Mosque. The fountain in the park that separates these two of the most famous buildings in Istanbul is pumping plumes of water high up into the air, children of many races and religions are playing together; and sparrows, ignoring all the human activity, are concentrating on their dust baths under the hedges.

All the visitors, tourists and local Turks, are mixing happily together, the Moslem women easily recognisable by their clothing, are mostly wearing long dark skirts or dresses, but it is their headscarves that make them stand out. Not to be denied as fashionable women, these scarves are a riot of bright colours and patterns, in shiny silk.

I go first to the Hagia Sophia, the immense Christian Church built an almost unbelievable fifteen hundred years ago, by the Roman Emperor Justinian. Having been converted to a mosque, with four minarets added when the Moslem Turks conquered the city in 1453, it is now a museum. Once inside the power and immensity of the building with its huge unsupported dome takes my breath away. As I wonder around the upper storey, I am struck by the stunningly beautiful Christian mosaics, which were revealed when thick plaster, put there by the conquering Turks, was removed from the walls. These mosaics sit comfortably alongside equally beautiful Arabic calligraphy declaring the Moslem love of Allah.

But the most poignant place for me is on the ground floor. At the centre of the back curved wall built to point, like all Christian churches, east towards Jerusalem, there is an empty space, where there would have been the Christian alter. And now, at a slightly odd looking angle just off centre, is the Moslem one, which points towards

Mecca. It makes this most holy area of the church/mosque look sad and out of balance.

Forty-five minutes later I thread my way through the teeming traffic, through the park, avoiding a drenching from the fountain when a gust of wind blows the plume of water in my direction, and I am standing outside the Blue Mosque. At the entrance porch as I slip my shoes into a plastic bag, now for the first time I am aware of being alone in Istanbul, and I hesitate to go in, feeling a bit awkward about entering a mosque for the first time in my life. I am startled as a hand touches my shoulder, and I turn quickly to see a young woman of about twenty dressed in smart navy shirt and trousers, and wearing a bright fuchsia pink headscarf.

"Excuse me lady. Is this your first visit?" She asks.

I nod my head.

"My name is Bikem" she continues, "and I am a student of French and English at the Galatasaray University in Istanbul. Are you English? Would you like me to show you the Mosque?"

"Thank you. You are very kind." I reply. "My name is Marie, and yes, I am English and this is my first visit to your beautiful city. I would be delighted if you would accompany me inside as I am not sure about what I should be wearing and how to be inside the Mosque."

"You are most welcome," she says. "First I will tell you that the real name of this mosque is the Sultanahmet, but it is popularly called the Blue Mosque because of the beautiful blue Isnik tiles which decorate all the walls. And do not worry about clothing. You already have your shoulders covered, and if you just put on your headscarf you will be good. Usually we do not object to the clothing of tourists unless they are too uncovered."

I soon see what she meant. As we walk inside I am struck immediately by the amazing patterns in different shades of blue, with whites and touches of other colours, which cover every wall surface. Once more I gasp at the size of another immense dome, this one so light and airy compared with that of the Hagia Sophia. It is magnificent, especially where the sunlight which floods into the building from the many windows high up in the dome, lights up many patches on the blue walls making them dazzle. Stunning! Every inch of the floor is covered with rich red carpeting, and most of the floor area is railed off, to be used only for men at prayer. Behind the rails there are many tourists, and many of them are wearing t-shirts and shorts. The barehanded foreign women stand out, but they seem to be accepted.

"Come this way," whispers Bikem, and she leads me through an inconspicuous doorway. We climb a steep and narrow stone stairway, and find myself on a balcony with small windows with screens, through which I can see everyone on the ground floor – visitors of both sexes behind the barrier, and men at silent prayer in their reserved area.

"Only the women and children are allowed up here, and they come when the Friday prayers are being led by the mullah." Bikem says. "The men down, and the women up here. I occasionally come here to pray, but I usually go to my local mosque."

We go back down and I spend a few more minutes gazing upwards at this amazing building. Outside, while I am putting my shoes back on, I thank Bikem.

"This has been very kind of you," I say. "Would you like to have a coffee with me."

"Yes please," she replies. "I have forty minutes before my next class, and I am very happy to do this. It is good for me to practise my English with you."

Over coffee taken outside in a busy street café I tell Bikem about the main purpose of my visit to Istanbul, and of my appointment at the British Consulate that afternoon.

"You will find that side of Istanbul very different from here," she says. "As soon as you cross the Galata Bridge you will see that that side of the city is more like Paris than Turkey. I would suggest that you take a taxi to Taksim Square, and then walk down Istiklal Caddesi, the main pedestrian road which used to be called the Grande Rue de Pera..."

"Now where have I heard that before?" my thoughts interrupt, but Bikem continues,

"...and you will see what I am talking about. I am sure that someone will show you the British Consulate which is just off the Istiklal Caddesi.

I hope that you find what you are looking for. Here, I will give you my telephone number." She writes down her name and a number on a sheet of paper in her note book, tears it out and gives it to me. "I must go now, but if you would like to meet me again while you are here, please call."

"I am only here for two more days, but if we both have time, I would be delighted to do so." I say. We smile at each other and I wave as she hurries off, soon to disappear into the crowds on the pavement.

After a light lunch I do as Bikem suggests, and take a taxi to Taksim Square. As we cross the Galata Bridge I look back out of the rear window and I see a view that looks vaguely familiar. In my memory I take away the modern bridge and replace it with an old wooden one and there it is! The view behind my father in his Bugatti. So he still lived here when he was a young man, and the photo has Grande Rue de Pera printed on the back! I get out of the taxi at Taksim Square and I find my way to the Consulate.

Even though Bikem told me of what to look out for, I am still surprised at the complete European look of all the buildings, and the numerous churches, which I find most surprising. If it were not for all the shop signs and the babble of Turkish conversations going on in the pedestrianised streets I would have, indeed, thought that I was in Paris. Even the old red streetcars, the only vehicles that still have the right of way here, look like traditional European trams.

I am quite nervous when I reach the British Consulate a few minutes before the appointed time, and I am waiting at Reception when a tall and good looking man in his mid-forties comes striding towards me.

"Good afternoon, Mrs Winton," he says in a slight Scottish accent. "I am Adrian Standish. Welcome to Istanbul, the most cosmopolitan city in Europe!" He does, indeed, make me feel very welcome, and we go straight to his office on the second floor, where he shows me to a comfortable leather arm chair.

"Thank you so much for searching your records for me," I say. "I do hope that you have been successful. It was a complete surprise to me to find my father's birth certificate. I never knew anything about his family coming from Istanbul, and I am completely staggered to see this part of the city looking just like home. Was this a European outpost or port in the past? The births certificate states that his father, my grandfather I suppose, was a shipping agent. Was his family in the shipping business?"

"Well, Mrs Winton," he says, "You have a lot of questions, and I hope that I will be able to answer them all, but first I have some good news for you. I have not only found records of your father's family and business in Istanbul, I have also found that you have a cousin still living here!"

"Wow! Have you really?" I am quite taken aback. I jump up and walk over to him, seated in his own armchair. "Who is it? Will I be able to meet this cousin?"

"Slow down and relax." Mr Standish chuckles. "All will be revealed in due course. First I want to tell you a little about the history of Istanbul, and the European community that lived here for hundreds of years until things changed in the 1920s, because it will help to explain how your family and hundreds of other Europeans lived for generations in the capital city of Turkey and remained separate Europeans."

"Really?" I ask. "Does that mean that I am not part Turkish?"

"Yes," he replied. "You are all British. I will explain that as I go along. I want to tell you about the uniqueness of the European community in Istanbul, or Constantinople as it was called until its name was officially changed in 1930.

The city was built by the Byzantine Greeks some six hundred years BC at the vital of crossroads of ancient trade routes between Europe and Asia, the Black Sea and the Mediterranean. This made it one of the most sought after and fought over cities in the Ancient World. The easiest land access to the Holy Lands and the Middle East was, and still is today, just across the Bosphorus, the narrow stretch of water which links Europe to Asia. The original city was built in the area where your hotel is, on a triangle of land, with sea on two sides and a long land wall on the third side. The narrow sea inlet on the northern side, called the Golden Horn, became a natural harbour."

"Yes," I said. "The Galata Bridge crosses the Golden Horn, doesn't it? And I could see the Bosphorus from there. So the city seems to be split into two!"

"You're right," replied Mr Standish. "It wasn't until the time of the first Christian Roman Emperor Constantine, who defeated the Byzantine Greeks in 320 A.D., and moved his capital to the city, that it was renamed Constantinople. Then for hundreds of years Constantinople was ruled over and fought over alternately by Greeks and Romans until they combined together to form the Byzantine or Eastern Roman Empire during which time, in 537A.D. the Christian basilica of St. Sophia, now called the Hagia Sophia, was built."

"Yes!" I interrupt. "I visited the Hagia Sophia this morning. "What a fantastic building. And to think that it was built so long ago. How did they do it? That was five hundred years before the Norman invasion of Britain, when we were living in little more than mud huts!"

"It is incredible, isn't it?" replies Mr Standish. "We all know what fantastic builders the Romans were, but what is really amazing is that it has survived, virtually intact, to this day!" He pauses to get back into his stride. "Back to Byzantines of old Constantinople. For nearly sixty years at the beginning of the 11th century Christian Crusaders took over, and in 1261 the Genoese helped the Byzantines to re-capture the city, then, and this is the important bit, the Genoese were rewarded by being allowed to build a walled city on the other side of the Golden Horn, as a trading colony, which they called Galata, and it was not long before they took complete control of all of the city's trade. In time Galata became a separate suburb of Constantinople, and it has been continuously populated by a mixture of Christian and Jewish Europeans. Initially there were Italians then Greeks and then increasingly, French, British, Armenians and many others."

"So, is that why all those grand buildings look European?" I asked, but I was still a bit puzzled. "Have Europeans been living in this part of Istanbul continuously since the 1200s? I can see that it unusual for Galata to have grown as a virtual foreign town within the Turkish capital city. It was more than just a community, wasn't it?"

"Yes, it does seem strange that the Byzantines allowed it, but that is just what did happen. By the 14th century the Ottoman Turks were attacking Constantinople and eventually defeated the last Byzantine Emperor in 1453. Although the Ottomans took over the Byzantine part of the capital city, the merchants living in Galata were still bringing huge amounts of wealth and profit to the city, and they were allowed to stay there; and, more importantly for them, they were allowed to keep alive their churches, their synagogues, their languages and their ways of life, they even were allowed to police themselves and make local laws. Another thing that made citizens of Galata unique was that every foreigner born here retained full citizenship and nationality of their forefathers, no one was registered as a Turkish national."

"So that must be why my father was registered as British, and had a full British passport," I speculate. I am really interested by now, I had almost forgotten why I had come to the Consulate, and I say, "I can see why the Ottomans allowed the traders continued existence considering the wealth they brought to the Sultans. It was to their advantage, but it is still strange to me that the Muslims would allow Christian/Jewish religions to remain and to flourish."

Mr Standish is well into his stride by now, and continues his little lecture. "You're right, it was all about money and taxes the European merchants were able to deliver. Unlike the European system of rulers and aristocrats inheriting power, whether they were intellectually suitable or not, the Ottoman Sultans created a system of power and control awarded only to those who proved themselves capable. Apart from the Sultan himself all civil and military leaders were hand-picked and trained as young boys. These boys of promise were usually chosen from poor Christian families or captured slaves, and raised as Muslims. In this way the Sultans avoided creating a Turkish aristocracy which might seek to rival or overturn the Sultans, and in the process they created servants whose only loyalties were to them.

So the European merchants living in Galata were not just tolerated for the wealth they created, but were actually welcomed as forming a vital part of this polyglot and multicultural city.

During the next hundred years or so, the richest merchants began moving outside the overcrowded wall encircled town, and started to build their homes among the vineyards on the hills above Galata, and this area became known as Pera. Here, as well as foreign Embassies, they built great mansions and gardens along what was to become the main street of Pera, the pedestrian area through which you walked today. Here let me show you and ancient map of Constantinople, or Constantinopolis as it was called then."

He gets up, walks over to his bookshelf, and pulls down a huge book, and lays it open on his desk. I stand up and come to look at the map which is reprinted on the first page. Its original was drawn in 1480, and to me it looks like a cross between a picture and a map. It is very interesting and very beautiful. Against a lovely background of the bright blue swirling waters of the Bospherous it shows, in picture form, the old walled city of Constantinople, with the Hagia Sophia dominating it. It also shows the inlet later called the Golden Horn, and the other side is shown the smaller walled city of Galata, with the Galata tower dominant. The garden area of Pera, drawn with little trees and plants, is shown to the north of Galata, and the main land of Asia on the other side of the Bospherous is shown as Turquia, with houses and mosques.

"That is so beautiful, as well as interesting." I say.

"I'm glad that you like it. It's one of my favourites too," says Mr Standish.

"But I still don't fully understand why the Turks, having conquered the city allowed the Europeans to remain. Surely they could have taken over the trading. After the Crusades they must have hated all Christians. Why didn't they want the Galata area as well the main part of Constantinople?"

"As I said, it was the wealth and taxes brought in by trade and shipping, of which the Europeans had full control. It was convenient to let the Europeans continue to dominate trade. The Sultan now relied entirely on this source of income. Their taxes to the Sultan kept him in wives, luxuries, and allowed him to continue warfare, and slaving into the rest of the Mediterranean and North Africa. Whilst the rest of Turkey was mostly populated by uneducated peasant farmers and fishermen, this European enclave produced almost all of the entire wealth of the country. And that's where the Beauvilles come into the story," he ended dramatically."

"Ah ha!" I exclaim. "My grandfather the shipping agent. Was he just a shore bound agent or did he own ships? Do you have records of where the Beauvilles came from, how long they lived here, and what sort of shipping business they had?"

"Yes. O.K. I'll just skip through the Crimean War when the British and the French helped to defend the Turks from Russian aggression, which the British did mainly to safeguard communications to their Indian Empire and the Far East. That was followed by the First World War, when this time the Turks sided with the Russians against the British and French. Not long after the First World War the Sultan was displaced, and the war hero Ataturk, their first president, brought modern Turkey into being. Despite all these volcanic changes in Turkey, and wartime restrictions placed on what became enemy citizens, the European community continued to thrive and prosper."

I try to stop the flow by butting in. "The Beauvilles," I say, "you were going to tell me about them."

"Oh, yes," he says. "Sorry, when I get onto my hobby horse about the history of Turkey I sometimes get quite carried away!"

"Sometimes!" I mumble under my breath.

"Sorry!" he says again. He puts on a pair of John Lennon old fashioned styled glasses that detract from his handsome looks and make him look a real geek, and I have to suppress my inner laughter.

"Now let me look at these notes. Before the British Embassy moved to the new Turkish capital, Ankara in the 1920s, this building was the Embassy, and everything about British people living in Istanbul was recorded here. Our records show a Johannes Beauville coming to Constantinople as Vice Consul for Malta in 1729. As a Maltese he was a British subject, and so all his family, births, marriages and deaths were registered here, and it was his great, great grandson Angelo who started the shipping business in the mid 1800s. Angelo Beauville was born on 2nd March 1848, and he had four sons: Philippe, your grandfather born 12th December 1870 and died on 2nd March 1924. Georges, born 22nd May 1872. Dominique born 28th September 1873, and Gerard born 13th April 1879. I don't have their deaths registered, so they must have left Istanbul. Philippe had two sons, another

Georges born on 23rd August 1903, who died on10th June 1954, and your father Jean-Pierre, born on 1st January 1906. I have no record of your father's death, but your uncle Georges died here in Istanbul on 22nd March 1952. He had one daughter, Alina Beauville who was born on 10th August 1933. In 1951 she married a Pietro Marino, an Italian citizen of Istanbul. She is now widowed, and she still lives in Istanbul today."

"Wow!" I gasp. I am more excited than I have been since I opened my chest seven months ago. "I can't take it all in. All those names and dates, they are all part of my family. Are you sure that Alina is my cousin? Do you have her address? Can I get in touch with her?"

"Slow down Mrs Winton," says Mr, Standish. "I have printed out all the information we have recorded here at the British Consulate, on the Beauville family for you. And, yes, I do know that Alina Marino is your cousin, because she came to see me two years ago with her father's birth certificate, and details of his brother, your father. She too wanted to trace the same information that I have given you. At the time she thought that she was the only one left of the Beauville family, and she left me her details in case I came across any other family notes! Shall I ring her for you?"

So there we have it, and after all the arrangements are made, and I have hugged and thanked a surprised Mr Standish, he calls for a taxi to take me to an address in the Beyoglu area of Istanbul where my newly found cousin Alina has an apartment.

The taxi takes me past the famous Galata tower, through the winding streets of the lower Galata area, and drops me off at the top of an alleyway with steps winding downwards. The driver then points to an old apartment block halfway down. I am a bit unsure of myself and hesitant as I pay him and walk down the steps, but as I get closer the apartment block I see a lady in front of it waving to me.

I hurry down. "Hello," I say. "Are you Alina Marino?" She smiles and says, "Yes."

"I am Marie Winton, and I think that we are cousins!"

I am meeting a very small and neat woman in her sixties, with a shock of dark hair massed around a face that still shows the beauty she must have been as a younger woman. She comes forward and gives me a hug, and says in perfect English, albeit with a strange accent that I cannot quite recognise,

"Yes, it seems that we are indeed cousins, and I am so happy to meet you. Please come with me to my apartment and we can talk about our families."

I follow her, wondering about her excellent use of English. My father spoke only French in his family, yet Alina's father and mine were brothers. We turn into the apartment building, take an aging and rattling open cage lift up to the third floor, where we go through an ornate door straight into her sitting room. I gasp. "Wow! What a fabulous view!" I cry. "That must be the Bospherous."

The water is as blue as any sea I've ever seen, and it is bustling with water traffic. I can see a container ship and a huge cruise liner that are about to pass one another, and a dozen or so smaller boats; pleasure boats, tourist boats and local fishing boats. I can also see two ferry boats that are weaving through all the north-south water traffic, on their routes across the Bospherous from Europe to Asia and vice-versa.

"This is just wonderful!" I exclaim again. "I'm sure that if I lived here I would sit at this window all day long!"

"You are right," says Alina. "I think that is wonderful too! And it is the main reason why I continue to live in this old building, with its bad plumbing and cracking walls, but, none of the modern apartments that I could afford have such a view. If you sit there by the window I will make us both a cup of tea. Would you like that?"

"Oh! Yes please," I say, thinking again about the 'Englishness" of my new found cousin.

There are rows of apartment buildings built on the hill between Alina's one and the bank of the Bospherous, but their roofs are below her window and her view is unobstructed. When I can tear myself away from that view, I look around the room. It is a large sitting/dining room, and it is stuffed full of Victoriana. The whole of one wall has floor to ceiling book shelves stuffed full of old and dusty tomes. Amongst the lumpy Victorian sofas and high backed leather armchairs I spot a beautiful antique pier cabinet, almost the twin of my father's one, which is veneered in beautifully patterned rosewood. The display window is shaped in what I can only describe as a fat violin! It also has two fine bronze figures on either side. Next to the pier cabinet there is a similarly beautiful and matching writing desk, on top of which rests an old and battered violin case. I wonder how it can be that the two brothers, her father and mine, have almost identical possessions? Did my father try to re-create his Turkish home in England?

Five minutes later Alina comes back into the room and puts a tray of English plates, cups and saucers, a teapot and a Victoria sponge cake down on the small table by the window. She sits down and as she starts to pour the tea she says, "I wonder where I should begin?"

"Well," I say, "the first thing that I must ask you is how come you speak such good English? I was expecting to have to talk to you in my rusty French, or even struggle in Italian."

She laughs, and she looks very pretty as she blushes as little. "Thank you for saying that, but you must remember that I grew up in a polyglot society. It is now fully Turkish in Pera and Galata, but when I was young we still had our separate ways. Your grandmother was French and my father and yours were brought up in a French-speaking home, and they went to French boys only schools."

"My grandmother lived with us for a while when I was little," I interrupt. "It was from her that I learnt my French."

"Well," Alina continues. "My father married an English speaking Greek girl, we spoke English at home and I went to an English girl's school. Then I met and married my husband who came from an Italian family. He spoke very little English and I spoke very little Italian, and we spent the fifty-five years we had together, speaking in French to each other."

"My Goodness!" I exclaim, "was everyone here multi-lingual? How did the society work?"

"The European families here was mostly English, French, Italian and Greek, although there were, of course, many other nationalities here including a large Armenian community. From the beginning of the 20th century it started to change when many wealthy Turks began to move here and send their children to European schools. When our fathers were growing up it was still a closed society, and the only way men and women were able to meet properly was at social gatherings. These were usually held, in turn, at the various Embassies, as they were then, until they were moved to Ankara. All the foreign Embassies acted almost like social clubs, they often held evening dances where young men and unmarried girls could mix, and be easily supervised or chaperoned. Not only was it a Victorian society, but they were also influenced by the Muslim culture which surrounded us."

"Maybe," I muse, "that could explain some of the reasons why my father did not trust his wives or me to be free to mix with men."

Alina looks at me curiously, but does not comment. Instead she talks about our two fathers again. "My father was always talking about his brother. They were such great friends and companions when they were young, and my father missed his brother so much when Uncle Jean-Pierre left Istanbul. Did you know that they went to school together in Constanta in Romania?"

"Romania!" I do not think that I could more surprised today, but I was wrong. "What were they doing there?" I ask.

"It was during the First World War when things were a little uncomfortable here for English and French nationals, because the Turks were on the German side. To make things easier the boys were sent away to a Romanian boarding school from 1915 to 1919. It was there that they both learned to play the violin."

"I saw the old violin case over there. Was that your father's? My father was a very good player. I still have his violin too. I can hardly take in everything that I am finding out about my father. It is so sad that he never shared any of this with us. I have only known and seen pictures of him as a fully grown man. And here you are with a whole different background for him than the one I thought I knew."

"Well where shall I begin?" she asks, and passes to me two old, faded sepia photographs. "Here are some close-up pictures of our two fathers together when they were children and young men. My father,

Georges, was more than two years older than yours, and, you may not know, they had different mothers. So they were, in fact half brothers!"

I am studying the photographs that Alina had handed me, trying to imagine my stern father laughing and playing as a boy and a young man. "These are wonderful!" I exclaim. "It's almost too much for me. Yesterday there was only my father and his mother and sister. Now suddenly there are uncles, aunts and cousins. It's hard for me to look at these pictures. Hard and wonderful at the same time. He looks so handsome. They were both so handsome, weren't they? How old were they in this second photo? And how come that they were half-brothers? I think that I have a hundred questions to ask you, and they all want to come out at once! I think the first one is – can I please have a copy of these photographs?" I stop babbling for a moment and I am looking at a photo of the two brothers. They are both standing in front of the Bugatti, and another vintage car that I don't recognise, at the old Galata Bridge. I was right. This is where that strange picture of my father was taken – the only picture of Constantinople and his boyhood that he kept!

I return my attention to Alina who is talking. "They were eighteen and twenty, and of course you can have copies. I have several more of the family which you may like to have too. Tomorrow we will take them to a friend of mine who has a photograph shop and ask him to make copies for you." says Alina. "For today we have plenty of time. Let's take it easy, have our tea, and ask our questions of each other one by one."

"All those names of uncles, aunts and cousins that Mr Standish told me about are confusing to me," I confess. "Have you ever drawn up a family tree?"

"Yes, I have," says Alina, and I will copy it out for you."

"How far back have you gone?" I ask. "Do you know anything about the first Beauville who came to Istanbul? Mr Standish said that he came here as a Vice Consul for Malta, let me see," I look at the print-out that he gave me, "1729. Do you know anything about him?"

"All I know, "says Alina," is what my father told me, and he said that Johannes Beauville was descended from one of the Knights of St. John in Malta."

"Really! A Knight of St. John. That's interesting." This visit to Istanbul seems to be revealing things to me about my family background almost minute by minute! "They were Crusaders weren't they? Knights Templar? Do you know any more about him?"

"No," replies Alina. "My father had a badge, a family crest, but I have never tried to find anything more about him. The family story of our parents, uncles and grandparents were always enough for me to try to follow.'

So for the next three and a half hours we chat together swapping family stories, comparing notes, and looking at old photographs, the family tree and the crest. Mysteries are unravelled and explained, such as my father's anger when we made unexpected noises when we were children. I learn from Alina that our grandfather died of a heart attack at the age of 54, and that her own father, too, died of a heart attack at the even earlier age of 51.

"I remember a time when I was seven or eight years old," I say, "my father was crying and crying, and Mum just said that someone had died. I didn't know who it was, but I was so upset to see my father cry that I went to school crying too. It must have been your father that had died. Dad never said anything more, but there must have been some continued contact between him and Istanbul. Was it you that wrote to him?"

"I think I did," replies Alina, "but I had never met him, he did not mean anything to me, so when I got no reply I wrote no more."

I reflect. "Your father's death must have been a shock to him too." I say. "No wonder dad shouted at us when we four children were playing noisily, and would always say that we were going to give him a heart attack. What with his depression he must have been terrified that he would also have a heart attack in his fifties!"

We continue chatting and I learn that her father and mine were always the best of friends, even though they were only half brothers. George's mother died when he was just a baby, and my grandfather married my grandmother Anna, who went on to have my father and Aunt Mariette. The three children grew up as a family, and when the two boys returned from Romania they completed school in Istanbul and then went into the family shipping business with their father, uncles and cousins.

"Alina, I ask. "Do you know about the family business, and what happened to it?"

"Well, this is the thing," she replies. "It all happened before I was born, but my father told me all about it, and the devastating shock to everyone."

"What shock. What happened?" I am on the edge of my seat by now.

"Well, this is the thing," she says again. I soon learn that it is her favourite expression. "Our great grandfather Angelo started his trading company way back in 1870 when he was just twenty-two years old. He had money from his father and with it he bought two small boats. To begin with he began his trading with oils, fruit, silks, that sort of thing, to Greek and Turkish ports as far as Cyprus in the Mediterranean, and then as his sons grew older and the business increased, he bought bigger boats which traded into the Black Sea to Constanta in Romania and Odessa in Russia. Then by the time my father was born they sold all their boats and put all their money in buying two large trading ships. It was at the time when the Bolsheviks were just rising in Russia, and the so called White Russians were leaving. Our grandfather and his brothers bought these two ships at a good price from a Russian company whose owners were selling up."

"My father has never told us any of this," I say, "and neither did my grandmother or my aunt. I wonder why? Do you know why they kept it a secret?" What was the devastating shock? I ask Alina.

"Well, their shipping business, Beauville and Sons, soon became very busy, and the family became very wealthy. We were one of the wealthiest families in Istanbul. They expanded their trade into all sorts of goods and were trading at all the main ports all around the Black Sea, and in the Eastern Mediterranean. They traded in Italy, Turkey, Greece, Lebanon, and as far as Alexandria in North Africa. It was arranged that the two ships would always meet and cross routes in Istanbul, so there was always one in the Mediterranean, and one in the Black Sea. To get experience in the business our fathers would often travel together in one or other of the ships to learn about the ways of all our trading ports.

Then the first of the tragedies happened, in 1927. Our grandfather, who was the head of the company, died suddenly of his heart attack. Our fathers were only twenty and eighteen, and they had to struggle with their uncles and cousins to keep their place in the company. Then the following year, in 1928, when one of the ships was docked in Odessa, the Russians made excuses to keep it there, and before anyone from the company knew what was happening and could recall the second ship, that docked there too. And then, this is the thing, the Bolsheviks, who had come to power with Lenin killing off the Tzar and his family in 1917, confiscated both ships saying that they were Russian ships, and that they had been stolen from the Russian people. There was nothing to be done. The British Embassy tried to help, nothing! And everything was lost!"

"Wow!" I exclaim. "Everything? Did they lose everything? Oh my goodness! What happened to Beauville and Sons?"

"Remember all this happened five years before I was born. All I know of it is what my father told me," she says. "He was the only one who remained here in Istanbul. After a couple years of struggling to get their ships back or compensation from the Russians, all the rest of the family, one by one, sold off all their remaining assets and left Istanbul forever. Your father, and his mother and sister, were the first to go, and because they were French speaking they went to Paris."

"Do you know what happened to them there?" I ask. "All I know is that he came to England from Paris in the late thirties. He must have kept some contact with his brother. You must have found our address in Eastbourne to let him know about your father."

"I really don't know much more about him, or how he lived after he left Istanbul, although there was some talk of a hotel in Paris. I believe that my father kept in touch with him a little. And I do believe I saw one or two envelopes with English stamps on them when I was a child, but I can't remember anything more of your father except that he was my Uncle Jean-Pierre, and he lived in England. Then my father died just after I was married when I was twenty-one, and, as I said, I never heard of my uncle again." She finished with a flourish, "Now, all of a sudden, here you are! It is quite wonderful to see you and to feel that I have family again."

"Wow!" I say again. "So my father went from being very wealthy, and a partner in the most respected firm in Istanbul, to being utterly downcast and virtually penniless. He and his mother and sister must have used what was left of their fortune when they sold up to buy the hotel in Paris. Then that failed too! It must have been so hard for him, having been so rich to suddenly have to struggle for every penny."

I do not continue with this line of conversation, and I change tack. "Do you have any children?" I ask.

Alina shakes her head sadly. "No." she says. "God did not bless us in that way, but we were very happy together always, until my Pietro died two years ago."

I am now curious about the rest of the family, and after a pause when I can see that Alina is thinking of her husband, I ask, "do you know where the rest of the family, the uncles and their children went?" I ask.

She is animated again, and the smile returns to her face. "I have very little details. Like knowing that your father went to France and then England, I know that Uncle Georges and Uncle Dominique went to Italy, and I believe that Uncle Gerard went to live in Colombia in South America. But I have no other information."

We are quite exhausted by then, and Alina makes us a light meal which we eat together quietly talking about her life in Istanbul and mine in England. When it is time for me to leave Alina calls for a taxi and we make arrangements to meet up again for lunch the next day.

It is dark by the time I take the taxi back to my hotel, my head is buzzing with all the excitement of the last few hours. I get out of the taxi at the Hagia Sophia. The air is soft and warm after the heat of the day, and the whole area is throbbing with people criss-crossing the road and the park between Hagia Sophia and the Sultanahrmet, which is gloriously lit from below by flood lights and from above by a full moon which brightens up the sky and stars. Seagulls wheeling all around the Mosque are performing a sweeping display between the six fluted, pencil shaped minarets, which point high into the night sky, their wings catching the light both from the flood lights below and the moon above.

As I leave the Mosque I cross the road once more, and make my way past an open restaurant with a raised platform at the back. Musicians are playing Turkish traditional music, and two men in long flowing white skirts and high pointed hats are performing a whirling dervish dance. They start of at a steady pace but as the rhythm of the music goes faster and faster they whirl around on the spot at great speed, their skirts billowing out fully, their feet a blur of movement. Just when I think that they are going to fly off the platform they slow down to a gradual stop. All the diners clap and I, who have been peeping over the wall to enjoy the show, move off towards my hotel.

I hear more music and I re-cross the road. I find myself looking down on another open restaurant in a sunken area below the Blue Mosque. I go down the blue tiled steps to walk along side it. Here the tables are close to the ground and all the diners are sitting on large plumped cushions. The entertainment here is a handsome man singing and his partner is performing a belly dance. This is certainly the high spot area for tourists! The real Turkish Delight!

Before I get much further towards the hotel, in spite of the lateness of the evening, I am stopped by one of several men touting for buyers to come to their carpet shop. "Beautiful lady, just to come this way. I have beautiful carpets to show you. You are English? I have brother in England"

I wave him away and say "No thank you." I have only been in Istanbul for less than twenty-four hours, and I could already have bought enough carpets to cover a football pitch! But good luck to them they work hard and their shops seem to be open from early morning to late at night to entice any tourist with a deep pocket!

At last I reach the peace and quiet of my hotel room where I start to relax and mull over everything that has happened today. It has been a day such as I have never spent before!

When I wake up the next morning I realise that my time in Istanbul is too short. I look out of my bedroom window on to the blue waters of the mouth of the Bospherous and the Sea of Marmara, and I wish that I had planned to be here a few days longer. Back in England when I made my appointment with Mr Standish at the British Consulate, I thought that a three day trip to Istanbul would be enough to consult with him and to see the sights, but finding Alina has changed all that. Now I find that I have only a day and a half left. The next morning I telephone Bikem and tell her that I have found a cousin. Bikem is very happy for me and says that she is still pleased to have met me. Then I go to meet Alina again. I meet her in what she still calls the Grande Rue, in front of the Church of St. Anthony of Padua, Istanbul's largest Catholic Church.

We kiss and hug in greeting, and I feel already that she is an established part of my life, and I know already that I am going to miss her when I return to England.

"My English girls' school was just near here, when I was a little girl," she says, "and we used to come here to this church to pray every day."

"It is a fine building, and those mosaics over the front doorway are beautiful. Is it still well attended?" I ask. "Are there still many Christian Churches here?"

"Oh, yes," she replies. "I still go every Sunday, and the church is almost full for the 10 o'clock mass. Although the whole city is Turkish now, the population is still very mixed, and all the churches are well attended. This one, as you know, is Catholic, but there are protestant, Greek Orthodox, and Armenian ones too."

We walk through a side street where Alina seems to know everyone, passers-by as well as shop owners, and we stop to have a coffee and a delicious pastry in her favourite pastry shop. She makes a great show of introducing me as 'family from England'. Even though she says that she does not like the Turks, and she never goes to the Turkish side of the city, she is friendly and chatters to them all in fluent Turkish.

After coffee, Alina takes me to her friend the photographer. He says that he would be pleased to make copies Alina's photographs, but that it will take a few days. Alina shrugs and says that she will post them on to me, then she tells me that she is taking me somewhere special. We climb into a taxi and she gives the driver directions. He drops us off at a large gate that looks like the entrance to a high walled park, and when we go through I see at once that it is a cemetery.

"This is the old Catholic cemetery of Istanbul, and this is where you will find all our ancestors," she says. It is a cemetery, unlike any I have seen in England. Most of the tombs are large and above ground, and many of them have statues of angels and such like on top. After weaving through the pathways we reach the section wherein our family are interred.

"Here!" she says triumphantly. "This is the Beauville plot." It is huge, and on top lies an almost life-size white marble model of a woman in repose. It is beautiful!

"Oh my goodness!" I exclaim. My speech fails me as I look closer at the tomb. All around the base are inscribed Beauville names and dates of husbands, wives and children all descending from the first Beauville Johannes who arrived from Malta over two hundred years ago. When I get my voice back I turn to Alina with tears in my eyes.

"Alina," I say. "Thank you for bringing me here. I did not know that I had such a family. And what a beautiful model, wherever did it come from?"

"Well, here's the thing," says Alina, using her pet phrase again. "This marble carving was ordered from Rome by the British Embassy, as it was then, for the British military section here, but when it arrived they decided that it was not suitable. This happened only a few months after our grandfather Philippe died of that heart attack. Remember the family were very wealthy then, and they offered to buy her from the Embassy. And here she is!

Now look at this tomb," says Alina, and she points to another large tomb, not so finely decorated, which lies opposite the Beauville tomb. "What do you see?"

I look at it closely. "Marino. That's your married name isn't it? Is this your husband's family tomb? That's strange that it should be so near ours isn't it?"

Alina is smiling broadly now. "This is where I met my husband. Romantic isn't it?" she laughs." We were both of us attending our family plot so many years ago, and bang! We fell in love!" The smile fades, and now she looks sad. "And now he is here and I come to talk to him when I am lonely." She bends down a picks a dead flower from the tomb, and I see the glimmer of a tear in her eyes. I take her in my arms and we have a long hug.

We are very quiet as we leave the cemetery. I have almost had an overload of excitement, experiences and emotion. We take a taxi back to Alina's apartment, where she makes us a fine lunch of her favourite Turkish food. For the rest of the day we swap personal details of addresses and phone numbers etc. and talk quietly of our two fathers, and how sad it was that they never met again after my father left Istanbul, or that our two families did not get a chance to know each other years ago.

When I leave at the end of the evening it is with many thanks and promises that not only will I return soon, but that I will bring my own family with me next time. We have a final hug and kiss and I am away!

As I am packing my suitcase I realise that I have not been able to visit any of the other highlights of Istanbul; the Topkapi Palace, the Archaeological Museum, the Grand Bazaar, the Spice Market, the Cistern and the Dolmabahce Palace. They were all on my list, but that got swept aside as soon as I learned of Alina.

So here I am, on the aeroplane going home with yet another explosive story to tell my family, and I resolve to bring them with me next time, not only to meet Alina, but to see everything else too! I really had no idea of what lay in store for me, and my family at home, when I first took off for Istanbul.

The opening of my chest certainly changed my life forever!

Afterword

June 1994

It is now seven months since my father's funeral, and I have, at last, got over the worst of the emotional shocks the contents which my chest had delivered, and, all the happy excitements of my discoveries in Istanbul After I came back buzzing with excitement of discovering my father's rather exotic roots, I decided to try to find my mother's English family. First of all I went to the Registry Office in Walthamstow, and after a little hunt I found Monica. She had been born some two years after Susan, on Christmas day 1918, just after the end of the First World War. And I wondered if their father James Harrison had served in that war and if he had survived it.

Armed with these details I carried on looking for a marriage of Monica Harrison in the same Walthamstow Registry Office and eventually found her. She married a William Ashton on 29th April 1942 (a simple Wartime marriage). I followed a trail to Colchester and eventually found her as a deceased widow, which was sad. I so wanted to talk to her about my mother, but it was not to be. But I did find her lovely two daughters Emily and Lizzie who still live in Colchester.

I also retraced my mother's steps and found the Thornton village church and all those de Courtseys! That was an exciting moment when I looked down on the effigies and tombs of my distant ancestors. And still the puzzle of Mary remains – who was she and where was she buried?

Now, after spending many hours re-reading and re-reading those documents and letters and thinking about the past, and the unexpected new future that those discoveries has led me to, I have decided to write my own addition to the family archives!

The circumstances of my birth did not weigh heavily upon me as a child. Although I grew up knowing that my mother had died when I was born, I just accepted it as a fact without realizing what that really meant. Our mother was never mentioned or discussed by my father or my stepmother Betty, and even my second Christian name, Susan, did not trigger any questions or comments. It was years before I realized that my second name, was the name of my mother, and I had been given it in her honour. I was only ever called by my first name, Marie, by everyone that I knew, and I only used Susan if I had an official document to complete. Now I am proud to have her name.

My father's journal reveals just how much he loved Susan, and regretted her death to an extent that it brought on a deep depression that lasted for years. And how he longed to bring up her children to love and honour her too.

Each time I read that awful letter from Susan to my father I am moved to tears, to read her most intimate thoughts. What an honest, open, passionate and courageous woman she must have been. For a letter written in 1944 it is astonishingly modern in expression and demonstrates her strength and ability to defy the conventions of the time to act not only as she did, but to openly talk about sex, even if it was in a private personal letter.

It is still hurts me to know just how unwanted I was, and how terrified Susan was at the thought of her oncoming labour. Although a large part of the blame rests with my father for her death, for not using precautions to prevent a fourth pregnancy, this knowledge does little to take away from me the feelings of guilt with which I have always lived.

But Susan's letter and those certificates, have, at last, opened my eyes to everything, and even most of my unasked questions are answered.

My father was a man of a very high, perhaps abnormally high, sex drive. Susan described him as a man 'who must have sex regularly to sustain himself', and he himself described his 'sins as his only way of survival'. He was brought up in a Victorian society, which was also heavily influenced by the Moslem culture of Istanbul. This meant that 'good' women were not freely accessible, and only sluts and whores mixed with men or gave themselves to men. He was first married to an 'unfaithful' wife, which would have been utterly unacceptable by him, no matter how he had behaved within their marriage. Was she unfaithful to him to pay him back for his own infidelities? In the 1920s/30s society in Paris it was usually accepted that many men had a mistress, and their wives would have had to accept it too. If a wife behaved in the same manner then it was she who was a slut!

He then leaves Paris, (no mention of any children, but who knows, there may be half brothers and sisters there? That might be another trail to follow one day), and he moves to London. There he meets our mother, Susan, who is passionate, sexy and of such an independent mind that she entirely disregards the conventions of the day. I am certain that he loved Susan greatly, but his background and culture might have made him secretly horrified at this freedom of hers in giving her love to him. He might also have questioned if this was usual and acceptable behaviour by women in his newly adopted country.

Susan sets up home with him, a married man, and has a child by him before he is divorced and free to marry her. And while it was wonderful for him, perhaps it also produces in him a paranoia about Susan meeting other men, and the possibility of her being passionate, sexy and independent with someone else. In other words, being unfaithful to him or leaving him for another man.

So perhaps he thinks that the best way to prevent that happening is by controlling her. And what better way to control her than keeping her busy having babies one after the other?

He has three sons in quick succession, and then within eighteen months of the third one, he has a daughter. Me. Who grows up with the same looks as my lost mother. Same independent spirit. Always resisting control, always stamping my foot and demanding to know 'why should I? and saying 'it's not fair!' (How well I remember the foot stamping and the pouting lip!)

So my nature is recognised and before I, too, can develop into a passionate, sexy woman, I have to be stopped, controlled and allowed no freedom with any boys or men so that I don't become pregnant before I am safely married.

That letter of my mother was the key that unlocked the mystery of my life. Why my father sought to control me to the extent that he did. It was not, as I had always thought, because I was like him – passionate and strong minded. (I have always identified myself with him, having had up till now, no mother to compare myself too.) No. I think that it was because I am so very like her, my mother. Not only in looks, but in spirit and temperament too!

As a child that defiant spirit had to be controlled and crushed, and then as I was growing, maturing and developing, my blooming sexuality had to be controlled and crushed too, so that I did not repeat what my mother had done – have sex before marriage, run away with man and have a child out of wedlock!

So what are my thoughts now about my childhood? My father's resolve to bring up his children to know, love and honour our mother faded as time passed. Was it because he did not want to hurt Betty? Was it because with the move to Eastbourne he became too busy and involved in making a success of his business venture? I think that the pain of my mother's death receded into a private corner of his heart and mind and all physical reminders of her were locked away in her chest. He knew that he had to go on, go forward, whatever the struggle.

So for me life was as it was then, and I grew to be a teenager before I started, just a little, to want to know something of my real mother. But those growing questions were never fully answered until now.

I remember how often I felt different from those around me, my brothers and my school friends even the foreign students. I wanted to be like the others and have what they had, that is the freedom to choose what they did, choose what they wore, and chose what career paths they wanted to follow.

For the first ten years of my life, in spite of my early traumas as a baby, I had, on the whole, a happy childhood. I was mostly unaware of my father's deep depression – only the outbursts of violent rage that caused us all to be very wary in what we said or did for fear of arousing his temper.

Although it was never talked about, I was aware from babyhood that my mother had died when I was born, but it took years to pass before I understood what that really meant. Unlike my brothers, I had never known our real mother and although Francine had mothered me for the first few months of my life, my step-mother Betty was my only mother that I remembered. My discoveries of, and admiration for, Susan take nothing away from the love and gratitude I feel for Betty. She could have abandoned us all when life with my father became unbearable for her, but she stuck it out, maybe out of guilt of the hurt she had caused Susan in the last few months of her life. But mainly, I think, because she grew to love us all, and always did her best for us, even if I was unable to recognise it for years.

After we moved to Eastbourne I deeply missed the love, care and protection of my Grandmama and Aunt Mariette, and then I got used to not having them around to watch over me. I also got used to not having the watchful closeness of my parents. As long as I caused no disruption to the workings of the guesthouse, School and College, which resulted in being shouted at, a spanking or a caning, I had freedom and playtime such as most children do not have a chance to experience today's modern and much more dangerous world.

I know that I did harbour feelings of denial and disappointment. I always felt that I was treated differently to everyone around me, including the students, my friends and, most of all, my brothers.

I did feel that I had been denied the love and attention of my mother and father; denied equality with the children who stayed with us in the guesthouse, denied the care and attention given to the students, denied the excitement that my secondary school friends had with their pretty clothes, parties and boyfriends; denied the normal expectations of growing up and learning to live and love as a young woman, and, above all, denied the chance to go to university.

During those teenage years of unhappiness and of feeling

unrecognised and unloved, I do not remember once associating my father's uncaring and harsh attitude towards me with the circumstances of my birth. The discoveries I have made from the documents in my mother's chest now lead me to the conclusion that my father did love me, but in a very different way from the way he loved my brothers. He loved me, but that love was tainted, and mixed with guilt. My very existence was a constant reminder him of his share in the responsibility in my mother's death. So he both loved me and rejected me at the same time.

From the time we moved to Eastbourne, I hardly remember any close care or affection by either of my parents. I now realise that this was mainly because they were so busy. In the early days of their business they really did work hard, every day of the week, from early morning to late at night. And in the end they did succeed, but it was at a huge cost to family life.

As I was growing older family relationships for me seemed to disappear altogether. Betty was never able to support me in any of my wants or against my father's domination, and I had very few meaningful conversations with either of my parents. From secondary school age and until I was twenty, apart from two girls from my class at school, who both disappeared from my life when they left school at fifteen, I formed no friendships with English people outside the College, I lived almost entirely with and amongst the students, and my friendships amongst them were always transient.

These documents show some of my father's ambiguous attitudes towards the women that he loved, but as a growing girl I knew none of this.

As a teenager my life became totally dominated by my father, whose own life was dominated by his powerful sex drive. He seemed to have no regard or love for me. His only expressions of love and care were to protect me from the lust of all men like himself – and to him that meant all males of all ages!

Without any real closeness I really felt that my father had become the all-seeing eye of "Big Brother" who was able to observe me at all times, even when I thought that I had evaded him. I tried and tried to win his approval with the contributions I made to the College, and to get him to accept me as grown up and responsible, but it never happened. And any future endeavours and achievements that I could have made for the College were lost because of his relationship with Emily, who became the main Administrator. She did not want me around either to interfere with her relationship with my father, or to become able to supersede or replace her in the College organisation.

At the age of eighteen, after two years of stalemate and doing nothing at the College, I eventually found myself a job in the Civil Service, and through that work I later met a local English boy, whom I married when I was twenty three. After my marriage I continued to live locally in Eastbourne, and I visited my parents regularly. As a married woman I lived in truce with my father for many years and I watched him mellow year by year. Raymond, John and I each had two children. I adored my two babies, and the happiest time of my life was when I was a young mother. For the first years of their lives my own life was taken up with being a mother; loving them, playing with them, reading them stories, and teaching them. They were two lovely little boys, who, in spite of the problems their father and I later caused them, grew to become delightful and caring young men.

My relationship with Betty also improved when I was married and was no longer putting her in the difficult position of defending me against my father. In retirement she became a soft and loving mother to me, especially when after nearly twenty years of marriage, I was going through the traumas of separation and divorce.

It was not until after I was divorced and Betty died, and I moved, with my father into this little house, that my father and I really talked to each other on a one to one basis, and I realised that in his old age he did, finally, respect and even admire me. It was these conversations with him that must have led him to make the final entry into his little journal.

That journal shook me to my roots and, reading it again, I am crying again at the love expressed for Susan and the four of us children. What a pity he didn't give it to me earlier and talk to me of our mother before he died. Nevertheless I had already forgiven his harshness to me, and in the final years of his life I grew to love him deeply. I know that I will miss him enormously.

Because of his obsession with sex my father had spoiled the lives of all the women in his life: his three wives, his daughter, and, yes, even his mistresses, Emily, who I now realise, got no real love or loyalty from him.

It seems that although he had loved my mother deeply, my father had been as harsh to her as he had been to all the ones he loved the most. Like he would do in turn to Betty, he humiliated Susan with repeated sexual encounters and casual affairs with other women, and shrugged it off by saying that a man must have his needs satisfied in order to live!

As a teenager and young woman my own relationship with my father was completely ruined by this obsession. My mother's last letter to him shows this obsession in the extreme, and what it led to. His journal shows how much he loved her and regretted his actions. That journal, and the photographs of my mother that he kept to himself, also revealed just how much I looked like and reminded him of her. Did that very reminder of her evoke the guilt feelings in him, and his blame in her death? While professing to love me, did that guilt cause him, consciously or sub-consciously, to reject me too?

I do not accept the ultimate control he had over me, and what I absolutely fail to understand is that after all the expressions of love and interest in an educated or musical future that he expressed in his journal for me in my babyhood, why, when I was growing up to be the very likeness of his lost love, did he then not take any interest at all in my education or my future at all, other than to preserve my virginity at all costs?

When I discovered those photographs of Susan as a young woman, and the shock that I felt on seeing that I was indeed 'the very reproduction' of her, I would really loved to have known what my father felt through the years that I was growing up.

In front of him he must have seen daily his Susan as a growing girl, yet he was unable to talk to anyone about his feelings. Certainly not to Betty who must have been aware for years that she was a 'stand in', and could not possibly match up to the paragon that Susan had become in my father's mind. And not to me, or to anyone else. We did not know how alike I was to my mother, as there were no pictures of Susan around for comparisons to be made. What did he feel on the day of my marriage when he walked down the aisle with almost a copy of Susan on the day of her wedding to him? (We were both twenty-three). He must have been full of so many emotions that he could not express. Poor Daddy!

Most of my questions are answered now, but there are some final ones that still remain unanswered, and I keep asking myself... why? He loved Susan so much, and here she was almost living again through me. Why wasn't he at least kind to me when I was a teenager? Was my very likeness to Susan a continual source of regret and reminder to him? Why did he have no real interest in my education, my future, my life? On a daily basis I was mostly ignored. He took more interest in the routines and schooling needs of the students than he did of me. Why did I seem to have no importance in his life? Other than his need to supervise any connection I had with the male sex, he hardly ever checked to see where I was, or what I was doing.

And, finally, why did he never tell us about his life in Istanbul? Was it because of the shock of losing all his family wealth? Was it his mother's wish that they should never speak again about Istanbul? Was it because he did not want to compare his lost wealth and comfort with his current life of working hard to scrape up enough money to live? Did he ever tell Susan about his early life? In later years he did sometimes talk about his boyhood and escapades as a young man, but he never mentioned where these escapades had taken place. He even owned his own car when he was just eighteen, and in the early 1920s that was quite something, but I always assumed that that early life was when he lived in Paris! Why did he keep Istanbul as a secret? A complete mystery!

Those questions will never now be answered.

Nevertheless, the father that I had sometimes hated as a teenager and young woman, became the Dad that I loved dearly when he was an old man. I eventually understood his lifelong desire to unite his children with bonds so strong that nothing could destroy our love for each other. His motto (borrowed from The Three Musketeers) "all for one and one for all" became a reality.

True, he loved us. But it was always a love given provided that we accepted that he knew better and that we should always do what he told to do or to follow his advice, even in his old age.

It was six weeks before his eighty-eighth birthday when he died. He had all beloved children around his bedside and he had, at last, spoken to me to of our mother, his beloved Susan, and of his happiness to be joining her soon.

I am thinking again about that devastating letter to father from Susan, as well as being shocked and saddened, I was also very surprised that my father had not destroyed it – if not many years ago, then when he had made the final entries into his diary in 1985. The fact that he did keep that sad and bitter letter must show how much he still regretted his loss, and perhaps some continued remorse that it was his actions that had caused her to feel so much pain.

In spite of everything I have learned in the past few months I am so glad that I can only think of him with love in my heart, and sadness at his death. I miss him. And although I never knew my mother I have learned so much about her that I miss her too. Is it possible to miss someone one has never met? I think it is. She has at last become a real person to me. My mother.

~~~

I was in tears again by the time I had finished writing my thoughts down. I printed out the document, read it through again, and then took it to my mother's chest, which was now mine, to add to all the other documents. I hope that one day that my baby granddaughter, Suzanne, will find it all interesting, when she, in turn inherits the chest.

Marie's Post Script Memo – 10th September 2009

Yesterday was my 65th birthday and my two sons David and Julian took me to London for a special celebration. We had lunch at the Ivy, a trip on the river, and an evening performance of my favourite show – The Phantom of the Opera. I had a wonderful and memorable day with them being thoroughly spoiled! So today was a bit of an anti-climax.

I was sitting quietly thinking what the 10th of September had meant to my dad, and everything I had discovered in my chest about my mother. I looked at the chest, sitting in its usual place in the corner of the room, covered with books' papers and odd bits, and I decided to give it a good polishing.

Then as I was rubbing particularly hard on a knobbly bit of carving...